HOME FIRES

A James Bay Novel

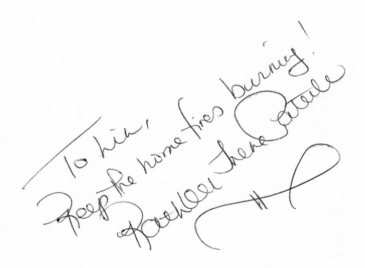

KATHLEEN IRENE PATERKA

DEDICATION

For my husband, Assistant Chief Steve Paterka of the Charlevoix Township Fire Department. Every woman should be so lucky to have such a heroic amazing man in her life 24/7.

ACKNOWLEDGMENTS

Many people provided valuable assistance in the creation of this novel. I am grateful to all of them.

Jenna Mindel and Christine Elizabeth Johnson, fabulous critique partners, authors extraordinaire, and the best friends ever. Long live The Queen of Hearts Club!

Cathy Chant and Edie Ramer, for their continuing encouragement, support and advice.

My beta readers: Larry and Kay Campbell, and Judith Ivan. Their feedback of the original manuscript was invaluable.

Chief Curt Thompson of the Charlevoix Township Fire Department. He patiently answered all my questions and allowed me to explore the Township fire barn, plus climb around on top and inside the fire trucks. Air horns are great fun!

Chief Paul Ivan of the Charlevoix City Fire Department. His personal '*behind the scenes*' tour of the Charlevoix City Fire Department and living quarters provided valuable information while researching for this novel.

Anne Victory, who took on the task of editing a burned-out manuscript and refining it into a blazing story; Karen Duvall, for her smoking hot cover artwork; and Amy Eye, the Queen of Formatting!

Most of all, to the brave courageous men and women who serve as first responders and never fail to answer the call when they're toned out by Central Dispatch, no matter what time of night or day. You are all heroes in my book!

CHAPTER ONE

ARSON SUSPECTED IN RECENT DUMPSTER FIERS

By: Charles Kendall
The James Bay Journal

JAMES BAY — Local police and fire officials ask
nmunity to be alert in the wake of
of dumpster fires in the downtown

aren't unusual this time of year,"
ief Ivan Thompson informed this
mertime. People get sloppy with
heir barbeque charcoal. But these
ally set."
nd-degree felony punishable by a
en years' imprisonment. Anyone
s asked to contact the James Bay
tment.

elve hours and already she was a
vn there would be no coffee in the
ould have made the journey north
on her favorite beans. How could
her mother have given up caffeine and switched to
herbal tea without saying a word?

"You need to take the next right," Irene Gallagher
said from the passenger seat.

"I haven't been gone that long, Mom," Rose teased.
"I think I still remember how to find the hospital."

Irene clung to her shoulder seat belt as they rounded the corner. "You might want to slow down, sweetheart. My car isn't used to going so fast."

Since when was doing twenty in a twenty-five mile-per-hour zone fast? Rose eased her foot off the accelerator and shot her mother a smile. Her best I-haven't-had-a-cup-of-coffee-since-yesterday-morning-but-I'm-not-complaining-YET smile.

"Watch out!" Irene gasped.

The cherry-red pickup loomed before them out of nowhere. Rose clutched the wheel and slammed on the brakes, but too late to stop the aging sedan. It smashed into the rear of the pickup. The grill crumpled flat against the gleaming bumper like a child's accordion.

"Mom?" Rose twisted in her seat and winced as the seat belt cut into her shoulder. She struggled to free herself. "Mom, are you hurt?"

"I think I'll live," Irene said with a grimace. "Too bad the same can't be said for my car."

Or his truck. Rose cringed as the driver slid from his pickup and leveled her with a furious glare. Who could blame him? She was the one at fault.

"Cecilia Rose? I can't... I think my seat belt is stuck."

"Let me try." She blinked back tears as she pushed aside her mother's fumbling fingers and grappled with the belt. One second of carelessness and look what had happened. All three of them could have been killed. Rose blinked harder but everything stayed a blur. The seat belt wouldn't unlock. "I'll come around your side and get you out."

2

Cutting the engine, she scooted from behind the steering wheel. Brilliant revolving lights registered against gleaming metal as her sandals connected with hot asphalt.

"Whoa, not so fast," a deep male voice rumbled. "Where do you think you're going?"

Rose glanced up into a determined face steeled with resolve. The driver of the pickup looked hot under the collar.

"That's my brand-new truck you hit."

"I—"

"Somebody should teach you how to drive."

She swallowed hard. "I'm very sorry—"

"Sorry doesn't cut it." He blew hard and shook his head. "Do you know how long I've had that truck? Two weeks and two days... and some woman takes me out in broad daylight in the middle of summer. Wintertime, I might understand, but—"

Some woman? Rose felt her own temper rising. He had some nerve. She wouldn't have hit him if he hadn't stopped so fast.

"This wasn't all my fault." Her words rushed between them. "You had no business stopping in the middle of the road without warning."

His eyes narrowed. "There's a stop sign at that corner, in case you haven't noticed."

"There is not," she shot back.

"See for yourself." He jerked his thumb over his shoulder.

Rose glanced past him, then swallowed hard as she spotted the gleaming red stop sign. Her face flushed. Since when had this intersection become a four-way stop? Obviously since the last time she'd been home.

"Looks like you've got a little explaining to do." He ticked off the offenses on his fingertips. "Failure to yield, following too close, plowing into my truck—"

"It's not like I did it on purpose." Her face felt hotter than the metallic red paint on his pickup. "I was distracted—"

"Doing what? Putting on your lipstick?"

She forced down an angry rejoinder. "I didn't see you."

He shot her a shrewd smile. "Another one to add to the list. Careless driving."

Rose steamed. The last thing she needed was to stand around arguing with some local yokel. She'd been taught how to drive by the best. Her own dad had been the instructor behind the wheel of the drivers' training car. "For your information, I am an excellent driver."

"I'd say that's up for debate," he drawled, staring at her with a look of amusement that caused a slow burn in the pit of her stomach. "We'll let the police figure things out. I called them from my truck. They should be here any minute."

"Fine." She shoved her hands in her pockets and glared at him. What a morning. A late start, no coffee, topped off by running—literally—into this idiot. It would serve him right if the Chief of Police himself showed up at the scene. Not that she expected special favors from local law enforcement, but Chief Dennis and her dad had been good friends. Small-town connections and a friendly face couldn't hurt.

"I hope you've got your license handy." He reached in his back pocket and drew out his wallet. "You wouldn't want them to add driving without a license to the list of offenses."

"Of course I have my license. Plus proof of insurance and registration. They're in the glove compartment. See for yourself." She gestured toward her mother's car—

Irene Gallagher waved through the front window.

"Oh, no." Rose's words hung like a sodden towel put out to dry in the hot June sunshine.

His eyebrows arched in a question mark. "Something wrong?"

"You might say that." Shamefaced, she nodded toward the vehicle.

He craned his neck and peered through the driver's side window. Irene's smile widened as she wiggled her fingers and gave him a little nod.

"Who's that?"

"My mother." Rose whirled on heel and headed for the passenger door. "Her seat belt is stuck."

"It probably jammed from the force of impact." His words floated from somewhere close behind. "Why didn't you say something?"

"You didn't exactly give me a chance." She leaned in the passenger seat and wrestled with the seat belt.

"Are you hurt, ma'am?" He crouched low beside the car. "Do you need an ambulance?"

"Thank you, young man, but there's no need for that."

"Looks like you could use a hand." He nudged in closer to Rose. "Let me help."

"Forget it," Rose muttered. "I can do it myself." A stranger offering assistance was a rarity in her world. Who did that anymore? He never would have stopped if she hadn't plowed into his truck.

Then again, if she hadn't hit him, there would have been no need for him to stop. It was her fault they were in this mess. Rose struggled harder, trying to unravel the twisted belt. If only he would get out of her way, she could fix things just fine.

"Sweetheart, perhaps it would be better if you let the young man try," Irene said after a moment.

"I've almost got it, Mom." Sweat beaded on her forehead but she wasn't about to give up. Not when she almost had things free. Not with him standing so close behind.

"Oh, Lord," Irene gasped. "Look at that smoke."

Billowing white smoke poured from underneath the hood. Rose sucked in a deep breath. The hair on the back of her neck bristled. "Come on, come on!" She gave the seat belt a desperate yank.

"Let me do it." He pushed past her to fill the passenger door and in an instant, the belt clicked free. "Ma'am? Think you can put your arms around my neck?"

Rose bit her lip. A hurried glance showed a tall, solid man with burnished blond hair, a steady gaze and arms that could easily cradle her mother. But with that knee so swollen and inflamed, one wrong move could mean intense pain.

"Be careful. She has a bad knee and can't move fast…"

In one fluid movement, Irene was up, out, and safe on the sidewalk.

"Would you mind grabbing her cane? It's in the back seat." Rose had no intention of going anywhere near the car. The way that smoke looked, the vehicle would soon be fully engulfed in flames.

There wasn't even a chance to thank him as he handed over the cane. Already he was at the front of the car, fumbling around the grillwork. In one quick swoop, he had the hood up. White smoke rushed from the engine, filling the hot summer air with even more heat. Rose eyed him as he labored under the hood. He didn't appear ruffled in spite of the rolling smoke. She shivered, remembering some of those videos on late night television where the cars suddenly burst into flames.

She backed farther away onto the grass and squeezed her mother's hand.

"Think I found your problem," he called after a moment. "Looks like the radiator hose broke."

"Would you please get away from there?" she urged. They'd exchanged words but that didn't mean he deserved to be roasted and toasted in front of their eyes. "Before the whole thing goes up in flames?"

"Calm down, the car isn't on fire." He stepped back from the hood and nodded at the muddy green fluid pooling on the street. "See that? Antifreeze on the exhaust manifold. That's what caused the smoke. It'll stop once the antifreeze runs out."

Rose scowled at the ten-year-old sedan Irene refused to part with. No doubt about it. The two of them were going to have a come-to-Jesus meeting about buying a new car before she left town. Maybe after today her mother would be ready to see the light.

He squatted next to his pickup and examined the rear end. Rose kicked herself mentally and held back a sigh. He hadn't been kidding about his vehicle. It looked like it still belonged on the showroom floor. Dollar signs ca-chinged in her head. There went her insurance rates. She should have paid more attention while driving. She should have listened to her mother's words of caution. Rose took a deep breath and steeled herself for the news. "How bad is it?"

"You rammed the trailer hitch. Looks like it got a little scratched, but no big deal."

"Thank God no one was hurt," Irene ventured. "You can always buy a new car, but you can't replace the people you love."

He joined them on the sidewalk. "The tow truck should be here soon."

"I suppose you called that in, too?" Rose said without thinking.

He cocked his head and flashed her a slow grin. "I did. The wrecker is on its way."

She eyed the swirling lights atop his pickup. Streets up north were filled with vehicles touting light bars. Maybe he made his living plowing snow. Maybe he owned the wrecker service, too.

"Let me know when you get it to the shop." Rose fumbled through her purse and fished for her wallet. "Will you take a personal check?"

"Nope." He wiped the oily dirt from his hands onto his clean jeans.

"I'm not sure how much cash I have." He had been a big help but this was no time to be playing games.

"I don't want your money."

He met her gaze head on with one eyebrow raised and a steady smile.

Rose straightened and pulled her purse strap tighter. Mr. Big-Truck should keep his eyes to himself instead of on her. Did he actually think she would flirt with him over a towing bill? If so, he had another think coming.

"I'll give you my mother's address. You can send the bill there and I'll stop by your shop and pay it."

"You will, hmmm?"

"Isn't that what I said?" She swallowed down a flash of impatience. "Just tell me where I can find you."

The beginning of a smile tugged at his mouth. "Okay, if that's what you want. You'll find me down at the fire station next to City Hall. You're welcome to drop by… but only if you want to say hello."

"What—?" She sputtered as her fingers gripped the soft leather of her wallet.

"He said he doesn't want your money, sweetheart. Isn't that right, young man?"

"Yes, ma'am." His face relaxed as he nodded at Irene. "Just doing my job."

Rose shifted on her feet. "But I thought you—"

"Owned the wrecker service? Not me," he said, nearly laughing now. "I'm a fireman."

She wanted to melt right into the pavement. After three years of practicing law, she knew better than to pass judgment on face value. A fireman. That explained the brilliant white and red lights swirling emergency warnings from the top of his pickup. She made a rapid reappraisal of the stranger beside them.

A fireman, a public servant—dedicated and committed, willing to help when needed, whether on or off duty. And from the look of his crisp jeans and dark blue t-shirt, he wasn't on duty today. A solid body with strong arms that could haul a fire hose, a thatch of thick blond hair razor clean against his neck, a sunburned tinge of red skin at the collar of his t-shirt.

She tried to keep her gaze from trailing any lower before he noticed she was staring.

"I'm sorry about everything. I mean, hitting your truck and for the way I acted. And I'm sorry I was short with you." Rose rushed the words. It was easier to apologize if you did it fast.

"Ditto." His face softened. "Guess I came across pretty strong myself. I just got this truck a couple weeks ago. You could say it's my baby." He squinted against the high morning sun. "You aren't going to be able to drive that car. I'd be glad to give you ladies a ride once the police finish up."

Rose eyed the shiny pickup. His vehicle was much too high for her mother to manage... not to mention fodder for the rumor mill probably now in full swing. Three cars had already slowed in the past five minutes, giving their little group a leisurely once-over. In James Bay, anything was fair game. The gossip would be flying by nightfall. And the sight of no wedding band on his left hand only made matters worse. *Knowing this town, they'll have us married off by morning.*

"I doubt my mother can climb inside." The tug of regret she felt refusing his offer of assistance caught Rose by surprise.

"It's this darn knee," Irene explained with a faint smile. "I'm having surgery tomorrow. Rose was taking me to the hospital for an EKG." She latched on to his forearm. "You are a real hero, young man. I don't know what we would have done if you hadn't stopped and put out the fire."

"It wasn't a fire, ma'am, just the radiator." The fireman's face reddened with each passing minute. "I didn't do anything."

Correction. He'd been nice enough to help, considering she'd nearly wrecked his brand-new truck. Plus, she really liked the way he smiled. Rose stepped forward and gently pried her mother's hand loose. "It's not like he had much choice, Mom. I hit him, remember?"

A patrol car with flashing lights pulled up behind Irene's car. Rose's spirits sank as she caught sight of an unfamiliar face behind the wheel. Just her luck. The officer couldn't be more than twenty one years old. A rookie on the force with something to prove.

"Got a little problem here?" The policeman strode from the patrol car with a curt nod for her and an easy smile for the fireman.

"Hi, Jerry. Guess you could say we had a little run-in."

"Looks like it. Say, isn't that your new truck? What happened?"

Her stomach fluttered. Definitely worse than she'd thought. The two of them sounded like friends.

"Not much to tell." The fireman cleared his throat. "I stopped. She didn't."

"I can't tell you how many people have blown through that stop sign since they put it up a couple months ago." The officer reached for his pen.

Rose rubbed her forehead with the heel of her hand. Guaranteed this would be one ticket she wouldn't talk her way out of. Especially once they found out she was a lawyer. Law enforcement personnel were always gunning for attorneys running afoul of the law. The last thing she needed was another traffic ticket, especially since she'd been stopped for speeding last fall. If she racked up any more points, she might be taking the bus to work.

A sleek white Cadillac slowed on the street, then cruised to a halt, pulling up behind the police cruiser. Rose groaned and steeled her nerves as their next-door neighbor and old family friend emerged from his car and joined them on the sidewalk. The Judge no longer presided from the bench, but that didn't stop him from speaking his mind. Hopefully His Honor wouldn't make matters worse or she'd definitely be doomed to using public transportation.

"Irene? Are you all right?" The Judge's voice rumbled with concern as he caught her fingers with a little shake. A thundercloud frown was reserved for the rest of them. "What's going on here?"

"We're all fine, Harvey," Irene replied. "No one is hurt... except my car, that is." She clucked her tongue in disgust.

"They had a little fender bender, Judge." The officer's hand tightened around the ticket book. "From what I understand, this young lady ran the new stop sign and—"

"That's not how it happened," Rose started. "I will admit I hit his truck, but that stop sign wasn't—"

"Cecilia Rose, I will handle this." The Judge silenced her with a firm voice that broached no rebuke. "Officer, have you already written the ticket?"

The baby-faced officer cleared his throat. "Not yet, Your Honor."

"Fine. I'm sure we can work things out, especially as my client has admitted responsibility." His black eyes zeroed in on the fireman. "Do you have a problem with that, young man?"

"My truck seems okay," he said with an easy shrug. "Besides, this town isn't that big. I suppose I can find her if I need something."

Rose pushed forward. "If you think for one minute that I'm paying for extra—"

"What?" The fireman smiled. Turquoise-blue eyes looked intently at her. "Or maybe you want to save me some time and grief and give me your name and address now?"

Irene clutched Rose's arm and pulled her aside. "I think we should let the Judge take it from here. He'll work things out."

Rose sputtered. That wasn't the way things worked in her world. She was no longer five years old and she didn't need the Judge, or anyone else, fighting her battles. She handled matters for her clients. She could handle matters for herself. "I think—"

The strength in her mother's hand came as a surprise.

"Let the Judge take care of it," Irene repeated.

Ten minutes later, Rose was still wondering how he had managed to pull it off. No ticket, no points, no public transportation. Merely a warning and the tow truck bill. A small price to pay for an act of carelessness. No harm done, save to her mother's car and a few dings to the fireman's trailer hitch.

Plus a few dings to her own stubborn pride.

"I'll drop you and Cecilia Rose off at the hospital, but I have a mediation scheduled for this afternoon," the Judge said as they stood watching the tow truck leave with Irene's car. "Why don't you call Lil and see if she can give you a ride home?"

"Good luck with your surgery, ma'am."

Rose frowned as the fireman headed for his truck with a backward wave. He was leaving? But she didn't even know his name.

And then he was gone.

"My, but he was cute," Irene said as Rose helped her settle in the front seat of the Judge's sedan. "Didn't you think so, sweetheart?"

"Mmmm," she said with a vague shrug. Perhaps her mother should consult a dictionary. Cute didn't come close to describing that fireman. After their little encounter this morning, she herself could of a few choice phrases without much thought. Conceited. Clever. Charming.

Quite the combustible combination.

The hospital was newly remodeled in that quaint up-north style, just like a good part of the downtown. James Bay, under the guise of progress with a capital P, was suffocating. People, drawn by the area's sparkling blue waters, clean pine air, and the lure of escaping the crowd, moved here every day... never realizing they brought the crowd north straight up the highway with them.

Rose shifted in the hard plastic chair. Any hope of finding a comfortable spot had disappeared, along with her patience. Someone had set the air conditioner on arctic blast. She would need to bring along a sweater tomorrow. They had scheduled the surgery for early morning. Who knew how long it would take? They could be waiting for hours. She rubbed down the goose bumps popping up on her arms and started a fresh mental list of things to remember.

"Don't you sit there worrying about your mama," Lil said with a firm shake of her exquisitely coiffed head. "She's a strong woman. She'll come through the surgery fine... especially now you're here."

With anyone else, Rose's ear would be fine-tuned for the slightest hint of disapproval, but not when it came to Lillian Gillespie. Her mother's best friend Lil—just like the Judge—had been one of the family since Rose could remember.

"Of course I had to come home. I couldn't let Mom go through this alone."

Lil's emerald-green eyes filled with understanding as she leaned in for a hug. "She misses you, honey," she whispered. "She might not say it, but I know she wishes you lived a little closer."

The older woman's words tugged at Rose's heart as the familiar rush of perfume flooded her senses. Crushed in Lil's embrace, Rose felt reduced to all of eight years old again. She closed her eyes and shut out the sterile surroundings. If only she could shut out the guilt as well. James Bay was a three-hour drive up the freeway from Grand Rapids, her adopted city for the past three years, and she didn't make the trip back often.

But James Bay wasn't home anymore.

No place was.

Lil drew back and settled in her chair. Her eyes settled with military precision upon Rose. "Are you eating enough? You look tired, Cecilia Rose. You need to take better care of yourself. Are you getting enough sleep?"

Rose couldn't hold back an ironic smile. No need for Lil to be so polite. She was well aware of how bad she looked. No amount of makeup could hide the dark smudges under her blue eyes. Her clothes hung on her lately, loose and unfashionable. She hadn't dared weigh herself in a month, afraid of the number she would see on the scale. But who had time to eat? Meals were caught on the run or eaten at her desk. There weren't enough hours in the day to accommodate the demands of a busy law practice, let alone deal with the stress of daily life. She was shrinking inside herself and she couldn't stop the process. Taking care of yourself meant making time for yourself. Time was a luxury she could ill afford.

"I'll sleep and eat more now that I'm home," Rose promised.

Lil lifted an eyebrow. "As I remember, you never were much of a cook."

"I'm home for the next six weeks. That should be time enough for me to learn." She had managed to avoid it for twenty-seven years, but there wouldn't be much else to do around the house besides playing chauffeur and nursemaid. Who knew? Cooking might actually be fun. Not that she believed it for a minute.

"I'll be over every night," Lil said.

"To do what? Help me?" Rose smiled. "You're a worse cook than I am." Lil's idea of a good meal at home was anything that arrived courtesy of a fast delivery service.

"Seems like you have talents we didn't know about. When did you teach your purse how to dance?" Lil pointed at the small clutch pulsating atop a woefully thin stack of magazines on the glass table before them.

Her cell phone. Last night's string of phone calls had interrupted their dinner and prompted more than one questioning glance from her mother. After the fourth call, Rose had set it on vibrate. Hear no evil, see no evil, answer no evil. But with her mother still busy being poked and prodded, the coast was clear and she'd turned it on. Rose snatched her purse, drew out her smart phone, and checked the identity of the incoming caller.

"Hi, Andy. Hold on a minute, will you?" She stood up. "Sorry, Lil, but I have to take this. It's important."

"Don't mind me, honey." She waved Rose away with an encouraging smile. "Go ahead and talk with your young man."

Rose merely smiled and slipped into the hallway outside the waiting room. Andy Sabatini was under thirty and definitely male, but that didn't mean he qualified as her young man. Not that Andy was about to let that stop him from actively pursuing the role. He'd already left two messages this morning. Apparently he intended to win her over with the same dogged persistence he practiced in following up with clients. "Okay, Andy, I haven't got much time. What's up?"

"You're killing me, Rose. How long do you plan to keep me waiting?"

Her former colleague had never been good at small talk. His brain was wired in one direction: winning. Rose knew he had targeted her as his next conquest. "Andy, I'm sorry. I don't have an answer yet."

"Rose, you know——"

"I can't talk about this right now. We're at the hospital."

"I thought the surgery wasn't until tomorrow."

"Mom is having some tests. An EKG, chest x-rays. They want to make sure everything is okay."

"What about you?" His voice slowed, softening. "You doing okay?"

"I'm fine," Rose said with a bravado she didn't feel. The hospital smelled faintly of lemon disinfectant and fear, and she would give anything to bolt out the door and hit the highway. But there was no going back. She was in it for the long haul. Six weeks of long haul.

"Rose, I hate to put the pressure on you but I need some kind of answer soon." Andy's voice was back up to warp speed. "They're breathing down my neck and I'm holding out for you. I want you with me, Rose. We make a great team."

How could she forget? They had been hired by the same firm from the same group of law-school graduates. But three years with the firm had proved enough for Andy. He had his eye on the bigger picture and he'd moved onward and upward to Washington D.C. with a cushy job working with the Department of Labor. Leave it to Andy to work his magic and come up with a job for her.

But he couldn't wave a magic wand and wish her into Washington. It was nearly one thousand miles away—five times the distance already separating her from home. Which, according to the world of Irene, was already two hundred miles too far.

"Think about it, Rose. Do you really want to spend any more time grinding out research memos or drafting pleadings for some partner who's going to end up taking the credit for your work? Trust me on this. Come out here with me and you'll have the chance to call your own shots."

It wasn't a matter of trust. She missed Andy. She missed having him directly across the hall in the cramped little office identical to her own. Rose shifted on her feet, closed her eyes and allowed herself a brief indulgence. From the get-go, his offer had sounded too good to be true. No more kowtowing to the firm. No more inane weekly meetings that wasted precious time. No more working her butt off trying to make partner.

"I know you, Rose. You would love it out here. It's just what you're looking for." His voice lowered. "And I miss you."

"Andy, that can't be the reason that I—"

"I know, I know." He cut her off. "Just think about it, okay?"

She swallowed down a fresh wave of guilt. Enticing as his offer might be, it definitely came with strings attached and she wasn't about to lead him on just to land a job. She'd rather be stuck researching case law and writing briefs for the rest of her life than give Andy false hope. He wasn't the man for her.

No one was. Not anymore. That part of her life was over. Dead and buried.

"I'll wait to hear from you. Don't forget, Rose, you're the one that I want."

Lil's emerald eyes gleamed with interest as Rose slipped back into the room and her chair. "Something serious?"

"Andy's just a friend," she said in a lighthearted tone that she didn't feel.

"Isn't it funny how some friends have a way of becoming much more than that? Especially friends of the opposite sex," Lil purred. "So, tell me. What's he like? Is he good-looking? Tall, dark and handsome?"

"Very handsome," Rose agreed, smothering a smile. Two out of three wasn't bad. Andy, blessed with smooth Mediterranean looks courtesy of his Italian ancestors, barely met her nose to nose.

"He treats you well?"

"The best," she affirmed.

"Then I say go for it!" Lil sat back triumphantly. "Obviously he's attracted or he wouldn't be calling. What's stopping you?"

One thousand miles and a heart that wasn't interested. "It's rather complicated. We worked together..."

"Ahh, an office romance."

"He's no longer with the firm. He lives in Washington D.C."

Lil nodded sagely. "A long-distance romance."

"It's not like that. Andy is… well, he's…"

"He's…?" Lil prompted.

Rose reluctantly nodded, hesitant to fill in the blank. *He's not Jeff. He never will be. No one will.*

"Say no more. I understand." Lil cocked her head in tacit understanding. "He's gay, am I right?"

Rose started to speak, then quickly decided to keep her mouth shut. Let Lil think what she wanted. Too bad it wasn't the truth. It certainly would make things simpler if Andy was gay. At least then if she eventually accepted his offer both of them would know there were no strings attached.

Up until a few weeks ago, she'd thought things were going fine. She worked hard, put in long hours. The firm was happy with her performance. But the message from the senior partners had been clear, despite their approval of her request for six weeks of unpaid family medical leave. She was an integral part of their team, and team players didn't walk away from their jobs. Team players found someone else to handle family emergencies. Team players stayed and worked their clients.

Team players made partner.

Rose sighed. This six-week sabbatical would probably mean at least another year grinding away for the firm. One more year of following the rules, schmoozing the clients and chaining herself to her desk. But how far could she push it? She was already working twelve-to-fourteen-hour days. Did she want to shoot for twenty? She'd already sunk pretty low. Pathetic, actually. A double espresso, comfy bathrobe and hefty Sunday newspaper now served as her regular weekend date.

But try as she might, she couldn't visualize Andy lounging in a bathrobe beside her. She doubted he could sit still long enough to read the Sunday paper. He'd have her out jogging at the crack of dawn.

Lil patted her hand. "It just takes time, honey. Sooner or later, the right man will come along."

"I'm not worried." And she wasn't. When was the last time she'd met someone new? Men didn't exactly stroll into her life. True, there had been that fireman from earlier today. But did he even count? Smashing into someone's prized pickup wasn't the best way to meet a man. Still, he'd taken it in stride. Plus, he didn't look like the jogging type.

More like someone who might fight her over the Sunday comics.

Once they managed to make it out of bed.

Rose blinked hard. When was the last time she'd even read the comics, let alone daydreamed about a man she barely knew? A man she probably would never see again.

The soothing pressure of Lil's hand steered her back to the hospital lobby.

"Don't think for one minute that you'll have to go through this alone. I'll be around whenever you need me. So will the Judge. You know how he can be. Once he makes up his mind, there's no stopping him. He'll camp out in your living room if that's what it takes."

Rose stifled a smile. With the Judge a daily visitor, she would definitely need to lay in an ample supply of coffee beans. His Honor broached no nonsense when it came to serious matters like his cigars and caffeine.

"There you are, you two." Irene hobbled back into the waiting room, leaning heavily on her cane. "I'm sorry it took so long and you had to wait on me."

"I haven't seen our girl in a while. It gave us time for a good chat," Lil replied with a firm pat on Rose's hand.

"Who were you chatting about?" Irene's bright eyes darted back and forth between them. "What did I miss?"

"Nothing at all." Rose unfolded herself from the chair and offered a steady arm to her mother. "Here, let me help."

"Thank you, sweetheart."

Love and guilt mingled with relief as the soft weight of her mother's slight frame sank against her. Rose blinked back hot, unexpected tears. How in the world was she going to do this? She'd never been good at nursing cuts and bruises, let alone assisting a semi-invalid. Six weeks of forced confinement in James Bay ranked at the top of the list of things she'd rather not do.

But how can I tell her no? She needs me. And I love her.

"Well, I'm ready to go." Irene took a deep breath. "I've already had enough of this hospital. No doubt I'll be mighty sick of it once I've been here a few days."

"Enjoy it while you can," Lil said as they headed for the door. "You'll have lots of visitors and they'll bring flowers and candy..."

"Ooh, candy, I like that idea," Irene said as they stepped into the sunshine. "Remember, milk chocolates are my favorite... just in case anyone asks."

Rose winked at Lil over the top of Irene's head. Her mother's fondness for sweets was well-known to all.

"I'll bring the car around." Lil left the two of them standing on the curb.

"Thank you for coming home, sweetheart." Irene's words were whisper soft. "Lil means well, she always does, but... well, I'm glad you're here."

One glance at the sweet familiar face wizened with pain and Rose's heart melted like chocolate in the warm sun. Impulsively, she reached out and hugged her mother close. "Don't worry, Mom, it will be okay. Things will work out."

"Of course they will," Irene replied matter-of-factly. "You're finally home where you belong. That will do for a start. Now all we need to do is make sure you stay here."

Rose's jaw dropped in protest. Then, on second thought, she clamped her mouth shut. Better to save her energy and arguments. She would need all her wits in the next few weeks. Her mother, Lil, and the Judge had always proved staunch allies. If they got wind of Andy's proposal, they'd be after her in no time flat to turn him down. Rose was straddling career choices that would impact her entire life. The last thing she needed was to spin her wheels battling counter tactics designed to keep her home.

So much for a leisurely sabbatical playing nursemaid and chauffeur, Rose thought to herself as she swallowed down a sigh. The next six weeks definitely were not going to be as simple as she had thought.

CHAPTER TWO

BAY BEAT

The James Bay Journal

WELCOME HOME! Ms. Cecilia Rose Gallagher, a native of James Bay and associate attorney with the prominent Michigan law firm of Arthur, LaCross and Mindel, P.C., is back in town for the next several weeks to assist her mother Irene Gallagher, who will be soon be recuperating from surgery. Welcome home, Cecilia Gallagher, Esq.!

"And the doctor said she came through the surgery fine?" The Judge's face flushed red with heat as he sank down in the chair next to Rose and brushed her cheek with a kiss.

"She's still in recovery," Rose replied. "They let me see her for a few minutes, but they said it would be awhile before they take her to her room."

The sight of her mother in post-op, hooked up to machines, drainage tube in her leg, had scared her more than she cared to admit. But Irene's color was good and she had even managed a groggy smile as the two of them held hands. Rose held back the tears as she left the recovery room. There was no time for crying. Now the surgery was a success, they needed to focus on the knee and regaining strength through physical therapy.

The Judge loosened the knot of the tie at his throat and fingered open one shirt button, then another. "Your mother is a strong woman, my dear. She'll pull through this fine."

Some things never changed, Rose thought as she offered him a cautious smile. Jeff's father had always proved a steady source of comfort and strength throughout the years.

"Where's Lil?" He glanced around, his gaze sharp and penetrating. "She knew I had motions in court first thing this morning. She promised she would be here."

"She's around. She decided to take a little walk."

"Probably down at the nurses' station, gabbing with her friends." The Judge settled back in his chair with a scowl. "She shouldn't have left you sitting here alone."

"Quit worrying about me," Rose chided gently. "I'm a big girl, remember? Besides, Lil deserved a break."

A retired nurse, Lil had proved a godsend this morning—patient and reassuring as the hours crawled by without a bit of news. Rose couldn't begrudge her a quick stroll. Her own legs were stiff and cramped, and she longed for a chance to splash her face with cool refreshing water. But the bathroom could wait. She wasn't going anywhere until her mother was completely out of danger and safe in her hospital room.

The day had been a long one, begun at four a.m. with the soft steady bong of the grandfather clock downstairs. She'd found her mother already up and moving quietly about the kitchen, feeding Bozo before they left for the hospital. The aging Red Persian seemed to sense something was amiss. He'd padded behind them through the rooms, his meows loud and protracted well before they left the house.

The Judge reached over and patted Rose's hand. "No worries, hear me? Your mother's knee will be good as new. Maybe even better, now it's made of titanium and plastic. We'll have her dancing in circles by the end of the summer. She's a strong woman, my dear."

"I know she is." She'd always admired her mother's strength of character in dealing with the day-to-day business of living, especially in the face of adversity. Irene and Michael Gallagher had been fine parents, the best a girl could ask for. Rose was an only child, named after her grandmothers, and the sole beneficiary of all the blessings her parents could lavish on the one child destined to share their love. And save for her parents' inability to fill the empty bedrooms of their large house with brothers and sisters for Rose, their little family of three had been happy and content.

Everything had changed one frosty winter morning shortly after Christmas. Home from college on winter break, Rose had just come downstairs for breakfast as her father came inside from shoveling snow. He sat down at the table across from Rose, smiled his thanks to Irene as she served him a cup of coffee, then suddenly clenched his chest and he grimaced with pain. The massive coronary took him down fast. Michael John Gallagher was dead before his coffee cooled.

They buried him a few days later with the winter morning sunshine glinting like diamonds against the new-fallen snow. Irene stood stalwart at the funeral, her hand clenched tight in Rose's own as the casket was carried into church, incensed, prayed over, and finally laid to rest. Rose marveled at her mother's strength as the town mourned the untimely death of one of their own. Irene never wavered, not even when the Judge broke down in her arms. Her mother's faith held them steady and firm. It was a lesson Rose never forgot.

She'd learned something else that day, too. Life offered up no guarantees. Her father had been a high school teacher and his last lesson, taught one cold December morning, was something Rose kept tucked deep inside her heart. If a good man such as Michael John Gallagher could be shoveling snow one minute, only to sit down and die, it was best to get on with the business of living. Dreams could be gone in a heartbeat.

Once upon a time, she'd blithely assumed she would live out her life in James Bay, practicing law with the Judge's son Jeff. His unexpected death had sliced her heart open straight down the middle. Jeff would no longer be there like they'd always planned. And she wouldn't practice law in James Bay, like they'd always planned. This town had turned its back on Jeff. Fair was fair. She'd turned her back on this town. Leave them to their talk. She was a practicing attorney now with a comfortable three hours' distance between herself and the wagging tongues of the gossipmongers of James Bay. Three hours away... maybe she should take Andy up on his offer. One thousand miles distance sounded even better.

A loud, shrieking buzzer pierced the quiet of the hospital walls, yanking Rose back into the present. "What's that?"

The Judge's gaze darted around the room as they came to a stand. "Best grab your purse, my dear. That sounds like a fire alarm."

"But I don't see any smoke." Rose sniffed the air. "I don't smell anything, either. Do you think it's a real fire?"

"There's no need to panic."

She yanked free of his touch. "What about Mom? We can't just leave her."

"I'm sure they have standard procedures for this sort of thing."

Even as he spoke, a harried looking nurse rushed through the room. "Out of the building," she said in a no-nonsense tone. "It's only a drill. Take the hall to the left."

All this commotion simply for a fire drill? No smoke didn't necessarily mean no fire. Why else would that shrill buzzer still be sounding? Her mother was in the recovery room, groggy with anesthetic, hooked up to machines. What measures did the hospital have in place to ensure Irene's safety?

Rose stood in the doorway and waved the nurse down as the hallway emptied out.

"Since it's only a drill, I think I'll stay where I am. My mother just came out of surgery and she's—"

"Everyone leaves," the nurse snapped. "That means you."

"But my mother—"

"Will be taken care of. You need to leave. Now."

Rose swallowed down a surge of annoyance at the insolence in the woman's voice. What did this nurse know about fire or smoke—or her mother, for that matter? Absolutely nothing. Rose backed up and plopped down in the nearest chair. "You can leave if you like," she said to the Judge, "but I'm not going anywhere until I know Mom is safe."

"You get out of that chair right now." The nurse folded her arms and leveled them both with an icy glare.

"My dear, I think it might be wise to do as she asks." The Judge gripped Rose's shoulder. "They'll take good care of your mother."

"I am not budging." Rose squinted at the nurse's identification tag and made a mental note.

"If you're not out of that chair in the next five seconds, I'll call security and let them deal with you."

"Totally unnecessary." The Judge grasped Rose firmly by the arm and yanked her onto her feet. "We're leaving, as requested."

"Did you hear her? That woman threatened me," Rose complained as he pulled her down the hall. "And what about Mom?"

"They aren't about to put your mother's life at risk. And as for whether there is actually a fire, obviously we are on a need-to-know basis. They want us out of here and I suggest we oblige them."

Rose squinted against the brilliant sunshine as they exited the building into the parking lot. Sirens wailed in the distance as she waited beside the Judge, watching as the fire trucks approached. The trucks were yellow, large, and loud, with air horns blaring and flashing red and white lights.

"Since when do they call out the fire department if it's only a drill?" she muttered. "Looks like I was right."

"Stand back, everyone stand back," came the call as first one, then a second fire truck pulled up in front of the entrance. A short stubby fireman tumbled out of the passenger seat, pulling on his fire gear as he raced past them into the hospital. A second fireman on the driver's side slid from behind the wheel and strode through the crowd. Rose's eyes narrowed as she spotted the tall, solid man. His determined face was steeled with resolve. Intense blue eyes filled with concern beneath a scuffed white helmet.

Rose drew in a sharp breath. She should have figured she'd eventually see him again. James Bay wasn't that big for their paths not to cross. But the sight of him today was somehow reassuring. Her anxiety vanished through the revolving front door along with the fireman.

The wailing alarm ended abruptly, filling the afternoon with an eerie silence. Seconds later, as if on cue, Lillian Gillespie emerged through the hospital main entrance. Rose exhaled a deep sigh as she caught sight of her mother's best friend. The gleam in Lil's eyes was a sure giveaway there was no need to fear. The hospital wasn't on fire. That fact would have been much too juicy for her not to share.

"Spill it, Lil," the Judge ordered. "What's going on?"

Lil pulled the two of them aside, far away from the visitors and hospital staff milling about the parking lot.

"This is hush-hush and completely confidential." She raised one finger to her lips and diamonds flashed on her rings in the brilliant sunshine.

"You're talking to two lawyers, remember?" the Judge replied. "We're officers of the court. There's no need to remind us about the rules of confidentiality. What happened?"

"Well, two doctors—both of whom shall remain nameless, mind you—decided to indulge themselves with afternoon cigars." The whisper of a smile appeared on Lil's face. "They were huddled up in one of the offices. It seems that little conference of theirs triggered the smoke detectors and set off the fire alarm."

Rose frowned. "I thought the hospital was a smoke-free area."

Lil nodded fiercely. "It is. But obviously those doctors forgot. Maybe all that smoke clouded their minds along with their better judgment."

"Ladies, as neither of you smoke, I wouldn't expect you to understand the pleasures of a fine cigar."

Rose couldn't help smiling as the Judge patted his jacket pocket. His fondness for cigars was well-known to all. And his taste in tobacco didn't come cheap. Everyone knew he paid a pretty penny to have his cigars custom made in the islands.

"At least we know Mom is safe. She should be out of recovery soon."

"Good Lord, where is my mind?" Lil shook her head. "They just took Irene up to her room. Sarah Mae Carter was one of the attending nurses. She grabbed me and let me know when I was coming out the door."

"Is Mom awake?"

Lil's head bobbed up and down without disturbing one hair on her perfectly coiffed head. "You can see her once we go back inside." She clutched Rose's hand and squeezed tight. "The doctor wants to talk to you, but not to worry. Sarah Mae told me that everything went fine."

Rose blew out a heavy sigh. Sarah Mae and Lil knew better than to discuss patients' private medical histories, but confidentiality be damned. This was her mother they were talking about.

The two firemen reemerged into the sunshine.

"Where's the fire? What's going on?" yelled an onlooker.

"Sorry for the inconvenience, folks. It was just a false alarm," the taller of the two firemen called as he pulled off his helmet. "You can go back inside now."

He turned then, not three feet away from her, and Rose suddenly found herself looking square into his eyes. He halted as their gazes locked and held. Mere seconds, perhaps, though it was hard to tell. She had the sudden sense the world's eternal timepiece had abruptly stopped ticking.

Then, giving a quick silent nod, he turned and was gone.

"Who was that?" Lil glanced toward Rose, an intense gleam in her eye. A longtime widow, Lil was always on the lookout for a good-looking man.

"Just someone I met the other day." Rose tried to keep the smile plastered on her face from growing any wider.

"Interesting... very interesting," Lil replied.

The Judge glanced back and forth between them. "Obviously I've missed something. What's going on?"

"Why, Judge, I thought you knew everything around town." Lil's eyebrows raised in high amusement. "For an officer of the court, you seem slightly clueless."

Rose smiled as she listened to the familiar banter between them that she'd heard all her life. "Come on; let's go see how Mom's doing."

She tucked a hand through each of their arms and led them back into the hospital. For the moment, life was good. The sun was shining, her mother had sailed through the long-awaited surgery, and the hospital wasn't on fire.

And for the last fact, she had professional reassurance taken on good authority.

Very good-looking authority.

Rose sank into the cozy window seat halfway between upstairs and down, resting her head against the wall. The house was quiet, save for the grandfather clock in the downstairs hallway ticking away the minutes. Fading sunlight filtered through the rose-mullioned window above her seat, casting a rainbow hue on the faded carpet runner. This little crannied nook with its bird's-eye view of the happenings in the house and neighborhood had been one of her favorite spots as a child.

Outside the window she could see the tree she and Jeff had climbed as children. They'd considered it *their tree*, though its roots were planted firmly on her family's side of the property line. It had been their private summertime childhood retreat, a cozy haven of shady green leaves offering shelter as the two of them explored the world of Popsicles and comic books. The tree was the one place they were safe from their parents: Jeff from the Judge's eagle eyes and Rose from her parents' benevolent gaze. She and Jeff had grown up together in the shelter of their tree, the only thing separating their two houses.

Now she was back home again... and Jeff had been dead so many years she'd nearly forgotten the sound of his laughter.

Rose curled up tighter in the soft cushions and pushed away thoughts of Jeff. He was dead and buried, just like any feelings she'd ever had for this town. The rumor mill surrounding his death had killed any sentimental longing she'd mistakenly felt for her hometown. James Bay wasn't home anymore. It was simply the place where she had grown up. Bad enough that her mother still lived here. Strategic planning was in order. Winters in northern Michigan could be harsh and unforgiving. Florida sounded nice. And what was the harm in trying? Her mother might prove receptive. At the very least, it would give them something to talk about for the next six weeks.

Her eyes drifted shut. She'd forgotten how comfortable the window seat could be. How long had it been since she'd indulged herself and spent some time in this favorite little spot? So long ago, she couldn't remember. She sank back farther in the welcoming niche, allowing herself the rare luxury of relaxing. Such a long day, but everything had worked out. The surgery had been successful. Maybe now things would finally begin to settle down...

And maybe someone would turn off that noise. Was it coming from outside? The screeching sound was like a shrieking alarm protruding on her daydreams.

Hopefully it would stop soon. Rose sighed and snuggled deeper.

The faint smell of smoke roused her to her feet.

Smoke?

That sound from below was the smoke alarm.

Fire!

Rose flew down the stairs and into the kitchen. Smoke filled the room, acrid and pungent, tearing her eyes and sucking the breath from her lungs. Every hair on her head felt as if it was standing on end. She threw an arm over her nose, fighting against the stench. Her eyes widened as she caught sight of the scorched tea kettle forgotten on the stove.

A hazy childhood memory of another smoke-filled room threatened... a hot summer night with the smell of cotton candy and the stink of smoke mingling in the air.

I can't see! I can't see! Daddy, where are you?

She snapped off the burner, but it took every ounce of courage she had to make a grab for the kettle. The heat was intense as her fingers connected with the black handle. She gave it a hard yank but the kettle wouldn't budge. It was melted to the coils of the electric stove.

Rose snatched the cordless phone from its cradle and stumbled out the door. She took deep grateful gulps of fresh air as she made the call to 911.

The fire department was only three blocks away, but the wait seemed interminable before the welcome sound of a wailing siren was finally heard. Rose watched from the front lawn of their corner lot as the first yellow fire truck approached. It filled the side street near the driveway. A fireman clad in full turnout gear slid from the truck and ran for the back porch. Smoke seeped from the kitchen window as a second fire truck roared in behind the first. Thank God she'd gotten out in time. *Stupid, stupid, stupid,* leaving the burner on under the kettle and walking away, sinking into sleep. The wail of the smoke detector had prevented a needless tragedy.

And the neighborhood gossips were already at it, fast and furious. Rose took in the gathering crowd of curious onlookers drawn by the sirens and lure of possible danger. News traveled fast in this town. Even her mother, stuck in her hospital bed, probably would know the full scoop within the hour. Rose cringed at the thought of the maternal recriminations sure to follow.

Somewhere in the crowd a dog barked, whining and straining against his owner's leash. The animal's yelp brought a rush of fear surging through Rose's heart. Bozo! Her mother's aging Red Persian was strictly an indoor cat and still inside, trapped. Anxiously she scanned the second and third stories of their hundred-year-old house. Who knew where that damn cat could be hiding? No access through the kitchen. She gave the front porch a wary eye. There'd be less smoke—hopefully no smoke—if she went in that way. She had to try. Her mother would be frantic if anything happened to her precious Bozo. Rose swallowed down a cold taste of fear and started toward the front steps.

"Whoa!" A strong arm yanked her away from the house. The rumble of a deep male voice held her captive. "Where do you think you're going?"

Rose looked up into familiar blue eyes. Dressed in full turnout gear of dirty yellow fire coat and pants with big black scuffed boots on his feet, he looked more like a battle-scarred veteran than the conquering hero. His eyes were like magnets, pulling her in, holding her close. For a moment she forgot her purpose. Why *had* she been headed into the house?

"My mother's cat." Sanity returned, quickly as it had departed. "He's inside the house."

"You stay where you are. We'll find the cat." Turning, he headed for the back porch and took the steps two at a time. He yanked open the kitchen door. Smoke rolled out the entrance as he disappeared inside.

"Cecilia Rose? What's going on?" The Judge stomped across the side lawn, still in his black suit. "What happened?"

What *had* happened? Rose cringed at the memory of the screeching alarm and her hasty exit out the back door. She shuddered in the Judge's arms as thoughts of the smoke-filled kitchen clouded her mind. Smoke was a swirling monster, worse than any flames. She hated smoke—blinding, choking, suffocating. No wonder she'd panicked and forgotten Bozo.

The fireman reappeared moments later on the back porch. His hands, clad in thick gloves, held the charred remains of the tea kettle melted fast to the element.

"I'm afraid you'll have to replace this," he said as he clomped down the steps. "It's not much good to you now."

"I was boiling some water." She cringed. The truth sounded lame. "I wanted a cup of tea. Then I sat down and... I guess I fell asleep."

"Better get yourself a whistling tea kettle. It's better than hearing a smoke alarm." His stern warning was curt but his eyes were framed by wrinkles of well-grooved laugh lines.

Was he making fun of her? Rose felt the blush climbing her cheeks. But if he was teasing, she had only herself to blame. Her forgetfulness had given him license to do exactly that.

She flashed him a quick smile. "Thank you for coming to my rescue again. I can't believe I did something so stupid."

Better that she said it first, leveled at herself, than to have him thinking it, silently or aloud.

"About the cat..." His eyes were intense as he looked at her.

Oh, God, Bozo was dead. She swallowed down a rush of panic. How would she explain his unfortunate demise to her mother?

I was too scared to think. I ran from the smoke.

"I did my best, but I couldn't catch him. That cat wants nothing to do with me. He's running all over the house meowing something fierce—I think he's telling me to get lost."

Rose gave a weak, shaky laugh. Bozo was safe. Thanks to the fireman, they had all survived.

The Judge's arm tightened around her shoulders. "You'll stay next door with me tonight, my dear. Give the house a chance to air out."

"What about Bozo?" Rose hesitated. The Judge had a long-running feud with their cat.

"He'll be all right. The fire's out and we opened up the kitchen windows," the fireman said. "You should go through the house and open the rest of the windows. Things will be aired out by morning."

A quick pressure on her arm caught Rose's attention.

"Stay right where you are, my dear," the Judge said. "I'm going back to my house to change, but I'll be back in a few minutes. Then I intend to take the two of us out to dinner."

"Call if you have any more problems," the fireman said as the Judge disappeared across the lush green lawn. "You have my number."

Rose frowned. She didn't remember exchanging phone numbers with him. "I think you're mistaken. I don't know how to reach you."

"Sure you do." He pulled off the scuffed white helmet and ran a hand through his hair, eyes sparkling bright. "911."

"Wait," she called out to the tall, receding figure as he headed for the fire truck. "In case I do call, who do I ask for? I don't even know your name."

"The name's Mike," he said. He stashed his gear in the truck and opened the driver's door. "Michael John Gallagher."

CHAPTER THREE

WEATHER WISE

The James Bay Journal

WEATHER ADVISORY: Hot, dry conditions throughout our area have prompted the Department of Natural Resources to issue an advisory for extreme fire danger. The threat of potential grass fires will continue until the current drought is relieved. The efforts of all James Bay citizens are needed to keep our community safe. Be vigilant and help prevent fires!

Chuck's Tavern and Grill was hot and crowded. Some faces were familiar, others not.

"Guess I've been away too long. I hardly recognize anybody in town anymore." Rose gave the Judge a weary smile as the waitress disappeared with their menus. James Bay in the summertime had its share of pleasures as well as drawbacks. For the ten blissful, beautiful weeks comprising most of June, July, and August, locals surrendered control of their town, as well as the restaurants, shops, and beaches.

"You already know the people who count." The Judge took a careful sip of his beer. His suit and tie from earlier were gone and his ample girth now sported an open-collared shirt paired with a navy blue blazer and slacks.

"I thought you were a martini man," she said with a thoughtful nod toward his frosted glass.

"It's true I love my martinis." The Judge took another sip of his drink. "But there's quite a bit about me you don't know, my dear. And now you're all grown up, I suppose it's time I let you in on some of my little secrets."

Rose smiled. "Secrets? Since when do you have secrets?"

"Don't we all?" The Judge matched her smile with a beguiling one of his own. "As for me, I enjoy a good beer now and then, especially on a hot day like this."

She chuckled softly. "You drink beer instead of martinis? Some secret."

His smile broadened as he leaned forward across the table. "Here's another for you, then. When you're dining at Chuck's Tavern, always order a beer. Creating a perfect martini is a true work of art. Unfortunately, our friend Chuck never attended that particular art school." He raised his glass in deference to Chuck, short sleeved and crew cut, hard at work behind the bar.

Rose followed his toast with a smile. Chuck's Tavern and Grill was a local establishment forged in the hearts of locals and resorters alike. Its Friday night all-you-can-eat fish fries bordered on legendary. She sat back in her chair and sipped her ice water, stifling a yawn. A nice quiet dinner, then home to bed for some much needed sleep were the only items on her evening agenda. It had been a long day, first with the anxious wait through her mother's surgery, only to be followed by that unfortunate mishap in the kitchen. And while it hadn't been a fully engulfed fire, the downstairs rooms in her mother's house still reeked of smoke.

Thinking of the kitchen fire turned her thoughts to something—and someone—else. How ironic was it that the fireman with those magnetic blue eyes should have the identical name as her own father... right down to sharing the middle name of *John*. Then again, *Gallagher* was a common enough last name, at least up north. Rose settled deeper in her seat. A mere coincidence, that's all it was. An unsettling coincidence.

A smile curled around her lips. What would Michael John Gallagher have to say about the coincidence when he found out?

"Maybe I haven't changed, but you certainly have," the Judge said. "You are a far cry from that little girl with dirty knees and pigtails I remember scuffling around in my backyard."

Rose ignored the slight tug at her heart. "That little girl is long gone. She grew up and went to law school."

"Speaking of law, how are things at the firm?"

"Firmly in place," she replied in a slaphappy voice, mimicking how she felt. Slaphappy, punchy, and sleepy, too. She struggled to keep her eyelids from drooping.

"You've done us all proud, my dear. If your father was still alive, I know he would be extremely pleased."

Even through the heavy fatigue, the rare compliment registered. Her old friend wasn't given to paying forms of false flattery. "Thank you, Judge."

Idle thoughts of a tall man with burnished blond hair and sparkling blue eyes returned to mind. What about that fireman? What would he think if he learned she was an attorney with a high-profile firm? He was completely different than the men she dealt with in her everyday world. *The suits.* Prancing lawyers with polished shoes and expensive wardrobes, roaming the carpeted corridors of the firm, gleefully choreographing testimony at scheduled depositions, hovering in the hallways of the Kent County courthouse. How long had it been since anyone remotely attractive and available had waltzed into her world? There had been offers, especially from Andy, but no man—a suit or otherwise—remotely sparked her interest.

Was this all there was left to her in the dating game?

Michael John Gallagher definitely wasn't a suit.

Forget that idea. They had nothing in common. What would they talk about? She was well-versed in legal jargon, but she'd forgotten how to carry on a decent social conversation with the opposite sex. She'd probably forgotten how to flirt anymore.

More important, did she want to?

Her clients, the firm, and never-ending community commitments stole every ounce of available energy. How could you expect to successfully master the dating game when each night brought you home exhausted and wishing for nothing more stimulating than a quick dinner; fragrant, hot bath; fresh sheets on the bed?

She didn't need a man to be happy. She'd settle for a good night's sleep.

"I have a question for you, my dear. What would you say about coming back to James Bay?"

Rose forced her attention back to the man in front of her. "But I am back. At least for the next six weeks."

"You misunderstood." He sat back in his chair, sharp black eyes trained upon her with precision. "I'm talking about you coming home and setting up law practice with me."

Rose nearly choked on her ice water. The Judge couldn't be serious. Was he actually suggesting she come back to live and practice law in James Bay?

"I know we've never discussed the matter, but I'm sure you will agree the idea has some merit."

"The two of us as partners?" She must be more tired than she'd imagined. Even when Jeff was alive, the two of them had never discussed the possibility of partnership with his father. Back then, with the Judge still sitting on the bench, the three of them setting up practice together had been a nonissue. And truth be told, that hadn't been such a bad thing, either. While she loved Jeff's father, the Judge had an uncanny knack for managing schemes that benefited him and a way of finagling exactly what he wanted.

And if I'm hearing him correctly, what he wants is me. But why me? And why now? He knows how I feel about this town. More than anyone else, he should understand.

"Yes, my dear, you and I as partners in a firm. That is exactly what I am proposing."

Partnering with Jeff's father. The thought sent a shiver snaking up her spine. Rose cast an uneasy glance across the table at the man with silvered hair and beguiling smile. The Judge was part of her past and her present. With the offer he'd just made, he could play a significant role in her future, too.

"Think of it, Cecilia Rose." He leaned closer across the table. "I have a large practice, but real-estate matters are taking up more and more of my time and I find myself in a position where I am no longer able to do justice to some of my other clients. I need help, my dear. I need you."

How was she supposed to respond? The Judge was nearly as dear to her as her own father. Plus he had helped finance her legal education. She was in his debt. But returning to James Bay to live and partner with him had never been part of the plan.

Or had it? Maybe he'd had the idea in mind all along, but hadn't planned to call in his markers until now.

"I wouldn't presume to ask you for a decision tonight." The Judge's face wore a tacit expression of quiet understanding. "I merely wanted to present the subject. I've been thinking about this for quite some time. And now, I believe it is time for you to think about it, too."

Clerking for her firm had been meant merely as a summertime job, but their offer following graduation had been too good to turn down. Admission to the Bar had gained her a position as associate attorney. There was a sense of security within the corporate ranks. Working for the firm provided a convenient out. There was no need for further explanation—to her family, friends, or even to herself. Jeff's death had seen the end of their dreams. There'd be no more talk of *when we grow up*. All that was left to her now was *what used to be*.

But she'd promised herself she wouldn't look back. If she wasn't successful, it wouldn't be for lack of trying. Her days were spent trying to fit in, to make some sort of niche for herself. Oftentimes she went home from work tired beyond exhaustion, convinced her efforts had gone unnoticed.

Unnoticed? Obviously not. With Andy's proposal, and now the Judge's, she'd just received her second job offer in less than a week. Rose felt a silly smile spreading on her face. The irony of it all was too delicious.

"Am I to assume you think it a ludicrous proposal?" The Judge sat back with a look of dismay.

"Not at all," she quickly replied. Her old friend and mentor's discontent was unsettling. But he knew how she felt about this town. He was Jeff's father. He had lived through the rumors just like she had.

So how could the Judge believe she would give serious consideration to any offer that brought her back to James Bay?

Yet maybe he wasn't so foolish after all. The Judge wasn't the type of man to resort to emotional blackmail. Or was he? If he chose to do so, it would prove difficult—if not impossible—to turn him down.

She owed him. Big time.

"There's no need for a hasty decision," he said as their dinners were served. "All I ask is that you give the matter some thought. We'll talk about it again soon." With a fond smile for her, he turned his attention to the food before him and began working his way through the platter of barbecued ribs.

Rose watched in fascination. The Judge's appetite was voracious, yet somehow he managed to maintain an air of dignity and refinement even while licking his fingers clean. She stared in dismay at her hamburger and side dish of coleslaw, no longer hungry. With the Judge's offer of a partnership on the table, she had some big decisions facing her. Could she accept Andy's offer and continue sidestepping his overtures toward an inevitable romance? Would it be possible to come back and embrace the town of her youth? Did she really wish to sacrifice her life and career to be stuck again in this small town and all its painful memories?

Rose rubbed her head with the heel of her hand. This was no time to be making any life-altering decisions. She couldn't remember when she'd felt so tired. The only thing she wanted was to crawl into bed and fall into a long dreamless sleep.

"Cecilia? Hello! I thought that was you." A distinct, clipped voice, filled with pleasure, echoed near their table.

Rose hadn't been away from town long enough not to recognize the voice that had haunted her since the first time she heard it in ninth-grade English class. She glanced up at the tall, spindly man with spiky brown hair and intense brown eyes. "Hi, Charles."

"Welcome home." Charles Kendall's face wore a look of open admiration. "You look wonderful."

"Young Mr. Kendall. How go things with the Fourth Estate?"

Charles Kendall's pale face lit up in animation. "Things are flourishing at the *Journal*. I'm Editor in Chief now." His proud announcement was made with a triumphant nod for Rose. "I have a staff of three and total editorial control."

Rose mustered up a polite smile and curbed the stir of impatience festering inside. She'd spent most of her high school career trying to put some distance between them, but somehow Charles always managed to find her. If nothing else, he was persistent.

"Looks like we've both turned out to be success stories." Charles beamed down at her. "You're an attorney with a big firm and I'm making a name for myself in the newspaper business. You've probably noticed the articles we've been running about the recent fires." His voice dropped in a low whisper. "I have it on good authority there's an arsonist at work in James Bay."

"Is that so?" Rose lifted her eyebrows in mild interest to hide her annoyance. Fire was the last subject she wished to discuss. The faint smell of smoke still lingered in her hair from the recent culinary disaster in her mother's kitchen.

"Watch the paper," Charles promised. "We'll be featuring more about it in the days ahead."

Rose cast him a thoughtful look. What exactly was he up to? Charles wouldn't stoop to manufacturing evidence just to boost the *Journal's* circulation. Or would he?

"We should get together while you're in town. I assume you're staying at your mother's?"

"Correct," she reluctantly acknowledged.

"Terrific. I'll phone you. When's a good time to call?"

Never flashed to mind. And he didn't plan on sitting down, did he? Charles already had one hand on the empty chair at their table. Its legs squeaked noisily against the scratched wooden floor. If he joined them, they'd be stuck sitting here at least another hour. There went her plans for a good night's sleep.

"Mr. Kendall, I must ask you to excuse us. Cecilia Rose has had quite the day and we were just about to depart for home."

Rose pressed her napkin to her mouth and hid a smile as she heard the Judge's voice ring forth with the weight of judicial authority. He hadn't sat on the bench for years but His Honor could still lay it on pretty thick when he wished.

Charles's face flushed dark red as he pushed the chair back under the table. "Another time, then."

Rose felt her heart soften at the discomfited look on his face. Charles had been an irritating presence long ago, but they weren't in high school anymore. Now she merely felt sorry for him.

"I'll be in town through the first week of August," she said. "It probably would be better if you wait until next week to call. Mom should be home from the hospital by then and I know she'd love to see you." As well as make a convenient buffer.

"Give her my best." Charles backed away from the table with the earlier confident look once more on his face.

"Thanks for interceding," Rose said to the Judge when they were alone again. "Charles can be a real pest."

"No thanks necessary, my dear." The Judge wiped the last remaining bit of barbecue sauce from his fingers. "I only told young Mr. Kendall the truth. You've been through a lot today and you need your rest." He gestured for the bill.

"Please, let me take care of dinner tonight." She reached for her purse. "You've already done more than enough for me."

"Absolutely not, this is my treat. Besides, I'll write off our little strategy session as a business expense."

"Strategy session?" Rose stood up from her chair with a frown. She caught a quick flourish of bills as the Judge thumbed two twenties from his wallet.

"Strategy, negotiations, whatever you wish to call it." He flashed her a brief smile. "Have you already forgotten? I'm in serious negotiations, my dear... with someone I hope will soon agree to be my new partner."

Rose trailed behind him as they headed through the crowd toward the cash register. She wasn't about to forget their conversation tonight. The Judge wasn't about to let her.

The market was as small and cramped as she remembered. Rose wielded her grocery cart down the narrow rows of canned goods stacked high in jumbled confusion and untidy display racks crammed at the end of the aisles. It seemed the recent spurt of James Bay remodeling mania had yet to touch the town's one grocery store. She steered clear of yet one more mini-traffic jam in the produce department and headed toward the meat display. Progress might be forthcoming in certain parts of town, but some things, like this grocery store, would never change.

"Hello there."

Rose veered her cart to the left as she caught sight of Michael Gallagher in front of the meat counter. The last time they'd met, he'd been dressed in fire gear. This afternoon he sported crisp dark blue jeans and a clean white t-shirt with the name and logo of the James Bay Fire Department. Obviously he wasn't on duty today. And had she merely imagined it, or had his eyes lit up as he caught sight of her?

She flashed him a quick smile and prayed he wouldn't notice the blush she felt climbing high on her cheeks. Something about this fireman left her feeling awkward, knock-kneed, and tongue-tied. *Almost like being back in seventh grade.* What was wrong with her, anyway? She wasn't in middle school anymore. She was a professional, accustomed to thinking and talking fast on her feet, in and out of the courtroom.

Rose glanced down at the package of steak in his hand. "Buying dinner?"

Too late. She groaned in silent mortification as she heard the words slide out of her mouth. Obviously he was buying dinner. Couldn't she come up with anything better than that?

"Just shopping for some things I need at the fire station. I'm running low on supplies."

"You buy your own food? But I thought the fire department would provide that..."

"You and everybody else in America. Nobody seems to realize firemen pay for their food and cook it, too." His eyes crinkled in a smile. "Speaking of cooking, you must be staying out of the kitchen—911 has been pretty quiet for the past day or two."

Rose's blush spread even deeper. He was teasing, and they both knew she knew it. This fireman was proving real trouble.

"Sorry, I couldn't resist," he said. "My brother's always telling me that my joking around will get me in trouble someday. He's probably right."

She hadn't noticed that dimple in his cheek until now. It played hide and seek against the dark blond stubble on his face.

"By the way, how's your mom?"

"My mom?" Reluctantly she pulled her gaze away from that intriguing dimple to meet his eyes.

"She did have surgery, correct?"

"Surgery? Oh, right." *Get a grip, Rose.* Here she was, babbling like an idiot. Then again, he probably already thought she was borderline crazy, what with nearly setting the house ablaze by cooking that ancient teakettle.

"The surgery went fine, thanks. She'll be home in another few days."

"My dad had surgery on his shoulder last year. It's hard, seeing your parents out of commission. Makes you stop and think about how lucky you are that they're still around."

Cute, courageous, and considerate, too. What more could a woman want? Memories from the past few days flooded her senses. A smoking car and a tall blond stranger coming to her mother's aid. A hospital alarm with a possible blaze and a stalwart fireman with scuffed white helmet sounding the *all clear*. Sleep deprivation sparking a stupid mistake, and once again, this fireman had been there to save the day.

"I know putting out fires is your job, but I'd really like to thank you. Maybe we could have dinner? My treat." Rose threw him a smile across the cluttered grocery aisle. "I'm free tonight, if that works for you."

He looked startled. Almost as startled as she felt, hearing the unexpected invitation slide smoothly from her mouth. But his response time was immediate. "Sorry, it doesn't."

"Oh." Her cheeks flamed as if they'd experienced a spontaneous combustion. "Never mind, it was just a thought."

She gripped the shopping cart so hard her knuckles hurt. Whatever had possessed her to ask him out in the first place? It wasn't as if she'd planned it. Now she had embarrassed them both. She gave the cart a sharp turn and veered to the left. Today's shopping excursion was over. She didn't need any more groceries. The only thing she needed was to get away from him, and fast.

But the shopping cart wouldn't move. Something held it back. Rose glanced down and saw Mike's hand gripping the handle, preventing it from veering even one inch.

"Wait a minute, okay?"

She took a deep breath and loosened her hold.

"I can't have dinner with you tonight. I'm covering for the chief down at the fire station. But I'll be off tomorrow. I could make it then."

Rose's eyes narrowed. More teasing? Did she dare trust that smile?

"Tomorrow night... would be fine."

"Good." He leaned back on his heels with a look of studied amusement. "So, where do you plan on taking me for dinner?"

"I... I hadn't really given it much thought." His question raised a valid point. Where *should* she take him? Not anywhere too expensive. This was only a thank-you dinner of sorts. She didn't want to give him the wrong impression. It wasn't as if they were going on a date.

"If you're planning to cook, let me know. I'll make sure the guys have a fire truck standing by." He broke out in a sudden abashed grin. "Sorry. Just forget I said that, okay? I'll try and watch myself from now on."

Rose felt her stomach do a little flip-flop. He actually was very cute.

"I'm sure you're a good cook," he added in a quick aside.

"To tell you the truth, I'm not." She returned his smile. "But then, you already know that, don't you?"

His eyes riveted on her own. "I suppose I do."

She hadn't forgotten how to flirt after all! Suddenly Rose felt all lit up inside, tingling with excitement. They were flirting with each other and it was tremendous fun.

"So, I'll see you tomorrow night, then?"

"I'll make sure I'm hungry." He released his grip on her cart. "How about I give you a call when I finish my shift?"

"I'll wait to hear from you." Rose wiggled her fingers in farewell as he steered his cart toward the checkout.

"Oh, wait!"

He turned with a patient smile. "Forget something?"

"You don't have my phone number. Let me write it down." She dug deep in her purse, scrounging for a pen.

"Don't bother. I've already got it."

"You do?" She glanced up with a frown.

"You called 911, remember? It's all in the fire report. Telephone, home address, plus your name."

Michael John Gallagher's eyes sparkled bright.

"I'll see you tomorrow night... Miss Cecilia Rose Gallagher."

CHAPTER FOUR

FIRE LABELED DEFINITE ARSON

By: Charles Kendall
The James Bay Journal

JAMES BAY—Fire officials have determined last night's fire that destroyed a large wooden shed on Martin Road was a definite act of arson. The fire was reported by Jim Bell, a local aviator who spotted the fire from his plane. James Bay firefighters were able to contain the blaze and keep it from spreading to the woods bordering Martin Road. "People need to be aware that this drought has intensified the fire danger," said James Bay Assistant Fire Chief Michael Gallagher. "If that fire had made it into the woods and crowned in the pine trees, we could have had a real disaster."

While no suspects have yet been named, the investigation continues. Residents are asked to contact the fire department with any information they have concerning the incident. Any tips will be kept strictly confidential.

Arson is a second-degree felony punishable by a $15,000 fine and ten years imprisonment or both.

Tommy Gilbert took the glass of iced tea Rose offered and drained it in one thirsty gulp.

"Thanks, Cecil. Man, I wish this weather would break. Mowing lawns is hot work, especially in this heat." He wiped the sweat from his face and neck with a rag from his back pocket.

"Why don't you quit for the day and come back tomorrow, Tommy? It's supposed to be cooler then. Mom won't be home from the hospital until Saturday and I don't care if you leave things like this tonight."

"Naw, thanks anyway, but it's not worth it. Joey will get mad if I didn't finish up. Now he owns the business, he likes to play the big man and tell me what to do."

Rose bit her lip as she refilled his iced tea. She didn't envy Tommy working for his brother. Tommy's older brother Joey had been her classmate for twelve straight years in school, and he'd been obnoxious and overbearing even back then. She could only imagine how demanding he was now, being the boss.

Tommy finished off the second glass of iced tea as quickly as his first and handed it to Rose with a crooked grin. "Back to the grind. I tell you, Cecil, never work for your brother... but then, you won't never have that problem since you don't have any brothers or sisters. Lucky you." He started down the kitchen porch steps but halted as a cherry-red pickup pulled into the driveway. "Hey, what gives? You expecting company?"

The two of them watched as Michael Gallagher slid out of his truck. He gave them a small wave as he headed toward them.

"Who's that guy?" Tommy's face scrunched in a frown.

"His name is Michael Gallagher," she answered coolly. "We were supposed to have dinner tonight."

And he was late. Nearly an hour late. In her world, people were on time or had a damn good excuse. Sauntering into a courtroom fashionably late didn't sit well with the judge or jury.

"Actually, I prefer Mike," he said as he neared the back porch. "Sorry, I didn't mean to eavesdrop, but I couldn't help overhearing." He climbed the steps and offered Tommy a hand. "The name's Mike Gallagher."

Tommy's face blossomed in a self-conscious grin. He wiped his hand clean against the back of his faded jeans, stuck out his hand and pumped Mike's own. "Tommy Gilbert. Nice truck. Is it new?" His gaze was riveted in rapt admiration toward the driveway.

"Pretty much. There aren't too many miles on it," Mike volunteered, with a fast smile for Rose.

"Mind if I check it out?" Tommy didn't wait for an answer. He stepped off the porch and headed for the truck.

"Sorry I'm late," Mike said. "I was at the fire station and just about to leave when the fire marshal stopped by. He just left."

Her heart softened somewhat. "That's all right," she said. Sometimes things happen. Everyone deserved a second chance.

"You ready?"

"I am." She'd dressed for their dinner in a short, sleeveless shift in a colorful swirl of salmon pink and lemon yellow. Her long black hair was pulled up, cool in a fashionable knot at the back of her head, though she already felt some strands pulling loose. Her feet were in sandals. She'd even taken the time to paint her toenails red with a bottle of scarlet lacquer filched from her mother's bathroom vanity. She couldn't remember the last time she'd spent her time doing something as frivolous and feminine as painting her toenails. But it was summer and she wanted to dress light. To think light and feel light.

Forget the law. She wanted to feel like a girl.

"I don't know..." he said. Rose caught the look on Mike's face as his gaze quickly traveled the length of her body. Was he preparing some long-winded tease? She silently vowed not to take any forthcoming compliments from him seriously. No matter what he said, she would *not* blush.

Mike glanced down at his khaki slacks and short-sleeved shirt, then back at her with a sudden doubtful look. "Guess I should have gotten more dressed up. You look so pretty, and I don't think I... well..."

"You don't have to change, not for me," she hastily replied. "You look perfect just the way you are."

He *did* look perfect. Perfectly wonderful.

Their eyes met, held and locked, and for one brief moment, she saw the hint of something in his gaze—a vulnerable, uncertain look she couldn't name or place. She tried to inhale, but it was hard to breathe. A shiver snaked up her spine. It felt as if the hot summer air had been sucked away by some strange eternal vortex. Something about this fireman left her unsettled and shy in a way she hadn't felt for a very long time. He was different than any of the other men she knew. He didn't carry a briefcase and he didn't wear a suit... unless you counted the heavy yellow fire coat, suspender pants, and big black boots with steel toes that were part of his regular ensemble whenever duty called.

They headed down the porch steps. Tommy Gilbert still hadn't started up the mower. He stood in the driveway, checking out the interior of Mike's truck through the open window.

"Nice truck," he said as they joined him near the driver's door. "How big is the engine?"

"V-8," Mike replied.

"Man, this thing is loaded." Tommy Gilbert whistled in admiration as he scanned the interior. "Check it out, Cecil. Air conditioning, four-wheel drive... hey, what's that?" He pointed to a large interior console with a microphone mounted directly to the right of the steering wheel.

"A two-way radio," Mike replied.

"Mike is a fireman," Rose informed him.

Tommy's eyes widened. He gazed up at the emergency lights fixed atop the truck. "That explains the light bar. You're with the fire department."

Mike nodded.

Tommy stroked the hood with a reverent hand. "Are you on call? Like, right now?"

"Twenty-four seven," Mike replied.

Rose shifted on her feet. Mike's admission seemed to have fired up her young neighbor's enthusiasm. The look on Tommy's face rang a warning bell in her mind. If she and Mike didn't leave soon, she'd find herself trapped in man talk and lengthy explanations of how the truck's various pieces of emergency equipment worked.

But Mike already seemed to have noticed her discomfort. "I'll be glad to drive." His gaze skimmed briefly over her short summer dress. "That is, if you don't mind riding in a truck."

She'd never given a thought as to which of them would drive. After the fender bender with his truck, her mother's sedan was still at the repair shop, which left only her own little sports car. With low bucket seats and cramped coupe conditions, it wouldn't exactly be a comfortable ride for someone built like him.

"It's been a long time since I've ridden in a truck, but why not? I'm game." She wiggled her fingers at Tommy and skirted around the hood to the passenger side, but Mike beat her to the door. He opened it with a flourish.

"After you, Miss Gallagher."

"Thank you, Mr. Gallagher." The unexpected chivalrous gesture gave rise to a sweet, heady rush of pure feminine pleasure that had long been forgotten, tucked away somewhere deep inside until this moment. Rose took Mike's hand and accepted the boost he offered with a grateful smile. Someone had taught him beautiful manners.

He slid behind the driver's wheel and turned the key in the ignition. Rose couldn't hide her growing delight as the truck rumbled to life. She'd forgotten how much fun it was to be in a truck, perched high in your seat, looking down on the world as you passed it by. Being in a pickup wasn't anything like driving in her little roadster, which neatly hugged every narrow curve and shoulder of the highway.

Tonight promised to be lots of fun.

"Remember what I said, Tommy," she called through the open window as they backed down the driveway. "Forget about the lawn and go on home. I'll see you tomorrow."

"See ya, Cecil."

"He seems like a nice kid," Mike said as he pulled out of the driveway.

"He and his family live a couple of blocks down the street." Rose gave a backward glance at her mother's house. Tommy Gilbert had resumed his position behind the lawn mower, pushing it with sweaty determination toward the dark blue pickup with *Joey Gilbert's Landscaping Service* advertised on the side panel.

Mike handled the truck with an expert hand as they rounded the corner and headed for downtown. "He must keep to himself, or maybe he's not around town much. He's hard to forget." His face instantly reddened. "Sorry, that came out wrong. I didn't mean to insult your friend or imply…"

"It's all right. You don't have to explain." She'd been around Tommy all her life. He was who he was and she was used to it. It always surprised her when other people saw the young man through different eyes than her own. His pockmarks and scars, short stature, and slight scuffle held no mystery for her.

"Tommy's had a hard time of it. Bad enough he's the baby of his family. And adolescence wasn't kind to him. That much is obvious when you see his face.

"You say he works for his brother?"

Rose nodded. "Tommy graduated from high school last year. He wanted to join the Air Force, and he's been waiting for them to call him up. He only found out recently they weren't going to take him, so he's back home now and working for his brother. They take care of lawns, do snowplowing in the winter, that sort of thing. I guess Tommy's using the summer to figure out what it is he wants to do with his life."

Just like she was herself, came the sudden thought. Both she and Tommy were spending their summer in the small town where they'd grown up. Both of them were trying to figure out exactly who they were and what they wanted out of life.

But life decisions shouldn't have to be so hard, especially when it was so hot.

Within a few minutes they were smack dab in the middle of the business district. Mike slowed the truck as they searched for a nonexistent place to park. Tourists were everywhere, wandering the few blocks of the downtown area. Strollers filled the sidewalks, pushed by absentminded fathers, directed by harried mothers.

"I'd forgotten how crowded town can get this time of year," Rose said as they circled the block one more time. She blew out a frustrated sigh at the backed-up traffic. Such was the price you paid to summer—or live—in James Bay. "Maybe we should swing around the corner and park up by the bank. It's not a far walk, just a few blocks. "

"Won't be necessary," Mike said with a quick grin as he pointed to a loaded minivan pulling out of a coveted parking space a few feet ahead. The cherry-red pickup was next in line—they won the rally.

"You timed that just right." Rose rewarded him with her best smile.

He shut off the engine and unbuckled his seat belt. "Made up your mind on where we're eating?" He opened the passenger door.

Rose hesitated as she slid from her seat and joined him on the sidewalk. City life had spoiled her. She'd grown accustomed to having a variety of available restaurants and nightspots to choose from, but her hometown offered limited selection. James Bay's few restaurants were sharply divided between cheap and pricey, with Chuck's Tavern and Grill squarely in the middle. But she'd been to Chuck's only a few nights earlier with the Judge.

"Are you hungry for something in particular?" Negotiating on behalf of clients had taught her you had better luck if all parties were involved in the decision-making process.

"Why don't we walk around a bit? I think better when I'm moving."

Was he crazy? It was much too hot out for a casual stroll, but she kept silent. She was the one who'd invited him out to dinner. The least she could do was be polite and play the gracious hostess. If Mike wanted to walk, then they would walk... right into a nice air-conditioned restaurant. She gazed back and forth from the t-shirt shop on her left to the nautical-themed gift shop on her right. "Where do we go from here?"

"Why don't we head that way?" Mike pointed down the block toward the lake, a cool shimmering oasis of blue. They started down the street, taking one block, then another.

"Hey, smell that? Mmmm, pastrami. My favorite." Mike halted beneath a pink striped awning with navy blue swirls proudly proclaiming "Diana's Downtown Deli." He peered inside the window, then straightened and grinned at her. "What do you think? This looks pretty good to me."

"Are you sure you really want to eat in there?" The delicatessen was unfamiliar to her. Just another new business venture, one that would most likely be shut down by season's end. Businesses in James Bay needed to turn a tidy profit in the summertime. Rent in the downtown district was expensive for shopkeepers, especially during the winter months without the tourist trade to sustain them.

Mike shrugged. "What have we got to lose? Worst-case scenario, we get a little heartburn. Come on, it'll be fun. We can grab some sandwiches and take them over to the park. Have a little picnic down by the water's edge."

A picnic in downtown James Bay sounded exactly like something a tourist would do. Rose gave the deli another once-over through the front window. It looked fresh and inviting, but a deli was a deli, no matter how you sliced it. And this place wasn't at all the type of place she'd imagined they would go for dinner. Was Mike merely trying to be nice? Did he think she couldn't afford to buy him a good meal?

But she *was* hungry. Best of all, there was no line at the front counter.

A little brass bell tingled above the door as they entered the shop. Tantalizing aromas of spicy meats and fragrant cheeses greeted them. Ten minutes later they were headed out the door with two large paper bags packed with sandwiches, chips, coleslaw, and drinks. Down the street the shimmering lake beckoned. Within minutes, they reached the marina and waterfront. Rose started for a picnic table but Mike shook his head and kept on walking. They ended up in front of a bench close to the water.

"How's this?"

"Perfect." Rose sank down on the park bench. She caught a breath of cool breeze drifting in off the lake as he dropped down on the bench beside her. Before them stretched the fresh blue waters of James Bay, which opened up farther out into Lake Michigan. The sun was halfway near the horizon, poised for its nightly plunge below the glistening waters far from shore. Together they watched nature's beginnings of the perfect summer sunset.

"Hungry?" Rose finally broke the golden silence.

Her words seemed to startle him. His gaze hung far out at sea. He turned back toward her and she caught a glimpse of something, a sudden longing in his eyes, a lost, lonely look cast about his face. Then, quickly as it had come, it disappeared, replaced by a rueful smile.

"Sorry about that." His voice betrayed his embarrassment. "I've been inside all day long filling out fire reports. I didn't realize how much I needed something like this."

She'd been inside all day long too, at her mother's bedside. The hospital was air conditioned, sterile, cool, and serene. The fresh lake breeze had blown the smell of antiseptic out of her head.

All she could smell now was pastrami.

Rose picked up one of the bags and peeked inside. "Are you hungry?"

"Starving." Mike pulled wax-paper-wrapped sandwiches from one of the bags and handed over a thick roast beef built on rye. "I think this one is yours."

Seagulls swooped and soared along the waterfront dock as the two of them munched in companionable silence. James Bay spread out before them, sparkling glints of gold in the fading evening sunshine.

Mike finished one of his sandwiches and rolled up the wax paper in a neat little ball before taking aim at the target several feet away. Kerplunk! He hit the trash receptacle dead-on.

"Good shot," Rose said, laughing out loud. "I couldn't do that in a million years."

"Bet you can," he said, urging her on.

"I was never good at sports in school."

"Ten bucks say you can."

His eyes had all but vanished, squinting against the brilliant rays of the setting sun. But his face wore an encouraging smile and Rose had the sudden irresistible urge to take him up on the challenge. Being around him made the years drop away and she felt like a teenager again, all gawky, giggly, and unsure of herself. Unsure except for one thing. She really really, really wanted to hit that target.

Rose wadded up her own wax paper scraps in a tight ball and took careful aim. Her thoughts focused, intent on the target. Imagine the bull's-eye, see yourself the winner, shoot for the goal. She let fly.

Ker-plop. It hit the ground several feet away from the large wire-rimmed basket.

From the pained look on his face, it was obvious Mike was struggling not to laugh.

"Don't you dare say one word," she warned as she bounced off the bench and retrieved the paper ball. Again she took aim, imagined herself victorious, and let the pitch fly with dead-on accuracy.

Thud. The second shot landed in the dirt, farther away than her first attempt.

"Come on, give it one more shot," Mike said with a grin. "What have you got to lose? Besides, you know what they say. Third time's a charm."

"Forget it." Rose turned her back on the garbage can and flashed him a saucy stare. "I already told you I was bad at sports. At least now you know I don't lie."

"Maybe not, but you *do* litter." With a quick flourish, he rose from his seat, scooped the wax paper ball from the ground and, taking quick aim, sank the basket.

"Show-off," Rose hissed sweetly as he dropped onto the bench beside her.

Mike stretched out his legs and glanced at her with an easy smile. "Thanks again for dinner. This was fun."

"If this is your idea of fun, showing me up shooting wastepaper baskets, I think you need to get a life."

"That might not be so far from the truth."

She shot him a sharp glance. Mike's face was flushed in the filtering light of the setting sun.

"I actually thought about calling you this afternoon and begging off. Don't get me wrong," he quickly added. "It's not that I didn't want to have dinner with you. But I got thinking about it, and, well, I guess…"

Mike rolled his water bottle back and forth in his hands, staring at it as if it were the most important thing in the world.

Rose swallowed hard. He'd almost called off their date? Whatever was troubling him, she was glad they were together tonight. "I don't know why you changed your mind, but just so you know… I'm glad you did."

He glanced over and searched her eyes. "So am I," he said after a long moment.

They sat there in companionable silence and watched the bay's calm waters grow dark as the evening sun lost its golden brilliance and melted into a fiery red. Boats drifted in on the horizon, returning from the deep waters of Lake Michigan to the safety of shore. Only the jarring call of the swooping seagulls interrupted the tranquility of the evening.

"Maybe you won't believe this," she finally said, "but in all the years I've lived in this town, this is the first time I've actually sat down here by the waterfront and taken in the view."

"It takes a transplant like me from downstate to get you to realize what you've been missing all your life?"

Rose eyed him in surprise. "Downstate? Is that where you're from? I guess I thought…"

"That I was from around here? I'll take that as a compliment." His face wore a satisfied smile. "I was born and raised in the city of Detroit. And I'll tell you something, Miss Rose Gallagher. If I'd been lucky enough to call James Bay my hometown, I never would have left."

"What made you move here?" Rose ignored the slight dig about her residence preferences, but the irony of the situation wasn't lost on her. She'd grown up in James Bay and left for the city... while he'd grown up in the city, only to eventually head north.

Mike's gaze was back out across the horizon. "I always wanted to live up north. When the opportunity came, I grabbed it. It's not often a job opens up around here for a fireman."

His story made sense. James Bay was hardly a metropolis by anyone's definition. There couldn't be more than two or three full-time men on the fire department. The other little towns surrounding them were the same. There would be few, if any, opportunities for a fireman to have a successful and lucrative career, monetarily or otherwise.

"What did you do in the city? Were you a fireman?"

"I put in ten years on the department before I moved north." Mike pulled his gaze from the water's edge and turned to face her. "My dad has an insurance business, but from the time I was a little kid, I wanted to be a fireman like my Uncle Steve. He retired after forty years with the Detroit Fire Department. I grew up listening to his fire stories. He died a few years ago, but he died a happy man. He spent his life doing exactly what he wanted—fighting fires. He loved it. Every minute of it."

Mike's words struck a responsive chord deep in Rose's heart. Her father had been like that. Consumed by his passion for teaching, for making every second count. He'd taught her to be the same. Setting things right for others in the pursuit of justice had totally consumed her back in the days before she'd joined the firm. Those days, she'd still been naive enough to believe she could make a difference. Things had changed somewhere along the line. She'd lost that edge, that passion for living, and it felt like there was no going back. Her world was filled with mandatory court deadlines and complicated legal briefs. Her voicemail backed up with clients clamoring for immediate attention. Her in-box overflowed with terse memos from the firm. The demands were constant. Higher billings. More receivables. Reductions in overhead.

Her stomach gave a sickening lurch. Was that really what she wanted for the rest of her life?

Mike's face was a quizzical question mark.

"I'm sorry, could you repeat that?" Rose felt the flush high on her cheeks. Lost in her own little world, she hadn't been listening. She hated it when people did that to her.

"What about you?" he repeated. "You're pretty much a mystery lady."

How could she not answer? Yet, how could she? Mike had been honest and open with her. He was a public servant who earned a public paycheck, while her annual salary was probably double, if not triple, his own. Deliberately, Rose decided to keep her career out of the conversation. Why spoil things between them? She was having too much fun for that to happen, though sooner or later, it probably would. Money eventually always figured into the picture, especially when men and their egos were involved.

"There isn't much to tell. I grew up in James Bay and now I live downstate." She threw him a fast smile. "End of story."

"Come on, there's got to be more than that."

She shook her head lightly. "Not really. My life is pretty uncomplicated." An understatement, if there ever was one. Dull and predictable, consumed with paperwork, with no time to herself. Queen of the microwave dinner brigade... if she remembered to eat, that is. She would probably end up suffocated someday under a stack of legal briefs. Death by deposition.

But it didn't have to be that way. She could take Andy up on his offer and make the move to Washington D.C. Her days would be spent in the shadow of the capital building if Andy had his way... and her nights would be spent in his arms.

Rose shifted on the bench. "Tell me more about your Uncle Steve. He sounds interesting."

"Don't change the subject," he warned. "Uncle Steve was a great guy, but he's dead. You, however, are very much alive."

There certainly were days she didn't feel that way. More like simply going through the motions. "I'm actually pretty boring. You'd be disappointed."

"I doubt that. There's a story buried in you somewhere, Rose Gallagher, and I intend to find it."

A nervous laugh bubbled out of her. "I doubt my story would be a best seller. Get up, go to work, come home, go to bed. Repeat the next day."

"You missed the part about being a devoted daughter," Mike gently reminded her.

"I think my mother would take issue with that statement," Rose said, dissolving in a fit of giggles in spite of herself. Devoted daughters didn't live two hundred miles away. Devoted daughters didn't pack up and move to Washington D.C. Devoted daughters lived right down the block or two streets over, close enough to share a ride to church or a Sunday-night supper.

Devoted daughters stayed where they belonged.

Rose sobered slightly. But where did she belong? Working alongside the Judge? Her mother definitely would agree.

"Sure you work, everybody works. But you took time off to help your mother. I think that ranks pretty high up on the devotion list."

She found herself suddenly glad for the cover of darkness. At least he wouldn't glimpse the hot flush rising on her cheeks at the unexpected compliment.

"I know something else, too," he continued. "You obviously don't spend much time in the kitchen."

"I object. That is not a fair assessment." Her laugh rang out on the soft evening breeze. "Setting an oven on fire shouldn't automatically disqualify me. For all you know, I might be a great cook."

"People who like to cook usually sample their own cooking." His voice carried a hint of gentle admonishment. "It doesn't look like you eat much at all."

Rose squirmed on the bench. She didn't need any reminders that her clothes hung on her, loose and ill-fitting, but when did she have time to hit the mall?

Obviously she needed to make time. When a man thought to add his two cents worth, it was time for action. That was one nice thing about living in the city. People simply didn't say such things. No one cared enough to comment.

"Don't think I meant that as an insult," he said. "Far from it. You're a beautiful woman, Rose. But you sure look like you could use an ice cream cone or two."

Though his face was lost to her in the setting sun, his voice was gentle, carried softly on the breeze blowing in off the lake. A part of her—a part deep inside that had been asleep for so long she'd forgotten how to daydream—sensed Mike was telling the truth. He hadn't meant the words to wound, yet they had. Perhaps it was the mere fact he was able to speak the truth that she found so unsettling.

"I suppose I have lost a few pounds in the last couple of months," she admitted after some moments. She hugged herself close in the growing twilight. "I was putting in extra hours at work, trying to get things settled before I came home. I guess I forgot to eat."

"So there's no need to worry. Your mom came through her surgery fine and she's going to be okay, correct?"

"She's coming home from the hospital on Saturday."

"Looks like you're in the right place after all." Mike came to his feet and offered her a hand. "Come on, let's go."

They were leaving already? Warily she took his hand and allowed him to pull her to a stand. She tucked her purse under one arm and frowned in the enveloping darkness. What did he mean, *she was in the right place*?

"Where are we going?"

"This town is loaded with ice cream shops. We're going to go get you an ice cream cone. My treat."

"Who said I wanted ice cream?" she asked as they headed away from the waterfront and back toward the lighted storefronts centering the downtown.

"Maybe you don't, but I do." Mike shot her a fast smile as they reached the top of the sidewalk. "Right now, the thought of a double-dip Mackinac Island Fudge cone sounds perfect."

A few minutes later, the two of them sat side by side in Mike's truck, ice cream cones in hand.

"Thank you." Rose sighed in contentment as she took another quick lick of her cone. The ice cream was delicious and the cool sensation of sweet peppermint flavored her tongue. "I can't remember the last time I did this."

"Eat ice cream? Lady, you sure live a sheltered life," Mike said from his seat behind the steering wheel as he licked fast in a circular motion around his sugar cone.

"It's not just the ice cream. It's everything—the whole shebang. Eating in the park, riding in your truck." She flashed him a shy smile. "My dad had a pickup. I loved riding around in it with him when I was a little girl. He used to take me fishing."

"You? A fisherman?" he scoffed. "That's a little hard to believe."

"It's true," she insisted. Her cone was melting and she licked faster to keep pace with the dripping ice cream.

Mike finished off the last of his cone and settled back in his seat, eyeing her with open interest. "Bet you didn't bait your own hook."

"You're wrong about that." Her voice and spirit rose to the challenge. "I'll have you know I've handled my share of wiggling worms. My dad taught me how when I was only five. I was quite the fisherman... or is it *fisherwoman*?"

"Okay, you win, I take it back," he said, laughing. "Think you'd be able to bait a hook today?"

"Well, it *has* been awhile since I've been out in a boat," Rose admitted. Some of her favorite childhood memories centered on being out on the lake with her dad in that little fishing boat he'd cherished.

"Where did you supposedly do all this fishing? Somewhere around here, or out in Lake Michigan? "

"It's a small inland lake not far from town. Mostly we fished for largemouth bass, but we used to catch perch and bluegills, too. I even hooked a turtle once." She smiled at the sudden memory. "My dad made me throw it back in."

"If you're trying to impress me, it's working." Mike's face caught in a lazy grin. "You wouldn't happen to remember the name of that lake, would you?"

Rose thought hard as she finished off the last of her cone, but came up empty-handed, just like a fisherman at times.

"Sorry, I don't. All my dad ever said was *Come on, Rosie, we're going down to the lake*." She swallowed hard, mingling ice cream cone and a bittersweet longing for the life that had disappeared.

"It's still pretty early. Are you up for a little ride? We could try and find that little lake you used to fish with your dad." He suddenly hesitated. "Or maybe you'd rather go home."

Go home already? No! She didn't want to go home. Not yet. Not for hours. She'd never expected to have such a good time with him. Being with Mike was just like breathing. She felt different tonight, in a way she hadn't felt in years. Tonight felt almost like being home inside herself again.

"Sure, I'm game," she replied. "If I remember right, that lake is only a few miles from downtown."

He threw the truck in gear and carefully pulled out into traffic.

"Take the hill and then the road heading out of town." Rose sat back in her seat and licked the last few drops of ice cream from her fingertips as they left the city lights behind for the quiet country darkness. Thoughts of her father and his little fishing boat tugged at her heart. Being home in James Bay, riding around in a pickup truck with another Michael John Gallagher, was bringing back memories.

"I think you would have liked my dad," she said. "He was a great guy. He taught high school here in town." His confident attitude, easygoing style, and relaxed, steady wit had made him popular among both staff and students alike. He'd known the name of every student at Bay High School, which was no small feat and amazed even Rose. The hot, hazy days of summer usually found him in the passenger seat of the local driver's ed car. She'd grown up hearing *Your dad taught me how to drive* from most townspeople anywhere near her age.

"He sounds like a great guy."

"The two of you even have something in common," she said with a shy smile. "You've got the same name."

"*Mr. Gallagher*?" He pulled his gaze from the road long enough to flash her a quick grin.

Rose shook her head softly. "His name was Michael, too."

Mike's head cocked in the dim green glow of the pickup's dashboard. His grin was gone, replaced by a thoughtful smile. "Michael Gallagher. Sounds familiar."

"Michael John Gallagher," she added quietly.

He shot her a hard glance. "That's some coincidence," he finally said.

"Maybe not such a coincidence. It's a strong name. One that can stand on its own... just like the man who wears it. It suited my dad." Rose hesitated. Her voice was low when she finally spoke. "I think it suits you, too."

For a moment only silence hung between them.

"I'll take that as a compliment," he said after a long moment.

"Good, because I meant it as one," she softly replied.

A furious beeping shattered the darkness. Rose sat up sharply as Mike gave the wheel a hard yank and pulled the truck over to one side of the road. The green glow from the cab's dashboard cast an eerie light in the truck's interior as Mike grabbed the pager from its spot on the bench between them. Rose tried hard to follow the electronic chatter. Mike's face was drawn with quiet intensity as they listened to a woman's voice flooding the cab.

"What is it? What's happening?" Rose finally dared to ask.

"That's central dispatch, 911. We're being paged out to a fire." With a quick pull on the wheel, Mike turned the truck around. Gravel crunched and flew as he pointed the pickup in the direction from which they'd come.

"A fire? But where?" She'd heard the same 911 page but most of the information had sounded like static.

"About a mile from here." His face was all business. "Sorry, but it looks like you'll have to come along. We're closer to the scene than we are downtown."

"But..."

Mike reached down on the console and threw a switch. The outside of the cab lit up, illuminated by brilliant flashing red and white emergency strobe lights.

"Hang on," he said. "We're going for a ride."

CHAPTER FIVE

FIREWORKS PRONOUNCED "DANGEROUS"

By: Charles Kendall
The James Bay Journal

JAMES BAY—The annual Fourth of July celebration may not prove much of a bang if local fire officials have their way. This reporter recently learned that Fire Chief Ivan Thompson is lobbying businesses that sell fireworks not to display them.

"People need to understand we're dealing with extreme fire conditions," Chief Thompson said. "Fireworks might be legal, but we don't want a situation getting out of hand. Until we get some good steady rain, the last thing we want is somebody shooting off something that could spark a flame."

An informal poll of local business owners indicates there are no current plans to pull fireworks from any store shelves in James Bay.

Rose had the eerie sense of being caught up in hell on earth as Mike's truck pulled up on the country roadside a safe distance from the blaze. Huge flames erupted in brilliant scarlet streaks against the night sky and thick black smoke rolled from the sprawling two-story framed structures. The heat was intense, staggering in awesome power. Billowing waves of acrid fumes pushed toward them. The stench caught in her throat as Mike threw open his truck door and slid out. He grabbed his fire gear stowed behind the driver's seat and slammed the door.

"Stay in the truck." He threw her a stern glance through the open window. "You'll be safe enough in here. I have to set up a fire command."

She would be safe enough—but what about him? *Don't panic.* Rose swallowed down a growing fear as she watched him head straight toward the flames. Mike knew what he was doing, she silently repeated in a low mantra. He was a trained professional. This was what he did for a living. But laying down fire hose and knocking back a blazing inferno certainly was a different job than the cool, sterile world of jurisprudence she lived in.

Sirens wailed in the distance. Within moments the scene was a complicated tangle of fire trucks, emergency equipment, and huge looming floodlights illuminating the site. Rose watched from the safety of the truck as dozens of men clad in fire gear and helmets materialized from nowhere, swarming the scene and laying fire hose.

She'd lost track of Mike. Some of the firemen had donned air packs and were headed toward the structure. Her eyes scanned the crowd, searching in vain. Hopefully Mike wasn't near the front of that roaring inferno or one of those men with an air pack strapped on his back. His monitor was still on the bench beside her. She picked it up and hugged it tight against her chest as she kept up her watch. Minutes ago, they'd been eating ice cream, swapping fish tales, and now they were in the middle of a scene straight out of hell.

Cars lined the narrow country road. A party atmosphere, fueled by the flame's intensity, rapidly developed as more people arrived each moment. The gathering crowd of onlookers grew as the flames shot higher against the night sky. Rose shifted nervously inside the cab of Mike's truck. How had everyone known? Where had they come from? The fire was miles from downtown. Were the flames high enough to be seen from James Bay?

"Stay back! Everybody stay back," a fireman called out from his post near the truck. Even with his gear on, he seemed familiar. Rose craned her neck and watched for a moment before recognition finally set in. She'd seen him with Mike at another fire, the one at the hospital that had proved merely a false alarm. But tonight was no false alarm. This fire was a raging inferno.

"Cecilia? I thought that was you."

A familiar voice burned into her consciousness. She offered a nervous smile through the open window. "Hi, Charles."

"What are you doing out here?" Charles Kendall's eyebrows bunched together in a frown. He shot a quick glance at the emergency lights flashing on the top of Mike's truck.

"I guess I'm like everybody else in town... here to see the fire." Rose scanned the swelling crowd held back by law enforcement. So many familiar faces, neighbors and folks from town, drawn by the excitement. If she wasn't witnessing it with her very own eyes, she never would have guessed so many people would come out to gawk at someone else's misfortune. "Where have they all come from?" she whispered. "How did they know?"

"I imagine lots of them have scanners, like I do," Charles said. "When you're a member of the press, you've got to get to the action quick." His frown deepened. "Whose truck is this? Are you here with somebody?"

"Hey, Cecil!" A familiar voice called out nearby. Rose looked up to see Tommy Gilbert struggling through the crowd.

"I heard the sirens and followed the fire trucks from downtown," Tommy said as he finally reached Mike's truck. His gaze was riveted on the flames before them, which the firemen were attacking with huge powerful streams of water. "What's going on? Do you guys know what happened?"

"Someone driving by saw the fire and called it in," Charles replied. "Looks like it will be a total loss. Too bad. These condos were nearly finished. Wonder if he'll be able to rebuild? I suppose that depends on the insurance."

Years of practice had accustomed her to tuning out Charles's voice, but something he said snagged Rose's attention. Someone else had been talking about condos recently... condominiums that were nearly finished and would soon be ready for occupancy.

"It sure doesn't look like there's going to be much left," Tommy agreed. "Man, look at that!"

An immense wall of flames shot up from inside the blazing structure as the second story gave way. The sky erupted in a cascade of burning sparks as the top of the building crashed down upon the first floor. A firestorm of glowing embers floated high above their heads, tingeing the air they breathed.

Where was Mike? Was he all right? Rose pressed the monitor closer against her heart and scanned the faces of the nearby firemen working the scene. She recognized no one except the Judge.

The Judge! He was right there at the edge of the fire line, his face a mask of concern and disbelief as he held forth in earnest conversation with a group of firemen. With a start, Rose realized one of the firemen conferring with the Judge was Mike.

Bits and pieces from the conversation she'd had some nights earlier with the Judge streamed to mind. He had sat there eating barbequed ribs and offered her a partnership. His suggestion had caught her off guard and she had barely listened as he mentioned his real estate deals. She watched with a sickened heart as heavy deluge guns sprayed water and knocked down the wall of fire. These condo units were owned by the Judge. It was his investment deal that had gone up in smoke and flames tonight. The smoke changed color as the flames subsided. Rolling clouds of heavy black misted into thick white steam.

Mike returned to the truck several moments later. His face was dirty under the white helmet. Soot stained his cheeks and disappeared down the side of his neck. His eyes were dark, shadowed with fatigue.

"You two know each other?" Charles's face wore a look of suspicious disbelief.

Mike pulled off heavy fire gloves. Ignoring Charles, his gaze centered solely on Rose. "You okay?"

"I'm fine," she reassured him. "But what about you?" She hated being there and wanted to go home, but not if it meant leaving him behind. The air was heavy, hot with smoke. It was bad enough just sitting there in his truck. Her lungs felt cloudy, trapped with acrid smoke. Enough smoke that she wanted to gag. But Mike seemed fine, as if it didn't bother him. How could he do it? He had been right there in the thick of things as he worked the fire line.

"Do you think you could find a ride back to town?" he asked. "Looks like I'm going to be here awhile." He opened the truck's passenger door.

"I'll take you home, Cecilia."

"Thanks, Charles," she reluctantly agreed. Rose reached for her purse and quickly slid out of the truck and onto the gravel roadside. Scanning the crowd for the Judge, she finally spotted him close to the fire scene, still deep in heated conversation with some of the uniformed personnel.

"I'm sorry to do this to you," Mike said, "but I can't leave. We'll probably be out here at least another two or three hours. The fire marshal is on his way."

"You think this fire might be arson?" Tommy's voice squeaked.

"It could have been electrical or poor insulation. At this point, we don't know. We need to find the source of origin." He focused his gaze sternly on Charles Kendal, who was busy scribbling away on a note pad. "All of that is off the record, understand?"

"Why didn't you let it burn all the way down? Looks like it's going to be a loss anyway," Tommy said.

"Evidence." Charles looked up from his note pad with a pointed smile. "Right, Officer?"

Mike's eyes narrowed underneath the white helmet. "Just remember what I said. This conversation is not for publication."

The smelly, charred remains of the burned-out condos hissed white steam and took center stage. The party atmosphere evaporated as the crowd slowly disbursed.

"Let's go, Cecilia. I have everything I need for my story." Charles tucked a protective hand under her arm.

A state police car with swirling blue lights pulled up close beside them.

"There's the fire marshal. I've got to go." Mike signaled with a weary wave of his fire glove to the tall, heavyset trooper emerging from the vehicle. "Thanks again for dinner," he added.

"You're welcome," Rose said. "Oh, wait. This is yours." Reluctantly she handed over his fire monitor, loathe to give up that small part of him she'd had tucked close to her heart. "You'll need this."

He nodded briefly, then turned and disappeared into the crowd of emergency personnel working the scene.

"Cecilia? Are you coming?"

Rose gave one last helpless glance around for the Judge. But just like Mike, her old friend was lost from sight. He'd been swallowed up in the midst of smelly white steam, black soot, and burly firemen. She blew a heavy, frustrated sigh and turned toward a waiting Charles.

She was running, trying to escape the flames. Surely around the corner she'd find some place to hide—but she smacked into a dead end, ablaze with crackling,

fiery red flames. The smoke intensified, gagging her...
All the air was gone and she was suffocating. A heavy
sensation pressed on her chest.

She couldn't breathe. She couldn't breathe!

A loud, protracted meow forced her eyes open.
Bozo was perched atop her stomach. His yellow eyes
gleamed as he watched her come awake. Rose
scratched the cat's head and waited for her heartbeat to
return to normal. No fire, no cause for alarm. She was
in the bedroom where she'd grown up, safe in her own
bed... and it was already past noon! She sat up in
dismay. No wonder Bozo had come investigating.
She'd slept away the entire morning. The cat had
missed his breakfast, but he didn't intend on missing
lunch.

"Come on, buddy, let's get you something to eat."
Rose threw back the sheet and crawled out of bed.
Bozo padded behind her, meowing loud rebukes.

Coffee set to brewing and Bozo's dish filled with
kibble, Rose headed back upstairs for her second
shower in less than twelve hours. She stood under the
hot needles of water. The taste of soot lingered in her
mouth and on her skin. She tilted back her head and
scrubbed harder, trying to wash away the acrid stink of
smoke. Half a bottle of shampoo later, her hair still
smelled. No wonder firemen wore helmets.

The telephone's shrill ring started as she stepped out
of the shower, but Rose ignored it. Whoever it was
could leave a message. She wrapped herself in a terry-
cloth robe and toweled her hair dry, then ran a brush
through the wet, heavy locks before they tangled. She
padded down the stairs, headed for the kitchen and the
coffee pot. Only after she'd poured her first cup of

coffee did she finally punch the replay button on the answering machine.

She recognized Mike's voice immediately as the message played. How did he manage to sound so alert? From the way things had looked when she and Charles left, Mike must have been up nearly all night working that fire. Maybe how to stay awake was something they taught in fire school.

"I was hoping to catch you at home. But obviously you're out and about."

Rose smiled. She *had* been out and about... down the hall in the shower trying to rinse the stink from her hair.

"I'd like to talk to you about last night."

Last night? Memories from the evening before flashed through her mind. She'd been having a great time until his fire monitor had gone off. Thank God no one had been hurt. The entire town had turned out to witness the blaze. So many people had been at the fire scene... Charles Kendall, Tommy Gilbert, the Judge.

Rose frowned as her thoughts inadvertently turned to the Judge. She'd been meaning to pay His Honor a visit. The two of them needed to talk. And after last night's fire, visiting the Judge would top her list of priorities today.

Mike's message finished with a polite request to return the call. Rose ignored it and headed back upstairs. She had a busy day in front of her. First she'd swing by the Judge's office and after that make her daily trek to the hospital. But as for returning Mike's call? She had no intention of doing so. The fire station was right downtown. Paying a personal visit sounded *much* friendlier.

The Judge's suite of offices occupied the entire second floor of one of the oldest buildings in downtown James Bay. Rose couldn't help a small smile as she stopped beneath the sign swinging high above the mahogany door's imposing entrance. *Harvey John James, Esq., Sole Practitioner, Licensed in Real Estate.* The Judge had always had a touch for the flair of the dramatic. The elegant, gold-embossed sign proclaimed his business title and address with a flourish. He *was* the law firm, as well as owner and proprietor of the building he occupied.

A sudden whoosh of cool air-conditioned comfort filtering from above greeted Rose as she pushed open the front door. Possible scenarios played out in her head as she slowly climbed the plush, carpeted stairs to the Judge's suite of offices. What would she say when they finally met? Last night's fire had been a living nightmare and she'd witnessed the devastation with her own eyes. It had to have taken a heavy toll on the Judge. With construction nearly complete, the condos were a total loss. She'd seen his face, haggard and shaken, as he'd spoken with Mike. The Judge had sported every year of his age last night and that scared her. The people she loved were growing older, whether she was there to bear witness or not. Living far away, it was easy not to think about it, but coming home brought a cold dose of reality. Eventually there would come a time when they would all be gone. Her mother, Lil, the Judge. She would be left all alone.

Rose took the few remaining steps with her heart fluttering like the hummingbirds buzzing at the feeder outside her mother's kitchen window. What in the world was the matter with her? Everyone in her world was very much alive. She forced a deep breath and a thin smile to her face. *Get a grip, Rose.*

Her smile evaporated as her foot hit the top step. The carpet in the spacious reception area was in desperate need of a good vacuuming and the glass coffee table wore a thin coat of dust. Normally the Judge was fastidious when it came to his surroundings. How could he have allowed things to sink into such a state?

And who was the young girl with the blank stare sitting at Judith's desk? She looked barely out of high school.

"Can I help you?"

"I'd like to see the Judge."

The girl blinked. "He's not here."

"Is Judith available?" The Judge's longtime legal assistant was a stickler for detail, but she must have taken a long vacation. The office would never have deteriorated like this if Judith were anywhere nearby.

"Who's Judith?" The girl's eyebrows scrunched together. "I thought you wanted to see the Judge."

"I *am* here to see the Judge."

"Who's asking?"

"Cecilia Gallagher. I'm an attorney from Grand Rapids."

"Is this about a case?"

"I'm an old friend," Rose coolly replied. "When do you expect him back?"

"I really couldn't say. He just left. He went to see his insurance agent. If you're a friend of his, then you probably know about that fire last night. I doubt submitting an insurance claim will do him much good, but I suppose he needs the money." The girl's voice dropped a notch or two. "My paycheck was two days late last week."

What kind of people were available for hire nowadays? This girl had no business dissing His Honor. She had no business working in a law firm, or elsewhere, for that matter. Rose held her tongue and anger in check as she fished through her purse for a business card. "Make sure you give this to the Judge."

The girl's eyebrows raised. "Arthur, LaCross and Mindel? That's the biggest law firm in Michigan." Her face beamed with respect. "You're welcome to stay if you like. I'll let you wait in his office. I'm sure he won't mind."

Exactly what had the Judge been thinking when he hired this girl? She looked like she couldn't be trusted to take an order at a fast food restaurant, let alone remember to hand over a business card. Did he really expect this young woman to take Judith's place, even if only for a few days' vacation?

"Make sure he knows I stopped by." Rose hurried down the stairs before she opened her mouth and said something she'd regret. She stepped out into the welcoming afternoon sunshine and gratefully pulled the heavy wooden door shut behind her. A receptionist with a mouth for gossip and an aversion to a dust rag didn't bode well for the Judge. And wait till Judith got back from her vacation. She would be livid.

"We're not sure what happened," Lil confided from her chair at Irene's bedside. "The Judge told us she retired, but it all seemed rather sudden, if you ask me."

"I told you, Lil, how Harvey chooses to run his business is none of *our* business," Irene said as she plucked a chocolate from the box on her lap. Her eyebrows pushed together in a warning frown. "Besides, I never much cared for Judith anyway. Remember how hoity-toity she could be? Maybe the Judge got tired of her attitude. Or maybe she asked for another raise."

"Ha! I'll bet that was it. You know how tight he is with his money." Lil nodded knowingly at Rose, perched carefully on a knockoff designer chair of stiff blue vinyl at the end of Irene's bed. "What do you think, honey? You deal with employment issues every day in that law firm of yours. Do you think Judith quit, or was she fired?"

Rose pondered Lil's question with a heavy heart. Whatever had happened, Judith definitely was gone. Had she disappeared for good? She could run the Judge's practice with her eyes shut. And someone needed to do something fast before the Judge's clientele deserted him in a cloud of dust.

"I think the Judge is going to have a lot to think about in the next few months," Rose finally offered.

Lil nodded sagely. "And that condo fire didn't help. Taking care of that is going to set him back a pretty penny. He was hoping to rent those condos soon."

"I wouldn't worry about it too much," Irene replied. "Knowing the Judge, he has plenty of insurance. He's always been savvy when it comes to money matters."

"Savvy?" Lil hooted. "More like a tightwad, if you ask me."

The Judge a tightwad? Absolutely not. Rose struggled to keep her composure as she felt the heat rise in her face. Lil had no business criticizing the Judge. After everything he'd been through—especially last night—he deserved their entire support.

"I think you're a little off the mark," Rose said. "The Judge is a wonderful man—"

"I never said he wasn't." Lil glanced at Rose with a patient look. "Honey, when are you going to stop looking at him through the eyes of a six-year-old? I know you think the man is a saint, and he is a good man, I'll grant you that. But that's exactly what he is… a man. He's had quite the life, as your mother and I both know. We've been right there as witnesses." Her eyebrows lifted slightly. "Oh, the stories we could tell. Isn't that right, Irene?"

"What do you think? Crème or nougat?" Gingerly Irene plucked another chocolate from the box and held it up for careful scrutiny.

"For heaven's sake, Irene, I don't know how you can eat those things. They're so fattening." Lil rolled her eyes and turned back to Rose. "I hear you were at the fire last night. Since when have you started chasing fire trucks?"

Rose coughed, hoping to hide the quick blush. "I only ended up out there by accident."

Irene dropped her chocolate and stared wide-eyed at Rose. "You were in an accident? Were you hurt?"

"I'm fine, Mom. And I wasn't in an accident. I was having dinner with a friend and his monitor went off."

"Firemen have monitors." Lil's green eyes glittered like emeralds. "This wouldn't have anything to do with that cute fireman we saw the other day, would it?"

Irene reverently popped a chocolate in her mouth and regarded Rose with a placid smile. "What fireman?"

Lil sighed. "For heaven's sake, Irene, I think the pain meds have gone to your head. Remember that nice young man you told me about? The one who rescued you and Cecilia Rose when your car caught fire?"

"The car was *not* on fire," Rose firmly replied.

Irene's face wore a bemused look. "Oh, him. Yes, now I remember. He was rather cute."

"You're both making too much out of this," Rose said. "We merely went out for dinner. It wasn't a date."

"You had dinner with a man and you think it wasn't a date? No wonder you're almost thirty years old and still not married. What is it with you young people?" Lil's eyes gleamed with mischief. "You might not be dating yet, but mark my words, honey... you soon will be. That fireman is going to ask you out. Just wait and see."

"Cecilia Rose doesn't need you telling her what to do," Irene said, then winced as the machine hooked up against her knee kicked in for another steady spin of flexing.

Rose came to her feet. Now would be the perfect time to leave. Her mother looked as if she could use the rest, while she herself could use a rest from any more questions. Plus, she still had one more stop to make. The fire department was five minutes away.

"I'll be back tonight." Rose brushed a quick kiss against Irene's cheek. "I'll stop after dinner and bring you the paper."

"Thank you, sweetheart." Irene smiled across the bed at Lil. "See what you missed, not having children? Isn't she the most wonderful daughter?"

"The best," Lil confirmed as she winked at Rose. "Go on now, off with you. Don't worry about your mama. I'll sit here with Irene and the two of us can have a nice little chat... about you and that cute fireman." Lil reached over and gently patted Irene's hand.

Her mother's affectionate smile was a bit lopsided. Obviously the painkillers had kicked in again. Rose headed for the door with one last backward glance. Irene's eyes were finally closed, but Lil hadn't moved. She sat there, a stalwart beacon and loyal friend. The kind of friend any woman would be blessed to have.

Rose slipped from the room and pulled the door shut behind her.

The fire department was only one block from the downtown business district. Second thoughts began to surface as Rose fed the parking meter. What if he wasn't working today? She glanced at her watch. It was already past two o'clock. Maybe she should have phoned first. She studied the fire station, an imposing two-story structure of sturdy red brick. No sign of Mike's truck. Maybe he had parked inside with the fire trucks.

There was only one way to find out.

Rose opened the door on one side of the building and stepped inside. She found herself in a cavernous garage filled with gleaming yellow fire trucks and emergency equipment. She peeked around the trucks, but only silence and oil spots staining the cement floor greeted her.

"Hello?" Her words echoed emptily around her. Why hadn't she phoned first? Obviously Mike wasn't here. She'd made the trip for nothing.

She turned to leave when she caught a glimpse of light filtering from a hallway in the far corner of the garage. Rose hesitated, then forced her feet in that direction. A moment later, she found Mike hunched over a layout counter with a thick stack of paperwork spread out before him. Pencil in hand, he stood making notes. Rose waited silently, loathe to disturb him. She hated it when she was at her desk and someone interrupted her when she was obviously busy.

Coming here hadn't been such a good idea after all.

She started backing up quietly as she could, but the slight movement seemed to have caught his eye. Mike glanced up from the counter.

"Hi." He looked surprised, though not unhappy, to see her.

"Hi," she replied. Mike looked scrubbed and fresh, and she caught a pleasant whiff of the lightly scented woodsy aftershave he wore. Casually dressed in jeans and t-shirt, he looked more like the relaxed, easygoing man with whom she'd shared a park bench and sandwiches than the grim fireman she'd left behind at the fire scene last night. It was only when she stepped closer that Rose finally noticed the weary look about his face and the telltale circles beneath his eyes.

She'd bet her law license he hadn't gone to bed last night.

"I'm sorry. I guess I should have called first," she said. "I didn't mean to disturb you."

"No need to apologize." The warm smile on his face encouraged her to continue. "I'm glad you stopped by." He put down his pencil and leaned against the counter. "I tried calling you earlier. I felt bad about the way things ended last night."

"Me, too." She flashed him a small smile. "It was fun driving around in your truck... until that monitor went off."

He gave a rueful grin. "Seems like that always happens, especially when you least expect it."

Was that regret she saw in his eyes?

Mike cleared his throat. "You managed to get a ride home okay?"

Rose nodded. "Charles Kendall brought me back into town." She rolled her eyes at the memory. If Lil thought the Judge was a tightwad, she needed to spend a little time with Charles. His current car was a clunker and hadn't wanted to start, but he'd finally managed to get the engine running. Their long drive home had proved three miles of cumbersome conversation. Charles, always the inherent newspaperman, was a stickler when it came to digging out the facts. He'd pressed hard for any and all details about her life—home, work, and love life.

"How well do you know that guy?"

Rose caught the fleeting glance of uncertainty in Mike's eyes.

"Charles? His family moved to town the summer before we started high school." She hesitated. "Why?"

"The two of you seemed pretty comfortable together last night." A small frown caught between his eyebrows. "Are you seeing each other?"

Rose burst out laughing. She'd rebuffed Charles for so many years, the idea of them as a couple seemed ludicrous. "Are you asking that question in an official capacity?" she teased.

Mike's face reddened. "Sorry, I didn't mean to pry. That's your business, not mine."

His reaction startled her. Did Mike actually think she was dating Charles? Better to set the record straight right now than to give him the wrong impression.

"I have never been interested in Charles Kendall and I never will be, no matter what anyone says—*especially* Charles."

Mike brushed her comments aside with a quick shrug. "Like I said before, that's your business, not mine."

She felt her cheeks redden. For a moment, she'd thought he had a personal interest in asking, but now she wasn't certain. When it came to dealing with matters of the law, she always felt so competent. How could she feel so clueless involving matters of the heart?

Mike picked up his discarded pencil. The look on his face suddenly was all businesslike. "I'm glad you stopped by. I'm the arson investigator for this district and I have a couple questions for you about last night's fire."

Rose frowned. "You want to question me? I don't know anything about that fire. What could I possibly tell you?"

"You probably know more than you think. You and I were first on the scene."

"All right," she reluctantly agreed. Being interviewed as a witness wasn't a role she was accustomed to playing. In her line of work, she usually was the one asking the questions.

He pointed down the narrow hallway to an open door. "The chief isn't here today. We can talk in his office."

It appeared she had no choice. Warily Rose followed him down the hallway and through the open door.

CHAPTER SIX

FIRE LEVELS CONDOS

By: Charles Kendall
The James Bay Journal

Another mystery blaze last night destroyed the nearly completed condominium project north of town. James Bay fire fighters rushed to the scene after smoke was spotted by a passing motorist. Fire crews managed to prevent the flames from spreading to the neighboring wooded area.

Assistant Fire Chief Michael Gallagher said the cause of the fire had not yet been established. An investigation unit will be searching the scene this morning. When asked by this reporter, Officer Gallagher declined to comment on the rumor circulating around town that the blaze is the latest in a series of arson fires plaguing our community. No suspects have yet been named.

The Bay Ridge condominium development project was owned by former Circuit Court Judge Harvey James.

The chief's office was dwarfed by a cluttered desk and overflowing file cabinets. Two chairs, both stacked high with fire magazines, faced the desk.

"Chief Thompson's not much for housekeeping." Mike quickly cleared one of the chairs by piling magazines in a corner of the room.

Rose perched gingerly on the chair and watched with a wary eye as Mike took a seat in the battered wooden chair behind the chief's desk. A hot blush seared her cheeks from his words moments earlier. She prided herself at being a quick read when it came to people, but she'd been wrong about him. How could she have thought he was interested in her? Officer Gallagher had made it quite clear he was interested in one thing and one thing only: investigating last night's fire.

"I'm not sure how much help I can be."

Mike's eyes were intent, flashing all business. "Just tell me what you remember. What the scene was like, who was there. Anything that seemed out of the ordinary."

"*Everything* about that fire was out of the ordinary." Rose shifted in her chair, remembering. Merely thinking about it gave her shivers. She hugged herself tight, trying to chase away the chill. Last night's smoke had been a seething monster, sucking the air dry, suffocating anyone and anything in its path.

"We've determined the fire was deliberately set."

"You mean it *was* arson?" Rose felt the goose bumps rise on her arms and the hair prickle on the back of her neck. The true scope of their discussion was growing clearer. Mike wasn't merely asking questions about a fire. He was conducting an investigation involving a working crime scene.

"There's a good chance whoever set that fire was in the crowd. You saw the people out there last night. Tell me what you remember."

Rose shifted uncomfortably in her chair. "Not much. There were so many people..." The memory of last night's inferno was seared in her mind, but the crowd was a different matter. Nearly the entire town had turned out to witness the blaze. Who did she remember? Everyone and no one.

"Just think about it," he urged. "What's that phrase? *The devil is in the details*. And you have a built-in eye for details, wouldn't you say?"

"I'm not sure what you mean." Not sure exactly, but Rose had the sudden feeling she was about to find out.

"People in your line of work have a way of getting at the truth. Especially when the truth suits their clients' interests."

She drew in a sharp breath. "You know I'm an attorney?"

Mike shrugged. "This is a small town, remember? Pretty hard to keep a secret. Yes, I know you're a lawyer. And to tell you the truth, I'm doing my best to overlook that fact."

Rose felt the blush ride high on her cheeks. She'd tried to keep her professional life from him but he'd known the truth all along. Law enforcement—police, fire, and first responders—tended to view matters in black and white and she'd butted heads with plenty of them when they took the witness stand. It was a love-hate relationship between attorneys and law enforcement, with many of them accusing her colleagues of setting up smokescreens and shielding their clients from successful prosecution within the law's subtle shades of gray.

How had Mike found out? A sudden suspicion came to mind. "Charles told you, didn't he?"

"In a roundabout way." His face crinkled in a wary smile. "It was in the newspaper a few days ago." Mike sat back in his chair. "How well do you know the Judge? Think there's any chance he might have been involved?"

Rose stiffened. He couldn't be serious. "If you're implying that the Judge set that fire…"

"Whoa, hold on a minute," he said. "I'd suggest you be very careful about putting words in my mouth. I'm not accusing anyone." He shot her a stern look. "Yet."

The chief's cramped office wasn't air-conditioned. Rose felt her temper rising faster than the heat rising between them. "Then what exactly did you mean? Because it certainly seems like that's the direction you're headed in."

Mike blew out a hard breath. "I'm not going to lie to you. Naturally the Judge is a suspect. He owns the property. That's the first place we start in an investigation." His eyes narrowed. "From what I understand, he recently took out a hefty insurance policy."

"Everyone has insurance. I don't see why you think that should bring him under more suspicion," she argued. "In fact, I'd think it would be odder if he *didn't* have insurance."

Mike shrugged slightly. "You can't alter facts. The Judge owned those buildings and they were deliberately torched."

She felt her face tighten. "There is *no way* he set that fire."

"Really?" The look on his face told her he wasn't convinced. "Because...?"

"Because he didn't, that's why." Rose flopped back in her chair and shot him an exasperated look. What was the matter with him? He didn't need to be so stubborn about it. "What you're suggesting is impossible. The Judge would never do something like that."

"Sounds like you know him pretty well."

"I've lived next door to him since I was two years old when we moved into my grandmother's house. Why, the Judge *is* this town. James Bay was settled by his ancestors. The town was named after his great grandfather."

Mike's eyebrows lifted. "Know why he isn't on the bench anymore?"

"You can blame that on this town, too." Rose gripped her hands together. "He was appointed to the bench when his son Jeff and I were in middle school. The sitting Circuit Court judge had died and the Judge was chosen to fill the vacancy. He ran for election himself when the term ended and he sat for a few years. But when Jeff..."

Abruptly she broke off. The last thing she wanted was to be having this conversation. There'd never been any need to speak of it aloud. Everyone in town knew the story and how it ended.

Everyone but Mike.

His eyes locked on hers in a bold stare, refusing to release her.

Rose took a deep breath. "His son Jeff was my best friend and we grew up together. We were only kids when we both decided we would be lawyers, just like Jeff's dad. We had everything planned out: four years of college followed by law school at the Judge's alma mater. Then back home to James Bay, where we would practice law together. At least, those were our plans... until..."

She broke off, stared down at her hands. She hadn't talked about any of this in so long. Telling the story left her oddly unshaken. Maybe it would be better not to say more. But Mike wanted the truth? She'd tell him.

"Jeff died," she said in a flat tone. "His mother found him dead in bed. He was only seventeen."

Even after all these years, it was still hard to believe. High school seniors simply didn't die in their sleep. Jeff had been there from the beginning, always just next door. They'd gone from tricycles to bicycles together, then moved on to cars. They'd received their letters of acceptance from the University of Michigan only the week before he died. Jeff's letter had been right there on his bedroom desk for all the world to see. Three days later it sat framed on display at the funeral home on the small table next to his casket. Jeff's death had sent her world tilting crazily out of control. How could she go on without him?

And yet somehow she had.

"Rose, I'm sorry, I didn't know..."

She lifted her head and met Mike's gaze, ignoring the sympathy she saw in his eyes. He felt sorry for her? Sorry for Jeff? It was a little late for that. What did Mike know about suffering? He was the one who'd started this, who'd insisted on knowing what had happened. Fine. She would finish the story and she wouldn't mince words, either. He was a firefighter. He could stand a little heat.

"You have no idea how cruel people can be," she said. "The rumors swirled after Jeff died. People said he'd been drinking, just like his mother."

"The Judge's wife was an alcoholic?"

Rose's eyes narrowed, remembering. "That's right. She was an alcoholic, though no one dared say it to her face. After all, people respected the Judge. But everyone knew she drank. She rarely left the house. It was never openly talked about until Jeff died. Then the talk never stopped. It was cruel and heartless, the things people said, all those rumors they spread about him and how he'd died."

"Wasn't there an autopsy?"

She nodded slowly. "Jeff died of congenital heart failure. It was a condition that had never been diagnosed. But no one cared about the truth. After the autopsy results were released, the talk really heated up. People in town said the Judge had called in his markers and had things hushed up. They said he'd paid people off to make it appear Jeff died in his sleep."

"Did he do drugs?"

Rose scoffed at the notion. "Jeff and I weren't interested in anything like that. But that didn't stop people from talking. They didn't care anything about

Jeff. Even though he was dead, his reputation was ruined." Her face hardened. "And no matter what I said, there wasn't anything I could do about it. Nothing is sacred... not when you live in a small town."

The memories flooded back, and Rose felt her heart pounding. She rushed to finish the story before it finished her.

"The Judge's wife died a year later. I was in college and came home for the funeral. I'm not sure what they listed as the official cause of death. She never left the house after Jeff died. My mother told me that the Judge did his best to get her some help. He tried convincing her to go away, to a rehab center like Betty Ford. But she wouldn't go. Her drinking was out of control and one day it was too late." Rose shrugged. "Maybe she died from drinking too much, but I think she died of a broken heart. God knows she had enough cause. But the fact remained that Jeff was gone and she was gone and the Judge was left to deal with this town on his own."

Rose took a deep breath and tried to clear her mind and heart of the sudden ache deep inside. "The man you see today is the man I've always known. The Judge is tough and crafty, and he doesn't mince words. But he's a good man and honest to the core. He's lived with his share of tragedy and he's gotten through it. The Judge is a survivor. And he deserves better than the way he's been treated by this town."

"Yet he's still here," Mike said softly. "He didn't run away."

"Like I did?" Her eyes met his in challenge. "Is that what you mean? This town has nothing to offer me. I'm happier exactly where I am."

His silence made her fume even hotter. Why should she have to prove things to him? The Judge was no arsonist. The sooner Mike gave up this ridiculous investigation of her old friend, the better off they would all be. Mike was chasing the wrong man.

"Thanks for the information," he finally said. "It was very helpful. Believe me, I didn't know."

"Of course you didn't know," she hotly replied. She tapped her sandal smartly against the cement floor. "You're not a local. You're just like everybody else that moves up here. After a couple of months, they assume they know everyone and everything about this town."

"I've lived here more than a year. I'm getting to know my way around."

"A year?" Rose scoffed, ignoring the defensiveness in his voice. "You could live here twenty years and it wouldn't matter. You don't know anything about the people in this town. Who are you to judge?"

"What about you?" he shot back. "You don't live here anymore. What gives you the right to tell me not to pass judgment when you've been doing exactly that for..." He checked his watch. "The past ten minutes. You've been sitting there passing judgment on me."

She sat back in stunned silence, her ears smarting under the rap of his stinging retort. But the trier of fact inside her heart urged her to listen to what he was saying. His criticism wasn't without merit. She'd purposely pointed a finger at him and it hadn't been a particularly pretty thing to do. Their staring match continued. Too proud, both of them, that's what they were. But her heart urged her forward. Why was she always so caustic and bold?

Say it, Rose. Tell him you're sorry.

The quiet between them expanded in the cramped, tiny office, bouncing off the dingy white walls and ceiling.

"I guess you're right," he finally said with a shrug. "I am an outsider. Guess I'll always be one, too." His lips pursed together in a tight smile. "Little towns are funny. It's not like growing up in the city, is it? But then, you wouldn't know anything about that, since you're from around here."

Silently she berated herself. It was impossible not to notice the wounded look in his eyes. He'd taken her words entirely to heart. She hated herself for it. She hated the way their conversation had gone, hated how she'd flung the words at him... words about Jeff, the Judge, and Mike's judging others. It had been a heavy ball and she'd lobbed it at a ready target with a steady aim. She would give anything to erase that haunted look on his face. Mike had only been trying to do his job. She shouldn't have lost her temper. She knew better than to allow herself to become emotionally involved. Once that happened, it was hard to detach.

But better to detach than to let your feelings carry you places you dared not go. That was a surefire way to be burned.

Could a fireman somehow douse that fire?

"I'll call you if I have any more questions or if anything else comes up," he finally said.

"That's it?" Rose gave him an uneasy stare. "We're finished?"

"Looks that way." Mike rose unsmiling from behind the chief's chair, his face bright red.

She stumbled to her feet. She didn't know if she was more embarrassed by the way she'd acted or the tone of their conversation. Better to get out of there fast than stick around and witness the hurt her words had caused him.

Rose turned on her heel and fled without a backward glance.

Their conversation haunted her well into the next day. What an infuriating man. She had wanted to talk, wanted to apologize, but then he'd gone and acted so aloof and professional, interrogating her about the Judge. She'd been so mad, hearing her old friend's character called into question. The Judge was like a member of her own family. If Mike thought things through, maybe he would understand her reasoning. Still, she shouldn't have come across so strong or insulted his handling of the investigation. The debate raged in her head, leaving Rose cringing as she remembered what she'd said.

Michael John Gallagher was all she could think about—the good *and* the bad. What was it about being around that man? He brought out feelings in her that she didn't understand. Maybe she should call him. Maybe she owed him an apology.

Maybe? Probably!

Apologize, every instinct urged her, yet Rose still didn't pick up the phone. She was still pondering the next evening when the telephone rang.

"Are we still talking?" Mike's voice was hesitant. "You ran out of the office pretty fast the other day. I wasn't sure if you were mad, or what."

Was she still mad? Did she have a right to be? She hadn't figured it out herself. "Yes, we're still talking," she finally admitted. "What's on your mind?" He put her right on edge with his attitude. One minute the cool and commanding public official, and the next minute lively and playful, only to turn moody and intense. The change in him was infuriating, exasperating, yet strangely appealing. Mike wasn't at all the type of man she was used to dealing with. With him, you never knew what to expect.

"You told me to call."

"I did?" Rose thought hard for a moment. Was he baiting her again? "I don't remember saying that."

"You said to call if there was anything else. I've got another couple of questions for you."

Rose nearly choked. Did he actually expect her to answer more questions after everything she'd said the other day?

"I know it's short notice." Mike's voice softened slightly. "I'd appreciate it, Rose. We're still actively working the condo fire file."

Did she have a choice? Mike had said the fire was deliberately set and that meant a criminal investigation. As an officer of the court, it was his duty to ask. As a citizen, it was her duty to comply.

But witnesses to be deposed had the advantage of being interviewed at a location of their choosing. If Mike insisted on asking further questions, then she would insist they meet on her own turf... within view of the Judge's house next door.

"All right, I'll answer your questions. But you'll have to come here. My mother came home from the hospital this afternoon. I can't leave the house."

"How about seven o'clock? I'm at the fire station till then. I can swing by on my way home after work."

Rose blew out a sigh as she hung up the phone. He wasn't giving up, no matter what sort of obstacles— verbal or otherwise—she threw his way. What was it about this fireman that caused her such concern? She glanced at the grandfather clock. Its hands inched toward seven o'clock. Mike would be here soon. If she hurried, she still had time to run a comb through her hair.

At precisely seven o'clock, Rose opened the front door and strode out onto the front porch. She flopped down in one of the wicker chairs lined up near the front steps and eyed the empty street. Lil and her mother were inside, and she wasn't about to answer his questions under their scrutiny. God knows what the two of them might start asking him.

She settled back in the chair and fanned herself with her hand. Normally the fresh lake breeze blowing in off Lake Michigan kept things cool, but that wasn't the case this summer. The heat this second evening of July was stifling and oppressive, stagnant in its ability to alter time and attitude. She pushed some stray hairs off the back of her neck. Maybe she should think about having central air installed inside the house. She could afford it, even if she didn't make partner this year. And if she took the job in Washington, her salary would be even higher. The house could be equipped with central air and her mother would want for nothing. She could even take up winter residence in a Florida condo if she wished. Lil could go with her.

Thank goodness for Lil. Her mother's best friend had proved a godsend today. Lil's luxurious sedan had provided air-conditioned comfort while transporting Irene home from the hospital. Rose was grateful for every bit of Lil's nursing expertise. Tommy Gilbert had also been invaluable in "Irene-proofing" the house. Together she and Tommy had converted the front den into a makeshift hospital room, complete with an adjustable hospital bed. A commode chair with padded arms was now installed in the downstairs bathroom. All the colorful throw rugs covering the hardwood floors had been gathered and stored, so as not to catch on the metal walker that her mother would be using for the next few weeks or longer.

Home calls from the visiting nurse and physical therapist would begin soon, perhaps as early as tomorrow. Considerable effort would be required on her mother's part, but the doctors had assured them that the flexible new knee would be worth it. Her mother hadn't complained, not even as Rose helped her from the wheelchair to Lil's car. Irene probably had thought no one was looking, but Rose had noticed the deep wince of pain that flitted briefly across her face as she settled back in her seat.

What was a little money spent renting a hospital bed if it helped speed her mother's recovery? What was the point of working so hard, if not to provide those you loved with life's little comforts? Her mother deserved whatever she could give her, and Rose could afford to pay the price.

She spotted the cherry-red pickup as it started up the small hill at the bottom of their street. Only a few minutes after seven o'clock. Right on time. There must have been no visitors at the fire station tonight.

Mike strode up the porch steps a few moments later. Rose took in his creased dark blue pants and crisp white short-sleeved shirt which sported that same strange-looking cross emblazoned over one pocket. He looked sharp and professional. She tried not to stare. What was it they said about a man in uniform?

"I thought we could talk out here," she said. "My mother isn't up to dealing with visitors."

"Sure, I understand," Mike said. His face wore an easy look of amiable concern. "Everything going okay?"

"She'll be all right."

"Glad to hear it. I won't keep you long."

Rose offered him a tentative smile and waved him into a chair. She was ready to forgive him, even apologize for her part in what had happened the previous afternoon. He'd said some harsh things, but so had she.

Something about this fireman made it hard to let go. They had to get things between them back on the right track.

Mike dropped down in the seat beside her.

"Cecilia Rose?" The front door cracked open and Lil's face appeared behind the screen. "Your mama says it's way too hot out here for the two of you to be talking on the front porch." Lil eyed Mike up and down with a frank, appraising look which melted into distinct approval. "Why don't you bring this nice young man inside?"

Rose bristled. She didn't want him inside the house. He'd already proved he had no fear about speaking his mind. He was here to question her, but her mother and Lil probably had plenty of questions planned for him... like insisting on hearing all the juicy details of how she and Mike had managed to meet up again. Rose grimaced, remembering the kitchen fire that had nearly set the house on fire. She'd managed to keep the news from her mother, but Mike's presence in the house would be like introducing a firecracker to a burning match. Her mother and Lil were masters in the art of interrogation. Who knew what he might say?

"Irene and I are having a little party to celebrate her homecoming and we could use the company." Lil pushed the screen door open wide. "No excuses, you two. Come on in."

Rose stood with a sigh. Mike held the screen door open and gestured for her to enter—then flashed her an outright wink.

"We'll be right there, Lil." She grabbed Mike's arm and pulled him aside as they entered the front hallway, waiting till Lil disappeared from view. "Listen, about that fire that started in our kitchen…"

"Yes?" His eyes sparkled with interest though his face wore an innocent look.

"I never mentioned it to my mother. I didn't want her upset." She wasn't used to begging for favors, but she'd do what she had to in order to keep him silent.

"You do understand what I'm saying, correct?" she hissed sweetly.

"I take it that you prefer I not mention the subject?" A soft smile played around his lips, taunting, inviting.

"Precisely." The last thing she wanted was her mother finding out, and he damn well knew it.

Mike leaned close enough for her to catch the light, inviting scent of recently applied aftershave. "I wouldn't worry about it, if I were you," he said. "Even if she does discover you nearly burned the house down, she already knows you're not much of a cook. After all, she *is* your mother. And mothers know everything."

The man was infuriating… absolutely infuriating! Had she actually considered apologizing to him? If it hadn't been for Lil and her mother insisting that he be invited inside, she would already be finished with his interrogation and Michael John Gallagher would be long gone.

"Just answer the question," Rose demanded. "You won't tell her, will you?"

"I thought I was the one asking questions tonight."

She didn't try to hide the open glare on her face.

Mike's eyes twinkled. "All right, you have my promise. I won't say a word." He crossed his heart with a flourish of his hand.

"Thank you." The words didn't come easily, but she was in his debt.

Trouble was, he knew it.

Reluctantly Rose led him onto the enclosed sun porch directly off the living room where Irene and Lil waited.

Mike had an extra wide smile for Irene. "Good to see you again, ma'am. I hope you're feeling better."

"Now that I'm home, I certainly am. Have a seat, young man."

Rose watched from the doorway as her mother nodded Mike to the wicker chair drawn up beside her, the very seat she herself had been sitting in until the clock had chimed seven. She'd given up her time tonight to allow Mike a chance to question her further. Looked like she'd given up her chair as well.

"What's your pleasure?" Lil's eyes gleamed with interest from her spot on the tasseled loveseat as she gestured with her glass. "We taught Rose how to make a decent martini. Neat, not too dry."

Now they were offering him drinks? Well, if *she* was the one playing bartender tonight, one drink was all he would get. He'd already shown he couldn't be trusted. The sooner he was out of the house, the better.

Ice cubes tinkled together as Irene raised her glass. "Lil likes her martinis, but don't you feel obligated to join her, young man. At the moment, I'm relegated to iced tea. My medicine, you know. But it's the right season for a nice cool drink. Lord, it's been so hot this summer."

"Iced tea sounds perfect." He shot Rose an easy glance. "If it's not too much trouble."

"No trouble at all." She forced a pleasant smile to her face and headed for the glass sidebar near the door. Grabbing the silver tongs, she piled ice cubes into a tall glass.

"Cecilia Rose? Perhaps your young man would like a little lemon," Irene said.

Her young man? Rose nearly dropped the glass. Where had her mother gotten that idea?

"Lemon would be nice," Mike said with a polite nod for her mother and a grin for Rose.

He was taking his sweet time getting down to business. And she'd like to wipe that silly smirk off his face. She glanced around the wet bar, but the lemon dish was empty.

"Sorry, we're all out of lemon." Served him right.

"Check the kitchen. I'm sure there are a few in the refrigerator," Irene suggested.

"I'll be right back." Rose grabbed the lemon dish and fled the sun porch. So, he wanted lemon in his iced tea? She'd give him lemon, all right. She found one in the refrigerator and whacked it with a sharp knife, returning moments later with mangled lemon slices in the dish. She splashed iced tea into the glass, critically chose the lemon slice containing the most seeds, and presented it to him with her most gracious smile. "Here you are, per your request. Iced tea, with lemon."

She whirled away and started for the loveseat.

"Sugar would be great. That is, if you have any?" Mike called out.

She took a deep breath and headed back to the side bar. *Naturally* he wanted sugar. Was there anything else she could provide to make his iced tea experience more complete? Guaranteed if there was, he'd probably think of it in the next few minutes—and no doubt he'd let her know. She had to get him out of this house and fast. No way in hell was she going to survive if he started questioning her in front of her mother and Lil. Asking him over tonight had been a mistake. A *big* mistake.

Lil settled back against the loveseat with a critical eye for Mike's iced tea. "I think I misjudged you. I took you for a man who enjoys a drink now and then. And what about you, honey?" She turned to Rose. "You're not drinking, either."

"Believe me, a drink is the last thing I need right now. If I had one, I wouldn't stop." Rose purposely stopped herself from looking anywhere near Mike. No doubt he was sitting there with a big grin on his face, enjoying himself immensely.

"I told you there'd be too much stress involved working down there in that city," Irene said. "Some people can't touch the stuff, honey. You of all people should know that. If you think you have a problem, maybe you should get some help."

Rose held back a sigh. "Mother, I am not an alcoholic. I do not have a drinking problem."

"Acknowledging is the first step of recovery," Lil offered.

Rose caught a flicker of mirth in Mike's eyes as he nursed his iced tea. He was obviously having a wonderful time and all at her expense. She could just wring his neck.

"I hope I didn't offend you, saying what I did." Lil nodded at Mike's glass. "It's none of our business if you choose to drink or not."

Mike's smile widened. "Well, ma'am, to tell you the truth, I do enjoy a beer or two now and then. But I'd have to say black coffee is mostly my drink of choice."

"For heaven's sake, Lil, leave the young man alone." Irene threw a hazy smile at him. "This medicine I'm taking must be playing tricks on me. I'm afraid I don't remember your name."

"It's Michael Gallagher."

"Michael Gallagher?" Irene drew in a sharp breath. "That was my husband's name." She slumped in her chair and leaned her head wearily against the pillows.

Rose jumped up from the loveseat and headed for her mother but Mike beat her. He crouched down close beside Irene's chair and gently cupped his hand atop hers. "Ma'am, are you all right?"

Irene's face was pinched white and her eyes were closed. Rose threw a worried glance at Mike. Suddenly she was very glad he was there with them, no matter how many questions he wanted to ask her.

"There's no need to fuss," Irene finally said. She opened her eyes and blinked once or twice at Rose and Mike, close together at her side. "It must be this medicine I'm taking. For a minute there I felt dizzy… all funny inside."

"Maybe we should call the doctor." Rose and Mike exchanged glances and he nodded.

"No, I'll be fine," Irene said firmly. "I feel much better now."

Lil pressed her fingers against the back of Irene's wrist. "Her pulse is steady."

Rose relaxed as the color slowly returned to her mother's cheeks. She tightened her grip on Irene's hand. "Please try not to scare us again like that. You had us all worried."

Mike stood up. "It's late. I should get going."

"You don't have to leave so soon," Lil said. "You haven't even finished your iced tea."

He picked up his glass and drained it in one quick swallow.

"You will come back and visit again soon, won't you?" Irene asked.

Mike nodded. "I'll do that, Mrs. Gallagher. You take care now, all right?"

"Thank you, Michael... or do you prefer Mike?" She reached out and caught his fingers in her own. "Somehow, calling you Michael seems right. That's the name my husband preferred."

"Then you go right ahead and call me Michael, ma'am. That will do me just fine."

Irene gave him a soft smile. "I look forward to our next visit. And I'll make sure Cecilia Rose has the iced tea ready."

Rose eyed him thoughtfully as she caught the hint of his smile. This fireman could be a real charmer when he tried. And he certainly was making the effort with her mother.

"Sorry if they came on a little strong," Rose said moments later as she escorted him onto the front porch. "My mom and Lil can be quite the pair."

He waved his hand dismissively. "Your mom seems real nice. And Lil is really something."

Rose eyed him as he stood there, one foot poised on top of the first step. He was leaving. Obviously he'd decided to put off asking her more questions until another time. It came as somewhat of a surprise to realize she was reluctant to see him go. He'd been pleasant and agreeable and—given the circumstances—extremely considerate. She'd have to remember not to take all his teasing so seriously. She'd been harsh with him yesterday in the chief's office and Mike hadn't deserved it. It was time for her to speak up, to let him know she was sorry for those words she'd flung at him in anger.

"Look, Rose, I just wanted to tell you I'm sorry about the way things turned out yesterday. Somehow we got off on the wrong foot. Those things I said about the Judge... well, I guess I was a little out of line. I didn't mean to offend you."

She felt her face flush as she heard his apology. She hadn't even had the chance to open her mouth. And his words were heart felt, that much was obvious. From what she'd seen, he didn't seem the type who tossed out empty words merely to smooth things over.

"I just want to make sure you understand what's going on here," he said. "It's my job as fire investigator to oversee every aspect of the investigation. Unfortunately, that involves asking hard questions. If I hadn't asked you about the Judge, I wouldn't have been doing my job."

"I know that." A grudging admiration for him grew. It must have taken considerable effort for him to pick up the phone and make the call that brought him over to the house tonight—all the while knowing he intended to apologize.

"Anyway, that's what I wanted to tell you." His eyes flashed dark with intensity. "So, what do you think? Is there a chance we might be friends again?"

"I think that could be arranged." She didn't even try to hold back the smile. He could be intensely appealing when he felt it worth the effort. And his tender concern for her mother tonight erased any lingering doubts in her mind.

Mike started down the steps.

"Wait." She reached out and tapped him on the shoulder. "I thought you said you had some more questions for me."

A half smile played round his mouth. "That's right, I guess I did. Well, you already answered the first one."

Rose frowned. "I did?"

"I wanted to know if you were still mad at me."

Still mad at him? What kind of official questioning was that? "What was the second question?"

"If you'd have dinner with me," he said. "I mean a real dinner this time. Not on some park bench." His voice dropped low. "And this time, I pay."

A sudden thrill leaped deep within her. Mike had asked her out. A *real* date.

"I would like that," she softly replied, smiling at the obvious relief that washed across his face.

"Great. I'm off for the next two nights. Maybe we could do something then."

The reality of her mother's situation returned to mind.

"I'm sorry. That won't work. I can't leave my mother alone for any length of time yet."

"Sure, I understand." He nodded. "You have to do what you have to do."

Rose brightened as a sudden thought came to mind. "Lil is a retired nurse. She's here nearly every day. Maybe she'd be willing…"

A steady grin spread over Mike's face. "Lil seems like the accommodating type."

"I'm sure she'll say yes. If all else fails, I'll bribe her with a martini."

His grin widened. "Better be careful, offering free booze. Remember what your mother said? They might get the wrong idea about you."

Rose's laugh of delight rang out loud.

"I'm going home and get some sleep. I'll call you tomorrow." He started down the porch steps, only to abruptly stop yet once more. Turning, he stared back up at her. "Rose."

"Yes?"

"No—I mean, *Rose*. I keep hearing people call you different names. Cecilia Rose, Cecilia, Rose. Which is it? You've never really said."

Her heart tugged at a sweet distant memory of a sunny afternoon long ago. The heat of the summer sun lingered warm on her arms and freckled her nose as the man who'd been the first love of her life carefully taught her the delicate intricacies of baiting a hook, casting out a line and reeling in her catch.

"You'll make a grand fisherman someday, Rosie sweetheart. It must be the Irish blood in you. Never forget, Ireland is an island of fisherman. And the Gallaghers are a fishing family."

"But you're not a fisherman, Daddy. You teach school." Even at eight years old, little Rosie's rational mind caught someone in a trap.

"I'm a fisherman at heart. And someday, Rosie, when I retire, I'll be a fisherman for sure."

The memory of her father's pet name brought back a flood of tender reminiscence. Fishing together had been their special time, the only time he called her Rosie. She'd give anything to hear that beloved voice calling her by his special name for her just one more time. *Rosie.*

She didn't dare say it. Her father's memory was too close and precious to speak aloud. But the notion that Mike cared enough to ask was already tucked away deep inside her heart.

"Why don't we figure that out as we go along?" she finally said.

Mike hesitated, then finally nodded, smiling at her in the growing twilight. "I'll say good night, then...."

"Good night."

The growing cover of darkness hid the pensive smile that lit up her face. Rose stood alone on the porch steps and watched as he climbed in the pickup, threw her a wave, and started down the street. Only after the pickup finally disappeared from sight did she turn and head back into her mother's house.

CHAPTER SEVEN

ANNUAL INDEPENDENCE DAY PARADE

By: Charles Kendall
The James Bay Journal

JAMES BAY—The annual Fourth of July parade kicks off Monday at 2:00 P.M. sharp. More than fifty entries are expected to participate in this year's parade. The VFW and American Legion will be represented, as will the Boy Scouts. The parade, led by the fire department, will feature bands, floats, bagpipers, and an honor guard. The parade route runs through downtown.

Residents are encouraged to turn out in full red, white, and blue regalia to celebrate the birth of our country. Patriotic commemorative buttons are being sold by the Kiwanis Club to raise funds for the library-remodeling project. The buttons, a new fund-raiser this year, are expected to be a local collector's item. They may be purchased from downtown merchants including the James Bay Bank, Bell's Drug Store, James Junior Wear, and Ramer Mercantile. Those interested in learning more about the buttons may contact Charles Kendall, Kiwanis button chairperson.

The phone rang while she was in the kitchen cleaning up the remains of their lunch. Rose grabbed it on the second ring before it could disturb Irene, who had finally settled down and was napping on the sun porch. "Hello?"

"You sound tired. Everything okay?"

Mike's voice breathed fresh life into her spirits. She hadn't expected caring for her mother to be as exhausting as a full-time job. How did professional caregivers do it? Every day left her physically drained, and dealing with the pain in Irene's knee kept both of them awake much of the night. Hours later, with her mother finally asleep, Rose had gone back to bed, only to discover sleep wouldn't come. All the *what-ifs* in her life kept her awake. Even when she managed to push aside the health-care concerns about her mother and the confusing thoughts about the path her career should take, her thoughts kept spinning. But this time, at the center of the whirling vortex was a tall, tanned fireman by the name of Michael John Gallagher.

"Mom's knee kept her awake most of the night." Rose struggled to hold back a yawn.

"Sounds like you need a nap." Mike's voice flooded patient and soothing over the telephone line. "What about tomorrow? I'm driving one of the fire trucks in the Fourth of July parade. I thought maybe if you weren't busy, we could get together, maybe spend the afternoon together."

Regret flooded through her as she heard his invitation. Any day but tomorrow…

"I'm sorry, but we do have plans."

"That's okay, I figured you might." His voice sounded flat. "It was short notice."

Did he think she was merely making up an excuse? "We do this special thing each year to celebrate the Fourth," she rushed to explain. "It's a neighborhood block party and it always ends up at our house. People come over and watch the fireworks. Our porch and lawn have the perfect view." She heard herself gushing and tried to tone down her enthusiasm. "I know it sounds corny, but it's actually lots of fun. You're welcome to join us."

She'd missed the annual party two years in a row due to work commitments. But she was here this year, and hopefully Mike could join them. The whole neighborhood usually turned out, with people wandering from yard to yard, sharing their barbecues, salads, and desserts before eventually ending up on the Gallaghers' yard or front porch. It was a fun time, a cherished childhood memory served up like a piece of Irene's famous rhubarb-cherry pie... a little slice of heaven.

"Thanks for the invitation. It sounds really nice, not corny at all."

She could already hear the *but* in his voice. Rose swallowed hard and steeled herself.

"But I'm afraid I can't make it. I'll be busy tomorrow night watching the fireworks."

She frowned and stared at the phone. Hadn't he heard her? She'd just told him they would be watching the fireworks, too.

"Our front porch has the perfect view. You can see them quite clear from up here on the hill."

He chuckled softly over the phone. "Guess I didn't make myself clear. I've got some free time after the parade, but I'll be working tomorrow night. I'm scheduled to be on standby with the fire truck down at the harbor. Hey, why don't you come down there? We could watch the fireworks together."

It sounded fabulous. What could be better than sitting next to Mike down by the lake, watching the night sky explode in brilliant colors of bursting shells? That would be the best view of all... especially with one of those strong tanned arms around her, holding her close.

"I'm sorry, Mike, I can't," she said. Regret lingered in her voice as well as in her heart. "Much as I would love to, I really need to stick around home. We have lots of people coming over and I can't disappoint my mom."

"No need to explain, I understand." He hesitated. "Maybe I'll stop by later, after the fireworks. That is, if the invitation is still open?"

"I would like that," she said with a growing smile. "And yes, the invitation is definitely open."

"Good, we'll leave it at that. You get some rest, take care of your mom, and maybe I'll see you tomorrow night."

Rose found herself humming as she hung up the phone. What was that little tune? She wasn't much of a musician, couldn't remember the lyrics, but the melody was soft and appealing and exactly fit her mood. Deprived of sleep, her world felt enchanted, soft and smoky around the edges.

All because of a fireman named Mike.

Rose wobbled along on Irene's old bicycle she'd unearthed from the garage. In dire need of an overhaul, the bike had seen better days, but it was good enough for the quick trip downtown. She was on a mission, and on this bicycle there'd be no need to search for a nonexistent place to park. The wire basket centered between the handlebars would provide lots of room for the barbequed chicken her mother craved. Plus, Irene's bike would provide a convenient getaway before the parade started. She would be back home with a hot tasty lunch before her mother missed her.

It seemed the entire population of James Bay, as well as the tourists, had been lured downtown by the holiday activities. Cars jammed the town center. Police directed traffic as the main street corridor was cordoned off for the upcoming parade. Crowds overflowed the sidewalks that were lined with flags, proudly displaying the colors of red, white, and blue. Excited voices of giddy children lifted on the breeze. Somewhere down the street she could hear the sound of bagpipes straining. The enticing aroma of barbequed chicken floated from the Kiwanis tent set up in Marina Park.

It was close to parade time, and traffic on the side street was at a near standstill. She waited in line for what seemed forever behind impatient customers hungry for chicken, but finally her turn came. Moments later, with a to-go box of hot, tasty chicken tucked safely in the bike's front basket, Rose kicked off for home. A red light at the corner forced her to stop. She straddled the bike waiting for the signal to turn green when the air was shattered by the eruption of a loud air horn. Startled, she glanced up to see a large yellow fire truck rounding the corner directly in front of her. A familiar face was behind the wheel. Mike's hand went up in a brief wave as he grinned at her through the truck's open window.

"Mama, look! That fireman waved at me!"

Rose shot a quick look at the little boy beside her hopping up and down on the sidewalk. His eager young face beamed as he pointed out the fire truck headed toward the library, the traditional starting point of the parade route.

The light turned green. Rose hopped back on the bicycle and pushed off into traffic. Mission accomplished, but she was taking away more than barbecued chicken. Tucked away in her heart was the sweet memory of a small boy's face as he spied a real live hero. She pedaled for home with a thoughtful smile.

Who said all the heroes were dead? Thank goodness little boys still dreamed of growing up to be heroes someday. And her very own hero planned on coming over to her house this evening. How lucky could one woman get?

Rose trailed her mother as Irene made the slow shuffle down the hallway, headed for the front porch. Even leaning on the cumbersome metal walker, every movement seemed a struggle. Watching was difficult, but her mother had the harder task. For a woman who had always been active and involved, recovery was proving a slow process. Rose tried not to think about the future. Her mother was growing older. The years ahead only promised more aches and pains.

Being three hours away made it easy to shrug off memories of home and the emotional burden those memories carried. Her mother needed help with the lawn? The garden? The house? No problem. Rose simply wrote a check. After all, wasn't that what money was for? Far easier to hire the job done and pay someone else to handle things than take the time and effort and make the journey home herself.

But this summer she'd had no choice. Hiring a housekeeper was an easy task, but her mother's surgery couldn't be ignored. How ironic that their roles were now reversed. Rose was home again, forced into the unfamiliar role of nurturer... a mother to her own mother. This might be just the first of age-related health issues needing Irene's attention—and a helping hand from Rose.

Her mother's surgery last week had done more than open up a knee. It had also opened Rose's eyes. She'd grown up in this house, spent most of her life in this little town. How many sacrifices her mother must have made, setting aside her own desires for the good of her family, her husband, and her child. Somehow Irene had managed to do it, while still maintaining her sanity and strength.

Devoted wife and mother. Such had been Irene Gallagher's chosen lot in life and it suited her well. She was good at it. Rose was good at things, too, but unlike her mother, she specialized in adults. She was good at drafting tight legal documents that allowed no room for maneuvering. She was good at providing the best in legal services for clients who trusted her. She'd be no good at dusting knickknacks, doing dishes, or changing dirty diapers. That was real work and not what she wanted out of life.

Her mother would eventually recover from surgery, but the slight tear in Rose's own heart wouldn't mend so easily. She had some hard decisions to make in the next several weeks and she needed to make up her mind. Should she stay with the firm and keep striving to make partner? Surely it would happen within another year or two. Or should she take Andy Sabatini up on his offer? The thought of working in the nation's capital was tremendously appealing, but Andy wasn't exactly Mr. Subtle. The job definitely came with strings attached. So far she'd managed to avoid leading him on, but a move to Washington would only intensify Andy's efforts in kindling a romance. She was safe for now with nearly one thousand miles between them. And even putting Andy's feelings aside, if she did choose Washington, that distance would be magnified between Rose and the people she loved.

The Judge's law offices were merely blocks away. Guaranteed that choice would make her mother happy.

But what would make *her* happy?

Why should the decision be so difficult? She was a grown woman with her thirtieth birthday fast approaching. She knew what was necessary to succeed. She'd purposely aimed in that direction. College, law school, clerking summers for the firm. For years she'd assumed her current position as associate attorney was the last piece in the jigsaw puzzle that had been her life for the past twelve years. But suddenly the future loomed uncertain and she found the mix to be strangely unsettling.

What would be so wrong with just staying put? Wasn't that exactly what she'd been working for since joining the firm? Making partner seemed an easy guarantee, and her dreams had soared no higher until Andy's phone call came from Washington D.C. His offer held such promise. Working at the Department of Labor, being involved in drafting and implementing employment law, she'd be fashioning laws that would serve to protect people and their loved ones. Finally she would have an opportunity to really make a difference in people's lives. Surely that would bring some focus to her life. And Washington D.C. was a beautiful city. An international metropolis. All she needed to do was tell Andy *yes*.

But if she did that, guaranteed there soon would be another question Andy would expect her to answer with a yes—as he placed a ring on her finger.

Rose pushed the thought aside. She'd never been one to settle, she didn't believe in taking the easier, softer way, and she wasn't about to start now. It wouldn't be fair to Andy and it wouldn't be fair to her. If she accepted Andy's offer and made the move to Washington, it would only be after the two of them had had a good, long heart-to-heart. But first she had yet to make up her mind. And there was still another offer on the table. It would be unfair not to give the Judge's proposal due consideration. It would bring her home to James Bay, to something else. And perhaps to someone else.

Deep inside, a memory beckoned. A smoky wisp of longing and desire for a man with sparkling eyes and a deep easy laugh. A man she had yet to see wear an expensive suit. A man whose usual attire was blue jeans or a fire coat. A man who lived in James Bay and from all appearances looked like had no plans to leave in the future.

"Cecilia Rose? Let's get your mama settled in a chair and then you can bring out the drinks."

Lil held the screen door wide open as the three of them headed onto the front porch. Rose fussed with her mother's favorite wicker chair, plumping the pillows behind Irene's back, gently propping up her leg on cushions as per the doctor's orders.

So many things to remember. Rose held back a sigh as she finally sank down in her own chair. Pills, pain, physical therapy. Some people devoted their entire lives to serving as a caretaker for someone else. How could they make such a sacrifice? How did you turn aside your own longings and desires? Feelings couldn't be shut off like a water faucet. Eventually the leaks would spring up somewhere. She'd be forced to rely on the expertise of a master plumber.

"How many fireworks do you figure we've watched together all these years?" Lil asked from her chair.

Irene's eyes squinted tight. "Too many for me to count. We're two old ladies, remember?"

"Excuse me? Did you call us *old ladies*?"

"You heard me," Irene replied with a quick wink for Rose.

"Speak for yourself." Lil straightened in her chair and fussed with the vivid silk scarf of red, white, and blue draping her shoulders. "I'm not ready for an assisted-living home yet."

"Well, given the shape I'm in, that might be where I'm headed. And last time I checked my calendar, you and I were the same age," Irene smartly replied.

Rose smiled as she caught the undertone of affection in her mother's voice. The two women had been bantering for as long as she could remember.

"Cecilia Rose? Move my chair a little bit closer to the edge, would you, sweetheart? I want to be able to see tonight's fireworks nice and clear."

"I think you're already close enough, Mom. We don't want you falling down the steps."

"Don't be ridiculous." Irene snorted. "There's lots of room to move this chair, at least another good three or four inches. If you don't, that tree limb will be in my way." Irene pointed toward the front yard and the offending braches.

"We are not moving your chair," Rose firmly replied.

"I think someone's learning what it's like to be a mother," Lil said. She shot Rose a fond glance. "Go on, honey, and do what your mama says. She won't fall off the porch. And if she does, she'll get over it. You know your mother. She's a tough old bird."

"For goodness sake, would everyone quit worrying about me?" Irene's voice edged with irritation. "I'm already so full of metal with all these staples and titanium in my knee, I doubt a little tumble off the porch would kill me. Besides, there'll be lots of people around here soon enough. No doubt someone will pick me up and stick me right back in my chair, good as new."

"What about that cute fireman of yours?" Lil glanced over at Rose with interest. "I'm sure he's nice and strong. Is he coming to our little shindig tonight?"

"I'm not sure," she carefully replied. "Mike has to work."

She had no guarantee he would show up tonight, and she'd already decided it was best not to think about it. If he showed, fine. But if he didn't? Well, she'd deal with the disappointment if and when that happened. It would be easier to handle if she didn't dwell on it now.

"That one is a real charmer, honey," Lil said. "If I were any younger, I'd go after him myself."

"I like your Michael." Irene settled back in her chair with a wistful smile. "He reminds me of your father."

"Mom, you have to quit calling him *my Michael*," Rose replied. "You're only saying that because of his name."

"That may be true, but there's something about him that I like very much," Irene said. "He's a nice young man, sweetheart. Very nice."

"You could do worse, young lady. *Much* worse." Lil wagged a manicured finger at Rose. "That fireman is a definite keeper and I'd make a move quick, if I were you. You'll only be in town for a few weeks. I say make a play for him fast before some other girl catches his eye."

"For heaven's sake, Lil, let Cecilia Rose be," Irene said firmly. "She's old enough to make up her own mind. She doesn't need the two of us giving advice on how to run her love life."

"Who said anything about me being in love with him?"

"Now that you mention it, *you* did," Irene replied.

Her mother's words brought a quick rush of color to Rose's cheeks. "I barely know him. We've only gone out to dinner once, and that didn't really count. It was only a picnic."

Sandwiches down at the waterfront, but she hadn't cared. Being with Mike was satisfying in its own way. It nourished her on some inner level she hadn't even realized needed to be fed—until now.

"Picnics can be more fun than sitting in some stuffy restaurant," Lil said with a breezy wave of her hand. Diamonds flashed on her fingers in the setting sun. "It all depends on the person you're with. And let me tell you, honey, I've seen the way he looks at you. I might not know much about some things, but there's one thing I *do* know and that is *men*. And that fireman is definitely interested in you, whether you know it or not. Heavens, he might not even know it himself."

"Lil, that's enough," Irene said, clucking her dismay. "It doesn't matter what you or I think. Cecilia Rose is quite capable of making up her own mind about dating Michael." She flashed a sweet smile in Rose's direction. "I'm getting rather thirsty. Would you please bring out the iced tea?"

"I thought we were having martinis. Cecilia Rose, why don't you fix us up a pitcher?"

"You'll be sloshed if you drink martinis all by yourself," Irene said. "I'm still taking my medication."

"Well, the Judge will be here soon. And Rose's fireman looks like he might just be a martini man, too."

Rose made a hasty escape for the kitchen. If the topic of conversation didn't change soon, she'd be diving into the martini pitcher herself. The last thing she needed was her mother and Lil speculating about Mike when he showed up tonight.

If he showed up.

CHAPTER EIGHT

REWARD OFFERED FOR INFORMATION LEADING TO PROSECUTION OF ARSONIST

The James Bay Journal

JAMES BAY—The Chamber of Commerce is offering a $1,000 reward to anyone providing information that leads to the capture and successful prosecution of the person responsible for the arsons plaguing our community. Contact the James Bay Police Department or Assistant Fire Chief Michael Gallagher for more information.

"Weren't the fireworks beautiful? I like the ones that flutter down in little gold sparkles. They're so pretty. They look like fairy dust coming straight from heaven."

"I bet our dog is under the bed. He hates those shells that explode in loud booms. Why they throw away money on something noisy that you can't even see is beyond me."

Muted strains of conversation wafted on the late night breeze as people started for home. The snack bowl supplies were nearly wiped out and the iced tea, lemonade, and martini pitchers had long since been drained. The front porch had been crowded all evening long with friends and neighbors, but the end of the firework display heralded the beginning of sleepy goodnights. Finally the porch emptied out, save for a few stragglers. Even Irene had gone in to bed. Rose couldn't keep her gaze from wandering to the one chair that had remained conspicuously empty all night long. Was Mike still on fire duty? There'd been no mishaps, no misfired shells or emergency scenarios, but he had never shown up. Only the Judge, Charles Kendall, and Tommy Gilbert still lingered on the porch, keeping her company on the hot summer night.

"Well, I suppose I will say good-night." The Judge stubbed out his cigar and reached for his jacket on the back of his chair.

"You're leaving, too?" Of all the people still surrounding her, the Judge was the only one she wished would stay. There was still a slim chance Mike might appear, and all night she'd been hoping to bring the two of them together. Once Mike got to know the Judge, surely he would drop this nonsense about her old friend being a suspect in the arson investigation. All the two of them needed was a chance to talk in a neutral setting. She couldn't think of a more perfect place than her own front porch.

"I'm sorry, my dear, but I need to go home and pack."

"Are you going somewhere?" Rose frowned.

"I'm flying to California tomorrow. My sister is ill."

"I'm sorry to hear that." No wonder the Judge looked so haggard and careworn. First the condominium fires and now his sister was sick. She gave him a tight hug, holding on for an extra minute. "Take care of yourself, promise?" Rose whispered in his ear.

He patted her back. "I'll only be gone a few days. We'll talk when I get back." He kissed her forehead and waved briefly at Charles Kendall and Tommy Gilbert. "Gentlemen, good evening to you both."

The cherry-red pickup pulled up in front of the house as the Judge started down the porch steps. Rose's heartbeat quickened as Mike parked the truck and opened the door. Maybe it wasn't too late after all.

"Sorry I didn't get here sooner," Mike said as he headed up the walk. A bulky paper sack was tucked under one arm. "The chief's wife was sick and he couldn't make it downtown tonight."

"You're here now, that's what counts." There was no need to force a smile to her face. She could feel it already firmly in place.

The Judge nodded at Mike. "Officer, I've been meaning to contact you. Have you any new information for me?"

Mike shook his head. "I'm sorry, Judge, I wish I did. We're still investigating."

"Certainly you must have some idea by now of who's to blame?" Charles spoke up from his chair next to Rose. "The Judge would like some answers and so would the reading public. How long do you expect us to wait?"

"As long as it takes." The porch lamp's cast a dim shadow across Mike's face.

"What's so difficult about figuring out who set a fire?" Charles shot back.

"It all depends on the evidence you find at the fire scene."

Rose caught the strained look of annoyance briefly cross Mike's face as he sank down across from Tommy Gilbert on the top porch step. He reached for the nearly empty bowl of corn chips and popped a few in his mouth before continuing. "Lots of times the evidence gets destroyed when the fire gets out of control. Take that abandoned boat warehouse down by the harbor. That place is like a tinderbox. If it ever caught fire, we'd never be able to save it. We've already requested permission for a controlled burn."

"I'm merely trying to satisfy our readers," Charles said. "People want to know. You should have some answers by now."

"Arson is a difficult crime to prove," Mike repeated. "It doesn't pay to rush this kind of investigation. You can't just look at the fire scene. Motivation is a big factor. Why does someone start a fire?"

"The first thing I would think would be for revenge." A frown bordered Rose's face even as she spoke the words. They were talking about the condo fires... but who would hold a grudge against the Judge? The man didn't have any enemies. Who would want to see him harmed?

"I think it's obvious we're dealing with a pyromaniac," Charles said with a challenging stare for Mike. "Have you considered that idea, Officer Gallagher?"

Rose's eyes narrowed sharply as she took in her old school nemesis. Charles seemed to be deliberately baiting Mike, a behavior she recognized from their days back in high school. He always acted like that when things didn't go his way, and he hadn't changed much throughout the years.

She made a mental note to self to skip their next class reunion.

"I'm sure Mike is investigating all the leads, Charles," she said. "He doesn't need you telling him how to do his job."

"What about the insurance money?" Tommy Gilbert piped up. "My brother Joey said lots of people set their own stuff on fire, just for the money."

Tommy's words made her cringe. The last thing she wanted Mike hearing was that people thought the Judge needed money. Rose shot the boy a sharp look, but Tommy seemed oblivious.

"You're forgetting something, Tommy," Rose chose her words carefully. "Setting a fire for personal profit is a dangerous sport. Someone would really have to need the money for them to take a chance like that."

She threw Mike a cautious glance. Hopefully he'd taken the hint. The Judge was more than financially solvent. His Honor was loaded. He had no reason to burn those condos to the ground.

Mike shrugged in the shadows. "Every one of the fires has been different. It's going to take some time and every available resource to help us solve the crimes."

"What about you, sir?" Charles turned his attention to the Judge. "You must have taken quite a hit in the wallet when those buildings went up in smoke. The condos were nearly completed. Another month or so and they would have been rented. You must want to know exactly who's to blame. Or perhaps there's some reason you'd prefer the criminal investigation be delayed... or not solved at all?"

The Judge's eyes glistened like two black marbles. "Young man, are you insinuating that I had reason to gain from that fire? Construction at that condo site was costing me considerable money every single day. Why would I want those buildings destroyed?"

"Precisely my question, sir. Why would you?" Even in the dim porch light, Charles's eyes gleamed with speculation.

"Charles, you have no idea what you're talking about." Rose waded into the mud being slung. "You know as well as I do that the Judge had nothing to do with that fire."

"I resent your allegations, Mr. Kendall." The Judge's face flushed dark with anger. "I warn you to be very careful. There are laws against libel in this state. You could have a lawsuit on your hands if any of this were to be printed."

"The *Journal* only prints the truth," Charles replied with a cool stare. "We've begun our own investigation. Our newspaper has an obligation to the community. *Someone* needs to solve these crimes." He shot a hard glance in Mike's direction.

Rose glared at Charles. She'd heard enough. First he'd been after the Judge and now he seemed intent on breaking down Mike's resistance. "I think you owe both the Judge and Mike an apology."

"Let me make one thing clear, Mr. Kendall. I stand to profit nothing—*nothing*—from that fire." The Judge's voice rang out with a sharp edge of authority. "The insurance will cover my loss. But since the *Journal* is carrying on its own investigation, I'm sure you know that by now."

Charles opened his mouth to speak, but the Judge cut him off with a quick raise of his hand.

"Furthermore, I have complete and utter confidence in our fire department. They are competent professionals, well-trained at their jobs. When they find the person responsible, he shall be held accountable. And make no mistake, Mr. Kendall. That person *will* be found."

"Thank you, Judge," Mike said. "We're doing the best we can."

Rose sat back in her chair, slightly mollified at hearing the Judge taking a stand in Mike's defense. After tonight, Mike would understand why she felt the way she did about her old friend. Surely he would understand why the Judge couldn't—and shouldn't—be considered a suspect.

The Judge's lips twisted slightly in a close-pursed smile. "So be it, then. Officer, I am satisfied to leave things in your capable hands. I plan on being out of state for a few days on family business, but I look forward to hearing from you upon my return."

"Good night, Your Honor," Tommy Gilbert called out as the Judge headed down the porch steps. The Judge lifted a hand in a brief farewell wave as he made the short trek home across the front lawn.

"What in the world were you thinking, going after him like that?" Rose turned on Charles with a furious glare. "You know he didn't set those fires."

"I don't know anything of the sort." A haughty look crossed Charles's face. "Besides, our circulation has picked up since the arsons started. Whoever the guy is that's setting these fires, he's good for business."

"What makes you think it's a guy?" Tommy Gilbert said from his seat across from Mike.

Charles shot Tommy a cool stare, then turned to Mike. "Correct me if I'm wrong, Officer, but isn't arson normally a crime committed by men? Women don't go around setting fires."

Witnessing Charles's blatant rudeness set Rose's nerves skittering on high. And she wasn't the only one annoyed. The irritation on Mike's face was apparent for anyone who cared to notice.

"I can't discuss the investigation," Mike replied tightly. "You know that."

"I'm not asking you to divulge privileged information," Charles retorted. "I merely asked a simple question."

"The evidence is down at the State Crime Lab. I'm hoping they'll be able to give us some direction or lead."

"That's all you've got?" Charles's voice filled with derision. "Those condos burned down five days ago. Our taxpayers deserve a better payout than that in you solving the crimes. So, tell me, Officer Gallagher— when can we expect some answers?"

Dealing with adversity was how she made her living, and Rose had had quite enough of Charles for one night. If he wanted a fight, she'd be glad to oblige. "Charles, why don't you do us all a favor and shut up. Mike doesn't need you grilling him. He'll answer your questions when he's good and ready."

Mike shot her a fast look, then looked back to Charles. "Like I said before, the investigation is not open for discussion. I can't talk about it."

Sudden words in his own defense put a smile on her face. Mike didn't need a spokesman or spokeswoman, either, speaking up for him. He could hold his own.

"Seems to me that there isn't much you *can* talk about." Charles's face wore an outright smirk and his eyes held a bold challenge.

The faint glow of the porch light provided just enough illumination for Rose to spy the flush of anger on Mike's cheeks. His eyes flashed as he glared at Charles. And poor Tommy, caught in the middle. She caught the worried stare as he nervously glanced back and forth between the two men.

"Stop it right now, both of you." Rose jumped up from her chair. There was way too much testosterone flying on her mother's front porch. "I've heard quite enough on this topic for one night."

The staring match continued a few seconds longer as Mike stood his ground. Charles finally shrugged, dropped his gaze, and stood up from his chair.

"Cecilia is right. It's getting late. Gentlemen, I propose we all get going and let Cecilia get some sleep."

Mike and Tommy settled back comfortably on the porch steps.

Charles's lips pursed in a thin line. He held his head high and stomped down the steps without another word. Rose watched him depart with an overwhelming sense of relief. He was still as arrogant, overbearing, and conceited as he had been in high school. She'd thought by now he would have learned the art of acting and speaking with prudence and decorum, especially given his position in such a public forum as the newspaper business.

"I don't like that guy," Tommy muttered as Charles's car engine choked, stopped, and eventually sputtered to a start. It backfired once or twice before the glowing red taillights finally disappeared in the direction of downtown. "What's he gotta be like that for? Acting so high and mighty."

"Forget about him, Tommy," Rose replied. "Charles will never change."

"Yeah, well, he didn't need to be so rude." Tommy glanced across the steps at Mike. "He made it sound like you don't know what you're doing."

Mike shrugged. "He has a job to do and so do I."

"Joey doesn't like him, either." Tommy gazed back at Rose. "People in town don't think much of the way he's handling that paper. He could drop those advertising rates, too. We're not some big city like Detroit or Grand Rapids. Heck, this is James Bay. Joey quit running his ad last month. Said he got more business from word of mouth than that pricey ad he had in the *Journal*."

Rose listened quietly. Tommy made a valid point. Charles could be stuffy and arrogant, but he was tolerable, when taken in small doses. Joey Gilbert, however, was another sort entirely. She still remembered his volatile temper from their high school days. Joey was the only one of Tommy's family she had never liked.

"You ever need any help down at the fire department?"

Mike shot Tommy a quick smile. "Sure. We're always looking for volunteers. Why? You thinking about being a fireman?"

"Are you kidding me? All my life!"

"Stop by the department sometime when I'm on duty. I'll show you around, let you see the trucks and equipment. You might change your mind when you see what's involved."

"I don't think so." Tommy's eyes flashed with excitement. "What about tomorrow afternoon?"

"I'll be around."

"Sounds great. I'll come down as soon as I get off work."

"See you then." Mike offered out his hand.

A big grin lit Tommy's face as he grabbed Mike's hand and pumped it hard. "I probably should get going. Joey's got us out working early tomorrow. We're trying to get stuff done early in the day before it gets too hot." Tommy came to a slow stand and gave his short legs a brisk rubdown. "Thanks again, Cecil, for inviting me. Your party was fun. I always have a good time over here."

"We're glad to have you. You've been a big help to me, Tommy, with everything you've been doing. I appreciate it and I know my mom does, too."

"No big deal. Glad to help. Your mom's a real nice lady." He gave a short wave and headed down the sidewalk.

"He's a nice kid," Mike said as they watched Tommy shuffle down the street toward home.

"That was sweet of you, taking the time to talk with him like that," Rose murmured in the darkness between them.

"You think I'm sweet, do you?"

"You know what I mean." She felt the telltale blush climbing her cheeks as she heard the flirting banter in his voice. How was she supposed to concentrate with him teasing like that? She struggled to continue. "Tommy tries so hard. Things can't be easy for him the way they are right now. He lives with his brother and Joey Gilbert can be a real..." She swallowed down the vulgar comment that immediately rose to mind. "Tommy needs something going right in his life. Being on the fire department might be just the thing."

"We're always looking for volunteers. I'll show him around, see what he thinks. But it's not just fun and games. Some people think all you have to do is drive the fire truck and spray water on some flames." Mike's face sobered. "Volunteers are just as thoroughly trained as a paid firefighter. Everyone goes through certification. And if Tommy's interested, there would be a lot of training involved before he could qualify."

"He could do it," she quickly replied. "People have the wrong idea about him because of the way he looks. Tommy was very sick when he was a little boy and ended up with a permanent limp. It's always been a problem for him. My mother told me that's what kept him out of the service." She frowned suddenly. "Would Tommy's limp stop him from becoming a volunteer?"

Mike shrugged. "I won't kid you. It's not easy passing the physical requirements. Hopefully his limp won't hold him back. The training alone takes over one hundred hours. If Tommy makes it through that, plus passes all the required tests, he could end up a certified firefighter."

"He'd be a great addition to the department. He's a sweet guy and he's very dependable. Plus, he's stronger than he looks," Rose assured him. "I don't know what I'd have done around here without Tommy. He helped me fix up the house before mom got home. We made the front den into a sort of hospital room and he got the bathroom fixed up so she can manage things herself."

Rose couldn't stop the sigh from escaping her lips. "Being home has really opened my eyes. I didn't realize taking care of her would be so hard."

"I know what you mean. It's easier to forget things when you're not there…" His voice trailed off.

The darkness hung between them and Rose had the sudden feeling he'd meant to say more. She watched as he reached for the corn chips, his hand searching the bottom of the bowl. "There's probably another bag in the kitchen if you're still hungry." It had to be way past midnight, but she didn't want him to leave. The two of them had barely had a chance to talk alone.

"I am hungry," he admitted with a rueful grin. "There was no chance for me to eat dinner. I had a couple of hot dogs before the parade."

"Why didn't you say something earlier? Come on inside, we've got lots of food left over." Rose stood up, then laughed as she saw the hesitation on his face. "Don't worry, I didn't cook it. There's no chance you'll be poisoned."

"That's not it." Mike shook his head as he came to his feet. "It's getting late and everyone's gone. Plus, I don't want to disturb your mom. I probably should go on home."

Her mother was fast asleep, and Rose wasn't about to let him get away, not yet. She grabbed his arm, holding him hostage before he could head down the steps for his pickup. "What kind of a proper hostess would I be if I didn't offer you something to eat? Besides, if my mother ever found out I let you go away hungry, I would never hear the end of it."

Mike grinned. "Well, since you put it that way... I sure don't want you to break any etiquette rules. And I don't want to upset your mother."

Rose halted as the soft purr of a car engine and flash of red taillights from the driveway next door caught her attention.

Mike nodded. "Isn't that the Judge's car?"

"I wonder where he's going so late at night." Her eyebrows knit together in a frown as the sedan pulled out of the driveway and started down the street.

"Looks like he's headed downtown. Maybe he forgot something down at his office."

"I doubt it. He's flying out to California tomorrow. What would he need from his office?"

Mike shrugged. "His Blackberry?"

"I doubt he's aware such things exist." She sighed as the car disappeared from view. "Come on, let's get you something to eat. A word of warning, though—my mom's asleep. We need to be quiet."

"Hey, speaking of your mom, that reminds me." Mike rustled around in the darkness and finally grabbed hold of a bulky paper sack near his feet. He handed it to her with a smile.

"What's this?" The sack was heavy in her hands.

"It's for your mom. Sorry, I didn't have time to wrap it."

"You got my mom a present?" Rose flashed him a shy smile. "That was nice of you. She'll be very pleased."

"I didn't think she had one in the house. And seeing as how you're home again, I thought it might be a good idea."

His words had her curiosity fully aroused. "Can I take a peek?"

"Go ahead."

Cautiously Rose opened the sack and peered inside. Her eyes opened wide as she spied the small fire extinguisher.

"You mad?" An abashed grin played around his face.

"That you consider me a fire risk?" Rose grinned right back at him. "You're a real tease, Mr. Gallagher, do you know that?"

"So I've been told," he replied softly as he held open the screen door.

A gallant gentleman, this Gallagher man, and a hungry one, too. She watched in silent amazement as he sat at the kitchen table and devoured first one, then another, then a third piece of cold barbequed chicken.

"You looked pretty cute on that bicycle today." His eyes sparkled thanks as she placed a large glass of cold milk before him.

"I'm surprised I even remembered how to ride it," Rose said as she sank down in the chair opposite him. She thought of the condominium high-rise that she presently called home. Its narrow, gated entry, marble lobby and ornate glass elevator weren't exactly bicycle friendly. And her building was located in the center of the city. Convenient for work and court appearances, but the only green spot was a tiny park two blocks down the street. Funny, she hadn't realized until now how much she missed the sweet fragrant smell of newly mown grass.

"The city is no place for bicycles," Rose finally said. "Too many cars."

And not enough time. In the oddest silent moments, she caught herself realizing how much she'd given up, how much she missed having time for herself.

Mike sprawled back in his chair with a smile. "I'll agree with you on that one."

She eyed him curiously. "What about you? Why did you move out of the city? Your family is still there, right? So, why the move north? Don't tell me you abandoned the city for bikes. All you do is drive around in that pickup of yours."

One look at his face and Rose knew she'd gone too far. When would she learn to keep her mouth shut? They'd been having a nice time, and now he'd clammed up. Now she might never know. "I'm sorry. I didn't mean to be nosy. Just forget I said anything, okay? Why you moved north is none of my business."

Apologizing never came easy for her, but at least the effort brought some reward. Rose watched as the hint of a smile crept back on Mike's face.

"You weren't being rude. You were just being... inquisitive."

She couldn't help but smile, too. Inquisitive was such a nice word for prying. Someone definitely had taken the time to teach Mike how to put a pleasant spin on things.

"I'm afraid my mother wouldn't agree with you. She always said I was a nosy little girl, and that I grew up to be a nosy woman."

His grin widened. "I knew there was a reason why I like your mom."

She couldn't keep herself from giggling. Whatever they were doing—conversing, talking, flirting—she thoroughly intended to savor every delicious moment that Mike sat in that chair at her mother's kitchen table. He was so different than the other men she knew, the stern suits she encountered daily inside the firm, or the dedicated debaters within the halls of justice. None of them made her feel the way she did now. Like she was sixteen again—lighthearted, playful, without a care in the world.

"My mom thinks you're pretty special. Lil likes you, too."

His grin returned full tilt. "The two of them are quite a pair."

"Lil is like the sister my mom never had. They grew up in James Bay. They went to school together and out on dates together. They even got married around the same time. Mom was there when Lil's husband died, and Lil was there when we buried my dad. Thank goodness they have each other to lean on. They bicker occasionally, but it doesn't really matter. Lil is family."

"They're lucky." Mike regarded her with thoughtful eyes. "And I think your mom's pretty lucky to have you, too."

A soft meow from the doorway interrupted them.

"Hey, Bozo. Here, kitty." The aging Red Persian padded over to the table to sit near Rose's feet. Picking him up, she stroked the cat's soft red fur as he settled in her lap.

"Bozo? Where'd he get a name like that?" Mike's eyes stayed trained on Irene's precious feline. The cat's yellow eyes focused cool and steady on Mike as he purred his pleasure at the post-midnight pampering.

"My dad named him. He said any animal with all that red hair deserved a name like Bozo. Mom couldn't come up with a better one, so it stuck. Right, Bozo?" Rose rubbed the cat's head affectionately. Her condominium didn't allow animals and she hadn't realized how much she'd been missing the companionship. Maybe she should think about finding another place to live. One that allowed cats. With space for bicycles.

"Anyway, Bozo is one of the family. My mom sets great store by him. He keeps her company when I'm not around." Her face dropped. "Which, according to my mother, is quite a bit lately." Rose sighed. "And I have to admit that she's right."

"Don't be so hard on yourself. You're here now, when it counts, and I'm sure that means a lot to your mom. Probably more than she lets on, and more than you know."

Mike's quiet reminder, gentle and insistent, settled soft in Rose's heart.

"I don't come home as much as I should. It's difficult to pull myself away from work."

"What type of law do you practice? Criminal defense?"

They'd never discussed the scope of her work. For all he knew, she could be a skillful litigator, a prosecutor whose days were spent convicting murderers, drug dealers—and arsonists.

"I don't have the stomach for criminal work. Most felons are constantly in and out of the system, working it for everything they can get. I stick with civil work and corporate law—employment law mainly. It's nice and clean, and fortunately there's lots of it. I have a good practice. It keeps me busy."

Abruptly her thoughts flashed on the white gauzy bandages covering Irene's knee. They would need changing come morning. They needed changing every morning until the wound was healed. What if that didn't happen? What if it took more time than she had? The firm was already impatient with her six-week leave of absence. She couldn't stay here indefinitely. Who would take care of Irene?

A tight smile pinched Rose's face. "I'm not a very good daughter, I guess. My mother deserves better than me. I know I'm busy, but I should try to get home more often."

"Don't should on yourself."

"Excuse me?" Rose frowned.

"It's something my brother Terry says. *Don't should on yourself.*"

"What exactly is that supposed to mean?"

"Don't let guilt get in the way of doing what you feel is right. Guilt doesn't solve anything. It only creates more problems."

Rose silently observed him across the table. How had he known she'd been thinking along those lines? "Your brother sounds like a pretty smart guy," she finally said.

Mike nodded and drained the last of his milk. "You couldn't ask for better."

Her curiosity got the better of her. "Do you have any sisters?"

"Nope, it's just Terry and me." Mike toyed with his empty glass. "He's a couple years older than I am. He works in the family insurance agency."

"So, you're the baby of the family." Rose flashed him a quick smile. "I suppose everyone spoiled you rotten."

Mike grinned. "Believe me, my mom is not that kind. She works in the business alongside my dad. She trained Terry and me fast. We were making our beds and doing dishes long before we started school."

A thoughtful look appeared on his face. "You remind me of her in a way," he said after a moment. "You both have careers, you're both centered and focused. But you're different than my mom..."

"Different?" She hoped so. For one thing, his mother had to have at least thirty years on her. "How so?"

"You're *much* softer around the edges."

He studied her, his eyes locked on hers, holding her close.

"I'll take that as a compliment," she replied in a voice barely above a whisper.

"Good. I meant it as one." Mike reached across the table and covered her hand with his. "Rose, I wish things..." He broke off suddenly and sat there a moment, shaking his head. "I don't know. It's been a long time. Maybe I should..."

His hesitation urged her on. "What was that you just told me? Don't *should* on yourself?"

His head came up as he met her eyes again. "So, you were listening after all."

"You bet I was." They held each other's gaze in silent understanding. The touch of his fingers, warm and pressing against her skin, set a delicious thrill surging through her as the grandfather clock in the front hallway bonged a quiet chime of two o'clock. Most of the world was fast asleep, but Rose felt as if she'd just come awake for the first time in her life.

"Cecilia Rose? Sweetheart, are you there?" The faint sound of Irene's voice floated down the hallway, accompanied by the louder jingle of the bedside bell "Cecilia Rose? I need help."

Bozo jumped off Rose's lap with a soft meow and padded out of the kitchen without a backward glance.

"I'm sorry." Rose reluctantly pulled her hand from Mike's and stood up. "She probably needs one of her pain pills."

"I should be going anyway. It's getting late." He neatly pushed his kitchen chair under the table and carried his empty glass and plate to the sink.

"You don't have to go. I'll only be a minute."

"No, it's late. I need to leave. I'll call you tomorrow. And don't forget what I said."

"About?"

His eyes filled with promise. "I still owe you dinner."

"I won't forget," she said with a shy smile.

"Thanks again for the chicken."

"You're welcome," she said, just as she caught another jingle of her mother's bedside bell.

"I have to go." Rose started for the hallway.

"Wait, you forgot something." Mike reached out and held her back.

"I did?" She looked at him in surprise. "What?"

"You forgot this."

His arms pulled her close. Rose caught her breath as she felt his hands cupping her face, his fingers drifting gently through her hair. She could feel his heart thumping steady against her own. She was adrift in a midnight world made up solely of the two of them. His eyes locked on hers, held her close.

Then he kissed her.

Rose lost herself in the lush sweetness of his lips. Willingly she surrendered to the pleasure of his touch. A rush of long forgotten sensation returned to mind. Of longing and desire, of something she'd yearned for and hadn't even known.

How long had it been since she had felt the welcome sensation of a man's arms wrapped around her? Since the smell of a man's aftershave mingled with her own perfume? So long, she couldn't remember. So long, she didn't even care. All she wanted at this moment was precisely this.

She kissed him back, enjoying it immensely.

From the hallway came the ringing of Irene's bedside bell again.

"Cecilia Rose? Where are you?"

The bell jingled some more, ringing through the hallway.

Damn that bell! Rose thought to herself as Mike suddenly let go. She made a mental note to hide it far from Irene's grasp the next time Mike showed up at the house. She tried to make her knees work again. Somehow her entire body had gone into shutdown mode, lost in the delicious sensation of being in his embrace. She wanted nothing more than to sink back into the crush of those strong arms, to feel those soft lips pressed hard against her own.

Suddenly she was finding it *very* difficult to breathe.

"I've been wanting to kiss you since the day we met. I thought it might be worth waiting for... and it was. You definitely know how to kiss. Thank you."

"Thank *you*." It was the only thing she could think to reply. For some reason, her mind didn't seem to be working. It felt weak, just like her knees.

From the hallway came a faint tinkle of the bell, followed by silence.

"Come on, I'll walk you. Don't want your mom giving up on you." Mike took her by the hand and turned toward the door. Willingly Rose allowed him to lead her down the hallway to the front den, presently serving as a makeshift bedroom.

"Cecilia Rose?" Irene's voice wavered from beyond the door.

"I'm right here, Mom. Give me a minute." She held Mike's hand tight as her eyes searched his own. She knew her plea was useless, but she still had to try. "Please don't go. Stay a little longer?"

"Sweetheart, I can't reach my pills." Irene's plaintive voice sounded, with a loud meow from Bozo taking up the chorus.

Rose glanced up Mike, eyes pleading. "Please?"

He shook his head softly and leaned in close enough to place one final kiss softly upon her lips. "I'll call you tomorrow, Rosie. You get some sleep."

Rosie. He'd called her *Rosie* without even knowing. No one had called her that in years. Not since she was a little girl in pigtails and another Michael John

Gallagher held her heart. She floated into her mother's bedroom as Mike let himself out the front door.

"I can't reach my pills," Irene fretted in the darkness.

"It's all right, Mom." Rose reached for the small bedside lamp. "I'm right here."

"I thought I heard voices. Isn't the party over?"

"Everyone's gone now. Yes, the party's over."

The party was over, at least for tonight. But Mike's kiss lingered fresh upon her lips. Rose hugged that special secret close in her heart as she flicked on the light and searched through the medications for the small prescription bottle with the pills that would banish her mother's pain.

"Here they are. Let me get you some water. Now take your pill, Mom and then let's get you back to sleep."

Kindness, tolerance and gentleness came natural when you felt happy and lit up inside. Rose smiled. Life would be wonderful if it was always as easy as this. She waited as her mother obediently swallowed the pill, followed by a few sips of water. Bozo jumped up on the bed with a soft meow and settled down in a comfortable heap close at Irene's side as Rose took the glass from her mother's hand.

"Thank you, sweetheart."

"You're welcome. I love you, Mom. Good night."

Rose bent and placed a soft kiss upon Irene's forehead. Just as she moved to turn off the light, a furious beeping outside the open window sliced through the silence of the still night air.

She'd heard the same noise once before and hadn't recognized it, but this time, Rose knew *exactly* what it meant.

"I'll be right back," she said in a hurried whisper.

She was out the front door and halfway down the porch steps as he flung open the truck door.

"Mike, wait! What is it?"

"We're being toned out. I've got to go." His voice cut through the still darkness like a knife. He threw himself behind the wheel and the truck's overhead light bar came instantly to life, swirling red and white zigzag emergency lights.

The insanity of the moment, the need for immediate response prickled the skin on the back of her neck. One minute he'd been headed home for much needed sleep. Now he was rushing off toward the unknown.

"Wait! Where's the fire?" She tried to keep the growing panic from her voice.

"There's a vehicle on fire down at the newspaper office."

With a screech of tires, Mike pulled a U-turn in the middle of the street. Rose stood and watched as the pickup roared off toward downtown.

CHAPTER NINE

EDITORIAL

By: Charles Kendall
The James Bay Journal

JAMES BAY—Citizens, be forewarned! An arsonist is loose among us, wreaking havoc throughout our fair community. I myself am the latest victim, with my own vehicle destroyed by fire. When pressed by this reporter, Assistant Fire Chief Michael Gallagher, currently assigned to lead the arson investigation, could give no assurance that he was close to solving the arsons.

How much more must our community endure before the fire department solves these heinous crimes? How much longer must we wait before residents are once again able to sleep safely in their beds?

This reporter can only pose the questions. When will the fire department provide the answers?

"How is your mom? Did her surgery go okay? I've been worried, Rose. You never got back to me, and I thought something must have happened."

Andy Sabatini's unexpected voice—friendly but questioning—on the other end of the telephone line ratcheted Rose's guilt up to an all-time high. She turned her back on the hallway door leading toward the sun porch, where Irene sat nibbling at her lunch. Her mother still had no idea about the career opportunities that had recently come her way and Rose was in no hurry to tell her. She had no doubt which one her mother would urge her to accept. Partnership in the firm would keep her three hours away. Andy's job offer required a plane ticket or a two-day car ride.

But the Judge lived right next door with a downtown office merely three blocks away.

"I'm sorry, Andy. I should have called you last week. My mother is doing fine. She saw the doctor this morning. Her stats are good and they finally took out the staples."

"Stats? Staples? Rose, what the hell are you talking about?"

Andy sounded as confused as she herself had been merely one week ago. Time changed things and she finally felt comfortable with the medical jargon, the smells and sounds of the hospital—even the sight of her mother's wound. Being a caretaker, she had little choice.

"Mom had staples from the surgery. Sometimes they use those instead of stitches."

"Glad to hear she's doing well."

She caught the tight pitch in Andy's voice. Patience wasn't exactly one of his virtues. "I know I should have called you, but it's been hectic around here. But believe it or not, I *have* been thinking about what you said."

"And…?"

She wavered slightly. "It's a big decision, Andy."

"Come on, Rose, you'd be perfect for the job and we both it. You're the one I want out here with me. Remember how it used to be, the two of us working together, side by side? It could be like that again. Just say *yes*."

For the most part, Andy was correct. The two of them had made the ideal legal team. She was methodical and precise with an eye for the slightest detail that could alter an agreement or change a stipulation. Andy was a people person, working with clients and brokering agreements that everyone could live with, leaving Rose to craft the final documents. His abrupt departure for Washington six months earlier had definitely left a hole in her life, public as well as private.

Truth? She missed him. Publicly and privately.

But not the way he missed her.

"I can't hold them off much longer. I'm getting heat from the deputy chief. The position needs to be filled. You're the one I want, Rose."

"I'm flattered by the offer, Andy, truly. Thank you." An unspoken sigh settled inside her heart. If only she had more time. It was such a precious commodity, especially in the legal field. But time was a request Andy didn't sound particularly amiable to granting. His offer meant leaving everything comfortable and familiar behind for a chance to embrace the world. Was that something she really wanted? The idea of accepting his offer excited and scared her at the same time.

Her position in the firm was relatively safe. Granted, the partners hadn't liked the idea of her abandoning her desk for a six-week leave of absence, but they'd had no choice. And eventually she'd be back. She would work even harder, show them that she still had the dedication, drive, determination—

everything required to make partner. Life in Grand Rapids certainly wasn't without its own complications, but unlike Andy's offer, there were no strings attached, romantic or otherwise.

"Rose? Are you still there?"

"I know it's a lot to ask, but could you give me a day or two? Things here are still a little unsettled. Just a few more days, Andy. I promise I'll have an answer."

Andy's long, frustrated sigh sounded loud and clear all the way from Washington D.C. "If it were anyone but you…"

"Thank you." Relief flooded through her. She'd forgotten what a good team they made. She'd always been able to talk him into nearly anything.

But paybacks could be hell.

"The end of the week, Rose, that's all I can give you. Don't forget."

She set aside his words of warning as she disconnected the phone. She'd successfully bargained a reprieve for herself, and for today that was enough. She didn't need her attention diverted. She had two important things facing her today: caring for her mother and her dinner date with Mike tonight.

"You're all dressed up, sweetheart." Irene's eyes lit up in a hazy glow of maternal affection. "Lil, doesn't she look pretty?"

Lil halted in her task, shuffling the deck of cards on the table between them. "Wow, you *are* all dressed up." She rewarded Rose with an approving smile. "I like that dress. It's got pizzazz."

The sixteen-year-old buried deep inside came alive as Rose twirled before her mother and Lil. The frothy silk concoction she'd purchased that afternoon had captured her attention the moment she spied it in the window of an exclusive summer shop downtown. She'd cringed at the price tag, but female vanity won the debate that had raged in her head. Why shouldn't she indulge herself? She worked hard, and what else was she going to do with the money, besides spend it on her mother and herself? Money was meant to spend on the people and things you loved.

And she loved that dress. Sleeveless and comfortable, it showed off her lithe figure to definite advantage. A pair of strappy fuchsia-colored sandals protected her polished toenails and feet. She drifted in an expensive cloud of her favorite perfume, one she saved solely for special occasions.

And tonight definitely was a special occasion. It was her first real date with Mike... and hopefully, their second kiss.

"Where are you going, honey?" Lil said.

"I've been invited out for dinner."

"I bet I can guess who's the lucky man." Lil's eyes twinkled as she peered over her reading glasses. "You're going out with Fireman Mike, aren't you?"

Rose smiled. "*Fireman Mike*? Is that what you're calling him?"

"You haven't heard the best part, Lil," Irene said with a wicked smile. "Ask her where they're going for dinner."

Lil's eyes glowed with anticipation. "Where's he taking you, honey? Tell all."

She felt her face redden. "Mike is cooking dinner for me."

"Fireman Mike is cooking for you? At his house? I'm impressed! Honey, that is one man you definitely don't want to let get away."

Rose's cheeks flushed a near perfect match to the brilliant sandals on her feet. Better to leave before the conversation got totally out of hand. She bent and kissed her mother, then Lil. "You two behave yourselves tonight."

Irene's gray curls flew in a brief nod. "Have a good time with your Michael. Lil's going to fix dinner, then we're playing cards all night."

"Excuse me? Did I hear something about me making dinner?" Lil shot Rose a playful wink. "I'm no cook. We're calling for takeout."

"Takeout is good." Rose zeroed in on the martini glass in Lil's hand. "I won't have to worry about Mike's pager going off tonight because one of you accidentally set the kitchen on fire."

"If you're referring to my inability to cook, you haven't offended me in the slightest. I'm proud of the fact that very few pots and pans know my name." Lil shuffled the cards with an expert hand, the diamonds on her fingers flashing in the early evening sun. "So it's settled then. Why don't we order a pizza?"

"For heaven's sake, Lil, I can't eat pizza and neither can you." Irene's eyebrows rose with mild exasperation. "The heartburn will keep us up all night."

"Quit being such an old frump. You said you wanted to play cards, and that's what I'm here to do...

play cards." Lil threw a quick wink and a little wave to Rose in the doorway. "Kick back and live a little."

"Very funny, Lil. You know I can't kick yet. But you do have a point. When the heartburn from the pizza sets in, at least I'll know I'm still alive."

Rose was still laughing as she headed out the door to the narrow, cluttered garage. She edged sideways past Irene's bicycle and took a seat behind the wheel of her own dark green sports coupe. The engine caught on the first attempt and started with a soft purr. She backed out of the garage and pointed the nose of the little convertible in the direction opposite downtown.

Mike's house was only a few miles from the city limits. The directions he'd given her over the phone last night were simple enough to follow. The evening sun danced warm on her hair as she left the residential area behind. It felt good to be alone and behind the wheel of her own car again. She felt the wind lift her hair, blowing it in the breeze. It was like being free as a bird, soaring down the open road without a care in the world.

Her jubilant mood quickly evaporated as Rose pulled onto the highway. The last time she'd driven this stretch of road had been with Charles Kendall the night of the condo fires. Now Charles's car was a burned-out shell of blackened steel, the latest casualty in the string of arson fires plaguing their community.

Charles could be a pest, but was that reason enough for someone to destroy his car? The irony of the situation rendered serious implications. Charles had been relentless on the Fourth of July in questioning the Judge about the arson investigation. Now Charles himself was a victim of the same crime.

Arson is a difficult crime to prove. Mike's words from that night pounded an insistent beat in her head. Evidence was often destroyed at the scene, burned beyond recognition.

What makes someone start a fire? Something else Mike had said on the Fourth of July flooded back to mind. *Profit... revenge... greed...*

Who stood to profit? The Judge was a victim. She'd witnessed it with her own eyes. His condo buildings had gone up in flames, brilliant against the night sky.

And the insurance money had paid off.

The tires screeched against the hot pavement as Rose hit the brakes. She'd been so consumed by thoughts of the fires, she'd nearly missed the turnoff for Mike's road. She backed up and turned the car around, then pointed its nose down the narrow dirt road that was lined with thick evergreens and led toward a small inland lake and Mike's driveway. Firmly she banished all thoughts of fire and Mike's ongoing investigation. She couldn't do anything about any of it, at least not right now, with the Judge in California. But once he returned, they were going to talk. He had made her a promise, and she would insist he keep it.

For tonight, the only thing she intended to concentrate on was having a good time with Mike. Hopefully that fire monitor of his would cooperate and remain silent.

Rose pulled in tight behind Mike's pickup and cut the engine. She undid her seat belt, trying to quell the growing disappointment as she eyed the dark blue sedan next to Mike's truck. She'd assumed the two of them would be having dinner alone. He hadn't mentioned inviting anyone else tonight.

Mike and another man strolled around the corner of the cabin as she opened the car door. Rose managed a graceful exit as the two of them approached. One look at the stranger standing at Mike's side and she knew exactly who his company was. Family.

"You must be Mike's brother, Terry." She extended her hand. "I'm Rose. It's nice to meet you."

"The pleasure is all mine," he replied.

There could be no mistaking the two of them as brothers. Terry, though slimmer and with thinning hair a darker shade of blond, looked like an older version of Mike. Both brothers carried themselves with the same friendly manner. She smiled as she glimpsed another pair of twinkling turquoise-blue eyes... though not with the same stellar blue intensity she'd grown accustomed to in her fireman.

"Mike didn't tell me you were coming for a visit."

"That's my fault. I got my weeks mixed up," Mike said. "I thought Terry was coming next week to do some fishing. He showed up a little earlier than I expected."

"Try a whole week early," Terry said with an easy laugh. "That's okay, Mikey. I know you've been busy. You ought to buy yourself a calendar."

"*Mikey*? He calls you *Mikey*?" Rose grinned at the notion.

"He *used* to call me Mikey. Isn't that right, Terry?" Mike threw a playful punch at his brother's shoulder.

"Whatever you say, *Mikey*," Terry said, jabbing back in reply.

It was hard not holding back the envy as she watched them joust in friendly camaraderie. Mike and Terry had something she'd always longed for. She'd always wanted brothers and sisters, to be part of a large family. Mike and Terry were lucky. They had each other.

Even better was the fact they seemed to actually *like* each other.

"I didn't mean to intrude." Terry's face wore a frank, open look. "Like I was telling Mike just before you drove up… how about I hop in my car and go back where I came from? I can come up any weekend, and it's obvious I'm interrupting something here. The last thing I want is to interfere with my little brother's date."

"Please don't leave on account of me—" Rose started.

"You're not going anywhere—" Mike chimed in.

Their simultaneous protest seemed so precisely timed that the three of them burst out laughing.

"Honestly, Terry, I would love it if you stayed." Rose didn't even have to mull it over. It was the truth.

"Rose is right. You're not going anywhere." Mike latched onto his brother's shoulder with a firm right hand. "You came up to fish, and that's exactly what we're going to do tomorrow. Fish."

"But tonight…" Terry glanced back and forth between the two of them.

"Tonight, Mike is going to make us dinner," Rose replied. "We'll have a chance to talk and get to know one another."

"Now I understand why you got your dates mixed up," Terry said with a quick smile for his brother. "If I were lucky enough to have a woman like this, I'd have forgotten my brother was coming up, too."

Rose smiled briefly at the unexpected flattery, though Mike ignored it. His attention was entirely focused on her little green sports coupe.

"Nice car." Reaching out, he ran his hand along the sleek hood. He glanced at Rose. "This yours?"

She nodded, then froze as his cool, studied look made her pause. Did he think she was trying to show off by buzzing over here tonight in an expensive car? She didn't know how much of a salary a fireman earned, but she doubted it was enough to afford a luxury such as her European sports car. Yet Mike must make a decent living. He drove a brand new truck and lived in a place like this. Rose glanced around the property. A small cabin nestled on a large shady lot, fronted by a sandy beach on Loon Lake, a sparkling, inland fresh body of water. Even with the economy the way it was and real estate prices dropping, lakefront properties in Northern Michigan didn't come cheap. Either Mike had money or he'd mortgaged away his life.

"Very nice." Rose glanced about the cabin in open admiration as Mike gave her a quick tour with Terry trailing close behind. The rooms were done up in handsome shades of reds and browns, creating an atmosphere both relaxing and appealing. A cozy living room had space enough for a wooden rocking chair, a man-sized leather chair, and a sleek modern couch. A fieldstone fireplace took up one entire wall. The front of the cabin sported a wall of windows and a sliding glass door opened onto what appeared to be a brand-new wooden deck that led to the lake just beyond. From her spot at the window Rose saw a small boat tied up to the dock at water's edge. Mike had told her once that he liked to fish, and from the looks of his boat, he'd told her the truth. Anyone dedicated to speed, to flying across the waves while looking flashy, would have no interest in a boat like that.

"Nice boat."

"It's not much, only a little fishing boat."

But it was obvious her words had pleased him. Rose noted the small smile tugging at one side of his mouth as they continued the tour.

She lingered a few moments in front of the massive bookcase near the front door. Thick volumes of history, biographies, and fiction were mixed together in an eclectic blend that surprised and delighted her. For some reason she couldn't name, she hadn't pegged Mike as a reader.

"You've got quite an assortment here."

"I like to read. It keeps me out of trouble, plus it gives me something to do on a cold winter night." He shared a sudden smile and Rose felt her pulse take off. Winter in the north country made for long cold nights. Nights made for snuggling in front of a blazing fire. A glass of wine and the comfort of a man's arms wrapped around her…

"Check out the computer. Mikey's got quite the setup."

Terry's voice close behind yanked her back into the present. Rose turned and followed Terry's finger pointing to a handsome wooden desk, upon which sat a top-grade computer and printer. Piles of paperwork were stacked in neat precision across the desktop. Though the monitor screen was dark, Rose heard the computer humming.

"Surfing the Internet?"

Mike didn't answer, but reached out and with a flick of his wrist touched the computer mouse. The monitor flashed to life. She leaned in close but Mike was faster. He pressed a button and shut down her view—but not before she caught a quick glance of the state police web site.

"You work at home, too?" She flashed him a sweet smile as her curiosity leaped into overdrive. Why had he been so quick to turn off the screen? Was something displayed there that he didn't want her to see?

"I've been trying to finish some fire reports. It's hard to find time down at the station."

"The arson investigation must keep you busy," she said.

He nodded. "Whoever torched Charles Kendall's car didn't do us any favors. We're getting lots of pressure to make an arrest—especially with all the news coverage the *Journal* is giving the story."

Rose hesitated. "Are you any closer to solving the case?"

He cast a guarded glance at her, then Terry. "I really can't say. The chief has the investigation under a pretty tight wrap."

"No problem, Mikey. We don't expect you to tell us what you can't."

With a flick of the mouse, he put the computer into sleep mode. "Thanks for reminding me it was on. I was working here at home when my pager went off, and Terry showed up just as I got back."

"There was another fire in town today?" Rose inhaled sharply.

Mike nodded again. "An electrical cord overheated and set some boxes on fire in some guy's garage."

She blew out a big sigh. She hadn't realized she'd been holding her breath. "So, it wasn't another one of the arson fires."

His face tightened. "Contrary to what you read in the paper, not every fire in this town is deliberately set."

"I'll remember that." Rose tucked his words away in her heart. The poor guy looked so tired. This was supposed to be his day off, yet he'd been out working another fire—in addition to being chief cook at tonight's barbeque, as well as playing host to an unexpected guest. Fighting fires, working up fire reports, trying to solve the crimes... the strain he was under would wear anyone down. And Mike was struggling, that much was obvious. The big dark circles under his eyes were the ultimate giveaway. How did he manage to get any sleep with that noisy fire monitor always going off?

She hadn't meant to stare, then their eyes met... caught and held.

"Think I'll go take a look at the boat and scope out the fish," Terry said with a knowing smile. He opened the sliding glass door and stepped onto the deck.

"We'll be right out," Mike said. "Let me get Rose something to drink."

Terry gave a wave and headed for the beach.

Mike took a deep breath. "What would you like?"

"I'm easy to please," she replied. "Whatever you have is fine." She trailed him into the narrow galley kitchen.

Mike suddenly paused, one hand on the refrigerator door, and turned to face her. "Sorry about the way things turned out."

"What do you mean?"

"Terry showing up like he did." He grimaced slightly. "I had this evening planned a little differently, but now he's here, I can't very well kick him out. It's okay if you'd rather leave. I'll understand."

"What makes you think I want to leave?" she asked softly. "I'm not going anywhere, unless you're kicking me out. Do you want me to go?"

"Not in a million years," he whispered and pulled her around the refrigerator door and into his arms.

Rose shivered slightly as his hand traced the curve of her cheek. It felt like déjà vu, and then she remembered. They'd stood together like this once before, in her mother's kitchen and she had felt the same rush of pleasure then as she did now, knowing she was about to be kissed.

His lips were warm as his mouth pressed hard against her own. She closed her eyes and surrendered to the sweet rush of desire.

"You smell so sweet." Mike's mouth murmured, soft against one ear. "Sweet as a rose."

She nestled closer against him as his lips nuzzled the nape of her neck. Delicious little zings sparked through her body, straight down into her polished pink toes. Mike was good at putting out fires, but he definitely knew how to start them, too.

"You do something to me," he whispered after a moment. His voice was husky with desire.

"Something good, I hope," she whispered back.

"Very, very good. I don't want to let you go."

"I don't want you to let go of me, either." But reasoning, the curse of attorneys, wormed a thread of logic through her longing and desire. If only they were alone. But they weren't. "Terry must be wondering what we're doing."

Mike abruptly let go and she suddenly found herself at arm's length. Rose stared in confusion as he yanked open the refrigerator door and peered inside. She'd never expected him to take her words to heart.

"Is something wrong? I didn't mean..." The uncertainty weighed heavy on her mind and in her heart. Why had he let go?

"What's your pleasure?" He searched through the refrigerator. "We've got beer, wine, pop. You name it."

Rose held back a sigh. He was deliberately ignoring her. The man could be so frustrating at times. "I'll have a pop. Diet, if you have one. Any kind. It doesn't matter."

Nothing mattered, except figuring out what in the world was wrong with him. What was it with this fireman? One minute he was smoldering intensity, filling her with a forgotten sense of feminine pleasure—then suddenly he was dousing the fire he'd kindled inside her with a cold stream of studied indifference.

If he kept this up, it was going to be a long night.

"Mike says you're in the family insurance business." Rose smiled her thanks across the picnic table as Terry refilled first her coffee cup, then his own.

"Yep, I work with Mom and Dad." Terry's eyes sparkled. "A load of fun, right? Not." He grinned. "Too bad I couldn't have been like Mikey here and done something important with my life. He always wanted to be a fireman. No going into the family business, not for Mikey."

Mike rolled his eyes. "Cut the crap, Terry. No use boring Rose."

"I'm not bored," she quickly assured him. "As a matter of fact, I'm finding the conversation fascinating."

She'd been nervous before dinner started. Things had been going so well in the kitchen, but the sudden coolness in Mike had confused her. Now he finally seemed relaxed again. Perhaps it was the beer he was drinking. And Terry's presence at the dinner table—à la the picnic table—proved steady and comforting. The food was delicious, but Rose merely picked at the steak and corn on the cob. Listening as the two brothers laughed and joked their way through dinner was better than eating.

"Being a fireman was all Mikey talked about when he was a little kid." Terry's eyes gleamed. "The whole family was pretty happy when he got through fire academy and joined the department."

Mike grinned. "That was a long time ago."

"I can't imagine being a firefighter. Facing those flames and breathing in that smoke." She shuddered and pulled her sweater tighter around her shoulders. "I hate smoke."

"When you're dealing with fire, you're dealing with smoke," he acknowledged. "That's one reason we wear air packs."

How did he stand it? Smoke was a swirling monster, worse than flames could ever be. She trembled slightly as a long forgotten memory seeped into her consciousness and the reek of sweet cotton candy mingled with the stench of smoke.

"Rosie? Want to take a try in the smoke house?"

"Yes, yes, yes!" She surrendered the sticky cotton candy to her mother and gleefully took her father's hand.

A fireman stood guard at the front door. He crouched low and met her gaze. "Ever been in a smoke house before?"

Rose gave a quick glance at the trailer behind him, then slowly shook her head.

"It'll be dark in there. And you're going to have to crawl. You be sure and stick close to your dad now, promise?"

She nodded and squeezed her father's hand tightly as the door clapped shut behind them.

It was like being enveloped in another world. The smoke house was dark and quiet, the screams of thrill seekers from the carnival outside muffled and distant. The universe shrank to a mist of swirling smoke, clouding her eyes, making her cough. She didn't want to be there anymore. She cringed back toward the door, loosening her grip on her father's hand.

"Rosie? Remember what the fireman said? Get down, sweetheart, get on your knees and crawl. That's what we're going to do. We're going to crawl through the smoke."

No! She didn't want to crawl. The house stank badly, like thousands of books of matches going off at once. She gagged, started to choke. She didn't want to be in the room anymore. She wanted out. Now!

She pulled away.

"Rosie? Sweetheart, where are you?"

Her father's voice wafted through the murky fog. He was lost to her. She couldn't see, and she no longer had hold of his hand. She was all alone... trapped in a swirl of smoke.

"Daddy? Daddy!" The smoke choked off her words. Rose stumbled backward and fell against a wall. Her heels scuffed on the hard wooden floor and her sandal came loose. She couldn't see, she couldn't breathe. Hot tears mingled with stale dust and acrid smoke. Her

sobs came faster, her breath in heavy gasps. She wanted out! Right now!

"Rosie, sweetheart, stay where you are. I'll find you."

She whimpered and hugged the floor closer. Her knee hurt where she'd banged it, and her sandal was gone.

"Rose? Hey, are you okay?"

She blinked once, then again, and found herself sitting on the picnic bench. She gave Mike a cautious smile even as she forced back the shudder building inside.

"For a minute there, you looked really scared."

"Sorry, I was…" She shook her head, trying to sort through the murky memory. "My dad took me through a smoke house once at the county fair. I hated it. All that smoke." She trembled slightly. "I pulled away and fell."

And they'd never found her sandal. She'd come out barefoot, crying hysterically. They were halfway home before anyone noticed she was missing a shoe.

"A smoke house can be pretty intense, especially for a little kid," Mike assured her.

"I couldn't see. The smoke blinded me."

"Smoke rises. That's why we tell people to stay low to the ground. If you're ever caught in smoke, get down on your knees and crawl."

Exactly the words she'd heard so long ago. *Get down on your knees and crawl.*

"That's what my dad and the fireman both said. Unfortunately, I didn't listen." Rose grimaced.

"Has Mikey told you any of his fire stories yet?"

"Fire stories?" She glanced uncertainly at Mike. "I don't think so."

"Come on, Terry, she doesn't want to hear that stuff."

"Sure she does." Terry turned to her. "Don't you, Rose? One of them is my all-time favorite."

Mike groaned. "Not that again."

"Sorry, but you've got my curiosity aroused." Rose challenged him with a smile. "There is no way you're getting out of this."

He let out a sigh. "It wasn't much, not really."

"Tell her about the maid," Terry prompted. He turned to Rose with a wide grin. "The fire started in a house not far from here...."

"One of those three-million-dollar summer homes down by the lake," Mike added.

"The owners weren't in town, but some of the staff was. The cook noticed smoke coming up from the floorboards. But instead of calling 911, she ran and got the housekeeper—"

"You've got it all wrong. It wasn't the cook, it was the housekeeper," Mike broke in.

"They took a look around, tried to figure out if there actually was a fire, but they couldn't tell for sure. So, instead of calling 911, they decided to get a third opinion. They got in the car and headed downtown—"

"You're getting it all wrong," Mike interrupted. He turned to Rose. "They knew there was a fire, but they were afraid to call it in on their own. So they went downtown to find the chauffeur. It took a while before they finally found him...."

"You're not serious?" Rose's face was a mask of bewilderment. "They actually left the house without calling in the fire?"

Mike nodded. "Smoke was rolling out of the basement windows by the time they got back. They went inside and tried to phone 911—"

"I love this part," Terry interrupted with a wide grin.

"But they couldn't dial out. The phone lines were burned clear through," Mike finished. "Lucky for them, the neighbors had already noticed the smoke and called in the fire."

Rose shook her head in disbelief. People's lack of common sense never ceased to amaze her. "What about the house? Did it burn to the ground?"

Mike shook his head. "We managed to save it. We were on scene with the trucks shortly after the call. There was considerable damage inside the house, but it could have been a lot worse."

"No thanks to the housekeeping staff," Terry said. "And people wonder why insurance rates are so high."

A low rumble of thunder growled across the lake. Flashes of heat lightning streaked across the night sky.

"Looks like it's finally going to rain," Rose said. "Maybe this heat wave will break."

"I don't think so." Mike cocked his head as if to catch a scent of the heavy air. "It's coming in fast but it won't be more than a sprinkle."

The rain started a few moments later. As he'd predicted, it wasn't enough to soak the ground, but it did push them inside the cabin—after Mike and Terry made a mad dash for Rose's car and put up the convertible top.

"If it wasn't so hot, I'd start a fire," Mike said as she came out of the cabin's bathroom, toweling her hair dry. He handed her a glass of wine and poured himself another beer.

Her gaze darted to the firewood stacked neatly near the hearth. There had been more wood outside, covered with a tarp. "Obviously you believe in being prepared."

"Mikey's a real boy scout," Terry said with a knowing grin as he picked up his coffee mug and took a careful sip.

"Darn right I believe in being prepared. I ran out of wood last winter and got caught out here with no heat." Mike snorted as he settled down in the cushy leather chair. "I don't plan on going through that again."

Rose chuckled to herself. The hearty dinner seemed to have warmed his insides and the beer had loosened his tongue. She listened as he started to share more of his fire stories. The sauna that overheated with the married couple inside—the married couple not married to each other. A former volunteer from the fire department who, in order to save himself the embarrassment of phoning 911 and having the whole town hear the page toned out, called a few fireman friends to request they bring a truck and help him extinguish the chimney fire roaring at his own house. The fireman who got so excited when the fire call came in, he backed the fire truck right into the side of the garage, effectively putting it out of commission for the next several weeks.

And when the fire stories began to lose steam, the family sagas started.

"Hey, remember when?" Terry prompted.

Rose nestled down in utter contentment, thoroughly enjoying herself as the two brothers swapped memories of their annual summer family camping trips up north, of ritual fishing trips with their mom and dad each fall, of spring break vacations to Florida and their grandmother's house. Back and forth Mike and Terry traded recollections, each seeming to try and outdo the other with his storytelling skills. Only when she finally noticed Mike's eyelids beginning to droop did she start thinking about going home.

"I think he's asleep." Rose nodded in Mike's direction. His head was back against his chair and his eyes were finally closed. "I should go."

"You don't have to leave yet," Terry protested.

She stood up from the couch. "He must be worn out from working all these fires. Besides, the two of you are going fishing tomorrow."

"Want me to wake him up so you can say good-bye?"

"Let him sleep. Tell him I'll call tomorrow."

"I'll walk you out to your car."

She grabbed her purse and cast a last hesitant glance at Mike. He was fast asleep in his chair and snoring softly.

"Now, that's real attractive," Terry said with a grin.

"You shouldn't make fun of him," Rose admonished as they headed for the door. "He can't defend himself."

The night air hung heavy and still after the earlier cloudburst. Mike had been right. The rain hadn't done anything but wet the grass. Rose felt the dampness clinging to her toes through her thin sandals as they made their way across the lawn.

"Guess I'll have to find something to read, now Mikey's asleep and you're going home. I'm still wide awake," Terry said as they neared the coupe.

"I wouldn't doubt it, after all that coffee you drank." She threw him a smile of thanks as he opened the driver's door. "Next time you should try a glass of wine. That always puts me right to sleep."

"I'll stick with coffee, thanks. I don't drink wine, or anything else." Terry smiled briefly. "I'm a recovering alcoholic."

His admission left her stunned. Terry, an alcoholic? But Mike's brother seemed like a regular guy. Nice and normal. She stumbled to find the right words. "I'm sorry, I didn't know. Mike never told me."

"No need to be embarrassed." His voice was warm and held no reproach. "I'm an alcoholic and always will be. The best thing I can do for myself every day is admit the truth. Admitting who I am helps keep me sober."

The driver's door was open, but Rose stood where she was.

"How long has it been? Since you quit drinking, I mean."

"I've been sober for over ten years," he replied. "Drinking cost me a lot. My job, my marriage. Getting sober saved my life."

Terry had been married? She glanced down at his hands—big, strong and steady, so like Mike's own. And just like his brother, his left hand was empty. No wedding ring.

"You were married?"

His face filled with regret. "Linda and I were married for a couple of years. She left me when my drinking got really bad. I don't blame her. She did what she had to do in order to save herself. It took me another six months of living in hell before I finally hit bottom. That's what it took, admitting I had a problem and it wasn't going away. Then I was ready to get some help."

He straightened slightly and squared his shoulders. "That's all behind me now. For today. That's what they tell you in recovery. You only have today. But I never would have made it through without Mikey and our mom and dad. The three of them stood by me and helped me learn how to start living again, once I got sober. Things were rough when I lost my job, but they were right there."

"I thought you worked in the family insurance business."

The moonlight caught the ironic smile on his face. "I was a pretty cocky kid when I was growing up. Thought I was too good to settle for working in the family business. Too good to stay home and work with my parents. But they're great people. After I lost my job and Linda left me, they took me back in, no questions asked, once I sobered up. They helped me get back on my feet." Terry's voice broke. He swallowed hard before continuing. "Family is important. I couldn't have done this without Mikey. He's a special guy."

A soft smile lit her face as she thought about Mike. Probably he was fast asleep by now, slumped even further in his leather chair. Was it any wonder? Being everyone's hero was exhausting.

She offered her hand. "It was a pleasure meeting you, Terry."

"The pleasure was all mine." He took her hand and kept it. "When Mikey mentioned you were an attorney, I was pretty surprised. I guess I thought…"

Memories of Mike's apparent disdain for members of her profession flashed to mind. Did his whole family have some unspoken grudge against attorneys? "You thought what?"

"That you'd be different somehow," he said. "I mean, different than you are. Don't get me wrong," he quickly added, "You're great, Rose, and I like you a lot."

"I'm glad to hear that," she softly replied. It was nice to know she had the older brother's approval.

"You put the smile back on Mikey's face. I didn't think any woman would be able to do that again." Terry's eyes filled with open admiration. "You're good for him, Rose, and it's pretty obvious the way he feels about you. I didn't think I'd ever see him smile like that again."

"I'm not sure what you mean." Rose felt the frown tugging at her eyebrows. "Did something happen to make him quit smiling?"

A sudden guarded look covered Terry's face. "You mean he hasn't told you?"

"Told me what?"

He shook his head. "Never mind. I said too much."

She recognized the concern registered in his eyes, as well as something else. The soft stab of pity sent goose bumps bumping down her spine. Mike hadn't shared much about his personal life and she'd respected his privacy. But Terry's words definitely had her curiosity aroused. "If there's something I should know, please tell me."

"It's not for me to say. Mikey needs to do it."

"Please, Terry?" She wasn't given to begging unless there was good reason. The unspoken knowledge hanging between them seemed good enough.

He wavered for a moment. "I'm talking about Katie," he finally said in a sad, quiet voice.

Her stomach dropped at the mention of a woman's name. Rose swallowed hard and dug deep for the courage to ask the question suddenly burning inside her.

"And Katie is…?"

"Mike's wife."

CHAPTER TEN

WEATHER WISE

The James Bay Journal

WEATHER ADVISORY: Hot, dry conditions continue to linger over the Northern Michigan area. Residents are cautioned that a *No Burn Permit* remains in effect for the foreseeable future and will be strictly enforced.

Rose lay sleepless, sheets tangled beneath her, in her childhood double bed. She tossed and turned as one thought drummed a steady beat in her head.

Why hadn't Mike told her he was married?

She wouldn't be able to sleep tonight. For a few seconds, she had the sudden impulse to sneak downstairs and filch one of her mother's pills. One little pill would never be missed. They'd been prescribed for pain, exactly what she was suffering tonight. She was in pain. Her heart was bleeding.

Why didn't he tell me he'd been married?

Over and over, her thoughts kept returning to her conversation with Terry. He'd reluctantly provided a few sketchy details, but only after she pressed, and only enough to give her a general idea of what had happened. Terry called them the perfect couple. Mike had given Katie his heart and a wedding ring. Their idyllic world had been destroyed one frosty December night by the loud blast of a gun. Mike lost his wife and their unborn son. Gone in an instant, all semblance of a normal life.

Rose flinched in the silent darkness. Technically Mike was a widower, but he still thought of himself as a married man. That lost, faraway look she glimpsed on his face now and then was all the proof she needed. The bullet that had ripped through Katie's body had torn apart his life.

Putting out fires was Mike's job, and according to Terry, Mike had done a good job extinguishing his emotions in the two years since Katie's death. He kept himself busy at the fire department, burying his tragedy in the smoke and soot of other people's misfortunes.

Looking back, everything made sense. An impulsive dinner invitation rendered in a grocery aisle weeks earlier, and his hesitation to share a simple dinner. The awkward silences. The unfinished sentences. No wonder he looked the way he did sometimes, as if he'd caught a glimpse of the gates of hell.

But he hadn't only caught a glimpse. Losing Katie had plunged Mike into a living hell on earth.

Cocooned in the private darkness of her childhood bedroom, Rose recoiled in a hot flush of horror as yet more memories intruded. She and Mike sitting at her mother's kitchen table in the wee hours of the night after the fireworks ended. Had his thoughts been on Katie while he'd been talking with her?

Had Mike been thinking of Katie while he'd been kissing her?

Rose hugged the sheet close as a piercing throb grew behind her eyes. She rarely suffered from headaches, but she knew she would have one tomorrow. Pain was a funny thing. It had a sneaky way of numbing itself into dull complacency, all but forgotten in the back of one's mind until least expected, only to come roaring back to the surface. Terry's words tonight had been a refresher course. She should have learned her lesson by now. She was not immune to happenstance or heartbreak. Tragedy and misfortune had already come calling twice in her life and taken away the men she loved. She hadn't expected she would have to relearn the lesson a third time.

But why should she be surprised? Bad things always happened in threes.

Rose rolled over in bed and smacked the pillow with a frustrated punch. She knew better. She was an intelligent adult. Sensible, practical, sure of herself. She should have trusted her instincts. She never should have allowed herself to get involved with him. Yet, how could she not? He'd woken something inside her that could not be denied.

Just when you thought everything was going smoothly, life had a funny way of showing you who was in charge. Once upon a time, Mike had been a husband and a father, while all she had to show for herself was a gilt-framed law degree and four cold walls surrounding her as she finished her billings for the day. If Jeff hadn't died, she never would have left James Bay. The two of them had daydreamed their childhood away with plans of opening their own practice. It had been a wonderful dream, but it died with Jeff. Since then, she hadn't given much thought to which way her life was headed. She'd chosen to take the easy path, wandering into the firm first as a summer intern and clerk, then as an associate following admission to the Bar. Now there were three offers on the table, distinct paths from which to choose. The lure of Washington D.C. and a chance to practice on a national level. The sharp, focused world of corporate practice and a safe, predictable life. Or return to James Bay, taking up the reins of a rural practice in amiable partnership with the Judge.

Her growing feelings for Mike only complicated matters further. He had made his feelings about living up north plain from the beginning. Choosing Mike allowed only one choice. Choosing home.

Was that something she was willing to do? That she wanted to do? Come back home and settle in James Bay? Practicing law with the Judge was a viable option, but choosing home and choosing Mike meant exploring avenues she wasn't certain she wished to visit.

Once Mike's life had held the promise of a child. Would that be something he would expect to have again? Rose had never had a craving to hold a baby in her arms. She had no desire for a little one of her own. No wish to wipe away milk bubbles or to be the one responsible for shielding tiny hands from things that could harm. Was a maternal instinct an inherent part of being a woman? If so, something definitely was wrong with her. Most women yearned to be mothers and care for a child, but adults were Rose's specialty. She liked solving their problems, winding things up in tight legal documents that allowed no room for maneuvering. Changing diapers, wiping runny noses, chasing after butterflies? That was *real* work and not at all what she envisioned for herself. She relished the quiet found each night as she locked her office door and left the worries of the workday behind. Until the next morning when the alarm clock rang.

Until these past few weeks, it had been enough. She had been content, her life complete. Now everything was different. She could no longer deny it. She could no longer push down the rush of emotions that she'd buried with Jeff.

Meeting Mike had spoiled everything.

One day you grew up and met a man. A good man. One who made you feel light and happy inside, safe and at peace. It was a feeling like coming home again, when you hadn't even realized you'd left home in the first place. She hadn't even been looking, but the unthinkable had happened.

She'd fallen in love with Mike.

But his heart still belonged to another.

The telephone's shrill ring broke the early morning silence as Rose headed into the kitchen.

"We need to talk."

She hesitated. She'd hardly slept, and from the gravelly sound of his voice, Mike hadn't either. Agreeing to see him might not be the wisest thing to do. She felt shaky and uncertain, still rattled by the midnight realization of exactly how much she'd come to care for this man.

"I'm not sure," she replied. "This isn't a good time."

"Then tell me when is. I'll come by and pick you up."

"I can't leave the house. My mom is here alone."

"We have to talk." His voice was firm and insistent.

"What about Terry?" Rose tried to buy herself more time. "I thought the two of you were going fishing."

"Terry can take care of himself. This is more important." Mike's tone softened slightly. "Please, Rosie?"

Her eyes misted over as she heard him use that special name. *Get a grip, Rose.* Normally she wasn't given to tears, but after last night, anything was possible. Her orderly world was going up in smoke.

How could she refuse him? She loved him.

"The physical therapist should be here by nine." She wiped away a few tears with the sleeve of her robe. "I suppose I could get away then…."

"I'll be over at nine sharp."

Rose eyed the small clock above the kitchen stove as she hung up. Not much time. She still had breakfast to make and her mother's knee to bandage. Plus, somehow in the next hour or so, she needed to find some way to put the emotional wreck that was now her life back into some semblance of working order.

Rose plucked two eggs from the Styrofoam carton and glanced at her mother. "Scrambled or fried?"

"Hey, gorgeous," a deep male voice rumbled from the hallway.

Rose looked up in surprise to see a stranger lounging against the kitchen door. The man was tall, with dark wavy hair, flashing black eyes, and a grin that screamed sex.

The eggs in her hand hit the linoleum with a splat.

"Good morning, George." Irene's eyelashes fluttered.

Rose squatted down and wiped the sticky yolks from the floor. So this was George, the in-home physical therapist that had been the hot topic of conversation between her mother and Lil since his appearance on the scene a few days ago while she'd been at the store. Rose eyed him suspiciously as she cleaned up the eggs. Good thing she'd laid in an ample supply of groceries. He didn't look the kind of man who could be trusted. She definitely was going to stick around more.

"Guess nobody heard me knock." He sauntered into the kitchen and patted Irene's shoulder. "How's my favorite patient today? Ravishingly beautiful, as usual." He wiggled his eyebrows.

Irene giggled in reply.

Rose glanced at her mother, then took a harder look. Good Lord, was her mother wearing makeup? It was only nine o'clock in the morning.

"George, this is my daughter, Cecilia Rose."

"Nice to meet you." He stared at her with apparent interest. "Your mother's told me all about you."

Rose barely nodded in reply. What on earth had gotten into her mother? Normally Irene was such a levelheaded woman, but she seemed to have completely lost her senses. She sat there at the kitchen table simpering at George like some ga-ga schoolgirl. Didn't she realize he was young enough to be her own son? She finished cleaning the eggs from the floor and tossed the messy paper towel at the garbage pail, hitting the target with a clean inside shot. Rose smiled to herself. Too bad Mike wasn't there to see it. He would have been proud.

Mike! If George was already here for therapy, then Mike would be here soon. And the last thing she wanted was him inside this house, chatting over coffee with her mother and George. He had told her he wanted the two of them to talk, and that's exactly what they were going to do.

Talk.

Alone.

The sooner they got this over with, the better.

Rose spied Mike's pickup through the kitchen window as it pulled in the driveway.

"Eat your toast, Mom. I'll fix you some eggs when I get back."

A puzzled look crossed Irene's face. "Where are you going?"

"I won't be long." Rose already had one foot out the door. She had to get going. Mike was out of his truck and headed up the walk. She pulled the screen door shut behind her and stepped out on the porch.

"Good morning." She swallowed down the sudden lump in her throat and forced herself to meet his gaze. *Be calm*, she reminded herself. Most of all, she needed to remain calm. Hot sudden tears threatened to spill out as his foot hit the first porch step, but she quickly blinked them back. She couldn't cry. She didn't dare. Tears would bring him up those steps in a second and all would be lost. She would be in his arms before they even talked.

Mike stopped midway up the steps. His eyes were wary and guarded.

She gripped the newel post. She would not cry. She wouldn't.

"Rose, are you okay?"

No, I'm not okay, she cried to herself. *Damn you for doing this, for making me fall in love with you.*

"I'm fine," she replied.

"I thought maybe we could drive down by the lake. It's quiet there and we can talk."

How stupid did he think she was? She wasn't about to get in his truck. He'd already taken her heart a captive prisoner. If she climbed in his truck, she would be completely at his mercy.

"Why don't we take a walk instead?"

Walking seemed a much better, a much safer idea.

"All right," he said uneasily. "If you want to walk, then that's what we'll do." Mike reached out and offered his hand.

Rose's heart raced as she stared at his hand. It was a man's hand, sturdy and strong, capable of keeping a fire hose steady. Was this fireman capable of steadying her heart as well?

Only one way she would ever find out.

Warily she reached out and put her hand in his.

Silence floated between them as they started down the street. It lingered in the hot air as they wandered down one block, turned the corner, and started down another.

"Whoa, careful there." His fingers tightened around her own as the toe of her sandal caught on the uneven sidewalk. Rose smiled her thanks. She'd stumbled but he'd kept her from falling. She kept her hand in his.

"That's where Tommy Gilbert lives." She broke the silence with a short nod at the aging three-story house on one corner of the second block. "It's his brother Joey's house."

"Looks like the place could use some paint," Mike said as they passed.

"It could use more than paint," Rose said as she scanned the Gilbert property. The untidy lawn, a child's tricycle overturned on the porch, the uneven hedges bordering the driveway provided diversion. It kept her gaze from straying where it shouldn't, to the man beside her.

Mike reached out and caught her arm as she started off the curb. "Can you stop a minute?"

"Yes?" She saw the questioning look on his face, the uncertainty in his blue eyes. Underneath the dark athletic tan, his face looked tired and strained.

"I want to tell you right now that I'm sorry about what happened last night." His eyes locked tight on hers. "I was going to tell you eventually. I'm sorry you found out like that."

"Please don't blame Terry," she quickly replied. The last thing she wanted was the two brothers fighting. "I was pretty persistent. I didn't leave him much choice."

Mike shook his head. "I don't blame Terry. I blame myself. I should have been the one to tell you. And I should have done it long ago."

"Then why *didn't* you?" She stood and stared, no longer caring that they were having this conversation on the street corner in front of Tommy's house. She couldn't hold back the torrent of words. "Did you honestly think something like that wouldn't matter?

It's an important part of your life, Mike. Why didn't you tell me you'd been married before?"

He sucked in a deep breath. "Guess I was waiting for the right place and time."

"There's *never* a right time for something like that," she replied. "Sometimes, no matter how much you don't want to say something, that's exactly what you have to do."

"I know that now. I'm sorry, Rose."

The miserable look on his face and the sorrowful look in his eyes was like a cold slap of reality. Who was she to be giving him advice about coming clean and setting matters straight when she herself was holding back information? Depending on what decisions she made about her career and her life—the people in it would be affected.

Plus there was that other little thing she wasn't sure she had the courage to mention.

The fact that she'd fallen in love with him.

Mike slowly shook his head. "I didn't want it come between us. Guess I was afraid it would make a difference."

"You were right," she said slowly. "It does make a difference." Until last night, this might have proved nothing more than a summertime romance once she left town. Mike might have been nothing more than a pleasant memory that surfaced every time she heard the wail of a fire whistle, every time she pulled her car over to allow a fire truck to pass. Shrill sirens would have brought back memories of a man who knowingly put himself in danger as he headed out in response to save someone's property or life. Everything had been different... until last night.

This was crazy. She couldn't be in love with him. They barely knew each other. It wasn't right. It couldn't be right. Mike was so different from the other men in her life.

But deep inside, her heart already recognized him for the man he was. Mike was the one man she'd been waiting for all along. He'd merely taken his time showing up.

"I didn't want to tell you until I knew how you felt." He hesitated. "I wasn't sure where things were going between us."

She turned and faced him. "Where *is* this going?"

"I don't know," he finally replied. "I was hoping you could tell me."

Hearing his story would be torture, but *not* hearing would be worse. Rose swallowed hard. The lump in her throat was back. "I think you need to tell me about Katie."

It hurt to speak his wife's name aloud. Even more painful was to see the look of anguish on his face, to know she'd put it there. Rose watched him fight his personal demons and her heart went out to him. It ached even further as she read the truth in his eyes.

He was still in love with Katie. But he also was in love with her.

"Is there someplace we can sit down and talk?" His jaw quivered slightly as he glanced down the street, the direction from which they'd come and the Gilbert family home.

"James Bay Elementary isn't far."

"Let's go." He reached over and took her head. Together they stepped off the curb and crossed the street.

The school sprawled out before them another block up the street. Rose looked around the playground. Once upon a time there'd been some benches here, but they were gone. Even the teeter-totters had been removed, perhaps for the summer season. The playground was an empty oasis of sand and swings swaying in the hot breeze.

Rose pointed to the heavy rubber swings. "How about those?"

She kicked off her sandals as her feet hit the sand. Rose sank down on one swing and tested it out, cautiously swaying back and forth. Mike finally joined her, taking a seat on the swing beside her. His long jean-clad legs splayed out before him as he warily scanned the heavy metal chains on both his swing and hers.

"Don't worry," she said, "they look solid enough." Rose scrunched her toes in the warm sand and twirled idly. Perhaps the playground had been a good idea after all. Maybe all Mike needed was time to relax—

"She had the prettiest eyes," he said abruptly. "Sparkling brown eyes that were always smiling. And curly brown hair. She was kind of chunky, always worried about her weight. I met her in the hospital. She was a nurse working in the E.R. unit. I got a little banged up during a fire run. Katie's face was the first thing I saw when they flushed the soot out of my eyes."

Mike's voice caressed each word as he spoke, as if he was holding his wife in his arms. Though she knew he was telling the story solely for her, Rose fought against the sudden impulse to stop him. She felt like a voyeur, as if she were eavesdropping on intimate matters meant only to be shared between a husband and wife.

"We got married right away. Both of us knew what we wanted and we figured there was no point in wasting time. It wasn't a big wedding or anything like that. Katie's parents and mine helped us out. We bought a house. I worked as much as I could, grabbing any overtime I could get. Katie had worked the E.R. for years. After we got married, she took the night shift. It brought in more money. It was a good year. We were happy. Especially the day we found out Katie was going to have a baby."

Both of them had stopped swinging. Rose sat scrunching her toes in the sand, quietly listening as Mike's story unfolded.

"Being pregnant wasn't easy on her. Katie wasn't very big, and her feet swelled up a lot. The doctor was worried about gestational diabetes. He kept telling her to cut back on working so hard. The E.R. is a busy place, especially at night. I tried to talk her into taking time off, but she insisted. She said she was going to work as long as she could, right up until the baby was born. Finally, I convinced her to switch to the day shift."

Rose chanced a peek at his face. Mike's jaw was clenched tight, his eyes boring a deep hole in the sand beneath his feet. He seemed lost in a trance, lost in the memory of a two-year-old nightmare.

"They told me she was laughing when she left work that night. She was talking about the dinner she was going to make for me. Why she stopped for ice cream, I'll never know. She must have been tired. It was past seven o'clock and she'd already worked a full twelve-hour shift." He spoke rapidly, shooting his words in no particular direction. "You know what they say about pregnant women, how you can't talk them out of anything once they get that craving. There was a convenience store right around the block from the hospital. That's where she stopped. That's where it happened. She made it out of the car and to the front door—"

"Mike, it's okay. You don't need to tell me." Rose reached over and gripped his hand tight, bridging the gap between their two swings. The words sounded hollow and lame to her ears, but what did you say when the man you loved was still in love with another woman?

"He shot her as she opened the door," Mike said. "Some guy, high on drugs. He'd just robbed the place and he was trying to get out. She was in the wrong place at the wrong time. Katie went in for ice cream and instead she got a bullet. "

Rose brushed away the tears with a quick swipe of her hand and searched her pockets for a tissue. The tears in his own eyes were breaking her heart.

"We had some life insurance on Katie." He took the tissue she offered and clutched it in his fist. "I paid off the house and gave some money to her parents. They're good people and even though they didn't have much, they'd helped us out when we needed it. I thought they deserved something. After all, they lost Katie, too."

She swallowed hard. His generosity and compassion came as no surprise. It was so like Mike, putting others first even after everything he himself had been through.

"What about the man who…" God, she couldn't bring herself to say the words. The last thing she wanted was to watch Mike's face crumble and his tears start again.

"You mean the guy who killed her?" Quietly he finished the sentence for her. "They got him, all right. But he wasn't some skid-row bum. His family had money and his parents bought him a deal."

Rose inhaled sharply. "He got off without doing time?"

"He was in prison, but not for long. The attorneys got together and plea bargained a reduced sentence without consulting us." He slowly shook his head. "Katie's gone forever, but the man who killed her only served one year."

Rose sat silently on the rubber swing. No wonder Mike had issues with attorneys. When it came to the issue of lawyers with questionable ethics, members of the Bar looked the other way. No one wanted to get involved unless someone made it personal.

"I tried staying put at first, after Katie… well, after the accident. But it was no good. Everywhere I looked, everything I touched, reminded me of her." Mike shot her a vacant smile. "When I heard about the job opening up here, I snatched at it fast. Once I got hired, I sold the house and headed north."

Things finally made sense. Katie's life insurance and the sale of their Detroit home had bankrolled the lakeside cabin, the new pickup, the expensive fishing boat. Mike had some nice things, but they'd been bought at an enormous price.

"Terry calls what I did *taking the geographic cure*. He told me moving away wouldn't solve my problems.

It's taken me awhile to admit he was right." Mike shrugged. "Guess I had to figure things out for myself. You can't escape yourself, no matter how far or fast you run. The problems will always be there, no matter where you go. Eventually the only thing left is to give in and face them."

Rose felt silent. *A geographic cure*. Is that what she had done? She'd left home and turned her back on James Bay and on all the dreams she and Jeff had once shared. Mike's words produced a quick, sudden stirring in her heart, a strange guilty longing for that which had been and would never be. Jeff was dead and he wasn't coming back. She'd run away from the truth.

A geographic cure was *exactly* what she had done.

"I used to love the city," he said, "but not anymore. That kind of life isn't for me. I'm happy here and I'm never going back."

Her mouth felt dry as the sand beneath her feet. If Mike was done with city living, where did that leave her?

"When I first came north, I was hurting," he continued. "Maybe I still am, in a way. But things are different now."

"Different how?" she finally asked.

"I feel more like myself again. I've got a nice little house. It's small, but it feels right for me. I can walk out to the end of my dock, do some fishing, do a little hunting. It's a great life. And the best part is, I'm living up north and getting paid to do what I love most. Fighting fires."

The mention of fire seemed to sober him slightly. "Though I could do without people like that Charles Kendall guy and his newspaper revving things up. But that goes with the territory. For the most part, I'm happy again. Especially these past few weeks. I've got you to thank for that." He turned to face her squarely. "Did you ever think about practicing law here?"

"You mean, in James Bay? Coming home?"

"Why not?"

Tiny flames of apprehension licked around the edges of her heart. After everything Mike had been through, this town must seem like paradise. But she had grown up living in paradise. If you weren't careful, the walls could dissolve into a living hell.

She scrunched her toes deep in the sand. It was time to confess. Mike had been honest with her and opened his heart about Katie. He deserved to know about the job offers she was considering. He deserved no less than the truth.

"Mike, there's something you need to know."

He was quiet for some moments after she finished. "Why didn't you tell me before this?" he finally asked.

Rose flushed. Why hadn't she told him? Possible answers seeped through her mind, curling like wisps of smoke around an evasive strategy. But her dad had always told her that when you were in the heat of things, the best tactic was to tell the truth. "I was afraid," she admitted. "Afraid of what you would say. Attorneys can be an arrogant bunch, trying to outdo each other, talking about their great careers and how much money they make. I didn't want you thinking that about me. I didn't want you to think I was bragging."

He took her hand and squeezed hard. "That's not you, Rosie. You could never be like that."

Why did he think she was such a saint? Mike had no clue who she really was, how polished and sharp, how professional her job required her to be. She didn't dare let down her guard, not even for a minute. Everyone in her profession was always looking for an edge, anything that would help them achieve the desired result for their client. She was no different. The law didn't award points for people who were patient, gentle, and kind.

"Have you decided what you're going to do?"

She shook her head. "The firm expects me back as soon as my family leave is over. I've managed to put off Andy for now, but I have to give him an answer soon."

"What about this guy?" Mike's voice strained in quiet intensity. "It sounds like he's in love with you."

"I don't feel the same about him," Rose quickly replied. "Andy is pretty hardheaded. He's used to getting what he wants. But If I accept the position in Washington, he'll have to understand his feelings aren't returned."

"So you are thinking about taking his offer?"

"I haven't ruled it out." She wouldn't lie to him. That wouldn't be fair.

"What about coming home?" he asked in a low voice. "The Judge offered you a partnership, too. You could practice law right here in town."

Rose stared at the sand beneath her feet. The longing in Mike's voice pulled at her heartstrings. She didn't dare look at him. She knew exactly what she would see. A silent, impassioned plea on his face, in his eyes, imploring her to stay.

"I haven't decided what I'm going to do," she finally replied. "I don't want to disappoint anyone. Especially my mother."

"Want to know what I think?"

Rose flashed him a quick smile. It wasn't difficult to guess what he'd say. "That I shouldn't disappoint my mother. That I shouldn't disappoint the Judge."

"Nope." Mike shook his head. "Remember what I told you before? *Don't should on yourself.* Your mom and the Judge are important, but they aren't who you really need to be thinking about right now."

Rose hesitated. "I'm not sure what you mean." If she shouldn't consider her mother or the Judge, then who was left?

"Don't disappoint yourself." Mike leaned across the swings and cradled her face between his two hands. "I think what you need to do is ask yourself one simple question: *what does Rosie want?*"

She shivered in spite of the summer heat. She knew the answer he hoped to hear, but she couldn't give it to him. Choosing Mike meant choosing home, and practicing law with the Judge. Was she prepared to make that decision?

No matter which choice she made, someone would be disappointed. Why did life's decisions have to be so hard?

"It's not that simple." She broke from his touch and forced herself to a stand. The hot sand burned her toes and she headed for the cool grass and her sandals. "I'm sorry. I have to go."

In one quick leap, he was off the swing and caught her in his arms. The wild pounding of his heart matched the furious racing of her own. "Listen to me, Rosie."

She closed her eyes, listening to the sound of his voice whisper soft against her ear, caressing her name. "I'm trying my best to figure things out. Please don't make this any harder than it already is."

"Listen to your heart," he murmured. "That's where you'll find the answers you need."

His mouth sought out her own. Their lips touched and opened, gently seeking that which the other craved. Rose leaned against the warm masculine scent that was him. His kisses left her breathless, wanting more, needing more. Dear God, would staying home be such a bad thing?

"Come on," he said hoarsely after a moment, loosening his hold on her. "We'd better get out of here before things go too far."

There was silence between them as they started for home. Mike had never had been part of her future plans—but neither was a return to James Bay. Only one decision would satisfy Mike. Accept the Judge's offer and move back home for good. Mike had already told her he was staying put. If she continued with the firm or moved to Washington D.C., their relationship would be good as dead.

George's car was still in the driveway as they neared the house. Rose cast a wary glance at another car, brand-new, parked along the curb. More company?

Mike halted as they reached his truck. He opened the driver's door and leaned against it, squinting at her through the brilliant morning sunshine.

"I'm headed home. Terry goes back to the city tomorrow and I need to spend a little time with him."

"Tell him I said good-bye." Her heart ached as she spoke the words. So much left unsaid. So much to be determined.

"I'll do that." He lifted her chin to meet his gaze. His eyes filled with tenderness and longing.

"Remember what I told you," he reminded her. "Your heart will never steer you wrong. When the time comes, you'll know what to do. You're a strong woman, Rosie."

He had such faith in her. If only she could be as sure about things as he was. She waited for the inevitable kiss but it did not come. She watched with growing disappointment as he climbed into his truck.

"Mike?" She held on to the driver's door and peered through the open window. *Tell him how you feel. Tell him you're in love with him.* She opened her mouth, but the words wouldn't come.

He buckled his seat belt.

"I want to tell you… I mean, I…" God, she couldn't say it. She couldn't tell him.

His eyes softened in understanding. "Don't be so hard on yourself. Give it some time." The truck's engine caught with a soft purr as he turned the key.

Rose watched as the truck backed out the driveway. What now? She was beyond help. Mike had set her heart on fire and even 911 couldn't rescue her now. Slowly she turned and headed back toward the house. Mike was right. Figuring out what she wanted was an inside job. Only if she searched for the answers within would she find serenity.

CHAPTER ELEVEN

TOWNIE TIDBITS

The James Bay Journal

Average temperature for the month of July: 89°
Average rainfall for the month of July: Trace
amount
Days without significant rainfall: 78

The kitchen door cracked open just as Rose reached
out to let herself in. George flashed her a quick smile.
"Your mom is on the sun porch."

Rose backed up against the railing, out of arm's
reach. She didn't trust him, not after the way he'd
acted earlier. "How did today's session go? Is she
making progress?"

"I wish all my patients were doing as well. Your
mother is one determined lady. That attitude will
carry her into a full recovery." He gave a brief nod.
"Nice meeting you." He bounded down the porch
steps and to his car.

Smiling, Rose shook her head as she stepped
inside the house. The brash young therapist from
earlier was gone, replaced by a consummate
professional. His flirting and amorous exuberance
must merely be an act, designed to get his patients
moving and back up on their feet. The joke was
definitely on her.

She found her mother on the sun porch, metal walker close at hand and Charles Kendall settled in a nearby chair.

"Oh, good, you're back. Look who came to visit us." Irene's face beamed with pleasure. "I never expected so much company this morning. First George and now Charles."

Rose remained in the doorway. She wasn't exactly pleased to see him again. Charles had set off a string of verbal fireworks on their front porch the night of the Fourth of July. He'd insulted Mike, irritated the Judge, and upset Tommy Gilbert. Until that night, she'd pegged him for nothing more than a blowhard, but she was no longer certain Charles could be trusted. The sooner he was out of this house, the better.

A sudden realization flashed to mind. "Is that your car out on the street?"

The smug smile on his face confirmed her suspicions. "She's a beauty, isn't she? I picked her up yesterday. She's fully loaded. And the best part is, the insurance company picked up the tab. Turns out our fire department is good for something after all. Since they didn't manage to save my car, I got a brand new one out of the deal."

Rose choked down a stinging retort. She didn't want to upset her mother, but Charles and that condescending attitude had no place in their house. His old car had been parked in its usual spot behind the newspaper office. By the time the blaze was spotted, the car had been beyond salvaging.

"You should take Cecilia Rose for a ride," Irene urged. "She doesn't get out much, now she's home with me."

"That's a great idea." Charles leaped to his feet. "How about it, Cecilia? Want to take a spin?"

She didn't want to go for a ride in his new car. She didn't want to go anywhere with him.

"I don't think so," Rose replied. "I shouldn't leave Mom here alone."

"I'll be fine, sweetheart," Irene said with a sweet smile. "Don't worry about me. I'm all worn out from those exercises with George. I plan on sitting here and reading my new gardening magazine."

Charles's face wreathed in a satisfied smile as he took Rose by the arm. She didn't pull away but reluctantly allowed him the small liberty. Good thing for him her mother was in the room.

"I'll have her back by lunchtime, Mrs. Gallagher."

"You two enjoy yourselves."

Rose gritted her teeth as he led her from the sun porch, but their foray came to an abrupt halt the minute her foot hit the back porch. "You can stop right here." She yanked away from his touch. "I have no intention of going for a ride with you."

"What's wrong, Rose?"

"You figure it out," she retorted. "I should think it would be obvious."

His smile dissolved in an uneasy frown. "All right, forget about the car ride. Have dinner tonight with me instead."

"You can forget that idea, too." Rose shook her head hard, feeling the hair from her ponytail tumble loose.

His face flushed an ugly red. "What's going on, Rose?"

Years of sparring with attorneys had sharpened her adversarial skills. She planted her sandals on the porch and stood her ground. "I don't owe you an explanation. I am not going for a ride in your car, and I have no desire to have dinner with you. That includes tonight, next week, and forever."

"This is about him, isn't it? That fireman." His eyes narrowed. "I know he was here this morning, so no use you trying to deny it. I saw his truck in the driveway."

"So what if he was?" Rose shrugged. "It's none of your business."

"What you see in that guy is beyond me." He spit out the words, more statement than question, with righteous indignation.

Rose felt like spitting right back in his face. Who did he think he was, telling her whom she could or couldn't date? Charles had been obnoxious and arrogant even when they were in high school, but his behavior this morning left a bitter taste in her mouth that no mouthwash would rinse away.

"You've sunk pretty low, dating someone like him. I'm surprised your mother hasn't said anything. I'm sure she expects more from you."

Rose felt her cheeks blazing. She'd tolerated Charles's boorish behavior throughout the years, but not anymore. They were through, as of right now. "Get out of this house."

"My pleasure." He started off the porch, then abruptly turned and gave her a hard stare. "Be careful, Cecilia. He's got you fooled. You might think you know that guy, but you don't know everything about him. Not by a long shot. Seems pretty strange, if you ask me, him showing up out of nowhere like he did... and suddenly he's the big hero, putting out fires, rescuing people. Well, I don't think he's doing such a great job. Last time I checked, we still had an arsonist in town."

Rose clenched her hands tightly at her sides. It took every bit of willpower she possessed to keep from slapping him across the face. Charles had no idea what he was talking about. How dare he make those kinds of accusations against Mike?

"Wait and watch. You'll be sorry, Cecilia. And don't say I didn't warn you." Charles squared his shoulders and stomped down the porch steps.

Her heart pounded as she watched him drive off in the direction of downtown. She'd made an enemy this morning but she didn't care. After all these years, she was glad finally to be rid of him.

"Where's Charles?" Irene's forehead wrinkled in a slight frown as Rose wandered back into the sunroom. "I thought the two of you were going for a ride."

"I don't think we'll be seeing Charles around here again." She sank into the cushioned wicker chair with a heavy sigh.

Irene laid aside her gardening magazine. "Did the two of you have a little spat?"

Rose struggled to keep her irritation from boiling over. Charles was excellent at manipulating people and Irene had always been subject to his charms. Even after all these years, her mother hadn't the slightest clue what Charles was really like.

"Don't judge him too harshly, sweetheart. He's very frustrated. The two of us had a little talk before you came home. Things aren't going well down at the *Journal*. These arsons are constantly on his mind. He would like nothing more than for them to be solved."

"So would the whole town," Rose mumbled. "Especially Mike."

"Your Michael seems like a smart young man. I'm sure he'll catch whoever is responsible."

"*My* Michael?" She shot her mother a wary look. "Who said anything about him being *my* Michael?"

"I might have a bad knee, but there's nothing wrong with my eyes," Irene said. "I've seen the way you two look at each other, especially when you think no one's looking. That young man is *definitely* your Michael. Don't try and deny it. And I'll tell you another thing. That young man is in love with you." Her eyes softened. "Do you feel the same?"

Rose squirmed in her chair, feeling like a teenager with something to hide. But what was the use in pretending? Patience had always been one of her mother's most valued attributes. She would never back down until she had some answers.

"I don't know how I feel about him, Mom. I don't know much about anything anymore. Lately my life seems very confused." Her conversation with Mike was too fresh, the pain in her heart still raw enough that she didn't dare talk about it. She didn't even want to think about it. Rose drew back her head and rested it against the pillows. Her gaze wandered the room, then traveled up along the ceiling. Paint peeled from the corner moldings. Maybe she would give Tommy a call this afternoon. Homes like this required constant maintenance. She didn't have the time or expertise, but she could afford to hire the work done. Tommy probably would be interested in a part-time job.

"I'm worried about you, Cecilia Rose."

Rose blew out a long sigh. "I'm fine."

"You try too hard, sweetheart. Always trying to do too much. You take care of me, you take care of everything. And just look at how thin you are. You need to rest more. I think after lunch, you should go upstairs and have a little nap."

"I don't need a nap. What I need is…" She felt the flush blazing on her cheeks. "Oh, never mind. I don't know what I need." Her conversation with Mike this morning had taken more out of her than she'd realized. And this sun porch was so hot. The noonday heat flooding the glass-enclosed room was stifling. The house was in desperate need of central air. Maybe while she had the place painted, she'd have air conditioning installed as well.

"I think you need some lunch," Irene replied. "Have we still got some of that roast beef left over from last night?"

Rose swallowed down her frustration. Fussing over food was the answer to everything in Irene's world. There were more important things in life than a roast beef sandwich.

"Are you happy. Mom?" The words popped out of her mouth before she could stop them.

"Happy? Why, of course, I am, sweetheart." A soft, puzzled look flitted across Irene's face. "Why shouldn't I be? My knee is on the mend, and soon I'll be up and moving around without this walker. I'll be happy about that."

"Have you ever thought about moving to Florida?" Rose said in a rush. "Maybe a little condo with an ocean view?"

Irene's eyes opened wide. "Why on earth would I want to move to Florida?"

"You're always complaining about the winters up here. How it gets so cold and there's so much snow. Just think of it, Mom. You could have green grass, blue skies, and fresh air all year round. I could set you up in a little place near the water. Let me do this, Mom. I can afford it."

Irene gave her head a firm shake. "I can't move to Florida. It wouldn't be home."

"You could make it home."

"But this is home. I grew up in James Bay. People knew my parents and my grandparents, too. They knew your daddy, and they know you. Don't forget that, sweetheart. My roots are here, and so are yours."

Rose purposely ignored the geography lesson. "I only want to make things easier for you. You've been stuck in this little town all your life."

Her mother sucked on her bottom lip. "You think I'm stuck?" she finally asked.

She backed off slightly. "Perhaps *stuck* wasn't the best choice of words. What I meant to say was…"

"Yes?" Irene's gaze centered on her, cool and steady.

God, what a mess she'd made of things. Why had she ever opened her mouth? This was all Charles's fault, setting her up for an argument in the first place.

"Cecilia Rose, I asked you a question. What exactly did you mean by me being stuck?"

She took a deep breath. So much for lunch and a nap. If that I-expect-an-answer-and-I-want-it-now look on her mother's face was any indication, neither of them was leaving the room until Irene was satisfied.

"I suppose I meant regrets. You've lived in James Bay all your life. You never left. Do you have any regrets?"

The pinched look between Irene's eyebrows softened after a moment. "One or two, I suppose," she finally admitted. "Everyone does, you know. I might be your mother, but I'm just as human as anyone else."

Rose straightened in her chair. She hadn't expected such candid honesty from her mother.

A wistful smile tugged at a corner of Irene's mouth. "Regrets? I always wished your father and I could have had more children. And I would have liked a different house… but *not* a condo," she added with a pointed stare.

Her mother's words left Rose totally surprised. Irene didn't like the house? Solid and stately, it had been built by Irene's own grandfather. Graceful and elegant, filled with antiques, their house was the epitome of her mother and it suited her well.

"You never told me you didn't like this house. I always assumed you loved living here. You grew up in this house, Mom. It's a beautiful home."

Irene nodded. "It *is* beautiful. But to tell you the truth, it took a long time before I felt like it was my very own. When we moved in, most of my mother's furniture was still in the house, and that wallpaper in the front hallway dates back to when I was in high school. You're too young to remember, sweetheart, but after your grandmother died and the house came to me, I wanted to sell it. Your father talked me out of it. He said this house was my legacy and that I eventually would be sorry if we let it go. Looking back, I have to say he was probably right. So we stayed put and I've grown accustomed to living here over the years. It finally feels like it's mine now. And it's *not* a condo," she added.

Rose struggled with the unexpected confession. How had her mother managed to keep such a secret bottled up all these years?

What else might there be that her mother was in the mood to share?

"Have you ever wished that you'd done things differently, if you could have done what you wanted with your life? You're so smart, Mom. You're one of the smartest women I know. Instead, you stayed home and took care of me. Are you sorry you never went to work?"

"Who says I didn't work?" Irene's eyes gleamed with soft challenge. "Raising a family is hard work.

And as for me not being able to do what I wanted, let me tell you something. Your father never told me what to do, not once in our marriage. Maybe that's one reason we got along so well. It's called respect. For one another, as well as for yourself."

"But what if things had been different? Don't you ever think about what might have been?"

"*What if* is a dangerous game to play," Irene replied. "I try and stay away from that kind of thinking. I made my choices early on, and I got exactly what I wanted out of life. I always knew your father was the right man for me. We started dating our freshman year of high school. And I wasn't about to leave this town, not if it meant leaving him behind."

Rose smiled as one of her childhood memories flooded to mind. Her father had always lauded the fact that he and Irene had been high school sweethearts.

"Your Daddy wanted to be a teacher. And I wanted…"

Rose held her breath, waiting for a reply. What *had* her mother wanted? Irene's flowerbeds and backyard garden were famous around town. Perhaps with some encouragement she might have had a little flower shop. And her mother was equally passionate about the written word. She would have made the perfect English teacher or librarian, surrounded by her beloved books.

"All I wanted was to be with your daddy," Irene said after a moment. "I knew I was meant to make my life with him. And I thank God every day for the time we had together. We had a good life and we loved each other. That's all anyone can ask."

"I suppose that's true." Rose mulled over her mother's words, chosen so carefully, lived so gracefully. What was wrong with her? Why couldn't she do the same?

"What's troubling you, sweetheart?" Irene suddenly asked. "Ever since you came home, you've been wandering around the house looking like some lost soul."

How did mothers do it? They seemed to be equipped with some instinctive radar that allowed them to keep close watch over their children's hearts, even before those same children—infants or adults—came to know and understand how they felt themselves.

"There's something I need to tell you," Rose said, and finally shared the news of Andy Sabatini's offer. The Judge's proposal needed no mention. Rose could already guess exactly which her mother would choose, if given a vote.

A thoughtful smile hovered about Irene's face. "Do you remember that time when your daddy and I took you to Washington D.C.?"

"How could I forget? It was wonderful." Her mother's words prompted a flood of happy memories. She'd been eight years old when they'd taken a trip in the family car to the nation's capital. It had been a special summer. Her father had foregone his normal summertime stint of teaching driver's education, and for two glorious weeks, they'd taken to the highway. They had traveled down the Ohio turnpike, spun through the rolling hills of Pennsylvania, and finally been rewarded by the majesty of Washington.

That same city beckoned to her now. One phone call to Andy and the job would be hers. There was nothing holding her back. Nothing except everything—and everyone—she loved.

"Do you know why we went to Washington that summer?"

Rose shook her head. She had only a child's memories of a special family vacation, but obviously her mother had seen it differently.

"I'd lost another baby that spring. You know your Daddy and I always wanted more children. I wasn't feeling too happy with myself, or anyone else for that matter. I insisted he take the summer off so we could go somewhere. I told him I wanted you to see something of the world. I said…"

Irene's voice quieted and her eyes misted over. Finally, after a deep breath, she continued. "I told him I didn't want you growing up like I had, thinking James Bay was the only place in the world."

Rose's heart softened as her mother's life opened up to embrace a young girl's dreams. Irene had sacrificed everything for one special man, for a heart that yearned for children. And the years drifted along.

"I'd been feeling selfish and mean for months, but all that changed once we got on the open road. Being with you and your daddy, my heart felt glad. I was happy again. Maybe all I needed was a little change of scenery. When we got to Washington, I took one look at all the people dressed up in their fancy clothes, going places and moving so fast, and I knew that place wasn't for me. I was mighty glad we had James Bay waiting back home."

Rose nodded, lost in memories. She'd forgotten the crowds of the city until now. No one stood still. No one listened.

"Do you remember visiting the White House?"

She nodded again as her thoughts turned to the majestic mansion. The people's house. The president's home.

"Jacqueline Kennedy lived in that house. She was little more than a girl herself when she became first lady. She had two small children and a husband with an important job and a country to run. But even with the world at her feet, something she said once got me to thinking. It didn't take me long to figure out Mrs. Kennedy and I had something in common. That stayed with me while we were in Washington, and long after we got home. And I knew then, if I had it all to do over again, I'd choose exactly the same as I had the first time around."

Irene settled back amidst the cushions. "Mrs. Kennedy knew how precious and important children are. She'd lost some babies of her own, you know. Even with all the important things happening in her life, she said—I can't remember the words exactly—if you bungle raising your children, whatever else you do doesn't really matter. And that set me to thinking. I thought about all the times your daddy and I tried, all the babies we lost, and the gift God gave us when we finally had you, our precious little girl."

Rose struggled to hold back the unbidden tears that threatened to spill down her cheeks. She knew her mother had had numerous miscarriages, but until today, they'd never discussed them openly.

"I tried my best to do a good job with you, sweetheart. All I ever wanted out of life was for you to be happy."

"I am happy, Mom," Rose assured her. "You did a wonderful job."

"But are you happy *now*?"

"I am," Rose said after a moment's thought, realizing she spoke with the truth. "I always wanted to be a lawyer."

"Just like the Judge," Irene added with a smile of her own.

Rose laughed through the tears that finally spilled down her cheeks. "Just like the Judge."

"Your daddy would be so proud. We always told you that girls could do anything, and you've grown up into a strong successful woman. Jacqueline Kennedy knew what she was talking about. I'm mighty glad I took heed of what she had to say."

Rose reached out and grasped her mother's hand. How much she loved this dear, sweet woman. The sacrifices she'd made had helped make Rose into what she was today.

Irene's fingers tightened around her own. "What I'm trying to tell you, honey, is that you mustn't worry about me. I'm happy in James Bay, doing exactly as I please. But knowing you are where you want to be, living your life the way you want, will make me even happier. I don't want to bungle raising you, even now that you're all grown up. So you take that job in Washington D.C. if that's what you really want. Follow your heart, honey. It won't steer you wrong."

Rose drew in a sharp breath. *Follow your heart.* An echo of the very same words someone else had told her just this morning.

"And, Cecilia Rose, one more thing…"

"Yes, Mom?"

Irene's eyes twinkled but her voice was firm.

"No Florida condo."

CHAPTER TWELVE

EDITORIAL

By: Charles Kendall
The James Bay Journal

JAMES BAY—The time has come to act. The safety of our community is in peril. Local fire officials have shown little initiative in solving the recent series of arsons plaguing our fair city. We take issue with Asst. Chief Gallagher's lackluster efforts in spearheading the investigation.

No longer do the citizens of James Bay dare sit by in silence, waiting for our public servants to respond. To date, no lives have been lost; these statistics could change at any moment. How long before this rampant epidemic of fires is halted? Let us join together and take back our town.

Citizens, a call to action! Proclaim your dissatisfaction with the current state of affairs. Demand the arson investigation be immediately turned over to qualified professionals of the State Fire Marshal's office. Telephone city hall and order the mayor to remove Assistant Chief Gallagher from the investigation before the arsonist strikes again.

The martini pitcher clinked across the room.

"Did you read that garbage they published in the paper yesterday?"

"Exactly which article are you referring to, Lil?" Irene said. "Seems garbage is about all the *Journal* prints lately. Worthless trash. The only thing that paper is good for anymore is recycling."

Rose glanced up from the book in her lap and surveyed her mother and Lil, facing each other over the card table. "I think she's referring to the editorial Charles wrote."

Lil slapped her cards on the table. Her emerald-green eyes glittered over the top of her reading glasses. "I still can't believe that Kendall character had the nerve to publish such a thing. It's one thing to complain about the way the fire department is handling things. But to launch a personal attack against Fireman Mike... well, it's just not right."

Rose felt her own temper simmering as she thought about the piece in yesterday's *Journal*. Charles had publicly called Mike's integrity and dedication into question. He'd practically accused Mike of gross negligence in overseeing the arson investigation. The whole town was talking. And she had no doubt what lay behind Charles's scathing editorial.

Jealousy was a powerful motive. Charles had made his feelings perfectly clear a few days ago. She stirred in her chair as she recalled their conversation on the back porch and the stinging words of warning he'd spit out as he stomped down the steps.

"Wait and watch. You'll be sorry. And don't say I didn't warn you."

How she longed for the Judge's return. His sage wit and savvy understanding had proved a steady source of comfort throughout the years. The Judge would know what to do about this mess brewing in town.

Irene laid her playing cards on the table. Her eyes were filled with soft understanding. "Don't worry, sweetheart. There are plenty of people in this town who know Michael is hard on the case. Never you mind what Charles is up to. No one pays any attention to what he writes, anyway."

"Don't be silly, Irene, of course they do." Lil shuffled another hand. "Most people are fools. If they hear it on TV or read it in the newspaper, they assume it must be true."

Rose slapped her book shut. "I think both of you are giving Charles far too much credit. He's simply after the publicity. He's like a pesky fly. He'll disappear once somebody swats him."

"I'd like to take a crack at him myself," Lil muttered and took a small, neat sip of her martini.

"He's certainly created controversy these past few weeks," Irene said. "The *Journal* must be selling lots of papers."

Lil sniffed. "We'll just see about that. He's already lost one customer. I canceled my subscription this morning."

"You're addicted to that paper," Irene said. "How are you going to live without your daily dose of who's getting married, having a baby, or got arrested last Saturday night?"

Lil pondered the question by seeking an answer in her martini glass. She brightened after a sip or two. "I just solved your recycling problem, Irene. You can save the newspapers for me." She flashed a triumphant smile as the telephone's shrill ring interrupted from the hallway.

Rose threw aside her book and headed for the door. Lil's voice, full of righteous indignation, trailed her down the hallway. "That Charles Kendall should be ashamed of himself. I'm surprised someone hasn't written a letter to the editor about this. For all we know, there could be shenanigans going on down at the newspaper office."

She chuckled as she grabbed the phone. Shenanigans at the newspaper office? Hard to imagine stuffy old Charles involved in trouble of any sort, except that which he brought upon himself.

"Hello, counselor." Mike's voice rumbled low and inviting.

Hearing his voice brought a rush of feminine pleasure surging through her, straight into her toes. "Funny you should call. We were just talking about you."

"In a good way, I hope," he replied.

"Definitely," Rose said with a laugh. "I've been defending your honor. My mother and Lil are having at it with Charles Kendall."

"He's at your house?" Mike's voice registered a verbal frown.

"No, we're bashing him in conversation."

"I'm glad to hear Lil is there." His voice lightened. "Think you could manage to sneak out for a while? I was hoping you'd have dinner with me tonight."

The unexpected invitation took her by surprise. "I thought you were working."

"I'm on duty through tomorrow morning, but that doesn't mean I can't have company. I'll give you a tour of the firehouse and cook you something fancy. That is, if you don't mind eating in the kitchen."

They'd never faced each other over a table for two in a crowded restaurant. They'd never sat through a movie or danced close together in each other's arms. They'd shared no real dates, according to any predefined rules. Yet she felt as comfortable and safe with him as if they'd been together for years instead of merely a matter of weeks.

"I would love to have dinner with you. What time?"

"Half an hour?"

"That should work. I'll check with my mom and Lil."

"See you then."

A large yellow fire truck was parked outside the station. Rose spotted Mike and another man coming around the truck as she drove up. The two men were locked in heated discussion. Mike lifted his hand in greeting and beckoned her over as she stepped onto the street. "There's someone I'd like you to meet."

The older man looked familiar to her. She'd seen him before. He had been at the hospital on the false-alarm fire run the day of Irene's surgery—and later that same afternoon as the fire department responded to the kitchen fire at her own house.

"This is Ivan Thompson, James Bay Fire Chief."

Rose offered her hand. Years of practicing law had taught her you could tell a lot about a person from the way they shook hands. "It's very nice to meet you."

Chief Ivan Thompson's handshake was firm, brief, and dismissive. He shoved a thin file of paperwork toward Mike. "Think about what I said. The two of us will talk soon." With a curt nod for Rose, he headed for his truck.

She peered at Mike, then the papers in his hand. "He certainly didn't seem happy to meet me."

"It has nothing to do with you." Mike tucked the sheaf of papers tight under his arm. "He's been trying to take some time off. His wife was diagnosed with a rare form of cancer last month. He doesn't like leaving her alone too long."

"Poor guy. Is she…" Rose broke off as the irony suddenly hit her. Mike, just like the chief, had been happily married once upon a time.

"Is she dying?" Mike abruptly finished her sentence. "I don't know. The chief's never talked about it and I don't want to ask."

A slow, irrational fear crept around the edges of her heart as they watched the chief's vehicle disappear around the corner. She chanced a quick peek at Mike. His face was in profile, his eyes hidden from view. Was he thinking about Katie? He hadn't lost her to some dreadful disease, but she was gone from him, just the same.

Suddenly she felt the warm touch of his hand on her own.

"I'm glad you're here. I could use the company."

"You're sure?" she asked quietly. In response, his fingers tightened around her own.

"I hope you're hungry. Dinner's nearly ready."

"What about the grand tour you promised me?" She trailed behind him into the fire hall.

"Patience, Rosie." His eyes twinkled as he threw her a quick glance over his shoulder. "You'll see it all soon enough."

"Patience isn't one of my virtues. I'm a lawyer, remember? We expect quick results."

Mike closed the door and they stood alone together in the cool, cavernous garage. She caught a quick glimpse of gleaming fire trucks and first response equipment.

"Patience has its own rewards," he said with a soft smile as he pulled her into his arms. "But if you want quick results, maybe you'll settle for this."

His uniform shirt was crisp against her skin. He smelled like fresh air, aftershave, and fabric softener rolled into one. His kiss was warm and inviting, and she felt the soft sweet urge of her body respond to the gentle press of his mouth upon hers. She kissed him back, moving deeper into his embrace. His lips lingered with lush sweetness, tenderly nuzzling, paying homage to her throat, her neck. His arms were around her, strong and solid as he held her close.

"You'd think I'd have more sense."

She felt a stab of disappointment as Mike pulled away. Why had he stopped? She'd been enjoying their kisses so much.

"This is a public place." A sheepish smile tugged at one corner of his mouth. "Anybody could walk in."

"You worried? The way you kiss, you have nothing to be ashamed about," Rose teased.

"You definitely know how to kiss as well." He reached down and took her hand. "Come on, I'll give you that grand tour before we get distracted again."

He led her down a narrow hallway, past open doors. Rose felt a quick rush of color flood her cheeks as she caught a glimpse of the chief's cluttered office. She and Mike had faced off against each other in that very room merely days ago after the nightmarish fire that brought the Judge's condominium project to the ground in a blaze of roaring flames. She tore her gaze from the chief's office as they passed. Their conversation that day had been filled with argument and innuendo. Hopefully her visit to the fire station this evening would result in much more pleasant memories.

Mike pointed out an imposing bank of electronic equipment, radios, and computers. Bright lights flashing red, yellow and green flickered alternately from the machines as electronic voices squawked randomly across the board. "This is our communications center, where we raise central dispatch."

"Central dispatch?"

"911. Central command," he said with a patient smile. "All our fire calls come through there." He led her up a flight of worn cement stairs to the second level and pointed to a large open room directly to their left. "That's where we hold our fire meetings and watch training videos."

"Training videos?" The idea sounded novel to Rose. "What's on them?"

"We've got a whole library on different subjects. The guys learn how to use hose lines, proper ventilation, ladder and apparatus use."

She'd never given the matter any thought until now, but his words made sense. How else were new firefighters supposed to learn?

"Training videos are great, but working an actual fire is the best teacher of all. Fire has a mind of its own. It does what it wants, when it wants. There's no way you can learn that sitting in school behind a desk."

"I can relate," she said with a knowing smile. "I was in law school for three years, but it wasn't until after I passed the bar that I began to realize how much there was I still needed to learn. Practicing law and working with clients is an education in itself."

"I graduated from the Fire Academy in Detroit," Mike replied. "Lots of colleges offer similar programs. Once you finish, you put in time on the job. Some firefighters take specialized training. Hazmat, things like that."

"Hazmat?" The unfamiliar technology was confusing.

"Sorry." He shot her a quick smile. "Hazardous materials."

It was impossible not to catch the determined lift of his chin, the serious look on his face. This was deadly earnest business. Fighting fires was a precise science, not some easy job that merely involved climbing a ladder or holding a fire hose. Thank God there were men willing to serve as skilled professionals. Those brave men who were the nation's heroes. Though their clothes were stained with soot and smoke, they had nerves of steel when it came to staring down a blazing inferno.

"Fighting fires is like anything else. The best teacher of all is practical experience. We try to provide that for our new guys."

"How exactly do you do that? Sit around waiting for the next fire call?"

Mike grinned. "That's not a luxury we can afford. The guys need the experience, so we give it to them. We set things on fire. Houses. Barns. Anything that burns."

"You are kidding." She stared at him in confusion. "You don't actually mean that you deliberately burn things down."

"How else are the new guys supposed to learn?"

"Isn't that illegal?"

"Not when it's a controlled burn. People donate junk houses or abandoned buildings to the fire department, which gives us a chance to practice. The new guys already know the practical stuff. How to roll hose, hook up to the engine, run the pumper, or use an air pack. When they're at a controlled burn, they get hands-on experience in a controlled environment."

"I suppose it makes sense," Rose said doubtfully. Who would set a fire on purpose?

Mike leaned against the brick wall. "Think of it this way. It's like learning how to fly an airplane in a simulator, versus being in the sky with the controls in your hand. If you crash when you're in the simulator, you can still walk away. But if you're really flying that plane, there's no room for error. Some of the young guys who've never seen a fire need the chance to get used to the flames. There's no telling what they'll do once they finally experience the heat and smoke. We've had some guys go through all the training, get their certification, and be gung ho to get to their first real fire. They strap on an air pack and work the fire. But then, once everything is over, they never come back.

"Every man has his own job at a fire scene. He needs to learn to do it fast and do it well—or get out of the way and let someone else take over. There's no time to teach when you're in front of a blazing inferno that's about to take down a fully engulfed building. It's hard to understand until you're out there, taking the heat and working the fire. We do the job as best we can."

Rose quieted, hearing the heat in his voice. Obviously Mike's patience was wearing thin over the unsolved series of arson. And Charles Kendall wasn't proving to be any help. His scathing editorial questioning Mike's competence had only added fuel to the fire and had the whole town talking. But better the townsfolk than the two of them. She didn't want to waste their time tonight thinking about James Bay or the gossip making the coffee-shop circuit. The two of them were alone, exactly the way it should be. Keep the town and the rumors at bay, far from the fire station and far from Mike. He deserved a nice quiet evening.

"What's the next stop on our tour?" she asked.

He crossed to a battered wooden door directly to their right and gave it a gentle push.

"And this is...?" Rose eyed him.

"Where we're having dinner." He waved her through the open door with a flourish. "Ladies first. After you, Miss Gallagher."

CHAPTER THIRTEEN

JOURNAL'S QUESTIONING OF ADEQUATE FIRE
SERVICES DRAWS RESPONSE FROM CHIEF

The James Bay Journal

JAMES BAY—In response to demands from local citizenry, James Bay Fire Chief Ivan Thompson appeared before the James Bay City Council last night to defend both his department and Assistant Fire Chief Michael Gallagher. Chief Thompson assured the City Council that despite Gallagher's lack of success in apprehending the person or persons responsible for the string of recent arsons plaguing our community, the investigation continues to provide new evidence on a daily basis. Additionally, Chief Thompson reports that the State Fire Marshal's office has been consulted and will be making recommendations for further causes of action in the immediate future.

While Chief Thompson's report seemed to appease some fears raised by local citizenry and the city fathers, this reporter still waits for an arrest to be made.

The gentle hum of an air conditioner greeted Rose as she stepped over the threshold. "Why, it's an entire little apartment of its own."

A narrow living room, crowded with furniture and a big screen television, spread out before them. Through a doorway off the entry she spied a kitchen table and bright, shiny stove. A door opposite the kitchen stood slightly ajar, giving a brief glimpse of a bedroom dresser. The overall effect was one of comfort and homey surroundings, rather than a working fire station. She turned to Mike with a delighted smile. "This is not what I imagined at all. It looks like a person could actually live here."

"We do." His eyes sparkled. "We're on duty for twenty-four-hour shifts. Did you think we spend all that time behind a desk?"

She trailed behind him as he gave her a quick tour. The first bedroom was spacious, with a large double bed and dresser, while the second was cramped with three narrow beds.

"The chief has his own room," Mike explained, "in case he's covering duty for someone. The rest of the guys sleep in the other room. We each have our own bed for when we're on duty."

Rose snuck a peek at her personal tour guide. The gleam in his eyes gave credible evidence of his love for the job. The tour was fascinating and the guide even more spectacular.

They ended up in the kitchen, a cozy room flooded with sunshine and the spicy smell of spaghetti sauce. Gleaming modern appliances stood aligned in precise array. Mike threw his paperwork on the kitchen counter as she took in the gingham curtains, clean kitchen towels, matching placemats on the table. It had a woman's touch. Were there any women on the fire department roster?

"This is nice." She smiled her thanks as he offered her a chair.

"The city council voted to have it redone last year. The chief's wife was in charge of the redecorating."

So that explained the feminine touches all throughout the living quarters.

"Don't tell me the chief's wife is in charge of floral arrangements, too?" Rose eyed the fragrant bouquet of fresh flowers sitting in the center of the round oak table. Snapdragons, gerberas, daisies. The colorful assortment transplanted the summer fields right onto the kitchen table.

"Nope, I did that on my own." Mike headed for the stove. "They're for you."

"You bought me flowers?" Her gaze lingered on his unexpected gift. When was the last time a man had given her flowers?

"I felt bad about the other day," he said from his station in front of the simmering pot. "I'm sorry you found out about everything the way you did."

Rose inhaled the summer blossoms, relishing the rich scent. Not only did he have beautiful manners, he was a true romantic. She looked up with a soft smile and shyly caught his gaze. "Thank you for the flowers. That was really sweet."

He shrugged in reply and turned back to the stove, but not quick enough. Rose caught the pleased smile on his face.

"You look cute standing there in front of the stove," she said. "All you need is an apron."

"I've got one around here somewhere," he replied. "One of the guys must have swiped it."

She giggled softly. Only a man utterly sure of himself could pull off wearing an apron with ease. She had no doubt Mike could handle an apron—even one with a flounce.

"I made a salad, too. Do you like garlic bread?" Opening the refrigerator, he pulled out a plastic-wrapped bowl filled with lettuce, tomatoes and crispy vegetables.

"That depends." A sudden rush of memory brought back the earlier delight of delicious, stolen kisses shared in front of a fire truck.

"Depends on what?"

"If *you* like garlic bread."

He frowned for a second, then a sudden smile lifted a corner of his mouth. He broke off two pieces of the piping hot bread. Mike's eyes gleamed with a challenge as he offered her one of the pieces.

"Come and get it."

Rose felt the hot flush rise in her cheeks as she joined him in front of the stove. She took the bread from his hand and sampled a tiny bite, never breaking her gaze.

"It's good," she said after a moment and nibbled another bite. They stood close together, shoulders touching. Her bare leg grazed his.

"Not too much garlic?" His voice was low.

"I *like* garlic." The bread was spicy, piping hot, and the zesty flavor gave her a sudden zing of courage. Up she went on tiptoe and kissed him.

Their bodies melted like butter as they pressed together, tasting the sweet pleasure of being in each other's arms.

"I like the way you cook," Rose murmured after a moment.

"And I like having you in my kitchen." His breath was soft and warm against her ears and he pulled her even closer, nuzzling her neck with delicious little kisses. He wanted her, just as much as she wanted him. Her insides ached, heavy with desire. She reached out and fingered the dark blond hairs peeping over the top of his shirt. She shivered as her fingers touched bare skin.

"You smell so sweet." His voice was smooth against her ear.

Rose inhaled sharply as she felt his fingers fumble with the buttons on her blouse. Big mistake, wearing this blouse. The tiny pearl buttons were a pain.

"Want some help?" She touched her hand to his.

He managed fine alone. She arched her back and sighed as his fingers cupped her breast.

"Hey, Mike. You around, buddy?"

The loud slam of a nearby door and quick heavy footsteps in the hallway forced them apart. Rose straightened her blouse as the kitchen filled with three young men. They were barely out of their teens and all of them sported matching yellow t-shirts with the fire department logo.

"Hey, guys." Mike gave them an abrupt nod.

Five seconds was all it took for them to take in the flowers, the simmering spaghetti and the perturbed look on Mike's face. Rose swallowed down a smile as they stammered and backed up through the doorway.

"Man, we're sorry. We didn't know you had company."

"Sorry, ma'am."

"No harm done, fellas. But as you can see, I'm a little busy. Why don't you come back another time?"

"Sure, Mike. Sorry again."

"Have a nice evening. See ya."

Rose wiggled her fingers in farewell as the three boys made a quick exit.

"Sorry about that," Mike said. A scarlet flush stained his cheeks as he headed back to the stove.

"Who were those boys?" She took her seat and bit her lip, trying to keep from laughing out loud. The last thing the poor guy needed was grief from her.

"Some new volunteers on the department. They show up almost every night."

"And do what?"

He shrugged. "You know how guys are. They like to hang around the fire station and see what's going on."

"I'm sure they got an eyeful tonight."

Mike didn't say a word. He laid out the silverware beside their plates in precise military fashion. The salad came next, followed by the crusty loaf of garlic bread, the spaghetti and sauce. Silently he took a seat and stared at her across the table.

"Mike, what's wrong? Are you upset that those boys stopped by?" The question had been burning inside her since the door slammed shut on their unexpected guests.

"It's not that." He let out a winded sigh. "Sorry, it's been a long day. No, guess you could say a long week."

He looked so tired. Probably he wasn't getting enough sleep. She wouldn't be surprised, with everything he'd been asked to do. Stepping in for the chief, heading up the arson investigation, dealing with newspaper reporters. She reached out and touched his forearm, her fingers lingering on the warm tanned skin.

"I'm sorry about everything that's been happening lately. Especially that piece Charles printed in the *Journal*."

"It's not your fault." He picked up his fork and swirled it through the pasta on his plate. "You didn't write it."

"Still, he had no right to say the things he did." Rose eyed Mike carefully as she struggled to find the right

248

words. There was no easy way to put it. "You realize what Charles is trying to do, don't you?"

"What's that?"

"Force your hand—or force you out."

Charles had the power of the newspaper behind him. Obviously he wouldn't hesitate to use it. Rose felt her discomfort rising as she watched Mike watching her. He seemed strangely unmoved by what she'd said.

"You can't just ignore it, you know," she added. "Everyone is talking about that editorial."

"Yep, I know. The guys at the coffee shop were kidding me about it today."

Her face flushed. How could he sit there so calm and cool with all the talk going on around town? "I hope you gave them an earful," she replied.

He shrugged. "Charles Kendall is a blowhard and I don't care what he prints. It won't stop me from doing my job."

"Don't forget this is a small town. If the *Journal* keeps running articles like that, people might start believing what they read is true."

Mike's eyes narrowed as he put down his fork. "That must put you in an awkward position."

"What do you mean?" She shifted in her chair.

"He's a local, right, just like you. Plus, he's a friend of yours. Maybe he's looking for you to take some kind of a public position on all this."

"This isn't about me," she replied. "Charles has made some serious allegations. Why aren't you defending yourself?"

"It's pretty obvious which one of us is the lawyer," he said with a grim smile. "Fighting is in your nature, but it's not in mine. My job investigating these arsons isn't to defend myself, it's to search out the evidence. When I have enough, I hand the results over to people like you."

She stared at him. "You mean to tell me you're just going to sit there and do nothing?"

Mike shrugged and speared some salad with his fork.

"Are you crazy? You can't allow Charles to keep on printing that trash about how incompetent he thinks you are."

She waited three, five, ten seconds, but the passive look on Mike's face never wavered. Rose felt like stomping her foot, not that it would do any good. Why did he have to be so infuriating?

He blew out a sigh. "Look, Rosie, I told you before: arson is a difficult crime to prove. Evidence often burns in the fire."

"Surely you must have collected *some* kind of evidence by now?"

His eyes were guarded. "Not enough to make an arrest. We're still investigating."

Rose sat back hard in her chair and eyed him with frustration. "But don't you see? That's *exactly* what Charles has been telling everyone: that you've totally mismanaged the investigation by not trying hard enough."

Mike's jaw clenched as he stared at her. "Is that what you think?"

She tried not to flinch under his steady gaze. "It doesn't matter what I think," she replied. "But surely you've narrowed down the range of suspects by now."

"As far as I'm concerned, everyone is a suspect until an arrest is made."

Mike was wrong. Not everyone was a suspect. "I hope you've already dropped your investigation of the Judge."

"I'm not ruling anyone out... including him."

"You can't be serious." This conversation was getting them nowhere. She'd made her position clear about the Judge's character. "You know he's not the one setting those fires. Why are you being so stubborn about this?"

"Why are you trying to tell me what to do?" he shot back. "You're a very bossy woman, you know that?"

Bossy? She sat back hard in her chair. Her cheeks stung as if she'd just been slapped. What gave him the right to call her bossy?

"Lawyers! What makes you think you have the right to interfere in official government business?" Mike glared at her across the table. "Did it ever occur to you that I might actually know what I'm doing? I am not a total idiot."

"I never said you were," she replied in a tight voice. Stupid and bullheaded, that's what Mike was. Investigating the Judge would only prove a useless exercise and waste valuable time in finding the real arsonist. In Rose-world, time was a precious commodity and not to be squandered or your billing timesheets would stack up empty.

"Anybody home?" A familiar voice filtered in from the next room. "Hey, Mike? You around?"

Mike threw down his fork and glared at the door. "Who's here now?"

Tommy Gilbert shuffled through the kitchen doorway. His eyes lit up in recognition. "Hey, Cecil! What you doing here?"

"Someone invited me to dinner." She glanced at Mike and saw the irritated frown tugging at one corner of his mouth. Obviously he wasn't pleased by this most recent surprise visitor, but Tommy's timing couldn't be more perfect. Officer Gallagher thought she was bossy? Fine. Let this fireman smolder about that for a while.

"Smells great. Hey, spaghetti? That's my favorite." Tommy yanked a chair from the table and took a seat. His gaze bobbed happily back and forth between the two of them.

Mike's sigh was barely noticeable. "You want a plate?"

"That would be great." Tommy's face shone with hungry delight. "Hey, Cecil, did he tell you the big news?"

News? She turned to Mike, only to find his gaze on her. Was that regret she saw written on his face? Maybe he was wishing he'd kept his comments to himself. As well he should have. Where did he get off, pointing a finger at her when she had only been trying to help?

Rose tossed her curls and turned her attention to Tommy. "What news?"

"I'm going to be a fireman." Tommy's voice pitched in a crow of delight as Mike passed him a plate of steaming pasta.

"You passed the test?" Her eyes widened. Tommy had been searching all summer for a new job but Mike had never breathed a word about recruiting him for a full-time position. She shot Mike a questioning glance.

"It's not official yet," Tommy said. "I've got to take some classes before I can actually work a fire. But I'm a quick learner. I'll pass, no problem. Watch and see."

"Tommy's joining our volunteer force," Mike said quietly.

"That's the same as a regular fireman, right? You said being a volunteer was an important job."

Mike pushed away his plate and leaned back in his chair. "We wouldn't have a department without volunteers."

"Volunteers go through the same training," Tommy said. "You go to classes and you get your own gear and helmet." He cast a keen glance at Mike. "What about my helmet? Will it be white, like yours?"

"Yours will be blue. That stands for probationary. Only the chief wears a white helmet."

"So how come your helmet is white? You're not the chief," Tommy said.

"No, but I'm the assistant chief."

A furious shrill beeping exploded through the room. Mike bolted from his chair and grabbed the monitor from its cradle on the kitchen counter as loud electronic static flooded the room.

"Hey, what..."

"Shhh!" Rose cut Tommy off as Mike listened with quiet intensity to the 911 page.

"Central Dispatch calling James Bay Fire Department. You have a report of a structure fire at 0135 Lakeshore Drive. Repeat, you have a structure fire at 0135 Lakeshore Drive, the Waller Boat Company. Reporting party indicates seeing flames through the roof. Central clear, first call, 19:45."

Mike's face hardened. "I've got to go. This sounds bad. I doubt I'll be back any time soon. You should probably go home."

"Hey, wait for me!" Tommy was already on his feet. Fruit and papers went flying off the counter as he made a grab for his baseball cap. "I'll go with you. I'll help fight the fire. Can I ride in the truck?"

"No. You're not a member of the department yet." Mike's gaze flashed to Rose and lingered briefly. "Sorry about this."

Frustration over their earlier heated discussion dissolved at the sight of Mike's troubled eyes. He was headed out to another fire. Rose waved him on. "Don't worry about it."

Mike slammed out the door as the station's rooftop fire whistle began to wail.

Tommy's eyes held a look of abject disappointment. "I don't see why he wouldn't let me ride in the truck with him."

"They probably have rules about those kinds of things. What if they had an accident while you were in the truck? I doubt the insurance would cover you."

"Who cares about some stupid old insurance?" He stuck out his chin. "I'm going to that fire. I'll drive my own truck. Once I get there, Mike will let me help. You wanna go, Cecil? I'll give you a ride."

"No more fires for me, Tommy," she replied. "You go ahead. I'll stay here and clean the kitchen, then head on home." Cleaning up would keep her hands occupied, as well as keep her thoughts from straying to the fire scene and the dangers awaiting Mike and the other firemen.

Tommy banged out the door, leaving Rose to survey the leftover remains of their dinners. The kitchen was a mess with pots and pans littering the stove and fruit and papers scattered over the floor. She scooped up the apples and pears that had rolled in all directions, then turned to gather the loose papers strewn in disarray. She stacked them on the counter, struggling to put them into some semblance of order when the sight of a familiar name leaped from the page.

Rose snatched up the city tax report, her eyes quickly scanning the page. Someone had been busy with a magic marker. Bay Properties, LLC was highlighted in yellow. Next to it, the name of the Honorable Harvey James, as its owner agent, was underlined in stark bold slashes of red. Her stomach gave a sickening lurch as she caught sight of the date and the money owed. The information was current, from the past winter season.

Delinquent.

If the paperwork was correct, the Judge was owner of Bay Properties, LLC.

And the Judge was also deeply in debt.

Her understanding and incredulity grew as she flipped through the file. Mike obviously considered the Judge a suspect—the prime suspect—in the arson fires. The proof was right in front of her, outlined in precise array. She read faster, her disbelief growing as she scanned Mike's handwritten notes outlining his interview with the construction manager on the condo project that had burned to the ground. Condos owned by Bay Properties, LLC. Work on the project had halted shortly before the fire, since the necessary funds to cover the labor and materials hadn't been provided. The Judge was out of cash.

There had to be some mistake. How could the Judge not be solvent? He had a flourishing law practice, which had to bring in a very nice income. Not to mention all the monies from his rental properties and real estate ventures.

But official tax reports didn't lie. Neither did exculpatory evidence. Goose bumps popped on her arms as Rose skimmed the evidentiary report on the vehicle fire that had destroyed Charles Kendall's car late the night of the Fourth of July. Evidence had been found at the scene of the crime. A half-smoked cigar, distinctly unique in make and design, had been discovered near the vehicle's burnt-out shell. Rose gasped at the implication buried halfway down the page. Those cigars were the Judge's signature brand, hand rolled for him and imported from the islands. Everyone knew how much he loved them. She'd ordered those cigars herself in the past as birthday gifts for him.

A flash of distant memory abruptly came to mind. A shadowy front porch late on the fourth of July and the soft purr of an engine as the Judge's car headed downtown. Could Mike be right? Could it possibly be true that the Judge was the one responsible for setting Charles's car ablaze? Rose struggled to comprehend the impossible. It made no sense. The Judge had no reason to set Charles's car on fire. Even more improbable was the other question that seared itself across her mind.

Why would the Judge torch his own buildings?

She hit upon the answer on the very next page. Mike had been thorough. Her hands trembled as she scanned the printed report from the Michigan State Police. Airline schedules—confirmed arrival and departure times for the Honorable Harvey James— spilled from the file. Validation of Michigan to Nevada flights. Confirmation of his arrival at McCarren International Airport, Las Vegas.

Las Vegas? She took in a sharp breath. If these reports were true, then the Judge wasn't in California visiting his ailing sister. He had flown to Las Vegas on July fifth and had been there ever since.

There was no mistake. Page upon page of documents stamped confidential listed gambling debts. The amounts were staggering. A roll of the dice and a spin of the wheel had caused her old friend's fortunes to tumble. Rose's cheeks flushed hotter, first in understanding, then in anger, as she flipped through the rest of Mike's file. He'd known all along that the Judge was deeply in debt, and he'd kept it from her. The Judge had played the slots, while Mike had played her for the fool.

No! It was simply too incredible, too ridiculous to believe. No matter what Mike thought, no matter what the papers said, she would never believe the Judge was the arsonist. Never in a million years. Rose crammed the paperwork inside the manila folder and slapped the file shut. She felt like a firestorm of emotions, a swirl of seething anger. This must be why doctors were prohibited from operating on members of their immediate family. Emotions got in the way. No matter what any official report said, she would never believe the Judge was responsible for the arsons. Not unless she heard it from His Honor himself.

And she wouldn't hold her breath waiting for that to happen. It never would. It simply wasn't true. After tonight, she would be able to prove it.

Mike was at another fire. The abandoned boat warehouse, a wooden structure, would probably burn to the ground. And if tonight's fire proved to be another in the string of arsons, Mike would have no choice but to admit the Judge was innocent. Maybe the Judge was a gambler and deep in debt—but, according to Mike's own files, at the moment the Judge was in Las Vegas and thousands of miles away. A person couldn't be in two places at once, even someone as crafty and wise as her dear old friend. Thank God the Judge had a geographic alibi. That would put a kibosh on any convoluted theories of guilt that could be stewing in that fireman's head.

She eyed the dirty dishes still on the table, the pots and pans on the stove and in the sink. Her first inclination was to leave them sitting. But a promise was a promise, and she'd volunteered to clean up. She got down to work before she could change her mind. Rose bustled around the kitchen, gathering the plates and silverware, rinsing dried spaghetti sauce from the dishes and pans. She kept herself moving and busy, allowing herself no respite or chance to think. Finally everything was put away and the counter scrubbed down. She punched the dishwasher button, bringing the machine to noisy life. Rose grabbed her purse from the kitchen counter and looked around the room, her gaze finally coming to rest on the kitchen table. She stared long and hard at the summertime bouquet. It had seemed such a charming, romantic gesture at the time, but now she could only wonder.

Maybe Mike had meant the flowers for another purpose instead. Had he meant to bribe her? Did he intend to buy her silence while romancing her as he went about his task of interrogating the Judge? Well, if that fireman thought she was going to keep quiet about what she'd seen tonight, he had another think coming. If Mike thought the Judge was the arsonist, she would prove him wrong. Dead wrong.

Rose stormed from the apartment and slammed the door with a satisfied bang, leaving the flowers behind.

CHAPTER FOURTEEN

BOAT WAREHOUSE FIRE LABELED "SUSPICIOUS"

By: Charles Kendall
The James Bay Journal

JAMES BAY—Another mystery blaze last night destroyed the Waller Boat Company warehouse on Lakeshore Drive. James Bay firefighters were unable to save the hundred-year-old structure, which was completely engulfed in flames by the time firefighters arrived. The boat warehouse fire has been officially labeled of "suspicious origin" as this paper goes to press.

"Come on, admit it. You're mad at me."

"Why would you think that?" Rose chose to ignore the strain in Mike's voice. He thought he was so smart? Fine. Let him figure it out. She wasn't the one with the clandestine file on the Judge.

Rose clenched her thin bathrobe tighter and stared at the *James Bay Journal* in her hand that she'd just picked up from their front porch moments ago. She reread the blaring headline touting last night's fire. With the Judge still in Las Vegas or California and the Waller boat warehouse fire labeled suspicious, maybe now Mike would believe her.

Maybe he would finally deliver that apology.

A slow sigh flooded across the telephone line. "I've lived with women long enough to know when I've got one mad at me."

His words made her hesitate. Once upon a time, not too many years ago, Mike had been a married man. Had Katie given him this much grief? From the little he'd shared about his wife, it sounded as if she had. Well, good for Katie! The thought brought Rose some comfort. Hopefully she'd been the spunky type, the kind of woman who gave as good as she got. This fireman of theirs could use a little downsizing of his ego.

"Is there a chance we can get together today? I'd like to see you."

"Sorry, I don't have time," Rose quickly replied. "I'm supposed to be helping my mom, remember? That's the reason I came home in the first place." Even if she wanted to—which she didn't—she wasn't ready to face him again. She was still seething about last night and how she'd discovered the thick file he had on the Judge.

"Tomorrow," he suggested.

"That's not a good day, either," she shot back.

The silence between them lengthened.

"Boy, you're really mad, aren't you?" he finally said.

Fuming, Rose held back the torrent of words stoking the fire inside her. Mike was no fool. If he gave it some thought, he could make an educated guess as to exactly why she was upset. He knew how she felt about the Judge.

"Obviously something's bothering you." His voice sounded weary with defeat. "I guess whatever it is will just have to wait. I don't have time to be playing games. I've been up all night fighting a fire. I'm tired and hungry. I'm going to climb in the shower, then grab some breakfast and get some sleep."

Rose's heart softened as a clear vision of his face rushed to mind. He was probably sooty and reeking of smoke, his eyes clouded with fatigue. Fighting fires was hot, heavy work.

"So, tell you what, Rose. When you're ready to talk, you give me a call. You know the number. And by the way, it's not 911."

Her mouth dropped as she heard the sharp click on the other end of the phone. He'd hung up on her? The man had some nerve! She slapped the phone back in its cradle and headed for the staircase. Call him when she was ready to talk? Mike had better not hold his breath. There weren't enough days in the calendar to mark the distance she intended to put between the two of them.

The shrill ring of the telephone stopped her mid-flight. If he thought he could simply call back and say he was sorry, he had another think coming. It would take more than a simple phone call. And he still hadn't apologized for calling her bossy the other night. Rose marched down the steps to her grandmother's antique cherry buffet and snatched the phone up. "You've got some nerve, hanging up on me like that."

"Excuse me?" The gruff, familiar voice gave a short cough.

"Judge?" Rose felt her knees grow weak.

"You sound a little out of sorts. Is everything all right?"

"I'm fine," she sputtered. "I thought you were someone else." She took a deep breath and tried to gather her wits.

"I didn't mean to call you so early, my dear, but I was hoping to catch you at home."

Rose quickly did the math. Las Vegas was three hours behind them on the clock. Good thing the Judge was an early riser. Then suddenly she remembered that he would have no idea that she was on to his true whereabouts. With a sinking heart, she forced herself to play along with his little game. "How's your sister?"

"My sister?"

Rose hesitated at his confusion. The Judge wasn't doing much better than she was in their verbal chess match. "I thought that's why you're in California," she reminded him. "Visiting your sister."

"Oh, yes, thank you. I believe she is doing much better. Indeed, from what I've been told, she will be just fine." His sentence finished in a firm, clear voice.

Rose frowned. If he'd called merely to cover his tracks and plant an idea as to how long he would be away, the Judge wasn't doing a very good job of playing a convincing role. "Is she in the hospital or home with you?"

"I'm afraid I don't understand, my dear. My sister is in California."

"Yes, I know that."

"But I'm right next door," he replied. "My flight got in late yesterday afternoon."

The bottom of Rose's stomach yawned in disbelief and suddenly her legs felt wobbly. She sank down on the cane-backed chair next to the cherry buffet and stared at the faded carpet runner beneath her feet. The Judge had come home yesterday.

And last night Mike had been toned out to the scene of another arson fire.

"Cecilia Rose? Are you still there?"

"Y... yes." She swallowed hard and forced down the lump in her throat. "Yes, I'm here."

"I was hoping the two of us could meet today. Could you spare a few minutes for an old friend?"

The sound of her heartbeat pounded hot in her ears. It felt as if she'd been sucked up in some bizarre parallel universe that resembled her hometown... only it wasn't James Bay. None of these people were doing what they were supposed to do. Mike shouldn't still be investigating the Judge. And the Judge shouldn't be home. Why wasn't he in Las Vegas, recouping his gambling debts?

"What time did you want to meet?" she asked.

"That, my dear, is entirely up to you."

Her mind raced in furious debate. She didn't want to meet with the Judge, but it seemed she had no choice. "Mom has physical therapy with George at two this afternoon."

"I will be in my office, waiting."

Rose nodded wordlessly and hung up the phone. She gripped the edge of the cherry buffet, blew out a deep breath, and forced herself to stand.

The Judge was home again. And last night, Mike had worked another fire scene. A fire that had been officially labeled of suspicious origin.

The arsonist was back.

Rose gave the empty reception desk a furtive glance as she trailed the Judge into his office. "Where's Judith?"

"Who knows?" He sighed as he sank down in the black leather chair behind the mahogany desk. "Speaking confidentially, my dear, I agreed to let everyone think she retired. But the truth is, I let her go."

"You fired Judith?" Rose stared at him in disbelief.

The Judge nodded. He pinched his nose, his eyes weary. "She was robbing me blind."

"Judith, a thief?" The thought was incredulous. "That sounds so…"

"Ridiculous? Yes, I thought so, too," he agreed, "until the truth was revealed to me. I never should have allowed her control of the checkbook. She was very clever in the way she did it, I will grant you that. She took a little here, a little there. Over the years, it all added up. Once I discovered what she'd been doing, I had no choice but to let her go."

Rose warily eyed her old friend. Judith had worked for the Judge for years. She ran his law practice competently and efficiently, without the assistance of additional staff or the benefit of a law degree. Now, merely on his say-so, the Judge expected her to believe that his longtime legal assistant had turned out to be a thief?

Rose's thoughts returned to the investigative file she had discovered last night and the records contained in the report. The Judge was strapped for cash, and now—by his own admission—he'd fired his former assistant.

A regular, generous paycheck went a long way in purchasing an employee's loyalty. Could it be that Judith wasn't the thief he hoped to make her out to be? Perhaps her desk was empty because he'd run out of money, she'd learned the truth and quit.

Rose glanced around the plush office suite with fresh eyes. A thin layer of dust covered the bookshelves, computer, and the desk separating them. Did the Judge lack the funds to pay a cleaning staff as well?

Such disloyalty to her old friend. She tried to shake off the foggy doubt from her mind. Before today, he'd never given her cause to wonder if what he said was true. But suddenly everything her dear old friend said seemed suspect. She hated feeling like this—doubting the Judge, doubting herself. Damn that fireman for causing her all this grief.

"I didn't ask you here today to talk about Judith. I want to discuss our partnership." The Judge's sharp black eyes narrowed. "Have you thought about my offer?"

"I haven't had much time," she said, hedging her bets. "You weren't very specific."

A frown of dismay encompassed his well-worn face. A face she'd known and loved all her life. "I was hoping you would have reached some sort of decision while I was gone."

But where had he gone? Had he made a hasty trip to California to visit his ailing sister? Or had he gone to Las Vegas, the gaming capital of the free world?

"Perhaps we should discuss finances. If it is a question of money—"

"No, that's not it." She cut him off quickly. Until today, she'd felt only love and respect for this man. He was as dear to her as her own father had been, and she owed the Judge more than she could ever hope to repay. His wallet had been wide open upon her acceptance to law school, and he'd refused to accept any reimbursement. How could she sit here and listen to him discuss his financial situation and the mounting debts he faced? She owed him everything. Everything, and more.

"I would insist we be equal partners," he continued. "Fifty-fifty, that is only fair. I will continue to handle the real estate portion of the business and you would handle the rest. Please say yes, my dear. I'd like to be able to tell my clients that you are on board."

"Buying into a partnership." Rose shook her head, frantic for time. "It's a big decision."

"I know it can be difficult when you are first starting out. Naturally you wouldn't have a tremendous amount of cash flow—"

"Do we need to discuss this right now?" The words tumbled out, sharper than she intended, but she couldn't stop herself. After reading Mike's file last night, she'd developed a suspicion of what was going on. She couldn't sit there and listen as the Judge admitted his gambling debts and how low his addiction had brought him.

"My dear, what has you so upset?" His face wore a puzzled frown. "Is it your mother?"

Hot tears prickled behind her eyes, threatening to overspill. She wouldn't cry, she wouldn't! She dabbed at them with the tissue he offered.

"Cecilia Rose, please tell me what's wrong."

If he had been a client, there would have been no difficulty maintaining a cool, studied composure. But he wasn't a client. He was the Judge. And that familiar loving tone in his voice, the soft paternal look in his eyes, brought every defense crashing down.

"What's wrong? Everything is wrong! I wish I had never come home." She lifted red-rimmed eyes to meet his gaze. "It's like the whole town's gone mad. Mom and Lil are in a constant uproar over something, and Charles isn't helping with those horrible articles he keeps printing." Her face scrunched in a deep frown as she fanned herself. "Even the weather is screwed up this summer. It's so damn hot outside. What happened to those cool summer breezes we used to have? Why can't things be the way they used to be? That's all what I want... things the way they used to be."

The other part of her wish remained unspoken. *Please don't let Mike prove me wrong about you.* Until today, the Judge had been her hero. His behavior had been above reproach, his ethics admirable, his words filled with truth. Until today.

If she could have any wish in this world, she would ask that the last two days be magically erased. Was that too much to ask? That the doubts and fears crowding her heart ceased to exist? That she never had cause to doubt this man again?

"We can't always have everything we want, my dear. You know that."

"Don't you understand?" She shook her head. "Everything would have worked out if only you'd stayed away just a few more days."

"If I had stayed away?" The Judge's voice deepened in a perplexing tone. "What is that supposed to mean? My dear, you are not making sense."

"Have you seen this morning's paper?" She lifted her gaze in a sudden challenge. "There was another fire last night."

He shifted in his chair. "I wasn't aware of that. Was anyone hurt?"

No more hiding in the shadows. No matter how bad the outcome, better to have things out in the open than to keep evading the issue.

If you have to make a move, strike on point.

"Mike thinks you're the one setting these fires."

"He told you that?" The Judge's words sliced through the hum of the air conditioner.

"He didn't have to. I saw his file on you. I came across it by accident at the fire station last night." She bit her bottom lip until it hurt. She'd already said way too much but she couldn't stop. "He's been investigating you all along. He thinks you're the prime suspect."

The Judge exhaled sharply. "Does he know that you've seen his file?"

Wordlessly she shook her head, waiting for him to speak. But contrary to her expectation, there was no bellicose bluster, no belligerent indignation. The Judge merely raised his eyebrows.

"You don't seem surprised," she finally said.

"Frankly, my dear, I would be more shocked to learn that your fireman friend *didn't* consider me a suspect," he replied. "He is only doing his job, and a difficult one, at that. He is trying to keep the entire town at bay while attempting to solve a series of crimes. I would assume everyone to be suspect in his book. Unless, of course, he should catch the culprit red-handed."

A small smile appeared on the Judge's face. "Do not worry, my dear. Let us trust him to do the job he was appointed to do, to protect our community and bring the arsonist to bay."

She wanted to stomp her feet, to kick and scream like a ten-year-old. Despite his soothing words and the kind, patient smile on his face, the Judge was holding something back. Where was the anger? The resentment? The rousing call to action at hearing himself unjustly accused? An honest man would protest his innocence to anyone who would listen. So, why not the Judge? Or perhaps he thought they were all fools?

Or maybe she was the fool, for believing in him all these years.

"My dear, you tend to take matters too much to heart," he said softly. "You've enough at home to worry about with your mother. Things will work out. They always do. You need to trust."

Trust? She hid her hands in her lap so he wouldn't see them shaking. Trust? Who was he to talk? Her belief in him had been shaken to the core.

"I'm very confused." She tried to keep her voice from trembling. "I feel like I don't know who I can have faith in anymore."

"But of course you do, my dear." The Judge reached across the massive desk and covered her hand with his own. "Never doubt it for one moment. You can always trust me."

CHAPTER FIFTEEN

LETTERS TO THE EDITOR

The James Bay Journal:

Dear Editor: The *Journal* ought to be ashamed. The editorial you published trashing our fire department was unjust, untrue, and uncalled for. These fine brave men fighting the fires are doing their best to keep our town safe. The last thing they need while trying to do their jobs is criticism from people like you.

You owe our firemen an apology.

Sincerely, Lil Gillespie and Irene Gallagher

"Pick-up for Gallagher!" The deep male voice boomed through the crowd at Chuck's Tavern.

"Thanks for letting me share your table, Lucy."

"Bye, Rose. Tell your mom I hope she feels better soon."

"I'll do that." Rose leapt to her feet with a smile for the girl she'd been chatting with for the past twenty minutes. Lucy's grandmother had been the Gallagher's housekeeper for years, and Rose and Lucy Carter had grown up together. Nowadays, Lucy worked on the *Journal* staff. Poor Lucy, having Charles for a boss, Rose thought to herself as she headed for the cash register and takeout counter.

A tall solid body dressed in crisp uniform blues blocked her way. Rose watched in disbelief as a tan muscular arm seized her dinner order.

"Excuse me, but that's my dinner you grabbed."

Mike turned with a cool stare. "Correction, I believe the man called *my* name."

Rose fumed. They hadn't talked since he'd hung up on her, and she was in no mood to be humored. She'd already waited more than twenty minutes in the hot, crowded restaurant. Who did he think he was, snatching up her dinner like that?

"That's my to-go order, and you know it."

"Got any proof?"

"I ordered fish."

"What a coincidence. So did I." The smile on Mike's face was docile and sweet. "Funny, both of us having a taste for fish tonight."

"Not funny at all," she shot back. "Give me that sack." She lunged for the bag but he held it high, a tantalizing three inches out of her reach.

"Hey, you two, take your lover's quarrel outside. But first, somebody pay for that meal." Chuck drummed his fingers against the bar counter, eyeing the two of them from behind the cash register.

Rose reached for her purse, but it was too late. Mike's hand already contained a flash of green dollar bills.

"You are the most obnoxious, arrogant man I have ever met," she growled as she watched him hand over the money.

"Careful now, Rosie," Mike warned. He grabbed her arm and guided her through the noisy throng of customers waiting for tables. "You don't want to say something you'll later regret."

"Don't you dare call me *Rosie*." She yanked free from his touch as they faced each other outside the restaurant door.

"Hasn't this gone on long enough?" His voice dropped, coaxing. "Come on, Rose. I don't get it. Why are you so mad?"

She shifted on her feet and leveled him with a tight stare. She wasn't about to give him the satisfaction of a reply. Mike thought he was so smart? Let him figure things out on his own.

Or perhaps he couldn't stand the heat?

Rose pushed down the small telltale voice that wouldn't cease. Mike was only doing his job. Plus, her snooping through the file he kept on the Judge hadn't exactly been an honorable thing to do. But at the moment, she wasn't in the mood to be proved wrong by anyone. By Mike, or herself. Not when it came to the Judge.

"I'm not going to stand here arguing with you. My mother is waiting for me at home."

"Just tell me why you're mad."

She glared at him. "Are you going to give me my dinner order or not?"

"First tell me what I want to know," he insisted.

"Fine, I'll tell you, but—" Rose broke off in heated reply.

Don't say it, don't say something you'll only regret...

She pressed her lips together. She wouldn't say it, she wouldn't.

Mike held the sack tight.

"I can't believe you hung up on me." The words shot out before she could stop them. "That was pretty rude."

His face reddened. "You were pretty rude yourself, if I remember correctly."

"You called me bossy."

"Did I?" He shrugged. "Well, you said I was bullheaded and stubborn."

Throngs of tourists wound uneven paths around them as their sidewalk stare-down continued. "So, is this where we leave things?" he finally said. "Stuck in limbo, waiting to see who's going to break down and *I'm sorry* first?"

She was close enough to notice the dark circles etched beneath his eyes. Was he even sleeping at night? A deep sadness tugged at her heartstrings, and for one fleeting moment, the overwhelming urge to reach out and take his hand flooded through her. Yes, Mike was aggravating, vexing, and annoying—but he was also dedicated and brave. And from the weary look on his face, his vigilant efforts continued. How long could he expect to keep up this pace?

Mike exhaled in a sharp breath. "You are one stubborn lady."

The blood rushed to her throat and colored her cheeks. If she was stubborn, it was only because he'd given her reason. Perhaps he should be the one to do the apologizing. He was the one who'd hung up on her.

"You think I'm stubborn? Well, Mr. Gallagher, that is my prerogative. Enjoy your dinner. I hope you choke on a fish bone." With a curt nod, Rose whirled around and hopped on Irene's bicycle, then sped off empty-handed toward home.

First one morning, then another, dragging into hot afternoons, melting into nightfall. Rose gave the silent telephone a furtive glance every time she passed. The temperature in her heart matched the hot, heavy air hovering over James Bay. And still the phone didn't ring.

What was she waiting for? Mike wouldn't call. He wasn't about to apologize. He had no idea what she'd done, that she'd discovered his file on the Judge.

This mess between them was all her fault. She'd known all along he'd only been teasing about the fish, but she was the one, bicycle pedals wildly spinning, who'd fled from the truth. She was the one who should pick up that phone and say she was sorry.

If she didn't do it, there would be no *them*.

The only thing between them was her foolish, stubborn pride. She hated that part of herself, the cool, calculating attorney who'd stood outside Chuck's Tavern peering down her nose at Mike. Why did she always insist on having the upper hand? Her parents hadn't raised her to be like this. She was so quick on the uptake when it came to analyzing legal briefs, but slow to internalize those undeniable truths concerning human nature. Truths like compassion, understanding, forgiveness... and love. Yes, love. There was no use in trying to deny it any longer. These few weeks at home had changed her. She felt softer, more vulnerable and exposed than she ever had in her life. Including her life with Jeff. One man had made the difference.

Michael John Gallagher had made the difference.

Call him, her heart urged, yet a nagging thought kept her hand from reaching for the phone. Sooner or later, the fire marshal would have enough evidence to make an arrest. Was she prepared to hear her old friend the talk of grocery store gossip? Was she ready to hear his reputation bandied about town?

Was she ready to visit the Judge in jail?

No.

She had no doubt they would figure out some way to make things easy on him. His stature in the community, his reputation from years on the bench would be factored in. But when all was said and done, even that wouldn't be enough to save the Judge. Evidence would convict him. Credible evidence, provided by Mike, would seal the Judge's fate.

And she wasn't ready to hear Mike speak those incriminating words. No matter how much her heart might long for the welcome sound of that fireman's voice, she wasn't ready to hear him label the Judge an arsonist. Not yet.

If only things could have been different. If only Mike hadn't insisted on carrying on his investigation. If only they had met in another place and time. *If only.* Two little words, whispering a painful truth inside her heart as the phone stayed silent and the days passed on, first one, then another, and then another two.

"For heaven's sake, honey, come away from that window and sit down. You're making your mama nervous."

Rose glanced over her shoulder at her mother and Lil. "Mom, am I making you nervous?"

"Not in the least." Irene studied her playing cards, then flashed a wide smile and laid down her cards to show a winning hand. "Ha! Look at that, Lil. You owe me a quarter. Pay up."

Lil slapped her cards on the table. "Put it on my tab. I'm tired of playing cards, anyway." Her eyes glittered as she turned her attention back to Rose. "Are you watching for someone special? We haven't seen much of your fireman lately. Where's he been keeping himself?"

"I guess he must be busy." Rose swallowed down the guilt. She'd been raised not to tell a lie.

"Too busy to make time for you?" Lil snorted. "And you never told us what he had to say about our letter to the *Journal*."

"I'll ask next time I see him." Rose turned back toward the window, hiding the embarrassed flush from her mother and Lil. Those two were masters in the art of dissecting the spoken word. She wasn't about to provide them with new material for speculating about her relationship—or lack thereof—

with Mike... especially since she had spent the past few days wondering about that very thing herself.

The sun porch's angle off the living room provided a convenient view across the narrow expanse of shady lawn to the Judge's house. She'd been watching the house for some time now, but so far only Tommy Gilbert had provided any entertainment. He was on his knees weeding and thinning the flowerbeds bordering their sun porch. Across the lawn, the Judge's drapes were drawn and his car was in the driveway. His Honor was home earlier than usual on a weekday afternoon, but for how long? And what was he doing inside that house?

Snatches of conversation drifted from the card table behind her.

"Did you remember to tell Cecilia Rose who I saw at the grocery store?"

"No, I forgot. You tell her, Lil."

Would the gossip never cease? Rose pressed her head against the window as cards were shuffled and the snap of a new hand dealt.

"Well, it was Danny Spencer." Lil's voice held more than a hint of excitement. "He had quite a bit to say about that little letter your mother and I wrote to the *Journal*. According to Danny, we have the whole town talking."

Despite her resolve not to listen, her ears prickled at Lil's news. If the town was abuzz over Mike and the arson investigation, wait till the gossips discovered whom he'd pegged as the number one suspect. That would certainly serve as kindling to set the rumor mill ablaze.

She forced her attention away from the Judge's house. "What are people saying? Are they for or against him?"

"Depends on who's doing the talking. One minute they agree with you, and the next thing you know, they're talking to their neighbor on the town council, insisting Mike be fired."

"That's ridiculous." How could they fire Mike? It would take a vote, most likely from the council members. But why fire him? He'd only been doing his job.

A fleeting thought flashed to mind. She'd been upset with him these past few days for the very same reason. Mike was doing a good job. *Too* good a job.

A flash of movement under the open window caught her eye, but it was only Tommy, still in the dirt on his hands and knees, weeding Irene's prized flowerbeds. She glanced back at the Judge's house in time to see the front door open and His Honor himself appear with a watering can in hand. Rose held her breath as she watched him move about the spacious porch, drenching thirsty geraniums and petunias spilling out of wooden planters lining the porch railing.

"Looks like the Judge is out and about," she murmured.

"Maybe we should invite him over. Lean out the window and call to him, honey."

"He's busy." Rose kept a wary eye on him as he sauntered around the porch with the watering can.

"Poor man. With all he's been through, it's a wonder he's not over here every night demanding a stiff drink. I don't know how he manages to stay so calm after losing that money."

"What money?" Rose whirled away from the window. "What are you talking about, Lil?"

"Why, the money from the condo fire, of course." Her auburn curls bobbed in a tight nod. "He had lots of money tied up in those buildings. I'm sure it set him back a pretty penny. He must be hurting for money."

"How do you know that?" Rose's eyes narrowed. Until now, no specific sums had been mentioned. How much money had the Judge lost when those buildings went up in flames?

"Figure it out yourself, honey," Lil replied over a newly dealt hand of cards. "The proof is sitting right there in his driveway. This is the first year I can remember the Judge hasn't bought himself a brand-new car."

Rose's gaze drifted back through the window to the Judge's sleek sedan parked near his house. Last year's model.

"That's right, he didn't buy a new car. That is odd, come to think of it." Irene's voice carried a hint of wonder.

"It wouldn't surprise me to hear he was flat-out broke," Lil said. "Danny Spencer told me Dorothy Harvey said the Judge is only waiting for the insurance to pay out—"

"How do we know for sure he's having money problems?" Rose demanded. "Did he tell you he was broke?"

Lil's eyes widened as she sat back in her chair. "Why, honey, please don't be upset. I didn't mean to make you mad."

"People aren't talking to be mean," Irene added.

"You know how things are," Lil said. "People like to talk."

"Nosy busybodies, that's what they are," Rose said in a tight voice. Exactly why she'd left town in the first place. "Cruel and malicious. Why can't people mind their own business? Everyone is too concerned with what everybody else is up to." She felt her temper rising, along with her voice. "What's the matter with people in this town?"

Irene's eyebrows lifted. "You might want to remember who you're talking to, sweetheart. Lil and I are part of this town. And so are you."

"I don't live here anymore," Rose said and added under her breath, "thank God."

"People talk, we all talk," Lil added. "It doesn't mean a thing."

"We all have opinions, and we like to give them." The hint of a smile flitted across Irene's face. "Maybe it's a bad habit we pick up during those long dreary winters. There's not much left to do but talk when the snow banks outside are piled up six feet high."

"There's no snow today," Rose shot back. "But that hasn't stopped everyone in town from talking about the Judge."

"He'll make out fine," Lil said.

"He's been through hard spots before." Irene's voice was steady and calm. "And if it's true he's having money problems, then the Judge is in the right place. He's where he belongs, right here at home, surrounded by people who love him. Things might not be going well for him now, but you mark my words: The Judge will manage. Something will happen. Someone will help him out and he'll have some money in his pocket again. Why, I wouldn't be surprised if we see a new car in his driveway soon." She sat back in her chair with a thoughtful gaze at her leg, propped up on cushions. "I think this knee is finally on the mend. Maybe it's time I put the pain pills away." She glanced at Rose with a steady smile. "Why don't you fix us up a pitcher of martinis? It's nearly five o'clock and I've had enough iced tea this summer to float me all the way to China."

Rose grimaced at her mother's words. Perhaps they could all use a good stiff drink. Alcohol wouldn't heal, but it might dull the anger and frustration simmering inside her heart. For now, it seemed she and Mike were the only ones who knew about the Judge's gambling habits.

"Is the Judge still out there? Call him, honey, and tell him we're stirring up a pitcher."

Rose glanced out the window to an empty vista. Tommy Gilbert was gone, finished with his weeding. And the house next door sat silent and still, with the front porch—and driveway—empty.

"His car is gone." Rose swallowed down a frustrated sigh. All that time spent watching, for nothing.

"Funny, him not coming around more often," Irene said. "It's not like the Judge to miss martini time."

Where had he disappeared to? Rose stared through the window in empty disbelief. No matter how much she wished things were different, it wasn't meant to be. No amount of watching would produce that car or the Judge himself. The man was beyond her control.

The shrill ring of the telephone echoed from the hallway. "You take care of the phone, honey," Lil said, "and I'll take care of the martinis."

Rose tried to force out the chilling chant that pounded in her ears as she hurried down the hallway. The Judge had disappeared again. What should she do if the town's fire whistle blew an alarm in the next hour or so?

"Rose? Is that you?"

"Andy, hi." Her alarm from ratcheted from high to extreme. When was the last time she'd thought about Andy, let alone given his job offer serious consideration? He deserved better than this.

"The under deputy was in my office this afternoon. I'm getting pressure for a decision." Andy's voice was no-nonsense. "The clock is done ticking, Rose. It's yes or no time. We're buried with work and I need your answer."

A loud rapping on the kitchen door echoed in the hallway.

"Andy, there's someone at the door. Can I call you back?"

"You can't keep putting me off, Rose. This job offer won't be open forever."

The warning signal in his voice couldn't be ignored. "Soon, Andy. I'll call you back soon."

"No later than tomorrow." His words were firm. "I need an answer by tomorrow, Rose."

Andy's demand had her backed into a corner, and she knew it. "I promise I'll call in the morning."

Familiar male voices rumbled on the back porch as she hurried into the kitchen. Her hand shook as she undid the metal latch and pushed open the screen.

"Hey, Cecil, look who I bumped into out in your driveway," Tommy said.

Rose and Mike warily eyed each other. Was it merely her imagination wishing and wanting it to be true, or did his eyes really hold a sign of peace?

Tommy beamed at Mike. "Thanks again for helping me load the lawnmower."

"No problem."

"Here's the bill for today's work." Tommy handed Rose a wrinkled invoice. "See ya, Cecil. See ya, Mike." He clomped down the porch steps with a backward wave.

Relief flooded through her as she glanced back at Mike. Relief that he'd come to the house, followed by sudden guilt. She should have made the first move.

"I'm sorry—"

"I'm sorry—"

Their apologies collided mid-sentence. Rose started to speak again, but Mike held up a hand, cutting her off. "If you don't mind, I want to say something about the other night. I was wrong. That's one of the things I came over to tell you."

Hearing his apology left her humbled and ashamed. Even after everything he had discovered about the

Judge, Mike was still strong enough—and man enough—to admit when he was wrong.

But she'd been wrong as well, and she should have told him so. She should have done it days ago. Only her foolish pride and Midwestern stubbornness had stopped her. But did it matter? Mike was back, right here in front of her. No matter what, they would work things out.

"Turns out you were right after all," he continued. "There was a double order in that sack I grabbed."

"Excuse me?"

A small grin tugged at a corner of his mouth. "At the restaurant, remember? You accused me of taking your fish."

Rose felt her heart clutch as she realized Mike wasn't offering an apology about the Judge. They were talking about fish. Stupid greasy fish.

"That's why you came over? To tell me you're sorry about the fish?"

"Not exactly. I've got something else to say, too."

She caught her breath as Mike reached out and drew her into his arms. She felt his heart pound through his soft cotton shirt, matching the wild racing of her own. His strong, tanned arms wrapped around her, enfolding her in that heady masculine scent. Her mind cried out in warning, but her heart overruled it. She closed her eyes and leaned into him, anticipating the soft brush of his lips against her own.

"Open your eyes," he said. "Open your eyes and look at me."

His voice was a gentle command, and Rose willingly obeyed.

"I love you," he said softly. "That's the other thing I came over to tell you today. I love you, Rosie."

The unexpected admission snatched her breath away. Rose buried her head against his shoulder. What was the matter with her? He loved her! She should be shouting from the porch steps or leaping cartwheels in the driveway like she'd done when she was eight years old. Instead, his words left her numb, with a strange sudden urge to cry. She blinked back the beginning of tears.

Mike's arms cradled her close. "I've been thinking about you ever since the other night when you left me standing alone on the sidewalk. That's not what I want, Rosie. I don't want to be some guy alone on a sidewalk." His breath was warm and soft against her ear. "I want you walking right along beside me, holding my hand."

Gently he lifted her hand to his lips and softly brushed each finger with the whisper of a kiss. "I know it sounds crazy. We barely know each other. Probably both of us could come up with a dozen good reasons this will never work out. Lord knows I've come up with plenty of them myself these past couple days. But I've lived enough of my life to know what I want. And what I want is *you*, Rosie. We have got to work through this. We have to fix what went wrong between us. Life is too short not to go after the things that matter."

Mike was no stranger to tragedy. He knew how short and sweet life could be, how fleeting the moments could pass. Both of them had their share of bittersweet memories. Thoughts of her father—another Michael John Gallagher—beckoned for an instant, followed by a swift wild longing for Jeff, of all that had been lost to her and all that might have been.

Rose couldn't fight back the tears any longer.

"Don't cry, Rosie," he whispered. "Please don't cry. I didn't come here and say all this just to make you cry."

He smelled of sunshine and aftershave, and she had no desire to resist as Mike's lips sought her own. She surrendered to the heady touch of being in his arms, of the warmth of his skin next to hers, of the hot sudden rush of molten desire. Her lips felt bruised when he finally released her, but she gladly would have suffered the pain and kept on kissing him. Mike cradled her close, their bodies warm, blending together as one. Nestled in his arms, she was exactly where she wanted to be, and she intended to never let go. Mike was right. They had to work through this.

"You're not the only one who's been thinking," she murmured. "I'm sorry about everything, too. So much of this is my fault."

Mike pulled back and gazed at her with searching eyes. "I'm not looking for any quick answer. You decide what you want, Rosie. I'll be right here waiting."

She closed her eyes and prayed for courage to make the right decision. Being in his arms felt right and good. But staying in his arms meant staying home—something she'd turned her back on years ago.

Mike had unlocked a door inside her heart, one she'd believed had shut forever. If she left town again, certainly the door would close for good. What was she going to do? If she couldn't make it right with him, she could kiss away any hope she had for a life filled with love.

"Why do things have to be so complicated?" Her words caught, muffled against the thin fabric of his shirt.

"It's not complicated for me. I've got what I want, right here in my arms." His hold on her tightened. "I'm a selfish man, Rosie. I want things to stay like this. Can you blame me?"

Far too late for any hope of an easier, softer way through. Mike was in love with her.

And she was in love with him.

"I meant what I said. You're the one with the timeline, not me. Love counts for something, but in the end you've got to do what matters most in your heart. Trust what it tells you. It will never steer you wrong."

She could no longer bear to meet his gaze. His eyes held a glowing love light, illuminated by the radiance of honesty and truth. Meanwhile, her own heart felt heavy and burdened with guilt. How could she bear to say good-bye? Mike had told her once that he had no intention of leaving James Bay. She wouldn't use tears to hold him hostage. She had too much respect for both of them to stoop to that sort of tactic. Better that she was honest with him now than to give Mike some false hope that would lead to future disappointment. If the two of them hoped for any future together, there were serious issues that needed to be addressed.

The first and foremost of which involved her dear old friend the Judge.

"What you said a moment ago," she started slowly, "about your heart and how it never steers you wrong. Did you really mean that?"

"Every word."

Rose took a deep breath. She had never been a gambler, but there's a first time for everything. Gazing into his eyes, she took a chance and rolled the dice. "Give up your investigation of the Judge."

A frown wrinkled his forehead. "What do you mean?"

"I know you think he set all the fires. I saw your file the other night at the fire station."

"You went snooping through my papers?" Mike let go of her and took a step backward against the porch rail. His face flushed a dark shade of red. "You had no business looking at those files."

"It was an accident." Her voice lifted in self-defense. "You and Tommy were in a big rush to get to the fire, and everything ended up on the floor, remember? I stayed behind to clean up. That's when I saw the file."

"A confidential file," he pointed out in a tight voice.

"It's not like I went searching for it," she said. "And if you don't want people reading things they shouldn't, the report should have been under lock and key."

"I was in the fire station, remember? I didn't see any reason to keep things locked up tight." His voice rang with a cold edge of fury. "You had no right doing what you did. What's inside that file is none of your business."

"Who are you to talk about rights?" She tried to stop herself from screeching. "What gives you the right to scrutinize the Judge?"

"It's my job." Mike's jaw clenched. "How much of that file did you see?"

"Enough to know he's considered your number one suspect. But you're wrong, Mike. He didn't set those fires."

His jaw clenched. "I told you before that this is a working investigation. It's not open for discussion."

"You know how I feel about the Judge." Rose knew she was treading on dangerous ground. Her professors had warned against this in law school. Emotions had no place in legal theory or argument. But when it came to Mike, she had to take it personally. And if he was serious about their relationship, he'd take it personally, too. "I am not asking you to drop the investigation," she said. "Only your part in it. Let someone else be in charge."

"How do you suggest I do that? I'm the arson investigator for this community. I can't hand the job to somebody else."

"Why not?"

His face clouded with annoyance. "There is no one else."

"What about the chief? Let him take over."

He shook his head impatiently. "He can't handle this."

"I thought the chief was the head of the fire department." She felt her impatience rising, right along with her temper. Why was Mike stalling? This conversation wasn't getting them anywhere except deeper into an unwelcome quarrel.

"It's out of the question."

"What about a conflict of interest?"

"Sounds like you're the one with the conflict of interest." His gaze softened slightly. "Come on, Rose, think about it. What if the story were reversed? Would you drop your defense of a client because the plaintiff and I happened to be best friends?"

"You're twisting my words." Her grip on the porch railing tightened. "I don't understand why you're being so stubborn about this. You know how I feel about the Judge. I can't put my feelings for him aside... just like I can't put my feelings for you aside, either. So if the two of us are going to be involved, I think you should step away from the investigation. Ethically, it's the right thing to do."

"You're lecturing me about ethics? I'm sworn to uphold the law, plus keep things confidential. You being an attorney, I would have thought that was part of your job description, too."

She stomped her foot in frustration. "I've seen the file, remember? I know about the hits the Judge took with his real estate ventures. I've seen the reports detailing his trips to Las Vegas. I know about his gambling debts. But you're wrong, Mike. No matter what kind of money problems the Judge has, I'm telling you he is *not* to blame for the arson fires."

He didn't believe her. She could read it on his face, a smooth blank surface. His eyes glazed over in stony disbelief. Rose fought down an urge to pound her fists against his chest and beat the truth into him. "How close are the police to making an arrest?"

Mike shrugged. "I'm the investigating officer, not the judge or jury."

"You're accusing a good man without any wherewithal. That rates pretty low in my book."

"You snooping around in private papers rates pretty low in my book," he shot back. "You're an attorney. You ought to know better."

"I ought to know better all right." The words were out of her mouth before she could think. "I should have trusted my instincts. I should have known better than to get involved with you."

His eyes narrowed. "Careful, Rose. Don't say things you don't mean."

"You think I don't mean it?" She heard her voice shake and fear prickle at her neck as she spit out the words. What was she doing? If she didn't stop, everything between them would be dead.

"Look, I know you're upset." His voice was low and urgent. "You're hurt, and now you're trying to hurt me. But I don't want to hurt you, Rosie. You know how I feel about you. I thought you felt the same."

She forced her gaze away. How could she have thought that she actually loved this man? She barely knew him. She felt as if she was being ripped in two. Did Mike believe she would stand by in silence while he collected evidence that led to an arrest? How could she visit the Judge in prison, all the while knowing Mike was the one responsible for putting her friend behind bars?

She couldn't. And she wouldn't.

"I meant every word," she coolly replied. "I'm sorry I ever met you."

She saw the angry hurt flash across his face. Instantly she regretted every word that had passed between them.

Take it back, Rose. Take it back quick, before it's too late.

Mike's eyes narrowed. "Ditto."

Too late.

Stupid, a stupid woman, that's what she was. She never should have allowed herself to become emotionally involved with this man. For the first time in her life, she understood how it felt to want to slap someone across the face. It would give her such pleasure to hurt him the way he'd hurt her. For a few minutes, for days, for weeks, she had believed she'd fallen in love with him.

Mike blew out a heavy sigh. "Obviously there's nothing more left for us to say."

Rose watched in silence as he turned and took the steps two by two. Her fists clenched in tight little balls as he backed his truck out the driveway. Her heart hardened as he took off down the street without a backward glance.

It took another five minutes grappling with the truth for acceptance and reality to kick in. The door to her heart had slammed shut. All that was left was to throw away the key. There was no reason to watch any further. Mike was gone and he wasn't coming back.

Rose steeled her shoulders and turned to the house. Mike would survive and so would she. She didn't need a man in her life. She was smart. Smart enough to earn a law degree. Certainly she could figure things out on her own. Shame on her for being so foolish to have once thought things would work out differently. It was time she took charge of her life. That fireman had proved a smoldering pile of emotional trouble from the very start. It was much better to halt things now than to go on pining for something that would never be.

The kitchen screen caught behind her and echoed through the house with a resounding bang.

"Cecilia Rose? Sweetheart, where are you? We're waiting."

"Coming, Mom."

She gave the phone a thoughtful eye as she passed, remembering Andy's words of earlier and how he expected an answer by tomorrow. Mike's visit, with the angry words shouted between them, had proved fruitful. At least now she finally knew exactly where she stood.

She had a major decision to make in the next twenty-four hours. And with one less person to worry about in her life, the decision would be all that much easier.

CHAPTER SIXTEEN

REWARD INCREASED

The James Bay Journal

JAMES BAY—The Chamber of Commerce and Downtown Development Authority ("DDA") have banded together to post a $5,000 reward to anyone providing information ultimately leading to the capture and successful prosecution of the person(s) responsible for the series of arson fires. Anyone with information should contact the police department or Assistant Fire Chief Michael Gallagher.

"Thank you for agreeing to meet with me, my dear."

Rose shifted in the plush upholstered chair. The Judge's phone call earlier inviting her to his offices tonight had been providential. She'd planned on paying him a visit anyway. Rose soberly eyed the Judge across his massive mahogany desk. The damning paperwork contained in Mike's file weighed heavy on her heart. The roster of back taxes left unpaid, the defaulted bank loans, the gambling markers.

Someday, possibly in the very near future, Mike would have enough evidence to arrest this man she had loved all her life. The Judge would be charged with crimes against their community. Turning her back on him now, when he needed her most, went against everything she believed, everything she had been taught. Her mind was made up. She would stand by his side, provide a legal defense to see him through his troubles… and then she would leave. There was nothing left for her in this town.

Mike had seen to that last night.

What a waste of time, indulging herself in such silly daydreams by imagining the two of them could make a life together. How could she have been so foolish? She'd allowed him to tangle her up in an emotional web that could have proved her undoing. For hours, days, weeks, Mike had had her under his spell. Until last night, anything and everything had seemed possible.

Now it was gone. Disappeared in a puff of smoke.

"I worked on this today. I hope you will find it agreeable." The Judge slid a neatly clipped sheaf of papers across the desk.

The heading marched across the page in capital letters. Her spirits sank as she flipped through the partnership agreement tying her fortunes to his. How could she sign this legal document? She didn't dare, especially now that she had seen Mike's file. What was she supposed to do? The Judge seemed oblivious to her dilemma, which offered no easy out. Either she signed or admitted the reason she couldn't… or wouldn't.

Damn Mike for the incriminating evidence he held against her old friend. Damn him for putting her in this position.

"I think you'll find the paperwork in order." The Judge settled back in his chair and eyed her with an affectionate gaze. "As you can see, my initial offer is still good. There is no need for you to make a monetary contribution. Your shares of the partnership—equal shares, my dear—have already been allocated. I have them here, already assigned, with your name on them." He tapped a closed folder to one side of the desk.

"You've certainly made it difficult for me to say no."

"I don't expect you to turn it down," he said with a confident smile. "I need your signature on those papers, Cecilia Rose. I will do whatever is necessary to ensure that happens."

Why was it so important she sign the partnership agreement? Why was he offering her an equal partnership in his firm? All she could provide was some experience and her law degree. A degree obtained with financial assistance courtesy of the Judge.

"You hesitate, my dear. I had hoped this would be an easy decision. Surely you don't intend to disappoint me?"

Rose felt the telltale blush creeping up her cheeks. She kept her eyes trained on the paperwork. How could she look him in the eye and admit she was loath to sign this document—any document—that tied her future to his? How could she confess what she'd seen in Mike's files? All the telltale evidence of the Judge's mounting debts. His lies, his deceit. How he'd played them all for fools.

How could she sit here in this chair and pretend to listen as her old friend rambled on, when all she wanted was the answer to one burning question.

How many fires have you set?

"Something obviously is troubling you, my dear. I had hoped to make the offer generous enough to set aside any worries you might have, but I see that is not the case." He rose from his chair. "Perhaps if I show you something, it will help convince you to think otherwise."

"What is it?" Rose eyed him warily. Did he mean to provide a written confession?

"A small memento, something I had planned to give you and Jeff long ago. I think perhaps you and I might put it to good use instead." His fingers closed around the car keys on his desk.

"You're leaving?"

"I won't be long. What I want is at home. Wait here in my office."

The Judge leaving would buy her what she needed... precious time alone. Rose eyed his computer, humming softly on the ornate credenza behind the massive desk. What had he been working on when she had showed up tonight? Had he been drafting a simple warranty deed for some real estate deal? Or had he been on the Internet, perusing the Vegas score sheets, checking the latest gaming statistics before he placed another bet?

Two or three quick clicks of the mouse and the information on the monitor behind him would be displayed for view. Would it be so wrong? She wouldn't be snooping, searching for incriminating evidence. His computer could very well contain valuable information that could be used to exonerate him.

But it could also contain files that led to his guilt. She had to be prepared if she wanted to discover the truth.

I have to know, one way or the other.

"Would you mind if I checked my email while you are gone?"

"Certainly you may. What's mine is yours, my dear." The Judge waved her into his seat and started for the door.

Rose settled in his chair, still warm from his considerable bulk.

"You look good in this office, my dear. Even that chair seems to suit you." The Judge cast her an affectionate smile from his stance in the doorway. "You know, that chair has seen me through many a long night studying case law. Sign our partnership agreement and I promise it's yours. A little gift from me to you saying *Welcome to the firm*. We'll put it in your new office next door to mine."

Rose fought down a wave of rolling nausea as he disappeared through the doorway. How low could she sink, actually contemplating snooping through his private files? Yet she couldn't shake the thought of how important it was to him that he obtain her signature on the partnership papers. Why was it so urgent? She stroked the chair's soft black leather. The Judge thought it so important, he was even willing to part with his beloved chair.

Enough! She didn't want to think about it anymore. Rose spun around and faced the computer. Her fingers flew over the keyboard, deft strokes that opened her firm's secure website and her own email account to life. Her in-box was nearly as empty as the last time she had checked her incoming mail. Clients had been forewarned for weeks prior to her absence, and her Out-of-Office Assistant was on. Quickly she scanned the few new messages.

A recent post from her secretary, Debbie, pasted a wistful smile on her face. Debbie and her husband had been trying for years to have a baby, and the news of an unexpected and most welcome pregnancy was a sweet answer to prayers. Rose hit reply and fired off a congratulatory email. At least something was going right in someone's life.

She swallowed down a nagging thought as she checked her remaining email. Both she and Debbie were nearly thirty, and Debbie hadn't had an easy time in her efforts to conceive. Precious years had been squandered on the fertility battlefield, but Debbie had finally won the war. The desire to cradle an infant close was one particular battle Rose had never aimed to wage. But being home again had opened her up in all sorts of ways she had never expected. A man in uniform labored on the front line, part of the fire brigade.

Twenty-four hours had passed since her frustrating encounter with Mike. Her heart still felt bruised and shaken as she remembered how he had stomped down the porch steps without a last good-bye. Sitting here in these offices only added to her misery. She and Mike had fought over the good name and character of the man in whose chair she sat tonight.

Rose straightened up. Better to focus on client emails and the firm bulletin board. At least those things could be controlled with a quick reply or a smart tap of the delete key.

Fireman Mike wouldn't be so easy to wipe off the monitor of her heart.

She scrolled through the emails trailing down the screen. Admonishments from the firm to partners and associates alike. Bill more time, push delinquent clients for payment, refuse work from those consistently overdue.

Delete, delete, delete. The action produced a small zing of satisfaction. She'd been away from the office so long, she'd nearly forgotten the pleasure that came from controlling her own little section of cyberspace. Her idea of normal had been altered this past month. Home brought its own rewards. No more rising before the dawn, roused to her feet by the shrill beep of an electronic alarm. The hot hazy days melted one into another with a dress code labeled casual shorts and t-shirts. Easy comfort versus a tailored three-piece suit.

Her world away from home was dictated solely by clients. It was a world of corporate meetings and cool rational heads, overriding impracticality and matters of the heart. The men and women in her firm were hardworking people and committed to their clients, but one motivating factor spoke the loudest truth.

Money moved it all.

She had loved working for the firm once upon a time, but five years spent with time sheets, accounts receivable reports and collection notices had muddled things in her mind. Billing enough hours would eventually render a partnership and commandeer a plush office space removed from distractions and annoyances, including people. But was it distance that she truly craved? Being home again had only served to remind her of how city life changes things. How it changes people.

Everyone was so busy, bent on achieving their personal goals. People at her firm rarely deigned to take the time to offer a smile or chat in the carpeted hallways. But what did working so hard gain you in the long run? Did it really matter how much money you made? Or what floor of the building your office was on? What type of car you drove?

A quick flush rose to her cheeks as she remembered the flashy sports car parked in her mother's garage. It had been hers after three years of long, grueling hours spent sweating at her desk. Three years of consistently high billings for the firm.

But when all was said and done, it was the firm's name, not her own, embossed on the vehicle's certificate of title. She didn't even own her car.

Rose shivered in the cool air-conditioned comfort of the Judge's office. If she refused his offer and stayed with the firm, would that be her fate? Never to own her own car? Always striving for the latest model? Doomed to end her days as one of those prancing practitioners expert at shrugging off others' selfish and boorish behaviors while blissfully ignorant of her own?

Had she forgotten the simple rules involved in the art of human kindness? It truly was an art form, one seldom practiced by members of her profession. Perhaps it was drilled out of them in law school. Practicality in all things. Close one file, open another. Keep your eye focused on the end result. Kindness doesn't count toward billable hours.

Did she really want to go back to working for the firm? Rose's hopes dimmed in the bright glare from the computer monitor. Was that what she wanted out of life?

A geographic cure offered another way out. But working with Andy in Washington D.C. would force other issues to the table. Andy was a seasoned attorney, dedicated and driven. The two of them had been an efficient moneymaker for the firm, due to Andy's brilliance and her own ability to work late most nights. Unless she was firm with him up front about her feelings, no doubt many late nights would again be involved.

Late nights when Andy would expect her to say yes.

The heavy slam of a door downstairs and the sound of raised voices sent her bolt upright in the chair. The Judge was back. Time was up. Rose stared at the partnership papers. He expected to see her signature on the dotted line. And Andy waited in Washington. She owed him a phone call and an answer before the day was through.

Resolutely she locked out thoughts of a fireman. She wouldn't think of Mike any longer. He'd made his choice. He no longer factored into if she should stay or go. Heavy footsteps sounded on the stairs and she heard the Judge shout out her name.

The time had come for a decision. Once there was a time when she'd known exactly what she wanted. Could she say the same today?

The Judge staggered through the office door, his face stained red, his black eyes bulging in panic. "We have to get out. That fool has gone and set the building on fire."

"Fire?" Rose jumped to her feet. "What are you talking about?"

The Judge halted inside the doorway and a soft puzzled look crossed his face. He stood there a moment, then gave a short gasp, yanking at his tie as he struggled for breath.

"Are you all right?" The words were automatic, accompanied by a sharp pang of fear as she rushed around the desk. Obviously he wasn't all right. His face was ashen gray. Something was very wrong.

He stumbled toward her but made it only a few steps.

"Judge!" Rose strained to catch him as he collapsed and sank to his knees.

He clutched at his chest. "I... I can't... breathe..."

A long-buried memory filtered to mind of a snowy winter morning and a steaming cup of coffee in her father's favorite mug. Cold black coffee that remained in his cup, taunting them as they returned home from the hospital later that day accompanied only by their grief.

The Judge was having a heart attack. Every second counted if he was to live. Rose struggled against his heavy weight to reach the phone.

"Get out," he told her. "Get out... now." His eyes closed as his body gave way and he crumpled to the floor.

"Judge!" Rose dropped to her knees and cradled him close, frantically searching for a pulse. It was thready and weak. He needed help, fast. She fought down a sudden surge of panic. Her hand trembled in another desperate attempt for the phone.

She smelled it before she saw it. It was an insidious scent, subtle yet pungent and enough to tear her gaze from the phone. Rose's eyes widened as she caught her first glimpse of the smoke climbing the walls and creeping across the ceiling.

The building was on fire!

Every single hair on the back of her neck stood up straight as she felt sheer terror rising inside her. *Get a grip, Rose.* But how? She was trapped, weighed down by emotions and fear, as well as the Judge's motionless body. He was too heavy and there simply was no way she could move him by herself. But she wasn't about to leave him behind, no matter what he might have done.

In the midst of swirling insanity, words she'd heard him speak merely moments earlier raced to mind.

Had the Judge himself set the blaze, then returned upstairs to warn her?

"Cecil?" A halting voice sounded in the midst of catastrophe. "Cecil, where are you?"

"Tommy! In here!" *Thank God.* Relief flooded through her at the welcome sound of her friend's voice. She hugged the Judge closer, sheltering him as best she could from the billowing gray smoke filling the room.

Tommy Gilbert staggered through the doorway, coughing and hacking. His eyes were wide with fear. "The basement is on fire. I can't put it out."

"We have to call 911." Rose sputtered against the acrid smoke as it intensified.

Tommy snatched the phone and punched in the emergency numbers, only to throw it to the floor. "It's no use. The phone is dead. The lines in the basement must have burned out."

"Help me, Tommy. I think the Judge has had a heart attack."

"Grab his shoulder. We'll get him out of here."

There was no time for gentleness. Smoke was pouring through the luxurious office. Rose shoved the Judge out of her lap and struggled to her knees. She grabbed one side of his coat collar with both hands. Tommy commandeered a position at the other side. The garage rooftop deck beckoned, a doorway to fresh air and freedom. They tugged and pulled, fear driving their efforts. Somehow the two of them managed to drag the Judge's motionless body across the threshold and onto the rooftop deck.

Rose sank down beside him. Frantically her fingertips searched for a pulse. For one heart-wrenching moment she had the sudden fear that they'd been too late, that her old friend was dead. Finally she felt his pulse. The Judge was still alive. She breathed in deep gulps of fresh clean air rolling in off the lake and hugged herself tight to stop the trembling. They were out of the building and safe for the moment.

"I'm going for help." Tommy rose from his knees. Tears stained his soot-smeared face, and his shirt was torn, singed black from fighting the basement blaze. "I can make it back down the steps to outside."

"No, Tommy, you can't." Rose struggled to a stand. "Don't go back in there. It's too dangerous."

He scurried toward the door through which they'd just come.

Rose started after him. "Tommy, don't be stupid. Come back here."

"You don't understand," he cried from the doorway. "I didn't start that fire to hurt nobody. He needed the money. I was only trying to help him, just like your mom said somebody should do."

Smoke rolled out in a menacing cloud as he yanked open the door.

"Tommy, are you insane? Get away from there!" It felt like she was screaming. He wasn't making sense. Nothing tonight made sense.

"I'm sorry, Cecil. I never mean to hurt anybody... not you, not the Judge."

Rose lunged for him, but he proved too quick. "Tommy, no!" Her scream echoed through the night as he disappeared through the open door.

She darted inside the office after him, fighting for every breath, choking in a blinding swirl of thick, stinking fog. The smoke was everywhere, filling each crevice of the once luxurious office space. No flames, but the smoke proved more terrifying than a raging fire.

The memory of another smoke-filled room on a hot summer night brought her heart to her throat. Nothing had existed in the smelly swirl of the smoke house, not even a sense of time or space. She had been alone that night, surrounded by smoke.

But she wasn't alone tonight. She heard Tommy hacking and coughing as he crashed his way through the Judge's office. Rose fought back her fears, flung an arm across her face to shield her eyes and nose from the bitter stench as thoughts of Tommy speared her on. Blindly she lashed out with one free hand, just as her father and the fireman had done that night so long ago. They had reached out for her and she would reach out for Tommy. He was somewhere in this room, hopefully still within her reach. Each gasp for breath singed her lungs, every instinct pressed her to turn back, but she forced herself forward. Where was he? She heard nothing human, only crackling and popping.

The sound of wood on fire.

How did firemen willingly face this monster of fire and smoke? How could Mike do this?

What would Mike do if he were here with her?

The sudden thought proved strangely comforting, even as she gagged and retched against the stinking fumes. He would never back down if he was the one looking for Tommy. And if Mike could do it, so could she. Rose stumbled forward another few steps.

"Tommy, where are you?" She tripped over a chair and cracked her knee against a solid piece of wood. The Judge's desk. She gasped from the pain and tried not to panic. She was blind, her vision limited to the murky brown smoke enveloping her. Even the sight of her own hand was lost to her in the smelly soot. She grabbed at empty space, then staggered another step, stopping, coughing, choking, spitting up soot. "Tommy! Answer me!" The smoke grew worse with each step she took. Every instinct urged her to retreat. The smoke and heat were too intense.

"Tommy, answer me! I'm not leaving without you."

Her voice gave out, replaced by a hacking cough. The acrid stench of smoke filled every pore of her body. Rose ventured one last step and reached out wildly, grabbing blind. Her hand hit something hard, firm and wooden.

She lashed out, pawing at the thing. Her hands searched high and low, running up and down smooth wooden grooves.

The hallway door. She'd finally reached the doorway, only to find it empty.

Rose pounded her fist against the wooden frame as hot tears streamed down her face, mingling with dirty soot. It was the end. She didn't dare venture any further, not if she had any hope of coming out alive.

Seconds later, a loud crash and an agonizing scream rose from the building, followed by a roar of flames and a menacing cloud of embers and sparks rolling through the hallway directly toward Rose.

Sheer terror kept her rooted in the doorway as she suddenly realized that she could die in here. No one knew she was in the building, except for Tommy and the Judge.

But the Judge was unconscious on the rooftop deck. And Tommy was...

Her resolve fluttered as she remembered the screams she'd heard as the front hallway steps collapsed, taking Tommy down with them. She had to make it back to the door. There was no other way out. She had to be strong. She had to do this. She had to get out.

But how?

Get low, a tiny voice whispered in her heart. Rose struggled to remember exactly what Mike had said. *Get down on your knees and crawl through the smoke.*

She sank to her knees and hit the floor, crying out in terror as her shoulder collided with a bookcase as she started to crawl. She kept going. She didn't dare stop. Frantically she felt her way around the edges of the furniture, groping for the way out. The smoke was blinding. She couldn't see a thing.

Crawl. Mike was right there with her, guiding her forward. *Crawl through the smoke. Let your heart lead you.*

Somehow she kept going, feeling her way around the edges of the room. And just as she feared her lungs would burst with one more breath of the sooty, smoky haze, Rose felt metal under her fingertips. She'd found the door's threshold and the freedom of fresh air.

In the distance, the town's fire whistle began to wail.

Rose held the Judge close as she waited the few interminable moments for the fire department to arrive. Cradling the old man in her arms brought a sense of comfort to a world that had gone up in flames before her very eyes. The heavy rumble of fire trucks from below announced their arrival on the scene. Shouts of men rushed up from the street as they labored to stretch the heavy fire hoses and hook up water lines. The fire department would save the day and maybe the building.

But there would be no saving the Judge.

Rose wasn't a doctor, but she knew her old friend was already gone. She hugged him tightly against her as a heavy aluminum ladder smacked against the rooftop's edge and a hoarse voice called out. She couldn't answer. Rose cradled the Judge even closer. She would sit with him until they forced her to give him up. Praying for his soul was all she could do. It was too late for anything else.

A thick gloved hand, then two, were steady on the ladder. Finally the fireman was on the rooftop. No suit of shining armor, but a heavy yellow fire coat and buffeted white helmet, air pack strapped to his back. He tore off the breathing mask and helmet and crouched down beside her. "Rosie?"

Only when she spied those turquoise-blue eyes did Rose finally crumple and the salty tears start to fall. Mike's arms wrapped around her and the Judge, holding them close. "Please, you've got to help him," she whispered.

"The paramedics are on their way. They'll help the Judge."

She clutched the front of his fire coat. "No, you don't understand. I'm talking about Tommy."

His jaw clenched. "Tommy Gilbert?"

"He's still in the building. I think… I think the front stairs gave way beneath him." The tears came faster as her thoughts turned to Tommy and the valiant stand he'd made against the raging fire. He had rushed back inside the building in spite of the inferno facing him, intent only on reaching the outside door, bringing help to her and the Judge.

Mike grabbed the radio from his belt and relayed an alert to the firemen below, starting the search for Tommy Gilbert. Rose shook her head and gave him a sad stare as he hit the squawk button, ending the page. She stroked the Judge's forehead.

"He's gone."

"Let me take him." Mike slid an arm under the lifeless body. "We have to get him down off the roof."

"Be careful with him," Rose whispered as she surrendered her hold. Paramedics joined them on the roof. She stood aside and watched as they strapped the Judge's body to a compact stretcher. He had been a large man in life, and death had not diminished him. His color was ashen, his eyes closed, but his face was quiet, filled with peace. Rose had no doubt his soul had already departed this world for another. An even better world than the tiny universe of his beloved James Bay.

Her turn came next. Rose grasped the ladder and began the long downward climb. She clung to each rung with trembling hands, but Mike was right beneath her, his body shielding her own from any slip or fall. *Baby steps, one step at a time...* she chanted the mantra in her mind as they inched down the ladder. Finally her foot reached the bottom rung. She put one foot, then the other, on the ground and stepped into the refuge of Mike's arms.

He led her away from prying eyes and the crowd of curious bystanders held back by plastic yellow barrier tape to the sheltering safety of a fire truck. Someone wrapped a blanket around her shoulders. Another fireman pulled Mike away to talk, a short stubby man with a white helmet like Mike's own. Chief Ivan Thompson, she noted as she pulled the blanket closer. Wordlessly she watched as an ambulance, with lights flashing and sirens wailing, departed with the Judge. Then Mike was back at her side. She leaned into him, taking no heed of his dirty fire coat or the smell of smoke he wore. The feel of his arms wrapped around her was all she wanted. It was a safe, secure feeling.

Like coming home.

"Rosie, sweetheart, I've got some bad news."

She squeezed her eyes shut and fingered away a few tears. She knew what was coming. She'd wanted to ask since they'd come down off the roof, but she hadn't been able to summon the courage to hear Mike confirm what she already knew. Finally, with a deep breath, she forced herself to meet his gaze. "Tommy's dead."

He nodded, his eyes flashing quiet sympathy. "They found his body in the basement."

Less than an hour ago she'd been sitting in the Judge's sleek leather chair. Now Tommy's lifeless body lay shattered and burned in the bottom of the building, and the Judge was headed for the hospital in an ambulance that—no matter how fast it went—would never succeed in bringing her dear old friend back to life.

"They've knocked down the fire. They'll bring his body out soon."

"Poor Tommy." She pressed her fingertips against her temples, as if she could squeeze the image from her mind. Her ears still rang with the sound of Tommy's scream as the staircase gave way.

"What happened up there, Rosie? Can you tell me?"

"He went back inside to try and get help. He was safe on the roof, but he ran back inside. Then, I think ... I think the front stairs collapsed beneath him." Rose's voice shook, barely above a whisper. "He tried to save us. Tommy tried to save the Judge and me."

"And he did that. You got out of the building alive."

"There's something else." She clutched at his forearm. "He said... before he ran back in the building, Tommy said..."

She halted, caught up in a flash fire of memory. The look of guilt mingled with terror on Tommy Gilbert's face before he bolted through the rooftop door was seared forever in her mind.

"What did he say?"

"Oh, Mike, he never meant to hurt anyone. He said he did it to help the Judge."

His eyes narrowed, two slits of brilliant blue mirrored in a dirty face. "Tommy told you he set the fire?"

Rose nodded. "But he didn't mean to hurt anyone, I know he didn't. And if Tommy hadn't shown up to help, I'd still be up there in that office with the Judge. Neither of us would have made it out alive." She shivered in the hot night air as she imagined that deadly scenario.

"Did he say anything else?"

The last half hour was a smelly, swirling haze of smoky memories, but some things she would never forget. "He said something about trying to help out the Judge... and something about my mother." She shook her head. "It sounded as if Tommy knew the Judge was having money problems. But how could he have known, Mike? How did Tommy know the Judge was deep in debt?"

"Maybe he overheard you talking. Who knows? Don't forget, you discovered the same thing yourself."

"Do you think—" Rose interrupted herself and concentrated hard. So much to take in. So much lost. "Is it possible Tommy was only trying to help the Judge? Do you think he believed that by setting the fire, the Judge would collect insurance money?"

Mike nodded. "We found the gasoline can in the basement."

"So Tommy was..." She broke off, barely able to bring herself to believe the thought suddenly sparking to mind. How could she speak such a thing aloud? Tommy was no longer alive and able to prove his innocence.

"Tommy's been our main suspect for some time," Mike quietly said.

"But you were investigating the Judge. I saw the file." She stared blankly at Mike, ignoring the implication behind his words. "I saw your file."

"I have lots of files. Various people were under investigation... including Charles Kendall."

"But I thought..." She shook her head.

Mike's arm tightened around her. "What?"

"You and I saw the Judge headed downtown that night, remember? And after Charles's car burned, you found one of the Judge's hand-rolled cigars at the scene. I thought the Judge had…"

"Torched Charles's car?" Mike finished for her. "I wondered about that myself. And I questioned Charles about those cigars. Turns out he filched two of them from His Honor's coat pocket. Charles dropped the cigar stub when he parked his car that night. But he wasn't the arsonist, Rosie." His voice quieted. "Neither was the Judge."

"So it was Tommy all along," she said. "Tommy was the one setting all the fires."

"Yes."

"If only you had told me." A wistful look settled on her face as she fingered away a few tears. "I thought you had enough evidence to arrest the Judge. If only you had told me the truth, we never would have had that terrible fight…"

Her voice trailed off as she reflected on the night they had fought and all the harsh, angry words flung out between them. Rose cringed, remembering all the things she had said.

Mike's arms tightened around her. "I told you once before that I couldn't talk about the investigation. I wanted to tell you, Rosie, but I couldn't."

"Cecilia Rose?" A familiar voice cried out from the crowd.

Rose glanced up and saw Lil, straining against the edges of the growing group of onlookers.

"I'm over here, Lil."

A fireman standing guard at the edge of the crowd held Lil back with a warning hand. He looked toward

Mike, who nodded his approval. Lil broke from the fireman's hold and scooted beneath the yellow emergency tape stringing the scene. Her eyes were frantic as she reached Rose's side and caught her in an anxious embrace.

"Thank God you're all right. Your mama has been beside herself ever since we heard about the fire. She knew you were down here with the Judge."

"Lil, there's something I need to tell you. " Rose drew back from the older woman's arms and grasped her forearms, steeling herself to deliver the news. "I'm afraid that the Judge…"

Lil's green eyes glittered sharply, then softened in sudden understanding. "Oh, honey, no. Not Harvey."

Rose bit her lip and nodded. Her own tears started anew as Lil wept in her arms.

Mike returned from a huddled conference with the medical personnel from the second ambulance still standing by. "Rosie? The paramedics want to take a look at you."

"There's no need for that. I'm fine." She took a deep breath to settle herself.

"Sure you're all right?"

The few remaining tears on her face disappeared with a quick swipe of her hand. "I don't need medical attention. I need to go home."

"Thank you for taking care of our girl." Lil's eyes glistened as she grabbed Mike's hand. "She's mighty precious to her mother and me."

"She's mighty precious to me, too," he said with a tender smile for Rose.

"Come on, honey," Lil said. "Your mama's waiting. Let's get you home."

Mike escorted them through the crowd to a police cruiser at the edge of the building. "Officer, these ladies need a ride."

"But what about my car? It's here downtown." Lil worried her hands in a knot as the young policeman opened the back passenger door and stepped aside.

"We'll get the car later," Rose replied. In the distance she spied her mother's bicycle, still chained to the streetlamp where she'd left it hours earlier.

Another lifetime.

"I'll drive your car home myself," Mike promised.

Without a word, Lil opened her purse, fished out her keys, and handed them over to Mike. "You'll find it over at the *Journal* office in their driveway," she said as she settled herself in the cruiser. "You can't miss it. It's parked in Charles Kendall's private parking space."

It was time to leave, but she didn't want to let go. Rose bit her lip hard to take away the pain of leaving him behind. She gripped his hands. "Thank you for everything. Thank you."

"Go get some rest," he urged. "We'll talk later."

Sympathy and sadness were there in Mike's eyes, as well as a promise. It was only seeing that promise of a hope for tomorrow that finally gave her the courage to let go of his hands and climb into the waiting car.

CHAPTER SEVENTEEN

OBITUARY: THE HONORABLE HARVEY JAMES

The James Bay Journal

The Honorable Harvey James, longtime Circuit Court Judge for the County of James Bay, passed away last evening of cardiac arrest.

The Judge was appointed to fill a Circuit Court vacancy and remained on the bench for nearly ten years. Following his retirement from the public sector, he made a distinguished career for himself specializing in the areas of business and real estate law.

The Judge, as he was affectionately called by all who knew him, was a native son of James Bay and the great grandson of its founding father, Horace Harvey James. His passing marks the end of an era for the James family's presence in our community. The Judge was predeceased by his beloved wife Mary and their son, Jeffrey. He is survived by his sister, Helen Murray, of Los Angeles, California.

Funeral arrangements are pending.

The morning of the Judge's funeral dawned hot, the temperature hovering at eighty with a promise of hitting ninety before the day was through. Rose held off dressing for the midmorning service as long as possible. The idea of donning a black dress and attending the Judge's funeral was not the ending she'd had in mind.

The past three days had been a blur. The phone never stopped ringing as friends and neighbors called to verify the news, and offer sympathy and their support. Rose took another phone call, too. Andy Sabatini had heard the news of the tragic events and extended his deadline another few days. Rose shrugged and returned to the somber business at hand. Making a final decision—a decision about anything—would simply have to wait. The only thing she cared about was getting through the next few days.

Wake services for both Tommy and the Judge were held the evening before their funerals. Rose stood soberly beside her mother, Lil, and the Judge's sister, Helen. She felt wooden and empty as the line of mourners moved past them, murmuring their condolences. Life would go on but it would never be the same. The two separate viewing rooms and the caskets laid out for display were grim reminders. But she was determined not to cry. No amount of tears, nothing anyone could say or do would bring the Judge and Tommy Gilbert back to life.

Even though Mike was on duty, he somehow managed to slip out for a brief sympathy call. Hand in hand they stood before the Judge's flower-draped mahogany casket and offered a silent prayer.

The second viewing room behind the front parlor held fewer flowers and even fewer people. Tommy Gilbert's graduation picture rested on top of the closed wooden casket. Rose and Mike took seats in the front row and spent a few moments in quiet meditation. She gave his hand a grateful squeeze as they finally left the room. No matter what type of spin the town gossips put on things, Mike knew the truth. He'd been up there on the roof with her that night. It seemed fitting and right that the two of them should be together to pay their respects and say their final good-byes.

Next morning, the funeral bells tolled. The church filled as friends and neighbors, former clients, plus a good portion of the legal community, crowded together in the polished wooden pews to mourn the Judge. Rose escorted her mother and Lil down the long center aisle toward seats reserved for them in the family's front pew. Irene's metal walker slowed their progress long enough for Rose to catch a familiar scent of spicy aftershave wafting from a pew. She chanced a quick glance sideways and spied gold braid on a smart black dress uniform. Mike sat at the end of the row of uniformed personnel. They had time to exchange only the briefest of smiles as she passed by his pew.

Irene and Lil sobbed through the service, but Rose found no need for tears. She'd faced the worst three days ago, and somewhere in a pew close behind sat a man who knew the truth. A man who held her heart. And even though there hadn't been a chance yet for the two of them to talk, knowing Mike was in the church brought a sense of peace and comfort. She could get through anything, even this sorrowful liturgy, knowing he was there. Rose stood between her mother and Lil, clutching their hands tight as the final prayers were read and the Judge was laid to rest.

Later that afternoon, she attended the service for Tommy Gilbert. This time, Mike sat beside her, holding her hand as the priest chanted prayers for the

319

dead over Tommy's casket. And when it all was over and Tommy Gilbert finally laid to rest, the two of them silently departed and headed for Mike's cabin.

Rose kicked off her sandals and flopped down at the end of the old wooden dock. Mike's boat was tied up to one side. She dangled her feet over the edge and splashed them through the warm water. Her somber black dress was gone, replaced by a pair of faded red shorts and comfortable t-shirt.

Mike joined her moments later. He'd swapped his dress uniform for a pair of khaki shorts, t-shirt, and sandals. His eyes scanned the horizon. "I don't think you'll be sitting there for long. Looks like it's going to rain."

"I don't care. It's so peaceful out here. Have a seat." She patted the dock. "The water feels wonderful. You should try it." She swished her feet in wide lazy circles as Mike sank down beside her. The hair on his legs was bleached by the sun, and she shivered as their bare legs touched. The feel of a hard muscular thigh as it brushed against her own brought the first flush of pleasure to what had been a most terrible day.

"What have you got in there?" Her eyebrows arched at the sight of the bulky sack at his side.

"It was down at the station. I brought it back last night." He handed it to her. "I think it belongs to you."

She weighed the heavy sack. "What is it?"

"Open it."

Rose's eyes widened as she peeked inside, then drew out the long wooden plaque. The edges were charred, but the embossed finish was still plain to read. *Gallagher and James, Attorneys and Counselors at Law*.

"We found it in the hallway outside the Judge's office," Mike said.

"He said he had something to show me. This must be what he went home to get that night." Her eyes misted over and she hugged the plaque against her heart. It still held a faint smell of smoke, but she didn't care. She'd thought everything was gone, but she had this. It would remind her of the Judge, of Jeff, and all the dreams they had shared.

"They read the Judge's will yesterday afternoon," she said in a halting voice. "He left his sister the house and everything in it. The rest he set up in a trust—all the property and his offices downtown. He put it in my name."

"He left his practice and the real estate to you?"

Rose nodded. "I doubt it will amount to much once I pay off his gambling debts. But I never expected anything to begin with. He was more than generous to me when he was alive." She swallowed hard. "I am going to miss him."

"He was a good man," Mike said.

Her gaze traveled across the still water, searching the horizon. Low gray clouds gathered far away as a soft rumble of thunder sounded in the distance. "I hope he knew how much he meant to me," she said after a moment.

"I'm sure he did." Mike reached out and caressed her back in long, even strokes.

"When someone dies, it's the saddest thing of all." Rose leaned against him and blew out a sigh. "It's the end of everything. There's no chance to go forward, no more chance for all the things you meant to do or say. All you have left are memories."

With the two funerals over, the world had lost some of its crazy tilt. Eventually things would have to return to normal. Life would go on. But it would never be the same.

"And poor Tommy." She shook her head mournfully. "He didn't have much of a life. He deserved so much more than what he got."

"It does seem like some people never get a break."

"He was the nicest one of the bunch out of the whole Gilbert clan." She turned to Mike. "Why did he do it? What made Tommy set those fires?"

"People do things all the time without thinking about the consequences. Look at the Judge. Smart as he was, he got in way over his head with the gambling."

"Setting fires is different than betting."

"Tommy had his own reasons for starting fires. With some people, it's a sickness. He started out small and the fires grew."

She stared at Mike. "There's no doubt about it, right? You're absolutely sure that Tommy was the arsonist?"

He nodded quietly. "We've been able to place him at every fire scene. Plus, every one of those fires started the same way. Tommy mowed lawns for a living. He always had his hands on a ready source of fuel."

Rose quieted as she thought of Tommy's old pickup. The bed had been jammed with gardening tools, weedwackers, lawnmowers... and cans of gasoline.

"We got called out to a small fire last spring in his brother Joey's shed," Mike said. "There was no power in that shed, no reason for a fire to start. Something was used to start the blaze. The burn pattern told us it was no accident."

What made someone start a fire? Mike had told her long ago. Profit, revenge, or a thrill. Tommy had started with the thrill of watching the flames grow, moved on to revenge by setting Charles's car ablaze, and ended by setting the Judge's offices ablaze to help him out with insurance money.

"Remember what I told you about what Tommy said that night? That he had set the fire because of something my mother said? I think I figured out where he came up with that idea."

Mike's arm around her tightened.

"The three of us—my mom, Lil, and I—were talking about the Judge and his money problems one afternoon. Tommy was outside in the yard. He must have overheard us while weeding the flower beds."

His eyes filled with quiet regret. "He was a nice kid. I always liked him. That's one of the reasons I let him hang around the fire station. I wanted to keep an eye on him. And who knows? Maybe some of this is my fault." He dipped his head low, his gaze centered across the dark water. "Part of me keeps thinking maybe I should have moved sooner with the evidence I had. But I kept hoping he wasn't the one. I kept hoping something would happen that would prove me wrong—"

"Don't do that to yourself." She pulled away and stared at him with frank appraisal. "You did what you had to do, and you never backed down. Don't start doubting yourself now."

Mike hesitated, then finally nodded.

"Did you hear the news about Joey Gilbert?" she said after a moment. "He's threatening to sue the Judge's estate."

"For what?" His eyes widened.

"Wrongful death. He's maintaining it was the Judge's responsibility to make sure the stairs were in proper working order."

"How the hell does he figure that makes any sense? His own brother Tommy was the one who started the fire that burned the stairs and caused them to collapse."

"Obviously you don't know Joey Gilbert," Rose said with a scowl. "I'll bet he's already found some plaintiff's attorney ready to represent him for a third of whatever they can get from the Judge's Estate. If that's the case, I intend to fight him every step of the way. The Judge would want me to do that. And so would Tommy," she added.

Mike nodded. "Yes, I think they would."

Thunder growled in the distance. Slow-moving clouds hung low to the shore.

"You were right," Rose said. "It is going to rain."

His eyes were thoughtful as he gazed toward the approaching storm. "It's beautiful here."

"My dad would have loved it. He always wanted a place on the lake."

He shot her a fast smile. "Know what I like most about this place? It's quiet. The city noises are gone."

There was no need for further explanation. She knew exactly what Mike meant. No car horns, no fire sirens, no people shouting. Only the soft splash of a wave lapping upon the shore, a growl of distant thunder, and from the nearby reeds, a frog croaking love songs to an absent mate.

So quiet. So peaceful.

And regrettably, not for her.

"I had a phone call from my law firm today," she said. "One of the partners in my practice session was in a car accident last night. He survived, but they don't expect him back for weeks. So, that's it for me. I'm going back."

Mike sucked in a hard breath and gripped her hand. "When do you leave?"

She hesitated. "Tomorrow."

"Are you serious?" His face looked like he had just been hit by a truck himself. "Are you coming back?"

Rose bit her lip hard. "I don't know. The firm needs me right now… no matter what I might decide to do in the future."

"What about your mom? She needs you, too."

"She'll be fine. She's getting stronger every day. And Lil has volunteered to stay at the house until Mom is back on her feet. I think it's a good idea. Those two need each other." She swallowed hard and clenched her hands together. "Probably more than ever, now that the Judge is gone."

"I can't believe that you're really leaving." Mike's voice was filled with quiet disappointment. His gaze focused out over the water. The lake glimmered like a mirror, flat and smooth.

"I know it's hard to understand." She scanned the sheltering shoreline, the small stretch of beach, Mike's little cabin. "This probably seems like paradise to you. Like a little piece of heaven."

"It *is* heaven, Rosie. Why would you want to leave?"

Why *did* she want to leave? Once upon a time, her reasoning seemed to make sense. But not anymore. Everything now seemed jumbled and confused. She needed space and time to put it all back together again.

"Think of the good you could do, right here at home. You could make a difference in people's lives."

"I don't have to stay home to make a difference. Grand Rapids is a nice city. And what about Washington, D.C.? I could make a difference there." She offered him a tiny smile. She'd have to come clean with Andy, but anything was possible with Mike at her side. Maybe it could work. "Have you ever been to

Washington? It's a wonderful city. You could be a fireman anywhere."

He stared at her a long moment. "You could practice law anywhere," he finally replied.

Rose's spirits sank. His eyes offered little hope.

"Everybody goes to Washington expecting they're going to change things," he said. "Maybe James Bay isn't as grand or financially rewarding as someplace else might be, but people here want you home. They miss you, Rosie. They love you. And love always counts for something."

"But it's not what I planned."

He grazed one finger against her cheek. "Sometimes life doesn't turn out the way we plan."

A shiver ran through her as he lifted her chin, bringing her gaze to meet his own. His head bent to meet hers and their lips touched, melting together, warm, moist, breathless. Rose closed her eyes and for one wild moment lost herself in the sweet insanity of his mouth hard on her own. How could she give him up? Dear God, what was she supposed to do? She loved this man.

"I love you, Rosie." His arms tightened around her. "I love you and I don't want to let you go. But I know I don't have any right to ask you to stay."

"If only things were different. Oh, Mike, I wish..." She broke off, struggling to hold back the tears. She hadn't cried yet, not in the past three days, and she wouldn't start now. If she gave in, all would be lost.

But how could she bear to leave him behind? How could she get through this and say good-bye?

"Did I tell you about the chief? He's retiring and leaving town."

"He's leaving?" Rose blinked hard and pulled back, searching Mike's face. "Why?"

"His wife was accepted into an experimental cancer treatment program out west. They're going out there so she can get the help she needs."

And Mike would become the new fire chief. It was inevitable. She struggled to be happy for him. He deserved every bit of success that came his way. If he stayed in James Bay, this was the only chance he would ever get to make an upward career move. There would never be another opportunity like this for him in this little town, and they both knew it.

If he followed her, things would be different. Mike was smart and deserving. No doubt he would quickly climb the ranks wherever they went—Grand Rapids or Washington D.C. But in a big city, he would end his career behind a desk, lost in a world of budgets and political firestorms, his fire gear stashed, forgotten in a closet. A job like that would drive some men mad. Especially a man like Mike. He'd always been clear about what he wanted.

He was a fireman. He wanted to work the fire, battle the blaze. If he stayed in James Bay, his fire coat and boots would remain at the ready. Every man—including the chief—responded to a fire call. No matter how many fire reports needed his attention, Mike would stand prepared to put his skills and courage, his very life, on the line when his monitor went off.

How could she ask him to give up his heart's desire, just for her?

She couldn't. And she wouldn't, no matter how she felt. It wouldn't be fair to Mike, regardless what his answer might be.

"They've asked me to step in as acting chief while the city council searches for his replacement."

She bristled at the words. What replacement? How could the city fathers have any doubt about who was the right man for the job? "But you're already Assistant Fire Chief. Naturally you're the perfect candidate. If they have any sense, they'll pick you."

"They can't pick me if I'm not here."

Her eyebrows knit together. "I don't understand."

His face was somber. "I'm not staying in James Bay."

"You're thinking about leaving? How can you do that? You love it here."

Mike gave her fingers a gentle squeeze. "I love something else a whole lot more."

Rose swallowed down a sudden lump in her throat. She couldn't let him do it. It was too much of a sacrifice and he would end up sorry.

"I'll go wherever I have to go, Rosie. All I care about is being with you and making you happy. I can fight fires anywhere."

"And I could practice law anywhere," she softly replied.

"I told you once before. I already know what I want. I want you, Rosie. And I'll do whatever it takes to make sure I've got you right beside me."

"No, Mike, I can't let you do it." She ducked her head, trying to hide the sudden tears welling up behind her eyes. He deserved so much more than she could ever give him. No matter how much they might wish things were different, she couldn't change herself. She was still the person she'd always been. She wasn't the woman for Mike.

"Lord, you sure are stubborn." He blew out a hard sigh and shot her a frustrated glance. "Why not give a guy a chance?"

"It won't work. You have no idea what you'd be giving up." Rose swiped away the hot tears flowing down her cheeks. The last thing she wanted was for him to see her like this, weepy and emotional. She struggled to keep things in perspective. They needed to be practical and sensible.

"A town is only a town, Rosie. It won't be so easy to find another woman like you."

Her tears fell faster. "You don't understand."

"Try me," he suggested. His hand ran up and down her back in long gentle strokes. "Come on, Rosie, spill it. What's really bothering you?"

She stared out across the water, listening to the sound of the waves crashing on shore in the wake of the coming storm. The truth would destroy them, but she had to tell him, if only for his sake. Finally she found the courage to meet his gaze.

"Mike, you want something I can't give you. I am not the soft maternal type, and I never will be. Don't you understand? I will never be like Katie." Rose halted as she saw his face harden. Had she gone too far? But he had to hear it all. She swallowed hard and, taking a deep breath, forced herself to continue. "I know how much you loved her. Eventually you'll end up comparing us, and you'll hate me for it. You'll hate me because I'm not her, and you'll hate me for taking you away from all... all this." She waved her hands in big circles of frustration.

"That's what's been bothering you?" he said with an incredulous stare.

She bowed her head and nodded.

Mike grabbed her shoulders. "You listen to me, Rose Gallagher, and you listen good. For a long time after Katie died, I sat around feeling sorry for myself. Some days, I even felt like life wasn't worth living any more. It scared me, feeling like that, thinking that I might actually give up on myself. But I didn't care what I did. I even took a sabbatical from the fire department. Then one day Terry made me come up north with him for a little fishing trip and we did some serious talking."

His face sobered. "I owe everything to Terry. He's the one who got me out and moving again. We were up here on that fishing trip when I found out about a job opening up with the fire department. Terry was the one who forced me to apply. When I got the job, I moved up north. At first, I didn't care. I put in my hours, came home, and chilled. The days drifted by, one into another. Then one morning, I realized I was feeling better, that there might be some hope for me after all, that someday I would wake up and life would be good again. And then, finally, one day it was, and that's how I knew life isn't done with me yet. I have proof."

"You do?" She couldn't tear her gaze away. The need to see the truth was too strong to resist.

"All the proof I need." He reached out and drew her close, one finger gently caressing her cheek. "You're right here in my arms."

The wild thump of his heartbeat matched her own galloping heart beat for beat.

"Katie was a wonderful woman, but she certainly wasn't the saint that sharp legal mind of yours has made her out to be," he said in a low voice. "She had a feisty temper and a mind all her own. She could go for days holding a grudge and not talking to me. And she had her little quirks, just like we all do." The hint of a smile played round his mouth. "She used to sleep with her socks on at night. I always hated that. Never could convince her to stop."

330

A sudden glint of mischief danced in his eyes. "Do you sleep with your socks on, too?"

Rose couldn't stop herself from giggling through her tears. "No, I don't wear my socks to bed."

"Good. At least that's one less thing we have to worry about." His voice filled with patience as he cradled her close. "Don't be afraid, Rosie. Everything will work out if we give it some time. And I'm willing if you are."

"But what if it doesn't?" She bit her bottom lip as all the unspoken fears and nagging insecurities rushed to mind. "You don't know the real me, Mike. The Rose you know is someone on vacation. I'm not usually like this."

"You mean you're not that decent, kind-hearted woman I made you out to be? You sure had me fooled." A big grin spread across his face.

His teasing coaxed the hint of a smile hovering around her lips. "What is that supposed to mean?"

"Quit underestimating yourself, Rosie. You're loyal and brave and fiercely devoted to the people you love. Remember how we met? You were driving your mom to the hospital when you rear-ended my truck. We stood there arguing and then her car started smoking under the hood. I took one look at you, so scared for your mother, scared silly for yourself... well, I think I fell in love with you that very minute, right there on that curb."

Rose smiled through the tears, remembering her first glance of this fireman. He'd been all business after their fender bender, ranting and raving till the radiator blew. He'd come out a hero.

Mike was right. There'd been sparks between them right from the start.

"And look how you stood up to me about the Judge. You were fierce, Rosie, fighting for someone you loved as you tried to prove me wrong. I admired you so much for that, more than I could ever tell you."

Was he actually saying none of it mattered? But even her father, another Michael John Gallagher, had had certain standards. Their house had been orderly, clean... and centered around her father. It had worked, in large part because of the concessions her mother had made.

Concessions like staying home and raising a family. Of being the perfect wife.

"I'm not like my mother," she voiced a quiet warning. At the very least, Mike deserved that much. "I don't even know if I want children. I've never thought about it."

He gave a slow nod. "We can talk about that."

"And I hate doing housework. Sometimes I don't even make the bed."

His eyes sparkled as he lifted his eyebrows. "You won't hear any complaints from me on that account."

She struggled to continue, in spite of the teasing. Better that he heard the whole truth now. Mike would never be able to say that she hadn't warned him.

"I work a lot of late hours. You would be coming home to an empty house. And I'm very independent. Sometimes I get mad when things aren't done the way I like them."

"Mmmmm."

The stoic look on his face hadn't changed since she first started talking. Rose thought hard. "I'm orderly and precise, practical in all things. Some men find that hard to deal with."

He merely shrugged. "I'm not all men. What else you got?"

She stared at him in confusion. Hadn't he been listening? "Isn't that enough?"

"More than enough." He leaned over to kiss the tip of her nose. "But none of it matters. I love you just the way you are."

"You might never eat again," she warned him. "I'm not much of a cook. Remember how I nearly burned down my mother's house?"

"No need to remind me. Your name is legend down at the fire station," he replied with a knowing smile. "Let's make a deal. How about you let me worry about the cooking? I know my way around a kitchen. I've been doing it for years in the fire station. I've even got my own apron."

"It's a good thing one of us does." Rose managed a shaky laugh, then sobered slightly. "Do you really think it's possible we can work things out?"

"I thought we already had. As far as I'm concerned, there's only one decision left to make—and that one I'll leave up to you. I'll follow you anywhere, Rosie. Wherever you are, that's home for me."

His words snatched her breath away. What had she done so good in her life to deserve such a man as this? Rose felt the tears start up again just as something splashed on her head.

"It's raining!" Laughing, she leaned back against the dock and opened her mouth to catch a taste of the cool, refreshing wetness.

"Come on, let's get inside." Mike, already on his feet, pulled her to a stand.

"No, wait." She stood planted on the dock and reined him in with one hand. "We've waited so long for this rain. Let's enjoy it."

"You're crazy, you know that? We're going to get soaked."

"I don't care." Rose leaned into the warmth of his embrace as the raindrops came faster, pelting them. She gazed up in wonder at the man beside her. He wasn't at all what she had expected for herself, this fireman with the slow steady smile, sparkling eyes, and a heart that saw the truth of all that was right and good with the world.

"Mike?"

"Yes, Rosie?"

Finally she found the courage to give voice to the words that had been locked inside her heart. "I love you."

"I love you, too." He laughed and hugged her close. "Come on, let's go get warm." He started toward the cabin.

"Wait a minute." She bent and grasped the wooden plaque from the dock, tucking it safe against her heart. "I can't forget this."

"We'll have to find you someplace special to hang that," he said as they reached the shelter of the cabin's front door.

Rose offered him a shy smile. "I already know the perfect spot."

EPILOGUE

ANNUAL INDEPENDENCE DAY PARADE

By: Charles Kendall
The James Bay Journal

JAMES BAY—The annual Fourth of July parade kicks off Monday at 2:00 P.M. sharp. More than 50 entries are expected in this year's parade, which will be led by the fire department.

Patriotic commemorative buttons are once again being sold by the Kiwanis Club to raise funds for the downtown beautification project. The buttons, a new fundraiser item last year, are hot collector items. They can be purchased up until parade time at the James Bay Bank, the *Journal* offices, or Ramer Mercantile. For more information about the commemorative buttons, contact Charles Kendall, Kiwanis button chairperson.

"I'm impressed, Rose. You've done wonders with the place." Andy Sabatini's admiring gaze wandered the office. "When I first saw it, I had my doubts. I never thought it would turn out looking like this."

Rose beamed with pleasure from behind her new desk. "Thanks, Andy. Decorating it was a labor of love."

"You're an amazing woman, you know that?"

The telephone rang. Rose shot him an apologetic glance. "Give me a second?"

He nodded, and she reached for the phone.

"Cecilia Rose? Sweetheart, is that you?"

"Hi, Mom." She settled in her chair and held up a this-will-just-take-a-minute finger for Andy.

"Why are you still at work? You promised me you would make it home this year."

"I'm leaving soon."

"Please be careful, sweetheart. I hate to think of you on the road in all that holiday traffic."

"I have someone in my office, Mom. I have to go." She shot Andy a conciliatory smile as she hung up the phone. "Sorry about that. You know how mothers can be."

"Totally understand," Andy replied as he came to his feet. "Don't get me wrong. I love my mom, but most days I'm glad she doesn't live anywhere near me. She has her own life and her own opinions. A couple thousand miles between us is a good thing."

"Moms... you've gotta love 'em." She stepped around the desk and into his arms. Andy had been a dear, allowing her the time she needed to make things right for all of them. "Thanks again. I couldn't have done it without you."

"You're giving me too much credit." He enveloped her in a tight hug. "I'm just glad to see you happy. This place suits you."

"I think so, too." She glanced around her new office with a satisfied smile. The decision hadn't been easy, but it had been a few months and she now knew she'd definitely made the right choice. How could she ever have had any doubts?

"So, I'll see you tomorrow?"

"Bright and early," she promised as she ushered him out the door.

Rose shut down the computer and gathered her car keys and purse, then took an extra moment for a final glance around the room. Sunshine bounced off gleaming polished windows. Fresh-painted walls and newly upholstered chairs lent a welcoming touch to the recently refurbished office space. Andy was right. The remodeling had been worth every penny.

She hurried down the stairs and gave a firm push on the heavy front door. Was it merely her imagination, or did she actually smell the enticing aroma of barbequed chicken?

The blast of a loud air horn shattered the afternoon. Startled, Rose glanced up to see a large yellow fire truck rounding the corner in front of her with a familiar face behind the wheel. Mike's hand went up in a brief wave as he grinned at her through the truck's open window.

"Look, Daddy, that fireman waved at me!"

Rose glanced at the little boy hopping up and down on the sidewalk outside the office door. His eager face beamed with excitement as he pointed out the fire truck to a man standing close beside him.

"That's what I want to be when I grow up," the little boy said. "I want to be a fireman, just like him!"

Pride and love flooded through her. Who said all the heroes were dead? Thank goodness little boys still dreamed of growing up to be heroes someday. Heroes like Mike.

"Daddy, look! He's stopping the fire truck!"

The little boy's voice hit a fever pitch as the heavy truck lumbered to the curb. The passenger door opened, and Rose reached up to grab Mike's hand. One quick boost and she was in the cab, settled beside him. She snapped on her seat belt.

"Nice outfit," she noted with approval. Mike's new dress uniform made him even more handsome. The chief's gold braid flashed brilliant in the July sunshine.

"Thanks." He shot her a quick glance. "Did Andy stop by?"

"He left a few minutes ago. We're all set to go fishing tomorrow morning."

"Did he like the office?"

"He loved it." She smiled to herself, remembering the astonished look on Andy's face as she gave him a guided tour of the Judge's refurbished suite of rooms that made up her new law office. She leaned across the bench seat and kissed Mike's cheek. "Thanks again for talking me into spending the money."

"It was worth every penny, putting that smile back on your face. And by the way, you were right about that sign." He nodded at the embossed wooden plaque displayed above the office's front door. "It looks perfect up there. The Judge would approve."

"Think so?" Rose wriggled with pleasure. The Judge had always tried to tell her she was meant to be at home. It seemed he had been right.

She wasn't so naive as to believe things would always be perfect. After all, this was still James Bay, the town where she'd grown up, with all the good and bad associated with small-town living. People still talked. Probably they always would. But she intended to counteract it with some positive talk of her own. No doubt the future would hold challenges and things wouldn't always go as planned. Life offered no guarantees.

But just as Mike had told her once, there was no such thing as a geographic cure. No matter how far you traveled trying to escape your problems, they simply followed behind you up and down the highway until you finally turned and found the courage to face them. Change couldn't happen unless you were willing to try. That's all that was needed to make some sort of start. The courage to try.

Mike's love had given her the courage to try again. She'd reclaimed her hometown for what it was... a small town, filled with ordinary people. Some good, some bad. Some generous, some selfish. All of them human to the core. But Rose was ready to give them all—including herself—a second chance. She could do anything with Mike at her side.

She'd grown to love the sight of him fussing in the kitchen. She'd gotten used to his squawking 911 pager that toned him out at the most inconvenient times. Who cared that they ate breakfast on the run or that the fire department saw more of him than she did some days? She had her share of late-night sessions sitting behind her new desk studying case law—just like the Judge. But they could get through anything, now they had each other. Life was good.

Mike's eyes gleamed with anticipation. "All set?"

"Are you kidding? I've been waiting all year for a ride in this fire truck."

"Let's get going, then." A big grin settled across his face as he threw the truck in gear and eased the truck away from the curb. Rose threw the little boy a wave through the cab's open window. The diamond wedding ring on her finger sparkled in the afternoon sun.

"Hey, Daddy, how come that lady gets to ride in the fire truck? No fair!"

"Maybe she's a fireman," the man answered. "Remember what I've always told you? Girls can do anything."

The little boy's words bounced around in Rose's mind as the truck headed for the library and the start of the parade route. Her, a fireman? She didn't have what it took to do Mike's job, not by a long shot. She wasn't the brave or daring type, and certainly not cut out for that type of work. But thank goodness that some men—and women—*were*.

Courage, compassion, and devotion to duty. Firemen had it all, twenty-four seven. And now Rose had one of these brave men as her very own hero for the rest of her life.

How lucky could one woman get?

ABOUT THE AUTHOR

Kathleen Irene Paterka fell in love with writing at a very young age. She was in her early 20's when she fell in love with her very own hero-husband-fireman Steve. **HOME FIRES** was inspired by the courage and devotion to duty she's witnessed throughout the years from Steve and his fellow firefighters of the Charlevoix Township Fire Department. None of them fail to answer the call when the monitor trips and they're toned out by Central Dispatch for a fire run. Kathleen is the author of numerous novels which embrace universal themes of home, family life and love, including the Women's Fiction series, "*The James Bay Novels*". She is the resident staff writer for Castle Farms, a world renowned castle listed on the National Historic Register, and co-author of the non-fiction book **FOR THE LOVE OF A CASTLE**, published in 2012. Having lived and studied abroad, Kathleen's educational background includes a Bachelor of Arts degree from Central Michigan University. She and her hero husband Steve live in the beautiful north country of Michigan's Lower Peninsula. Kathleen loves hearing from readers. You can contact her via her website at www.kathleenirenepaterka.com.

If you enjoyed **HOME FIRES**,
check out these other titles in *The James Bay Novel series* by Kathleen Irene Paterka:

The James Bay Novels

FATTY PATTY
(#1 – available now!)

HOME FIRES
(#2 – available now!)

LOTTO LUCY
(#3 – coming soon!)

FOR I HAVE SINNED
(#4 – coming soon!)

Non-Fiction:
FOR THE LOVE OF A CASTLE
(available now!)

Coming in 2013:
ROYAL SECRETS

Turn the Page for a free bonus read!

LOTTO LUCY
Book #3 in *The James Bay Novel series*

LOTTO
LUCY

A James Bay Novel

KATHLEEN IRENE
PATERKA

LOTTO LUCY

A James Bay Novel

KATHLEEN IRENE PATERKA

CHAPTER ONE

I'm a cash-only girl and I've never been a gambler—with my money or my life. So when Kris Henderson and I stroll into Pete's Place, our small town's gas station/convenience store to pay for my gas, Pete Kelly's suggestion I buy a lottery ticket has me chuckling and shaking my head before the words are out of his mouth.

"Aw, come on, Lucy. Whatdya got to lose?" His craggy eyebrows lift high. "It's only a buck."

"Sorry, Pete, but you're talking to the wrong girl. I don't gamble." When you live in place like James Bay, ticking off the wrong people can come back to bite you. But Pete—a fixture in our town for the past seventy years—and I have always gotten along. I like Pete just fine. Thing is, I like my money more.

"What's the big deal?" he says. "Do yourself a favor and buy a ticket. Besides, you're in the Lottery Zone."

"And what's that supposed to mean?" I ask.

"The Lottery Zone." He straightens behind the counter and points upwards. "See that? The salesman from the State Lottery Commission stuck it up there a couple days ago."

Kris and I glance up to see a neon-glo sign swaying above our heads. LOTTERY ZONE glitters in bold swirls against stripes of yellow and black.

344

"It's some damn promotion they've got going," he says. "If I don't ask for the sale, you don't pay for the ticket."

"Sorry, I don't gamble. You should ask Kris." I nod at my colleague. "Spending money is her hobby."

"Hey, speak for yourself," she spits in protest. "Besides, I'm broke."

Pete eyes me over the cash register. "You never know, Lucy. Buy a ticket, and you could end up the lucky winner. You could even get your name in the headlines on the front page of that paper of yours."

Kris and I trade glances, then laughter. As reporters for *The James Bay Journal*, it's our job to write the news, not make it.

Pete rolls his eyes. "Maybe you girls think it's funny, but I don't. My sales are down, and I've got a quota to meet. You want the state to yank my machine?"

Now it's my turn to roll my eyes. Pete's Place has the busiest gas pumps in town, not to mention the best prices on beer and wine. Hard to believe his store doesn't do a thriving business selling lottery tickets.

"Sorry, Pete, but I'm only buying gas today." I scrounge through my latest purse, digging for my wallet. The oversized leather pouch resembles a duffel bag and things inside have an odd way of disappearing. Today it's my wallet that's a no-show.

"You could save yourself some time and hassle if you paid at the pump," he says.

Kris snorts. "And use her credit card? Lucy would rather die than break out the plastic."

"It's only for emergencies," I say, trying not to sound too prissy.

She eyes me suspiciously. "Define *emergency*."

Too bad someone hasn't defined the word for Kris. Maybe then she wouldn't have a problem keeping her own credit cards tucked safely away where they belong. But my colleague isn't sucking me into playing semantics today. We spent too much time gabbing over lunch and I'm running late. The Hospital Foundation's latest ribbon-cutting ceremony starts soon and I'm scheduled to cover the story.

"I prefer to operate on a cash-only basis," I say. "If I can't afford it, I don't buy it."

She huffs a long sigh. "There's your problem, Lucy. Why are you so scared of spending money?"

"The better question might be, why don't more people feel that way? Too much easy credit gets people into trouble. Thanks, but no thanks." I come up with my wallet and slide my last two twenties across the counter. With payday still another week away, and the price of gas soaring higher than the scorching summer temperatures, I can't afford to bask in thinking I've got money to burn. I've never lived on easy street. In fact, there's a For Sale sign on the front lawn of the house where Grandma raised me. Plus, a mortgage still due, and no takers in sight. The way I'm going, I'd need a million lottery wins to get me out of my money mess.

Pete counts out my change, then dangles the bills just out of reach. "Whatdya say, Lucy? You've got seven dollars here. That equals seven chances to win. All it takes is one ticket."

"Sorry, Pete, but you're wasting your breath. Like Grandma always said, *the best way to double your money is to fold it in half and stick it in your wallet.*"

"That Grandma of yours didn't know everything," he mutters.

I'll have to give him credit. When it comes to being successful in business, my old friend Pete learned the secret a long time ago. Never give up. But two can play at that game.

"Pete, how long have you known me?"

He scratches his bald head. "Pretty much all your life, I guess."

"Exactly," I say. "Now think back a few years. Remember when I won the Miss James Bay Contest my senior year of high school?"

He frowns. "Can't say that I do."

I cluck my tongue, holding back the smile. "How about last year when I landed the biggest trout in the annual fishing tournament and won the thousand dollar prize?"

The furrow in his brow deepens. "I thought Bob Campbell took first place last year." He hesitates. "Or maybe it was the year before?"

Poor guy, he still doesn't get it. "It was last year, Pete," I say gently. "Bob won the contest, not me."

"But you just said—"

"I was only kidding," I say, suddenly ashamed of myself for egging him on.

He peers over the cash register. "What about that Miss James Bay thing?"

"Pete, honestly, can you see me entering a beauty contest? I'm the unluckiest person you'll ever meet. So me buying a lottery ticket would be like throwing good money away. Guaranteed I wouldn't win. I never win anything."

"Seems like I remember you winning some scholarship or something to the university," he muses.

"Partial scholarship," I correct him. Though a lot of good it did me. The money barely made a dent in my student loans. Four years later, I'm still paying the bills, the most recent of which arrived two days ago. It's still unopened on my kitchen counter where I tossed it. I haven't worked up the nerve to rip it open and see how much the interest has accumulated.

Kris plucks a candy bar from a display and shoves it on the counter. "What's the big deal, Lucy? Buy yourself a ticket. It's only a dollar."

"And so is this chocolate," I reply. "Buy your own candy."

"Come on, Lucy, please? I'm a little short on cash. I'll pay you back."

"Where have I heard that line before?" I push the candy bar back at her.

Kris eyes the chocolate with a woeful face. "Just so you know, I'm holding you personally responsible if my blood sugar plummets and I keel over. My family is hundreds of miles away. Who'll take care of me?"

"I'll drive you to the E.R. myself," I promise, trying not to smile. My colleague Kris Henderson is irreverent, witty and everything I wish I could be myself (spiky blond hair excluded). But Kris hasn't lived here very long. And though I've spent twenty of my twenty-five years in this little town, that doesn't mean I'm naive enough to believe I've earned local status. That right is reserved solely for people like my father and Pete, both born and raised in James Bay. You could live in this town for fifty years and still be merely a *local wanna-be*.

I turn to Pete with an open palm. "Could I please have my change?"

"Sure, Lucy, no problem. You want your money, here's your money." He slaps the bills into my hand. "Glad to oblige. After all, it's not like you owe me. At least, not much."

"Owe you for what?" I ask warily. That sly smile on Pete's face has stripped away some of his seventy-plus years and I suddenly have a funny feeling I'm being set up.

"No big deal, it was just an interview," he reminds me. "Remember? You came waltzing in here a couple days later, thanking me for all the great quotes I gave you, and telling me how people were writing letters to the editor… plus how that Kendall guy that runs your paper actually gave you a compliment. But don't let that get you feeling guilty, Lucy. You keep your money. Like I said, you don't owe me. It was just an interview."

Maybe if he hadn't fetched up that hilarious hound dog expression, my mouth and wallet would have stayed shut. But Pete and I have been friends since I got my driver's license and started pumping my own gas. And all kidding aside, Pete makes a good point. I *do* owe him. That interview he gave me last month about the escalating price of gasoline had some colorful quotes about the little man getting screwed.

My story made the front page above the fold and generated a slew of heated letters to the editor.

Letters to the editor sell papers. People buy extra copies, happy to see their name in print.

"When's the last time someone told you what a great salesman you are?" I say, laughing. "All right, I'll buy a ticket. But only *one*," I warn him.

"Thatta girl, Lucy." He waltzes behind the lotto machine. "You want to choose the numbers or you want an easy pick?"

"Oooh, let me pick the numbers." Kris snatches a coupon and grabs a pencil stub. "We can use our birthdays. Pete, what month and day were you born?"

I squint at the plastic beer clock 3-D display over his shoulder. I'm due at the hospital in ten minutes, plus I still need to drop Kris off at the *Journal* office. "Just give me what you've got."

"One easy pick, coming right up." The machine spits out a ticket, which Pete presents me with a flourish. "Big jackpot drawing Saturday night. Sixty-five million dollars."

"Thanks, but I won't hold my breath." I trade him a smile for my ticket and change, and throw them in my bag where they settle in the mess pooled at the bottom.

"Don't forget to check your numbers, Lucy," Pete calls as we head out the door. "Who knows? You might get lucky."

Me, lucky? I'm still laughing as I drop Kris off downtown, then head for the hospital. People like me have two chances of winning the lottery. Slim and none. Like Grandma always said, *the only sure bet is the one you make on yourself.*

I'd like to bet that I'll make it out of this town someday, but so far the only thing I've ever won is that partial scholarship. One journalism degree later, my hometown connections landed me a job on the *Journal* staff. Being back in James Bay working for the local daily isn't the career fast track I intended, but it keeps me near Grandma and plus, it's a job. Lots of people my age with college degrees flip burgers for a living. And while being a journalist might sound important, I doubt it pays much better than a stint behind a hamburger counter.

Winning the lottery? Maybe other people have time to sit and around dream about hitting the jackpot, but I need to hustle faster than someone slinging hamburgers if I want to keep my job. With the internet and cable news available 24/7, newspapers are becoming paper dinosaurs, headed for extinction. But until that happens, I've got things to do.

Like make today's interview on time.

Like finish my latest article on the re-zoning of Loon Lake.

Like visit Grandma at the nursing home.

Talk about a reality check. Each time I visit, it get harder to force myself to walk through the door. Grandma took up permanent residence at Whispering Pines six months ago and she won't be going home. A flashy *For Sale* sign decorates the front lawn of the modest house where she raised me. I dread the day the sign comes down. Blessing or curse, it will mean the house is sold and mark the end of everything important in my life. But I've run out of options. The monthly bill from Whispering Pines averages seven thousand dollars and Grandma's savings account is almost tapped out. The balance dwindles with every statement and it's nearly disappeared.

Just like Grandma's mind.

"You girls want another beer? More iced tea?"

Kris hoists her empty beer mug and salutes our waitress. "No thanks, Nettie. I've got a date with a camera and eighty high school seniors, and my eyeballs already feel a little loose." She slides me a sideways grin. "That would make quite the story in Monday's *Journal*. ***BOOZED UP REPORTER BASHES BACCALAUREATE***. Detailed coverage, see page three."

I stir up a smile with my straw, then drain my iced tea as I conjure up a mental picture of the *Journal's* managing editor, scowl firmly in place. "Who knows? If it helps circulation, Charles might give you a raise."

"Like that's going to happen." She shoves her mug aside. "Two beers are my limit, but somebody ought to buy Charles Kendall a six-pack. That man needs to lighten up."

I lose my battle fighting off the giggles. My own life lightened up earlier this year when Kris joined the *Journal* staff. She covers the crime beat, court docket and schools, while I focus on municipal and non-profit groups.

"Whoa, Lucy, check out the guy at nine o'clock." Her eyes disappear in a deep squint. "He looks familiar. Do we know him?"

Chuck's Tavern and Grill is standing-room only for a Saturday night. I scan the crowd. "Where?"

"Halfway down the take-out line." She nods toward the cash register. "Definitely your type. Baby-faced, casually dressed, up-north appeal."

"I'm not interested in dating tourists," I say with a sniff. Summertime in Northern Michigan means warm sunny days and crisp cool nights. Those of us who live here year round have some names reserved for these eight to ten weeks of summer. *Pure heaven. Tourist hell.*

"No, I'm sure I've seen him before. I think he lives around here. See the guy I'm talking about? Blue jeans, brown hair, white polo shirt."

I crane my neck and swivel in my chair, but the only thing in my line of vision is a crowd of hungry strangers jostling for take-out.

"Wait, I've got it," Kris crows in triumph. "Remember the interview I did last month about that kid's camp on Loon Lake?"

Her words alone are enough to raise goose bumps on my arms.

"Please do not mention that place in my presence." The last thing I need on my night off is hearing about Loon Lake. Bad enough Charles forced me to cover the rezoning issue for The Journal during working hours.

"That guy is their new camp director. His name is Max Graham. And Lucy, he is perfect."

"Perfect for what?" I ask, though I already suspect I won't like what I hear.

"For you, naturally. You're two of a kind. Just look at the poor guy, all alone, ordering take-out on a Saturday night." Kris leans closer. "We should ask him to join us."

"No, I don't think—"

"Come on, Lucy, loosen up. You'll never know unless you ask. I bet he says yes." She aims a high beam smile directly at the take-out counter. "Will Lucy Carter find love and happiness in the arms of a stranger ordered up from the take-out line? Talk about a terrific feature story."

"Don't you dare!" I grab her arm mid-air. Kris is always sniffing around for the next splashy feature that will get her name above the fold, but I'm not putting my reputation on the line as a romance guinea pig to further her career. "I am not interested," I hiss.

"You're never interested." She slumps back, throws her hands in the air. "You drive me crazy, Lucy, you know that? I swear, if you weren't my best friend... " She shakes her head. "Girl, you need to get a life."

"I have a life, thank you very much." My voice sounds as stiff as my spine.

"Could have fooled me. When's the last time you went out on a date?"

"I don't remember. Besides, when do I have time? I've got a job—one that keeps me busy most nights."

"My point exactly," she says. "You're way too busy taking notes in the back row at those boring commission meetings. You're missing out, Lucy."

"That's not true."

"No? Turn around and take a long hard look at Max Graham. The man is living proof. Go on, I dare you."

I sit and stare at her in stony silence.

Kris's eyes hold a challenge. "Or maybe you're scared to face the truth?"

"My life is perfect the way it is, thank you very much, and I don't need any distractions. Especially the male variety."

She lets out a long sigh. "I'm only trying to help."

"What makes you think I need help?" I ask, chin tilting higher. Sometimes my stubbornness amazes even me.

"You're twenty-five years old and having dinner with a girlfriend on a Saturday night." She rolls her eyes. "How pathetic is that?"

"Speak for yourself." I fling my straw across the table, missing her nose by a good inch.

"I'm happily involved, remember? And if I wasn't, you'd do the same for me. Isn't that what friends are for?"

Kris is right, of course. But then, she doesn't need my help finding dates, since she's been involved in a long-term same-sex relationship since college. I've never met her friend Toni, but I've heard all about her.

"Don't you dare write a story about this," I mutter as Kris waves Max over. There's no escaping the inevitable. I've been taken prisoner in a crowded bar and grill.

Or maybe not. I straighten as he nears the table. Tall, lean build, warm brown eyes, engaging smile. Definitely a 7.5. Maybe even an 8. I note the slight limp slowing him down.

"Kris Henderson, right?"

"Nice to see you, Max." Her voice oozes charm. "This is Lucy."

He turns a 120-watt smile on me and sticks out his hand. "Max Graham."

Warm handshake, firm grip. My fingers tingle at his touch. "Hi. I'm Lucy Carter."

His eyes widen slightly. "Lucy Carter from The *Journal*? The Lucy Carter covering the Loon Lake issue?"

I squirm under his heated gaze. Being a reporter in a place like James Bay makes you small-town famous. Which can be a good thing or a bad thing, depending on the reader's politics and/or point of view. "That's me," I admit.

His smile broadens. "Nice to finally meet you. I've been reading your by-line all winter. I'm one of your fans."

I'm guessing my face is as red as the grease pencils we use to mark up the *Journal*. When I envision my reading public, it's not people like Max who jump to mind. More like Pete Kelly and the gas station crowd.

"You're doing a great job on the rezoning story," he says. "Let's hope the County Planning Commission notices."

"Thanks." I swallow down the compliment. Max hasn't quit staring since Kris introduced us and it's a little unsettling. I feel lost without my notepad. Call me a control freak, but things are much more comfortable when I'm the one conducting the interview.

"There's something different about you, Max." Kris eyes him thoughtfully, then brightens. "You shaved your beard."

"It itched." He scratches his chin and grins. "Plus, camp starts in a week. I don't want to scare the kids."

I blink. Nothing about Max Graham could be conceived as scary. Beard or no beard, he would attract kids.

And women. *Definitely* women.

He turns to Kris. "I've been watching for your article about camp, but I haven't spotted it in the *Journal* yet."

"It's scheduled to run on the feature page soon."

"I appreciate that. We could use the publicity." He brushes a hand through thick brown hair grazing his collar. "We still don't have a full roster yet. Hopefully if enough people read the article, we'll fill up for the rest of the summer."

"I'll talk to our editor and see what I can do," she promises. "Look for it next week. I'll get you some extra copies." Kris flashes me a pointed smile. "I'm sure Lucy would be glad to deliver them personally."

My mouth drops open. There's a fine line between helping things along and blatantly promoting, and my ex-friend Kris just crossed it. I stare at my empty glass, kicking myself for not taking Nettie up on her offer of more iced tea. I could use some cooling off.

"Lucy's great, very accommodating," Kris continues. "She's always willing to help out. Isn't that right, Lucy?"

Subtlety isn't one of my colleague's most endearing qualities and being put on the spot isn't one of my strong points. But with Max watching, there's not much I can do but acknowledge him with a gracious smile.

And glower at Kris when he's not looking.

"Sure, I'll be glad to play delivery boy," I mumble.

"Thanks. I suspect I won't get into town much once camp is in full swing." He steps aside as Nettie pushes past him and gathers our empty plates. "I'd better get going."

Kris grabs his arm. "Why don't you sit down and eat here? We'll keep you company. Right, Lucy?"

That's a maybe, depending on if she plans to stay. Kris grew up with three brothers and she's a natural when it comes to chatting with the opposite sex. Unfortunately, I am not Kris. And since I'm an only child, I have no brothers. Plus, no dad. When it comes to men, I operate best armed with notepad, pen and a long list of questions.

Nettie levels Max with a dark scowl. "I've got people lined up waiting for tables. If you're eating, find yourself a chair and make it quick."

"Take my seat, Max. I've got to get going." Kris grabs her purse. "Lucy will keep you company. Oh, and could you give her a ride home? I've got eighty high school seniors in caps and gowns waiting for me to immortalize them for the *Journal* archives. God knows how long that will take." She throws some bills down, tosses us a brisk wave and scoots out the door.

"Is she always like that?" Max asks as he settles in her chair and scans the menu.

"You mean, bossy?" I say, watching with an evil eye as my ex-friend departs.

One corner of his mouth turns up. "I was trying to be polite. But seeing how you mentioned it, bossy works."

"It goes with the job. You get used to not taking *no* for an answer." I fiddle with the paper wrapper off my straw and keep my eyes low. It's safer that way. As I told Kris earlier, I don't need distractions. And Max's warm steady gaze providing heat across the table is a distraction. A very tempting distraction.

"Know what you want?" Nettie is back, armed with check pad and pen, and a pointed glare for Max.

"I'll have the fish and chips." He hands over his menu and shoots me a smile. "How about you?"

"I already ate, thanks."

He eyes my empty glass. "Buy you a drink?"

"Nope, I'm good." I squirm in my seat, simultaneously cursing and missing Kris. If he plans on ordering a big meal, this could prove a long night.

"I don't like to drink alone. At least let me buy you a glass of wine."

"I already said no." The words come out flat and firm, faster than I expected, and immediately I regret them. Max seems like a nice enough guy. There's no need for me to play defense. "I don't drink," I add softly.

"Okay. Sure, sorry." He sits back slightly, uncertainty registering in his eyes. "Would it bother you if I do?"

Now I'm the one surprised, not to mention impressed. Nobody's ever asked my permission before. Usually they press me for the reason I don't drink, why I've never touched alcohol, why I never will.

I have no desire to end up like my mother.

But from the look on Max's face, I've definitely inherited her sharp tongue.

"I'm sorry, I didn't mean to be rude. Go ahead and have your drink."

"You sure?" He eyes me hesitantly.

"Absolutely." I shake my head so hard, I feel my ponytail swing.

"Make it a beer." He smiles up at Nettie. "Whatever you've got on draft."

She doesn't budge. "Let's see some I.D."

"No problem." He pulls out a leather wallet and flashes his driver's license. "I'm legal."

"Barely," Nettie says with a sniff and turns away.

Barely? What exactly is that supposed to mean? He has a day's worth of stubble grazing his chin, but so do teenage boys. "How old are you?"

"Why?" Max asks. "You worried?"

The sparkle in his eyes catches me off guard, as does the zing shooting straight down my spine and into my toes as I realize he's flirting with me. The thought is intriguing, exhilarating, and utterly ridiculous. Doesn't he know I'm romantically challenged?

"You've got the rules mixed up," I loftily inform him. "It's supposed to be the other way around."

His eyebrows lift.

"It's a woman's prerogative to keep her age a secret," I explain, "not the man's."

His eyebrows rise even higher, but one corner of his mouth turns up. "That's rather sexist, don't you think?"

"What I *think* is that you're trying to evade the issue." I tap his wallet with one finger. "Exactly how old are you, anyway?"

"Old enough to know better and young enough not to care." He slides his wallet into his pocket. "How's that for an answer?"

"Not nearly good enough," I shoot back.

He props an elbow on the table, leans forward, chin in hand and squints a smile. "You're a very nosy woman, Lucy Carter. Anybody ever tell you that?"

"All the time, but I never let it stop me. I'm a reporter, remember? Being nosy and persistent is part of the job." Keeping up a sober expression is proving hard work. Who knew I'd enjoy hassling him like this? "Not to mention I have access to records," I add. "I can always check you out with the DMV."

"Touché," Max fingers his forehead in mock salute. "Okay. I'll tell you mine if you tell me yours," he says as Nettie plunks a plate and beer in front of him. He waits as she disappears, then turns to me with a cocky grin. "You first."

"Twenty-five," I challenge.

"Twenty-two," he says, devouring a French fry.

Three years younger than me? I stink when it comes to math, but even I can figure this one out. Max is barely out of college. *If* he went to college. Do people need degrees to work at summer camp?

He eyes me casually as he spears a piece of fish from his plate. "You have a problem with younger guys?"

A problem with him being younger? For having no degree? For making my toes curl, and suddenly wishing I'd paid attention while the other seventh-grade girls primped in front of the bathroom mirror? *Yes, I have a problem.* With a ponytail scrunched high atop my head and glasses perched on my nose, I'm not exactly the kind of girl men are interested in. My closet is crammed with banker boxes full of books instead of fashionable clothes. Keeping up with the latest styles requires time and money, and I have neither to spare. I'm plain old Lucy Carter. No man would look twice.

Who cares?

Sitting across from Max, I suddenly realize someone cares.

Me. I care very much. Until now, my femininity or lack thereof never seemed particularly relevant. But sitting here any longer will only prolong the inevitable. Why make Max suffer?

"Sorry, but I've got to go. It was nice meeting you." I bounce up, chair screeching against the scarred wooden floor. "Enjoy your dinner."

"Wait, you're leaving?" His eyebrows arch as he leaps to his feet. "What's wrong? What did I say?"

"Nothing," I stammer. "Believe me, it's nothing."

I'm the one who's nothing. And if I stay any longer, Max will figure that out.

"Look, Lucy, I'm not sure what's going on, but I didn't mean to say something to make you mad. I get joking around sometimes, but I don't mean anything by it. I guess it comes from being around kids. Don't hold that against me."

"Never mind, it's okay." I grab my purse.

He sighs. "If you're that intent on getting home, give me a minute. I'll get this in a to-go box and meet you at the door. My car isn't far." He flags Nettie over.

I swallow hard, not an easy task when the inside of your mouth feels as parched as the Sahara desert. "That's not necessary. I don't live far."

"No problem. I'm parked right around the corner."

And my apartment is just down the street. Damn Kris Henderson. Now I have to 'fess up and admit the truth. Why did she ask him to drive me home? Kris has a big heart, and an even bigger mouth. First thing Monday morning, she and I are going to have a little chat and establish some ground rules.

Rule No. 1. No messing with Lucy's love life.

"I don't need a ride." I ball up my fists, jam them in my pockets. "I live right here downtown, one block away."

His face scrunches up like he's trying to figure out why he got an incomplete on a final exam after pulling an all-nighter. "But I thought Kris said... "

It's worse than I thought. Max still doesn't get it. No wonder he didn't go to college.

"She lied," I blurt out. "She told you that I needed a ride because... well, because she thinks I need some excitement in my life. And I guess she thought that you... that you might... "

We stare at each other for what seems like forever as he ponders my explanation and I ponder diving under the table. But the thought of crawling around on top of those crunchy little peanut shells littering the floor isn't one I relish.

Then suddenly he gets it, and the sympathetic look that washes across his face is more than I can handle. A man feeling sorry for me is the last thing I want. *Lucy's Pity Party* is an exclusive club with sole membership limited to myself and the occasional guest, like Kris.

"Look, Lucy, it's okay—"

I hold up a hand, suck in a deep breath, blink back hot tears threatening to spill over. I am not going to cry. I refuse to be reduced to tears, especially in front of a man.

"Honest, Max, you seem like a nice guy, but I can fend for myself. I've been doing it for years." I fling my purse over my shoulder and head for the door...

He grabs my arm before I make it two feet.

"Did I mention how much I hate eating alone? It's a hang-up I've had since I was a kid." His voice softens and his hand on my arm loosens a bit. "Come on, Lucy, stay and keep me company. You'd be doing me a favor."

And he smiles. Actually, merely one corner of his mouth lifts, but it's good enough to qualify as a smile. Maybe Kris is right. If I leave now, I'll never know what's got me scared, why I'm constantly running away from life instead of embracing it. And if nothing changes, nothing changes. If not now, when will I learn?

Maybe my first lesson is standing right in front of me.

"I'll even share my French fries," he offers.

My eyes narrow. "Are you trying to bribe me with food?"

"Only if you think it will work." He grins and I feel the Lucy-deep-freeze beginning to defrost.

"I wasn't kidding about hating to eat alone," he adds. "Plus, I'd appreciate a chance to pick your brain and find out what you think about the re-zoning on Loon Lake."

"I'm not allowed to have an opinion," I say. "I'm covering the story for The *Journal*. I'm supposed to be neutral."

A flat out lie. When it comes to Loon Lake, they can turn the place into a swamp, a desert or a firing range, for all I care. I fought from the get-go not to be assigned to cover the story. A conflict of interest, I argued with Charles Kendall, citing my family history. But, as usual, the *Journal*'s Managing Editor blew off my concerns.

"At least tell me the latest," he says.

I drop my purse on the table and plop down across from Max. "What do you want to know?"

"The Planning Commission recently passed the application on to the Township Engineer for review and approval. Think they're close to a resolution?"

"Maybe." For once I'm not in the loop with the Township officials. I thought it odd they're being so closed-mouthed, but seeing how it's Loon Lake, I haven't pushed the issue. "Why do you ask?"

Max leans forward. "You might say I've got a vested interest in the matter. Our camp is surrounded by the property they're debating."

"I think I'm beginning to understand." The Loon Lake rezoning has been controversial from the beginning, and it's not going away anytime soon.

"It's a disaster waiting to happen." He shakes his head in disgust. "Our camp has been around for fifty years. If the rezoning passes, we might as well board up the cabins and call this our final season."

I get what he's saying. If money makes the world go around, Northern Michigan has been spinning out of control for the past ten years. It wasn't like this when I was growing up. It used to be that a family cottage on the lake meant an idyllic summer retreat. But times have changed, and inheriting property uncaps the land value. In this economy, especially with lakefront property taxes soaring, heirs are desperate to sell. That's when developers with cash in hand swoop in like ugly black crows and buy up the property. With more than enough acreage for a Planned Unit Development, the PUD application was filed one month ago.

"They're trying to force us to shut down," he says. "Once they do that, they'll grab our property, too. They know there's no way we can run a boy's camp smack in the middle of mega-mansions and an eighteen-hole golf course."

Like it or not, I get the point. Loon Lake is an inland lake, and one of the last pristine bodies of water in our region. Jet skis, powerboats, thirty-five foot cruisers will destroy it.

Not that I care. I've hated that lake since I was five years old.

"Hey, I've got an idea." Max straightens, brightens. "Why don't you come out and see the place for yourself? I can give you a guided tour. We'll hike the property."

I swing my head so hard, my ponytail whips in my eyes. "Sorry, Max, but you're talking to the wrong girl." Loon Lake is the last place on earth I want to visit. "I hate bugs and dirt. I hate anything to do with the great outdoors."

He chuckles. "Obviously your parents didn't send you to camp when you were a kid."

"No, they didn't," I say flatly. Summer camp is for kids with loving parents who can afford it. I had neither.

"Come on, Lucy, at least give it a try. What have you got to lose?"

The thought of a path overgrown with slimy moss, of dark hiking trails winding through the forest brings a shudder down my spine. Who knows what dangers might lurk beyond the tree line?

"Did I mention snakes?" I add. "I hate snakes."

Max grins. "I've seen some garter snakes around camp, but they won't hurt you."

"You're right," I agree with a fierce nod. "Because I won't be around to give them a chance."

"It's not the jungle, Lucy. It's only a summer camp."

His eyes gleam and I know he's teasing, but somehow it's okay. He's having fun *with* me, not *of* me. There's a huge difference between the two and Max seems to understand the difference.

Being with him feels safe.

"The famous Lucy Carter, afraid of snakes. Who would believe it?" He grins, shakes his head. "You come across so brave and fearless in those articles you write."

"It's called literary license. I use it to full advantage."

"Okay, forget about hiking the property. Come out and see what we've got to offer. I'll even throw in dinner." His eyes crinkle in a smile. "Roasting hot dogs over an open camp fire. No one in their right mind could call that dangerous."

"Depends on how sharp the stick is that you're cooking them with," I say with a quick smile. I can almost hear Kris cheering me on from the sidelines. Max is trying so hard to be nice. The least I can do is meet him halfway. Plus, there's a free meal involved. "Okay," I relent.

"Great. I'll call you at the *Journal* and set something up."

"Give me a few days." Reporter or not, I'm still a girl. And before I go anywhere near that camp, I intend to pay a visit to our local hardware store and buy myself a pair of thick rubber boots. A pair of boots a snake can't bite through. I'm not sacrificing my toes to some slimy reptile.

"I can't wait to show you around. You'll love the place, Lucy."

"Don't be too sure about that," I warn him. Poor Max. He has no clue what he's gotten himself into. Unfortunately, I do. And while I knew this day would eventually come, I didn't expect it to arrive so soon. I was counting on having another twenty or thirty years—or better yet, never—before facing the truth.

But being a reporter means following leads, taking risks, and facing facts. I guess it's time I did just that.

I'll start with Camp Call of the Loon.

Maybe then I'll find the courage to finally face Loon Lake.